Motherfaker

Motherfaker

Anna Brook-Mitchell

MACMILLAN

First published 2026 by Macmillan
an imprint of Pan Macmillan
The Smithson, 6 Briset Street, London EC1M 5NR
EU representative: Macmillan Publishers Ireland Ltd, 1st Floor,
The Liffey Trust Centre, 117–126 Sheriff Street Upper,
Dublin 1 D01 YC43
Associated companies throughout the world

ISBN 978-1-0350-7301-6 HB
ISBN 978-1-0350-8929-1 TPB

Copyright © Anna Brook-Mitchell 2026

The right of Anna Brook-Mitchell to be identified as the author of this work has been asserted in accordance with the Copyright, Designs and Patents Act 1988.

All rights reserved. No part of this publication may be reproduced, stored in a retrieval system, or transmitted, in any form, or by any means (including, without limitation, electronic, mechanical, photocopying, recording or otherwise) without the prior written permission of the publisher.

Pan Macmillan does not have any control over, or any responsibility for, any author or third-party websites (including, without limitation, URLs, emails and QR codes) referred to in or on this book.

1 3 5 7 9 8 6 4 2

A CIP catalogue record for this book is available from the British Library.

Typeset in Sabon by Palimpsest Book Production Limited, Falkirk, Stirlingshire
Printed and bound in the UK using 100% Renewable Electricity
by CPI Group (UK) Ltd

This book is sold subject to the condition that it shall not, by way of trade or otherwise, be lent, hired out, or otherwise circulated without the publisher's prior consent in any form of binding or cover other than that in which it is published and without a similar condition including this condition being imposed on the subsequent purchaser. The publisher does not authorize the use or reproduction of any part of this book in any manner for the purpose of training artificial intelligence technologies or systems. The publisher expressly reserves this book from the Text and Data Mining exception in accordance with Article 4(3) of the European Union Digital Single Market Directive 2019/790.

Visit **www.panmacmillan.com** to read more about all our books
and to buy them.

For the incomparable Lynn Brookfield

Chapter One

The couple in the window are fraudsters.

They look innocent enough, I know. Her – twiddling the stem of her over-blackcurranted Kir Royale. Him – pinching the handle of his compact espresso cup, like Gandalf borrowing Frodo's mug. He styles it out, confident he has the purchase required to take a smug sip. Anyone passing might observe them and think: *Look at that chic pair gazing out over the harbour. What blissful lives they have!*

Absolute hoodwinkers.

And I know this to be true because the offspring that accompanied them here – the ones they pretend don't exist – circle my table on their scooters like a loud and obtrusive merry-go-round. On a normal day, I would find this highly irritating but it is especially irk-inducing this morning because I am trying to pay attention to the text I've just received. The one telling me my marriage is over.

The kids continue to orbit. I feel like a specimen in a centrifuge.

I scroll back through the recent messages. Clingy paragraphs from me; spartan one-liners from Sean. I see it now: I'm the candle that won't blow out and he's the enthusiastic birthday puffer, determined to extinguish, make his wish and move on to the next bit.

'Here we are, then. A nice latte.' The waiter – a former student whose name I can't quite remember – shuffles closer to avoid being mown down as he places my drink in front of me. I reread that final message again.

> I'm sorry. It's over. I'm not coming back to Guernsey at all.

A slight intake of breath from behind alerts me to the waiter side-eyeing my phone screen. I look up at him and his cheeks redden. It sparks a memory of this very same face – a bit younger, more pimpled – guilty after being discovered copying his neighbour's work during a GCSE mock.

'Thank you for delivering this to me so efficiently,' I say, nodding to my coffee as I turn my phone over to conceal the earth-shattering message. I hope my politeness will deter him from gossiping, but the way he sashays to the counter, grabs his mobile and starts typing doesn't fill me with confidence.

One of the children bashes my table, sloshing my coffee onto the saucer. I glare at the parents, expecting an intervention. They just smile at me like I should think this the most adorable scenario in the world. The perfect heart shape that had previously topped my latte is now a sad, misshapen Pac-Man.

Sean and I would spend Saturday mornings sitting in the window those two have hijacked, choosing which boat we would buy if money was no object. A part of me hoped we might get one ourselves one day. Nothing fancy. A bright-bottomed fishing boat for day trips to Herm – cosy jumpers, sandwiches and perfectly brewed Thermos tea for two. But Sean isn't really a boat person. Or, it seems, a me person.

I wipe latte off my Lavazza biscuit and place the napkin between my cup and saucer. It turns from white to light brown as it absorbs the liquid.

For the briefest of moments, I feel an urge to stick my leg out and send that little girl head first over the handlebars of her stupid scooter. But I'd never actually do that. For one, she's not wearing a helmet, so the pink star-shaped sunglasses pushed up on her head – not quite high enough to appear stylish – would leave an indentation.

'Look at me! Look at me! Look at me!' says the little boy, balancing no-handed for a millisecond, as if this feat were akin to performing in the Cirque du Soleil. The couple make those fake impressed sounds perfected by parents the world over and snap back to their conversation, their progeny left to the supervision of strangers who – luckily for them – don't have the heart to act on the impulse to trip them up.

'Your children should be wearing helmets,' I say, downing my coffee.

The look of disgust Kir Royale gives me is as undiluted as her sickly drink. She turns back to Espresso. 'What a Karen.'

As I stand, my chair skids with more momentum than I'd intended. It smacks into the boy, who propels into his sister, who clonks her head on the corner of a table.

Kir Royale and Espresso are up on their feet, scowling at me and coddling their children.

'I didn't do it on purpose!' I step towards them to reinforce my innocence.

Crunch.

The star sunglasses lie shattered beneath my Birkenstock. The girl wails, the boy laughs, the parents coo.

I squeeze my phone like a stress ball and use the remnants of my overdraft to buy their children an apology lollipop.

Chapter Two

My name isn't Karen, by the way. It's Barri. Elegant written down but when spoken aloud – which is how names tend to be used – people just hear 'Barry', which sounds like the name of a gruff lorry driver from East London. Or a Chuckle Brother.

There is a world in which a thirty-five-year-old woman named Barri makes light work of it. She's tall with the svelte body of a weasel. Eats Nordic yoghurt. A party animal who also loves wholesome activities like getting up early to go on a trail run or socialising. Whereas I . . . well, that lorry driver – whack him in a generic smock dress, give him curly reddish hair, wide calves and, if the practical shoe fits . . . I often think about how different life would have been if my sister Lara (svelte weasel type) had been named Barri and I Lara, but still, we move.

'Ah well, none of us ever thought Sean would come back, eh?'

I hope my mum didn't summon me here just to impart that brutal nugget. I fidget in my chair. This is not a comfortable house; there's only one chair you can squish into and my mum usually sits in it – the rest of her furniture is all hard edges, flaccid cushions and creaky wood. But this room does – even on this murky November day – have an incredible view over the craggy cliffs to the zigzag sea beyond.

Mum rummages in the bureau, her petite frame almost engulfed by it. Her toned physique suggests a lifetime of aggressive Pilates when, in reality, she barely walks to the end of the street. She plonks down at the table opposite me, a serious expression on her face.

I didn't tell her about Sean, of course. Nosy Waiter must have decided it was in the island's best interest for everyone to get the memo. For a moment I'm convinced Mum's going to provide some helpful advice. Instead, she slides two small pieces of brown tatty paper across to me. 'What do you make of these, then?'

They have 'Premium Bonds' emblazoned across them. Hardly a mystery. 'Premium bonds,' I say. 'Old ones.'

'Weird, eh? I called the NS&I and here's the odd thing: they weren't your father's.' I ignore the disdain in her voice at the mention of Dad. 'I tried every single name they could possibly belong to. None of them match. The NS&I woman got ever so grumpy with me as I couldn't understand her accent. Very thick, it was. I told her she sounded Scottish but she insisted Irish. I think she was lying to me.'

'Maybe Lara can help,' I offer, rather than question that poor Irish girl's possible motives for pretending to be Scottish.

As if cued, my sister and her children bluster through the back door. Lara, all slinky-haired and efficient, deposits name labels and PE kits in front of me and Mum springs up to put the kettle on. They don't bother to offer me one, but that's just because they know I'm particular about tea.

'The stick-on labels didn't work, then?' I say.

'Yes, you were right. Happy?' To give Lara her credit, she grimaces at the tone she adopted, no doubt having remembered that my husband has, just this day, officially abandoned me. By text message.

> I'm sorry. It's over. I'm not coming back to
> Guernsey at all.

Along with the premium bonds, Mum has strategically left an architect's brochure on the side, the page open on their offering of chic garden buildings. She clocks Lara's eye-roll.

'What? It would be like having a live-in au pair you don't have to pay for!'

I open my sewing box, having been instructed by Lara to bring it along for this very purpose, and get to work stitching the labels on Harry and Luke's shorts, T-shirts, joggers and sweatshirts.

'There's no space in the garden for an annexe,' says Lara. 'And even if there was, we can't afford it.'

'I'd sell this place—'

'You OK to pick Luke up from his football on Thursday and walk him down to Dave's office?' Lara asks me. 'Our au-pair-in-training here has her book club.'

I pretend not to notice the look of horror my nine-year-old nephew gives his mum at the news that he's going to be forced to spend fifteen whole minutes in the company of his weird auntie.

'Yes, fine,' I say.

The buttoned-up Fred Perry polo and bucket hat combo Luke is sporting today is, as my Year Elevens would say, vibey. He looks like he should be egged-up to the eyeballs at a festival, sloshing a warm plastic pint about and picking fights with people who look at him the wrong way. He clocks me studying him and gives a dispassionate wave. His hand is covered by an oversized goalkeeper glove.

After Luke was born, we had to endure two years of Dave bragging about how strong his family genes are until Harry, with his big old mop of red hair, came along. Seven now, Harry's natural disposition is that of a fifty-five-year-old man concerned he doesn't have enough money saved for his retirement. He sits bolt upright on a hard wooden chair – the most brutal of the house – like a burdened puritanical king.

My sister examines the premium bonds. 'I'll speak to my editor and see if the *Press* can do an investigation to find out who they belong to.' She loves pretending she's Louis Theroux when, in reality, the most exciting story she has ever reported was when someone kept dropping unwrapped Werther's Originals on L'Ancresse Common. Her headline read: 'It's Only a Matter of Time Before Someone Chokes and Dies!' Sean and I nearly choked and died from laughter when he read it out to me over breakfast.

Mum gathers up the premium bonds. 'If we find out these are worth something, you, Dave and the boys can go on holiday! It's so expensive going away out of term time.' Lara places her cup down and squeezes Mum's hand. I'm relieved I wasn't offered a tea – there's a layer of oily scum on the surface of hers.

'I can only travel during school holidays too,' I say.

'Yes,' my sister replies, 'but that was your choice.'

Lara's reproduction was etched into her destiny; Mother Nature's fallopian tubes and hers are entwined as one. By comparison, my need to earn money is an irresponsible choice, a by-product of which is the inability to go away during school holidays without remortgaging my house.

When Mum leaves the room, my sister turns to me. 'I can't believe the man ended it with a fucking text?!' Despite Lara lowering her voice for the F-bomb, Harry tuts. Luke, still wearing his goalkeeper glove, bashes the remote control without success. 'I mean, I know he's not over here but would a phone call have killed him?!'

I shove my sewing work towards Lara. 'Not the neatest, but they won't come off in the wash.'

'At least it should be pretty clear cut given . . .' She clears her throat. '. . . And I know an excellent lawyer.' Lara inhales the smell of Luke's freshly washed sweatshirt and clutches it to herself. 'I just don't understand how after all these years and all that bullshit –' Harry flinches again – 'he condensed his abandonment of you into a couple of hurriedly typed sentences.'

'I thought you said you could only pop in briefly today?'

Lara sniffs. 'Yes, well our playdate got cancelled. Some child-hating madwoman hit their kids with a chair or something. Poor little Olivia had to be checked out for concussion.'

'Oh no . . .' I pull Mum and Lara's tea mugs towards me to take through to the kitchen.

'And then the cruel woman stamped on her sunglasses!'

'Well, I'm sure she reimbursed them,' I say over my shoulder.

Well over market value.

My tiresome colleague Yolande offers me a biscuit. 'And then, when Lara said Sean had been messaging you for months expressing his intention to come back to you, I was all like, "Oh no, that makes it *so* much worse!"' I take the Hobnob, give a curt thank-you and return to my marking. But my aloof biscuit acceptance is not enough to deter Yolande.

'Lara is absolutely fuming. She never liked him, as you know . . .'

The way Yolande dresses is a style I like to refer to as 'peasant-core' – oversized structured skirts teamed with oversized structured shirts in muted browns and beiges. Like a forest-y *Handmaid's Tale.* Yolande thinks this makes her look stylish, but as it's impossible to determine what shape she is under all that, it gives a disconcerting impression. She continues to complain about how my husband abandoning me has impacted my sister while I imagine how a human body shaped like a hexagon might look . . .

I nibble the dry biscuit and glance at the kettle. My crusty nemesis. Dare I make a cup of tea? We have to top it up once used 'to ensure the staffroom kitchen is a considerate place for all' but I can't tolerate the stagnant, limescale-infused liquid lingering in there after the morning kettle rush. To combat this, a while ago, I started pouring out the topped-up water and refilling it for my fresh brew, topping it up again afterwards as per the mandate. A passive-aggressive notice appeared on the corkboard: *Wasting water doesn't contribute to the Victor Hugo High School's commitment to be 100% carbon neutral.*

Not one to be deterred, I settled on using the fetid kettle-swamp to water the plant on the windowsill. Very eco. This ultimately resulted in the death of said plant – I maintain from limescale poisoning rather than over-zealous watering. Following a heated discussion with Julie, the highly irritating headteacher and self-appointed Prime Minister of Kitchen Conduct, I reluctantly agreed to cease and desist. It seems as if this staffroom must be a considerate place for all unless you are me.

Just as I'm about to step towards the kettle and risk it for, literally, a biscuit, Julie strides through the door, her clumpy courts accentuating her wide gait. She insists we arrive fifteen minutes early every Monday for a team meeting, which she refers to as a 'Huddle'. The most irritating thing – other than the early start and the use of the word 'Huddle' – is that she makes us stand up for the whole thing as she claims it 'energises us all for the week ahead'. She has her arm around Suzie Martel, the other English teacher, who recently returned from maternity leave. Suzie is a shirker. Constantly finding excuses to dump more work on me, or leave parents' evening on the dot when there are chairs and tables to be put away. I imagine this will get worse now she has yet another child flumped in a nursery somewhere.

When I'm made Head of Key Stage Four, my first action will be to initiate some kind of rebalance for those who are constantly covering for colleagues with childcare responsibilities. Yes, the world isn't set up for mothers to thrive at work, but child-free people should be gifted the odd lemon drizzle thank-you cake every now and again for picking up the slack, don't you think? Yes, even Yolande.

I'm pulled out of my thoughts by laughter in the room. Julie is regaling everyone with a 'hilarious' story about how her little boy ended up in the doctor's because his penis got an infection from him touching it too much. I ask myself whether this is suitable content for Monday Huddle but I remain silent.

Julie clocks my expression. 'Barri's staying very quiet. Maybe she had a similar issue with her bits!'

Wow. 'No,' I reply, 'I was just thinking how relieved I am I don't have kids.' The best way to make a room full of parents uneasy is to challenge their life choices.

Afterwards, Julie pulls me into her office to 'have a little chat about the Key Stage Four gig'. She sneezes loudly as she unlocks the door, spraying germ particles over the handle and spattering the 'headteacher' nameplate with tiny droplets she doesn't wipe away.

I have never seen her without a cold. I would have gone to my GP for further investigation by now to eradicate the likelihood of HIV, hepatitis and the like, but she insists her current symptoms are 'a new infection picked up from nursery'. In principle, I admire people soldiering on through illness as it shows a tremendous commitment to their work. However, when she coughs exaggeratedly and fails to make any attempt to cover her mouth, I re-evaluate. Would it be antisocial to open the window? A huge, freezing gust swooshes rainy leaves past the glass. Better not. I dislike Julie, but not enough to kill her off like a sickly character in a Charlotte Brontë novel.

Julie sits at her chaotic wooden desk and indicates for me to take the chair opposite. 'I'm so sorry for that little joke I made about you at Huddle. I hope it wasn't an overstep.' Her affected Americanisms are from when she spent six months in the States thirteen years ago.

'It's fine,' I say, desperate for her to cut to the chase.

'No, I'm going to tell everyone to keep the baby talk to a minimum in the future.'

'My colleagues' vocabularies are basic but I wouldn't

diminish them to talking like babies, Julie!' I sit up taller. If being Head of Key Stage Four affords banter like this, Julie might grow on me.

She ruins it with her saccharine smile. 'Not everyone can have children and we totally should be mindful of that.'

'I have no idea whether I can bear a child,' I say, trying not to be distracted by the dribble of mucus oozing from her nostril. 'I just choose not to have one.'

She laughs. 'Ah, don't worry, you'll change your mind!'

'Ah, don't worry, I won't!' I am desperate to slide the box of tissues towards her. She creates a hammock with her hands and rests her chin on it, which somehow creates a frame for the snot.

'Well,' she says, with the profundity of a prophet, 'you should give it some serious thought. You might wait too long and then have to live with that regret for the rest of your life.'

Does she really think this is new information I haven't already considered? I lean forward, then remember she's a germ factory and recoil. 'My life is, and will continue to be, fuller and richer without a baby,' I say, forcing a smile.

Julie's face flushes with outrage . . . or is it consumption? 'In what way is *your* life fuller and richer than mine?'

Her emphasis on the word 'your' accompanied by the accusatory finger point cuts deeper than I'd care to admit. I look down at my lap. 'I thought we were here to discuss Key Stage Four.'

'Yes.' Julie clears her throat – from 'overstep' awkwardness, not the potential tuberculosis ravaging her lungs.

'It was a tough decision, but there was another candidate who just pipped you. At this stage, it came down to tiny things, but in the end . . . well, we've offered the role to Suzie.'

I whip my head up to glare at her. 'Your best friend, Suzie Martel?!'

She smiles. 'Well, we're friends. I wouldn't say—'

'She's just taken most of the year off!'

'She hasn't been on holiday; it's hard work having a newborn.'

I scratch into a groove on the side of the desk with my thumbnail, tempted to etch it into a cock and balls.

'I'm sorry, Barri. I know it's a disappointment.'

The mucus globule suspending from her nostril is now the size of a mini lightbulb. I fiddle suggestively with the tissues. She doesn't notice.

'I didn't see Suzie Martel stepping in to play Titania in *A Midsummer Night's Dream* when that Year Eleven went into labour, did you?' I ask, crossing my arms.

'No, and I agree she would have been much better casting for the role of a fairy queen—'

'I think the reviewers would disagr—'

'Suzie didn't step in because she was with "that Year Eleven" at the hospital. And she actually knew her name.'

No doubt Julie will relay all this to Suzie later. The pair of them laughing over a glass of Prosecco, delighted in my painful rejection. I shunt the box of tissues towards her. 'I suggest you blow your nose.'

Julie doesn't hear me. She's distracted by a personal message on her phone, making that annoying muttering sound while she reads.

Assuming we're done, I stand up.

'Barri. Do you think you could cover homework club at

lunch? Caius has a temperature and I have to pick him up from nursery.'

I clench my fists. 'Yes, fine.'

But everything's not 'fine'. Sean is gone and my promotion has been usurped by a less talented, less committed, half-rate teacher from Milton Keynes!

I look back at Julie, who grimaces as she finally detects the salty presence of moist mucus on her top lip. She scoops all of the green sticky bogey away with a tissue that is conveniently beside her elbow since I shunted the box to her. She doesn't even need to look up from her phone to locate it; a prime example of the unacknowledged, unseen and unappreciated value I add to this school on a daily basis.

And as I watch in fixated horror as she places the gunky tissue on her desk instead of the bin beside her, I have a moment of flawless clarity.

It's time to get the fuck off this island.

Leave behind the un-binned snotty tissues and start to actually make something of my existence. I'll go to all the places other people visit and then bore me about afterwards. Settle somewhere new. Where no one will know me or Sean, or that our marriage ended with typed text instead of spoken words.

In what way is your life fuller and richer than mine?

All right, Julie; it isn't. But it will be.

Barri Brown's getting off this rock and she's never looking back!

Chapter Three

The second I left Julie's office last Monday, I called the estate agent and instructed them to put Mon Petit Rocher on the market as soon as possible. My little cottage is small fry over here, but I'm chain-free. An easy win and I know it will sell. The one next door sold in a matter of hours to a buy-to-let landlord. Given the dearth of affordable rental properties over here, that's not actually a bad thing . . . as long as it's someone local who benefits from it.

To chivvy things along with my house sale, I spent some time in Town buying various items to 'stage' my property like they do in those American real estate TV shows. Blankets, flowers, tasselled cushions . . . the stuff people go cock-a-hoop for that I'm indifferent to. I thought it made everything feel homely, but when the well-groomed, shiny-foreheaded estate agent came round to do the valuation earlier this week, she cast her eyes over the candles, vases and potpourri and then took in Sean's action figures, gaming chair and *Alien* movie poster, wrinkled her nose and said it gave off a 'confusing energy'. I told her what I found 'confusing' was why she expected me to trust her taste when she had intentionally brushed her eyebrow hairs to stand vertically and then laminated them to her face.

Despite our differing opinions – and her being too easily offended by some well-meaning eyebrow feedback – she suggested an asking price of more money than I could ever have hoped for. Half will go to Sean, of course, but there should still be more than enough to go travelling, with a small deposit left over for wherever I decide to settle.

I want to go to every continent. Even cold ones, where the only babies will be of the penguin variety. No annoying scooters will disturb my peace as I sip a glass of oaky Chardonnay in Napa Valley. Parents won't screech at their children to stop fighting while I relax on the white beaches of Costa Rica. I'll master Muay Thai, picturing Suzie's smug face as I punch a pad in Phuket, and I'll grin from ear to ear as I ride in the front seat of a jeep in Zambia . . . not like the time I went to that safari park with Mum, Lara and the boys and was forced to sit in the middle, despite it being just as much my right to look at the lions as theirs. When in Fes, I'll enjoy a peaceful traditional hammam and, afterwards – while parents across Europe are doing 'bedtime' – I'll venture up to the rooftops to watch the sunset and listen to the call of the muezzins echoing across the city. The calls to prayer will resonate like an anthem: Barri Brown is here and she's thriving in her No Fucks Given epoch.

The only time I've felt a slight pang of sadness over the past week was when I cycled past Belle Greve Bay on the way to my swim yesterday . . . ormering season starts in January, so still two months away. I'll miss that feeling of pure calm, wading out in the freezing cold and turning a rock over to discover the rough exterior of a sizeable ormer underneath. The sound of it clinking against others in the bucket, ready to be taken home to cook.

But nothing is stopping me from taking a bit of Guernsey with me. An ormer shell tucked in my pocket like a mascot – its pinky-green oil-slick interior glimmering while I island-hop in New Zealand, eat street food in Ho Chi Minh City and attach a big brass padlock to the top of the railings at Montmartre. BARRI etched into it. A name so elegant when it's written down that it stands alone, with no requirement for another next to it. Smug couples can point at my padlock and say, 'Poor Barri, all alone in the world.' People with more common sense might remark, 'Yes, Barri, you back yourself!'

But none of this can happen if I remain a salaried rat race runner. It's time to rip off the wax strip and quit this job once and for all.

On Sunday evening, I light one of my new candles, the scent of vanilla wafting through the living room, and sit at the dining table with my laptop and a glass of red. I take a deep breath, close my eyes in zen preparation, open them again because I can't touch-type, and begin.

I've heard writers on Radio 4 talking about a 'flow state' and thought it was nonsense but the words waterfall out of me. Every nit-pick, observation and irritation I've fixated on means I've been drafting this resignation letter in my head for the past seven years.

I begin with general feedback. For example, how the school would benefit from a one-way system. Yes, it is impractical to turn left and circumnavigate the entire school when one is only going a single classroom to the right, but I truly believe it would help tackle the sedentary lifestyle the students are forced to have during the school day . . . and encourage some of my colleagues – for example, the sweaty biology teacher – to improve their cardiovascular health. I'm not exaggerating when I say that psychologists could use the water patterns on the back of Mr Bell's shirt to evoke emotional responses in patients.

I spend half a page on Yolande and how someone that indiscreet shouldn't be allowed to be a school counsellor, and I double down on Suzie's complete lack of English acumen. I also provide a list of all of the shirkers in the faculty and to whom they owe lemon drizzle thank-you cakes. All those allotted to me, I suggest splitting among non-shirking staff.

It's 3 a.m. by the time I get to listing all of the potential diseases Julie might want to get checked out for. I'm particularly proud when I bookend that section with 'a definite case of Ignorantboreoffitus'.

Three quarters of a bottle of wine to the wind, I pepper in a few bullet points that casually call into question whether her first-class degree from Oxford actually exists. Like that time at the PTA quiz when she insisted JFK was O. J. Simpson's dad, making her team lose by one point. Mr Bell was so annoyed to miss out on the winning prize – a meal voucher for four at China Red – he insisted we address this American history faux pas during morning Huddle. Without blinking, Julie looked him in the eye and claimed she never said it at all. Such conviction, the other members on her quiz team nodded in agreement, which irked Mr Bell even more. I'll admit I admired her ability to style that one out.

While the kettle boils, I watch the printer regurgitating my words, wishing I could seal the warm sheets with wax, like in a costume drama. I glance at the cooker clock:

5.30 a.m. Despite the lack of sleep, I feel a need to burn off all my wired energy, so I grab my swim bag and shove it and my Thermos into the basket of my trusty pushbike, Melva.

On my way to the bathing pools, I stop off at school to deposit my letter in Julie's pigeonhole. Yes, it will be awkward working alongside one another for the remainder of the autumn term but, fully in the knowledge that the students are about to be lumbered with a sub-par teacher like Suzie Martel, Julie will be so desperate for me to impart all the literary wisdom possible to my students, she will have no choice but to grin and bear it. I won't let on about the extensive revision notes I've prepared for the students until I email them through from the airport departure lounge.

The strong sea wind blusters directly into the pools today, but once I'm in and ploughing through the freezing saltwater it doesn't matter one bit. It must be the adrenaline from my letter-writing because I finish my lengths five minutes quicker than usual. I climb out and wrap myself in my Dryrobe; my favourite present ever from Sean. Camo print because I'm 'like a drill sergeant'. The absolute delight on his warm, beardy face as he said that, wrapping me up inside it. The memory is a jellyfish sting.

There's no one else at the bathing pools this morning – my solid preference as no pleasantries need to be exchanged; no conversation about whether we can or can't see bloody France. (I can't.)

I find a spot behind the wall that shelters me from the worst of the wind. As I pour tea from my Thermos, I search Skyscanner and spot the cheapest flight to Nashville I've come across all week *and* it's leaving the day after term ends.

Positive this is a sign, I scrabble about in my bag for my credit card.

It's important to me that the first place I visit as a solo traveller isn't somewhere that will make me think, *He would have loved it here*, which is why I've settled on Music City. I've always wanted to go . . . I even have a pair of never-worn cowboy boots in my wardrobe. I love the idea of strutting down the street in them as I hear incredible tunes travel through every open door and window, tapping toes at the Grand Ole Opry, or flooring the gas pedal of a convertible Chevrolet as I zoom through the gates of Dollywood.

I'm just waiting for a verification code from my card provider to approve the payment for my flight when my screen changes to alert me that I have an incoming call. Annoying timing aside, I'm impressed the estate agent is up and at work already.

I left her a couple of voicemails yesterday evening with some questions about the viewings we have coming up. Lots of interest as predicted. I visualise all that money being wired over to me like a scene in an espionage thriller. Although I don't anticipate the real-life transfer will require secret codes, a laptop in a metal briefcase or a special Swiss bank account key, receiving my half of the pot will be just as thrilling to me!

'There was a remortgage on your property a few months ago, Ms Brown.'

The estate agent's abruptness disarms me for a second but then I chuckle. 'Remortgage? That's impossible.' No wonder she's at her desk so early – can't manage the simple workload in her core hours.

'It's true. Spoke with your mortgage adviser this morning.'

I stretch out my tight calf, trying to ignore the peanut of alarm calcifying in my stomach. 'Right. Yes, I left her a voicemail . . .' I pause my movement. 'Wait, is she allowed to discuss my personal—'

'Not really, but we go to the same gym. Found ourselves face to face doing a side plank and it just kind of came up in conversation. Really took my mind off the ab shake.'

The estate agent sounds breathless. I imagine her heading out of the leisure centre, gym bag on her shoulder, invigorated by the exercise and gossip in equal measure.

'He's taken the lot, apparently. Your husband.'

I grip the railing as another swimmer heads down to the water, skinny and purposeful in her swimming cap. I clamber along towards the sea hoping the waves will mask my conversation.

'I don't understand how that's . . .' I perch on the edge of the concrete platform at the far end of the pool. 'Sean can't do that without my permission. Can he?'

'How should I know? Speak to the bank or a lawyer or something.'

I spring up again. 'There's no need to be snappy. I know you didn't appreciate the eyebrow feedback, but—'

'I've hardly slept. You left me seven voicemails at 3 a.m.!'

'Well, that's your own fault for having your phone beside your bed!'

Swimming Cap Woman sits on the side of the pool, eyeing me with interest. I lower my voice and turn to face the sea. 'There's got to be some kind of misunderstanding . . . a clerical error—'

'No, she's positive. Checked it several times, she said.'

There's absolutely no way Sean would do that behind my

back. I ignore the little niggle telling me I also thought there was no way he'd end our marriage. I squat down and rest my head against the cold metal of the railing as if this change of position might somehow pivot the conversation.

'In terms of the immediate need for liquidity, I don't need to be a mortgage adviser to tell you you're fucked, Ms Brown. But, as it goes, that's also word for word what she said before she turned away to plank in the other direction. That you're fucked!'

The trouble with a small island is that the talent pool is limited. I suspect Fallaize and Flood Estate Agents has fallen victim to this fact. Forced to hire this unprofessional young lady who is now enjoying my misery with her hard-abbed contemporaries. If I wasn't so tired of writing letters, I'd be drafting a very strongly worded one to her employer.

Oh God, the resignation letter, freshly typed and sitting in Julie's pigeonhole! The bit where I compare her posture to that of Kermit the Frog. When he's not being puppeteered . . .

I hurtle off on Melva, wondering if I can get a fine for breaking the island speed limit on a pushbike.

Arriving at school flustered and covered in sweat, I head straight for the staffroom and grasp at the air inside Julie's empty pigeonhole. Yolande, a nosy rectangle today in a structured shoulder-padded dress, regards my red face, wet hair and camo-print Dryrobe teamed with sockless burgundy brogues. Feigning calm, I shuffle towards Julie's office, sprinting as I turn the corner.

She's in there with Suzie, who looks so bloody glowy. That's what nearly a year off followed by an instant promotion does for you. The letter sits unopened on the desk.

I knock, enter, and beeline for the envelope without giving them time to take in my ridiculous appearance. 'So sorry to interrupt. I left a letter for you but my circumstances have changed so I need to—'

Julie's hand shoots out to grab it before I can get there. Her grubby ink-stained fingers tarnish the white of the envelope as she feels its weight. 'Wow, whatever it is, you certainly had a lot to say . . .'

I think about the section where I compare her unsightly mastication to that of a barely weaned baby sucking on dry Jacob's crackers. She opens it, pulls it out, applies her reading glasses . . .

'STOP!'

Julie looks up at me in alarm.

'I'm pregnant!' I shriek.

Chapter Four

Julie stares at me open-mouthed. Even her moustache hairs look aghast. 'How is that . . . I mean . . . wow, Barri . . . that's . . . fantastic news.'

My grip tightens on the back of the chair I'm leaning on, knuckles white, as I try to pinpoint when this plan – if we can call it that – formulated. I struggle to come up with an answer.

But it doesn't matter. In a minute they'll realise that I can't possibly be serious given how often I've banged on about not wanting children. They'll laugh, and then I'll laugh, and I'll snatch the letter out of Julie's hand before she has a chance to open it, dash to the nearest toilet and shove it in a sanitary bin.

But as I rise onto the balls of my feet, poised to lunge for the envelope, I'm thrown by a dog-summoning high-pitched *Eeee* sound coming out of Suzie's mouth. She and Julie turn to each other, grinning. And then . . . Julie joins in with the noise. Admittedly, it's not as pure and bell-like as Suzie's, making me wonder whether Julie has a nodule on her vocal cord.

I cover my ears with the heels of my hands while they

squeal, arms glued to their sides, waving their hands like excited T-Rexes, and it dawns on me that despite having said I don't want a baby multiple times – including in this office only last week – neither of these two, or possibly any one for that matter, has ever believed me.

I want to shake Suzie by the shoulders and demand that she uses her brain. I want to march round to Julie's desk and move her mouth open and closed like a ventriloquist's dummy: *But Barri, that's crazy; you're always saying you don't want kids.*

But I don't shake Suzie, or ventriloquise Julie. I just stand there. And the longer I do, the less I want to tell them it's not true. And – disturbingly – the more convinced I become that I could actually pull this off.

While Suzie monologues about 'baby mammas', 'milky smells', and 'little squidges', I realise how poetic this is. Paid maternity leave is my chance to redress the balance for all the holidays gifted to favoured sisters and promotions granted to less-deserving colleagues. The stitched PE kits, patronising comments, last-minute lesson covers and extra homework clubs. Certainly better than a lemon drizzle thank-you cake.

It's nowhere near the cash injection I was expecting from the house sale but it still means I can leave. I'll have to scale back my plans a bit. Maybe head to Nashville and travel around the southern states for a few months before settling somewhere new. I've been thinking a lot about Edinburgh of late. That university visit where Dad's grin got bigger and bigger as we wandered the cobbled streets. *I can just picture you here, Bazza.* There's something quite apt about finally getting to live there.

But faking a pregnancy?! There's still time to stop this

now. Come clean. Say, *I'm sorry – I'm feeling delicate about Sean, the promotion.* They might gossip behind my back, but out of pity more than anything.

My stomach twinges as I remember the conversation with the estate agent this morning. *He's taken the lot, apparently. Your husband.*

The sound of upbeat country music in my brain segues into a bagpipe mash-up as I come to realise the truth: I don't want to stop. I want to cut and I want to run.

I tell them the letter was to announce my pregnancy. It is multiple pages because I'm so moved by the experience of becoming a mother (they lap this up) but I've reconsidered and I'm uncomfortable sharing my news yet. Their faces break into concern. A flurry of questions. I reassure them everything is OK. The first scan looked good.

'When's your due date?' Julie asks.

I do a quick calculation. 'Thirtieth of June.'

The two of them exchange a look. 'Why on earth did you have a scan at eight weeks?!' Julie asks, concern knitting her brow. 'There's nothing wrong, is there?!'

I curse my rudimentary mathematical skills, reassure them there's nothing wrong and make up some nonsense about 'gut feelings and maternal instinct'. They both nod at me like I'm their cult leader.

'Oh Barri, anything you need at all, I'll be here.' Suzie goes to grasp my hand, pauses when she remembers I'm not a toucher, and opts to wiggle her fingers at me instead, which makes me feel worse than the touching would have.

'Would you be kind enough to cover for me when I go for my next scan?' I ask her.

'Of course!'

'It's on a Monday, so I'll miss Huddle . . .'

'No problem,' replies Julie, beaming.

This is so easy . . . their instant warmth, the kindness, the relief that they were right: that deep down I'm a conformer just like them. In The Club. Ironic, because I've known for a while I never want to join it . . .

It was Liberation Day, nearly six months back and I'd been in Town watching the cavalcade of Union-Jacked military vehicles pass along the seafront. I pretended I didn't recognise the group of Year Tens drinking down the side of a gazebo on the other side of the road, where a trio of enthusiastic musical theatre students attempted an Andrews Sisters-style version of 'Wannabe'.

It was a gorgeous spring day. Sean had been a bit out of sorts when I left him that morning, so I was surprised when he found me in the crowd and suggested we go for a walk.

We headed on round the cliffs to Fermain – one of my favourite places on the whole island with its lush greenery surrounding the cliff path, and the clear blue sea splashing onto the shimmering pebbles below. Feeling my body tugging for a swim but knowing that Sean wouldn't be keen, I suggested we stop at the cafe there for a sandwich and a bottle of cider to enjoy the view instead. My treat.

Just as we were about to tuck into our well-stuffed crab sandwiches, a woman asked if she could sit on the other end of our double picnic table. She was trying to present as a lone person out for a peaceful walk, ready to partake in a solitary coffee. Little did she know that I clocked her and her family from all the way up on the cliff path. A loud husband, several primary-school-aged children, and a precocious preschooler.

She held my gaze with resolve but her eye gave a twitch. *A tell.* I rested my elbow on the tabletop, ready to decline—

'Yeah, sure,' said Sean.

The woman moved quickly. She summoned her brood and yelled at her husband in the queue that they had table six. Before I had time to correct her that she had *half* of table six, the whole family moved in and took up the lot.

Sean, who would usually share my disdain, seemed to enjoy his proximity to this chaos, laughing along with the precocious child's silly jokes. 'Brutus,' I muttered under my breath, trying to pretend my bum wasn't going numb from having only one cheek on the end of the bench.

As I observed the grimacing mother, I had a moment of realisation. She wasn't pretending she was family-free to manipulate me into letting them share the table. Her eye twitch wasn't a tell. She was a kidnap victim desperate to alert me that she was being held hostage by her own family and needed rescuing. We met eyes for a moment across the table. Her expression said: *I don't know how this happened, but none of it is my fault.*

The dad reminded me so much of Sean with his easy, fun smile and lolloping posture. He behaved like he was one of the kids, leaving all the discipline and un-fun decisions to his wife while he got to have all the glory. He was Fun Dad – here for the weekend to entertain us all and display to the world what an awesome father he was! Everyone else in our vicinity was taken in by this display. I knew in my soul it didn't occur to him to let his wife stay on the beach to read her book while he brought the kids up for lunch. Every time they referred to her conspiratorially as 'silly Mummy', my heart bled for her.

I watched Sean appraise this man with something akin to hero worship. I could see him thinking to himself: *Yes, this is the father I will be. Fun and adored by my children. A hero and a clown in equal measure. Look at how the public loves him!*

It was at that moment that I gained diamond-cut clarity. Sixteen-carat solitaire.

I would never have a child.

If I had a baby, I would gain a dependant. Someone who relied on me for everything for every hour of the day. I would wash and scrub and blot and comfort and empty and load and wipe and worry and feed and wake and coddle and cuddle and rub and teethe and dab and mop and jiggle and juggle and sterilise and wean and Sean would . . . befriend.

On our walk back up the hill, Sean turned to me, saying, 'Maybe we should have one,' fondly remembering his new hero, Fun Dad.

This came so out of left field, I snorted. But rather than laugh along with me, Sean launched into an impassioned monologue.

Silly Mummy.

'Can we change the subject?' I asked.

Silly Mummy.

He wouldn't let the point go, claiming what wonderful parents we'd be and how this island is the perfect place to bring up a child.

SILLY MUMMY!

'Where's this come from all of a sudden?'

Sean shrugged. 'We're not getting any younger and it's . . . I think it's something I want. A mini you and me running around. It would be funny. And cute.'

That old chestnut is not as appealing when you know you're the one who would be doing all the 'running around' after this adorable and hilarious fictional toddler.

I felt like I was being pranked on a reality TV show. Sean had never shown any interest whatsoever in wanting children. He was always indifferent to Luke and Harry and barely acknowledged his best friend Ish's son, despite being his godparent.

Whenever we'd discussed having a baby in the past it was always me not wanting one and him giving me an uncharacteristically passive 'I'm happy to go along with whatever you want'.

But not that day. That day, he was determined to convince me to change my mind. His speech segued into his views on bottle vs breastfeeding. Something I couldn't give a flying fuck about so long as it was not me administering either.

'Breast is best,' said Sean, as if this childish rhyme were the gospel of Jesus.

I stopped walking and looked at him. 'The very idea of another human drinking from me – gifted the immunity I have built up over years of enduring colds, flu, coughs and sneezes – disgusts me.' Off his protestations, I continued: 'I don't want another human sucking the life force out of me, burning my precious calories so that they can get stronger. I understand it is the most natural thing in the world for some people but it doesn't feel natural to me, Sean. It feels . . . leechlike!' I grimaced at my own turn of phrase. Sean looked so dejected, I felt the need to point out that none of this should have been a surprise to him.

He just shrugged, a look of hurt on his face. 'I always thought you'd change your mind.'

I may have made a guttural sound of frustration upon hearing that nugget.

'You're not even willing to think about it?' he'd said, scuffing his foot against a loose stone.

'Think about it?' My raised voice drew a look from a couple getting into a car parked along the side of the road. I lowered my volume. 'I'm thirty-five. The rapid demise of my fertility is embedded in my head like a microchip.'

Despite society forcing me to give my fertility the same consideration as men purportedly give the Roman Empire, I knew I was extremely lucky to be in the camp of not wanting children, rather than wanting and not being able to have them. But in that moment, I realised that I was in a new situation I'd never considered. Sean wanting and me not. He left for the UK soon afterwards. Picked up an extra project at work to keep busy. He said he just needed time, promised that he'd come back.

I thought I'd be enough. But I wasn't.

The school bell brings me out of my thoughts and I'm acutely aware that I'm still in my Dryrobe-bather combo. 'I'd better go and change,' I say, pointing to my attire.

'Yes, silly Mummy!' Julie says. We all laugh. Thrilled with my natural ability to pull this off, I swivel on my brogue.

'Oh and Barri,' Julie adds, smiling.

I swivel back.

'We'll need a signed copy of the medical certificate as soon as possible.'

Fuck.

Chapter Five

My brother-in-law's pupils grow so large, it is as if a cartoonist has shaded them in. 'Oh God. Is it Lara? The kids?'

'No, they're fine, why would—'

Dave leans against the wire fence, thumps his heart with his fist and takes deep, dramatic breaths. In hindsight, I suppose it does come across as a little intense that I've tracked him down to the edge of a five-a-side football pitch on a freezing floodlit Tuesday evening.

Finally, he gathers himself. 'What are you doing here, Barri?'

His intimidating teammates laugh, no doubt picturing Barry from EastEnders.

'Do you . . . er, fancy a drink?' I ask.

'Bit of a downgrade on his Mrs,' one of Dave's friends mutters, prompting sniggers from his pals. I'm transported back to Year Nine when Azem Divjak and his mates assumed I discussed a poem about Bosnia to win his heart when in fact I only picked it because it had the phrase 'scratch your crotch' and I wanted the opportunity to be crude in a public setting.

I scuff my foot on the astroturf, imagining the scratches it will cause to my body when it swallows me up.

'Pipe down, lads, she's my sister-in-law.' Dave guides me

further along the pitch. His eyes scan over my frumpy dress, thick grey tights and Doc Marten shoes. I pull my duffle coat around myself.

'Why are you here?' he asks.

'Well . . . you're a dab hand with . . . if somebody needed to . . . create a document . . .'

Dave glances again towards his mates who have started kicking the ball around again without him. 'What kind of document?'

'On the computer?'

'Can we chat about this another time? Maybe on Thursday when you drop Luke off?' he says.

Inspiration strikes. 'I'm writing a TV show.'

On Radio 4 recently, a screenwriter described how even important people – heart surgeons, high court judges, etc. – are willing to talk if you tell them you're researching something that might be on television. They fantasise about boasting at dinner parties, describing how they offered the scientific nugget that aided a huge plot twist. I'll easily hook in an over-confident IT middle manager like Dave. Especially when I weave in a 'Netflix is interested'.

'What your protagonist should be most concerned about is the electronic footprint.' Dave takes a big gulp of IPA. He's put on a matching black tracksuit over his football kit. The hood of the sweatshirt is so plush, it sits proudly around his neck like a travel pillow.

I shuffle in my chair – far too low for the height of the table – so that I can position myself as far away as possible from his sweaty-socked foot, which taps confidently within a red slider.

'What do you mean by "electronic footprint"?' I ask.

'Well, if he's –' the assumed maleness of my protagonist does not irk me in this instance – 'paid someone online to forge documents – the police or the dodgy private investigator, or that clandestine monk who used to be a hacker – they'd be able to find that.'

I have gone to town on the plot of my fictional TV series! Dave seems so into it that I'm tempted to pitch it to actual Netflix. I look at the list of questions on my notepad. 'I've heard of something called the dark web . . . would my male protagonist try that?' I ask.

'Yeah, maybe . . . but police are on there, like, all the time, posing as buyers and sellers. He could get in all sorts of bother if he stumbled across a Fed. Even at work, Keith was telling me—'

'So the medical certificate he needs to forge . . . the one to prove he has psychotic episodes and can't remember murdering anyone . . . ?'

Dave drums the table with his fingers while he considers. 'I think his best bet is to find an actual doctor who can do it for him. Keeps it all more legit. There would be a witness, but as he's a serial murderer already, he can just kill them too if he needed.'

My phone springs to life, making me jump. I grasp at it, hoping it's Sean getting back to me. I tried him several times earlier to ask him about the remortgage, but I haven't been able to get through.

It's not Sean, just an alert from my bank telling me that I'm in my unarranged overdraft following the round of drinks I purchased and have been charged. As I type another message to Sean to reiterate that I'm sure it's some kind of admin error and to please get back to me, I notice Dave eyeing the menu's selection of expensive sharing plates and sliders. I spring up. 'You've given me so much useful intelligence, I'm desperate to get home and get started.'

'No problemo. I'm well impressed you're doing this to be honest. Didn't know you even watched TV – always imagined you sitting there reading Dostoevsky or something.' He stands too, putting on a duvet-sized puffa coat, but pauses, grinning at me. 'This was actually all right, you know. We should hang out more.' His blatant insincerity is offensive to both of us. I give him a thin smile and nod once.

'While I've got you, Barri . . .' He busies himself with his coat again. 'This granny annexe thing. Lara says she's not entertaining it, but she brought home this brochure the other day and . . . well, you're on your own now so I wondered whether you'd consider having your mum to—'

My death stare silences him.

The next morning, I unstick a photo of Sean and me from the fridge and lay it beside my infuriatingly silent mobile phone. Being forced to confront the reality that my partner of ten years is no longer obliged to pick up the phone to me is gut-wrenching. But there's also a stab of concern that he hasn't jumped on the phone to clear this up.

If he was in some kind of financial difficulty, it would be simple to conceal that from me – apart from one shared account, we've always kept our finances separate, which I don't think is abnormal in this day and age. But he'd been working round the clock . . . why would he need money that desperately? It has to be a misunderstanding. Sean may be a lot of things. Impulsive, cocky, unable to hang washing out in a timely manner . . . but he is not a thief.

I force my brain to mull over Dave's advice from last night instead . . . well, not the murder of a doctor bit, but everything else. I don't believe that a single Guernsey police officer is currently lurking on the dark web conducting an elaborate sting operation on the off-chance they might snare a secondary school teacher faking a medical form. But I can't make up a doctor's name; the island's too small for that. Nor can I fake a certificate with a real doctor's name. What if Julie knows them, and mentions it in passing? I'd be found out immediately. Dave's right; I need the legitimacy of a real doctor.

I pick off the grit-covered Blu Tack from the back of the photo of Sean and me and repurpose it to stick up a picture I took of Dad in Edinburgh, tartan beret on his head, grinning with his arm around Greyfriars Bobby. I stand back to admire my new fridge photo as I call Mum to tell her I'm coming to The Soup.

'Why on earth would you want to do that?' She's always on at Lara to pop along. I guess she's less keen to show off the oddball daughter.

To those in the know, The Soup is an institution. For five Guernsey pounds, you get a bowl of home-made soup, bread with golden Guernsey butter, a pudding, a cup of tea, a biscuit and an experience that can only be compared to that of a pure and hearty hug without ever having to hug anybody. Outstanding value.

The Soup cannot and will not begin until every paying guest is in their seat. Don't ask me why; there is no sensible answer. Even if we only verbally agreed it this very morning, it is expected that I adhere to the one sacred rule: never be late. This plays in my head like a mantra as I frantically pedal around the lanes, lost because one of the roads is up.

I sprint into the church hall at a quarter past twelve to be greeted by twenty-three fuming, wrinkled faces, all glaring at me from their U-shaped table, like a geriatric board dissatisfied with a company's financial results. In fairness, their rage is justified. Many of them survived starvation during the German occupation and grow anxious about any obstacle in their path to a full stomach. I creep past, muttering sincere apologies for my tardiness. Mum stands in the kitchen doorway, her head lowered for the shame I have brought on the family. I place myself beside Gladys, usually a jolly lady, who was a pal of my granny's. She glares at me, po-faced.

Everyone relaxes as soon as the bread comes out, followed by the steaming soup, which is a delicious-smelling lentil and bacon. I leave them to chatter about the road being up and the headline in today's *Press* – a freak wind knocking someone's breakfast off the table – and choose my moment.

'Has anyone had to go to the doctor recently?'

Absolute jackpot.

I hear about ailments, moans and how doctors don't have time to chat like they used to. As I drill down into these various GPs, paying particular attention to those who have traits of laziness, unconventionality or downright incompetence, I shortlist three promising candidates to be potential medical form signers. Eager to get cracking, I decline pudding – a delicious-looking sticky toffee.

'You keep looking after your figure like that, next time you'll keep your man.'

Cheers, Gladys.

Dr Taylor is younger than I was expecting – thirty-seven-ish, with American teeth and eyes that don't blink enough. His office is a bright room towards the back of the surgery and is filled with Formula 1 memorabilia, family photos, and a novelty portrait of a dog.

One of my OAP informants told me through wheezy breaths how Dr Taylor gave her an inhaler last year but didn't bother to show her how to use it. The poor woman had been breathing in plastic-infused air for months, wondering why her new medicine wasn't working until her granddaughter showed her how to press the button on the top.

A doctor who wants his patients in and out as quickly as possible will cut corners where he can. Someone like that could be corruptible, or – perhaps this is wishful thinking – might sign a maternity form without bothering to check whether someone is actually pregnant.

He looks at his watch and then at me, assessing how quickly he can get this over and done with. I begin gently by spinning a yarn about finding it hard to sleep because of the stress of work. 'Does your wife have a stressful job, doctor?' I glance at the photograph of the nuclear family on his desk, hoping she might be a stay-at-home mum who didn't get maternity leave herself.

'Stress doesn't cover it; she's a registrar at the hospital.'

Damn. A double medical family means two people who have sworn an oath and two people who might discuss their moral outrage about being asked to lie. I glance up at the signed photograph of Lewis Hamilton on his wall. Worth one more try.

'The trouble is, I'm in a spot of bother. I got a few too many speeding tickets and the stress is affecting my sleep,' I say.

He starts busying himself with some files on his desk in an efficient manner.

'So you're not one to bend the rules, doctor? You never speed up the Val des Terres pretending you're Lewis Hamilton at Monaco?'

He stops. Meets my eye. 'A speeding driver killed my brother last year.'

I remove Dr Taylor from my selection process and leave with a sleeping pill prescription and a reminder that if I want to have children, I need to think about it now. I'm tempted to retaliate with a dig about the inhaler, but given I unintentionally stirred up painful memories of a dead brother, I leave it.

Next on my list is Dr Tostevin. The Guernsey surname concerns me, but I've got no idea who she is so decide she's worth a punt. One of the old boys at The Soup described her as 'very alternative', which makes me think she might be down for a bit of law-breaking. I wait outside the surgery for her, hovering on Melva like a middle-aged teenager up to no good.

I'm just contemplating giving up and trying another day when an actual teenager skids up beside me on a bike. I double-take and – when recognition dawns – I'm suddenly flashing back to last year, my classroom and poor Lottie Le Page's hair aflame, me trying to work out how to use a fire extinguisher and my class descending into chaos.

The culprit: one Callum Le Brocq.

I picture the short-for-his-age Year Ten student we expelled last year for his dangerous classroom pyrotechnics. Puberty has now taken Callum full force. He towers over me, despite being on one of those low-slung BMX jobbies.

'Jeez, Le Brocq. You won't have any issues buying booze for you and your mates.'

''Cept everyone here knows how old I actually am. Shithole rock,' Callum says, meeting my eye so directly I'm forced to look away for a moment.

'Visiting from the UK, are you?' I ask, wondering if he can detect the hope in my voice. He moved over there with his dad shortly after his expulsion, so I'm surprised to see him back here. Callum doesn't respond. He just looks at me, sniffing out the weakness I'm displaying to him.

'What you doin' here, miss?'

'I just had an appointment. Heading off now. Unless you fancy going up the shop and getting a Panda Pop with me?'

'You a paedo?'

I hold my hands up and nearly topple off my bike. 'No, no! It was just a joke! An amusing reference to us both looking so funny hanging out on our bikes like an awkward pair of oversized teens. I mean, I know you are a teen but, anyway . . . Panda Pops . . . well, they don't exist any more, but they were these—'

'You're waiting for someone, eh?' He studies me.

'No.' My heart jogs as I witness a pink-haired lady in Doc Martens heading out of the surgery saying her goodbyes to the receptionist.

'Her, is it? I did say you always had this gay thing even though you're married.'

The mention of my marriage is a gut punch. So much so that I leave it far too long to respond. His eyes narrow. '*Were* married then, is it?'

I meet his eye, poker face back on. 'I'm still married, Callum. Not that it's any business of yours.'

Callum leans back in his saddle, using the handlebars for balance. 'I wouldn't have said Tostevin was your type, though, eh?'

So it *is* Dr Tostevin. A lean body that I very much doubt has birthed a child and a free-thinking, liberal aura. Very promising indeed.

'Stop perving and come on.' Callum grabs my handlebars and cycles towards the doctor, dragging me behind him. My legs scramble along the ground in an attempt to not fall over.

I notice the Bible society sticker on the back of her car and the 'God of Rock' sign I assume is a spin on the Monsters of Rock logo. She must be part of the Tostevin-Gill clan, this home-schooled feral family who live near the airport. They're distantly related to Dave, and my nephews often talk about a happy-clappy wedding they were all forced to go to where 'the pink-haired lady started singing and just wouldn't stop'.

The 'Choose Life' badge on her hessian book bag is the final nail in the coffin. Dr Tostevin is not a liberal alternative. She is a right-wing Christian rocker.

'This is Ms Brown and she wants to hear about the Word of God,' Callum says, before cycling away as fast as his newly grown man's legs can take him.

What feels like four hours later, I tear myself away from the pink-haired doctor, determined that even if she was 100 per cent on board with my plan and would, in fact, pay me ten thousand pounds to allow her to fake my maternity form, I wouldn't let her. People with such extreme views on eugenics should not be doctors. I make a mental note to tell all her patients from The Soup to switch healthcare professionals immediately.

This just leaves Dr De Jersey. I have such a good feeling about Dr De Jersey! Dr De Jersey has the highest rate of patient deaths on the island. It's all private healthcare over here, so a doctor losing patients whether by death or desertion should be more inclined to jump at the chance of gaining one – plus an imaginary foetus. Money in the bank.

I arrive at the practice to find a very bored receptionist playing Candy Crush. She buzzes through to Dr De Jersey but there's no response. We wait for a further five minutes while I pretend to be interested in photos of her two-year-old – is there no escape? – before we simply knock on Dr De Jersey's door.

We call an ambulance out of necessity, but it is clear he has been dead for a few hours. I suppose it's poetic that he, too, died on his own watch, like many, many of his patients before him.

Chapter Six

The bumps at least are easy enough to come by – just a quick Google search. The seven foam-padded cushions, each one plumper and heavier than its predecessor, arrive wrapped in enough plastic to end the world. I line them up in size order in my hallway to greet me each morning and evening, like a disturbing prenatal nursery. A poor woman's Tate Modern. A sinister teddy bears' picnic.

After a week of getting used to the presence of Liesl, Friedrich, Louisa, Kurt, Brigitta, Marta and Gretl, on Saturday morning I decide to try little Gretl on for size. The larger bumps have several thick Velcro straps to go across my back and some extra tie cords for added security. The biggest one, Liesl, even has a protruding belly button to add a realistic touch underneath clothing in the latter stages. Gretl just has one band that attaches comfortably around my waist with a slim strip of Velcro.

Once she's strapped on, she looks foreign but not unpleasant . . . like I've recently eaten a meal that hasn't been digested. Not too scary. I spin through the living room, acclimatising to the feeling. After a few fun rotations, my belly catches a wedding photo on the sideboard. It topples to the floor and the glass smashes. Its new position in the room allows me to appraise it with fresh eyes: me laughing as Sean licks wedding cake off my nose. It's the most un-us photograph I've ever seen, and I've displayed it in our home for the past five years without realising.

That whole wedding was an un-us blur to be honest. After the initial excitement of getting engaged, it all began to feel rushed, despite the fact we'd been together five years at that point. I loved Sean. He was the light after Dad dying. But it felt wrong to be getting married anywhere other than Guernsey. The more Sean pointed out that the University of Southampton was where we both met, and that it would be easier to do it in a place that came along after Dad, I started to see his rationale. After all, Southampton had meaning for both of us, whereas for Sean this island isn't special; it's just somewhere he moved to be with me. But I had this niggle inside the whole time that Dad would want it to be here.

The day itself wasn't memorable. I just have these little flashes of discomfort that wriggle through me when I think about it. The unspoken tension between Sean and his mum; Mum and Lara begrudging the cost of the flights and the fact that we didn't do it in the school holidays, meaning Luke, Dave and Harry couldn't even come. Generic dress, generic dinner, generic guests; no headspace for the personal touches. We could have curated it, kept it small, made it ours, but Sean was all about the big romantic gesture. He didn't want to stop the momentum of the sweeping love story.

This photograph captures the only moment of that day I actually enjoyed. Eating cake. I touch my chin, remembering the feel of Sean's beard bristles microneedling it as he leaned in to lick the icing.

I pull my phone out of my pocket. Still no response from him. Since the remortgage revelation, I've been asking myself whether me not wanting to have a baby was the only reason he left. But what else could it be? He was so often in the UK for work, and he's from there originally. I assume when I said I didn't want a baby, he concluded there was nothing keeping him here any more. The life we had together wasn't enough for him; I wasn't enough.

The money must have been to set himself up permanently. Maybe he's in his home town of Crawley, but I honestly have no idea. He refused to tell me, even when we were still communicating, which consisted of him messaging to say we were fine – work was busy; he needed to think – but not answering any of my questions . . . and then that text telling me it was over.

I bring up Sean's Facebook page. The small profile photo of him holding a stein of beer in front of his face hasn't changed since he left nearly six months ago. I click on his profile despite knowing it won't reveal a thing to me given he unfriended me the day he left. At the time, I put this down to his needing space. I see now how naive it was to think he wasn't pulling away even then, but it wasn't abnormal for us to have sporadic contact when he was away working. His job – selling medical equipment to hospitals and healthcare trusts – is demanding at the best of times. He was constantly on the road, meaning all communication was brief and distracted. But it never mattered because when he was back here and it was just the two of us, we'd click into place again.

My husband's online life not being instantly revealed to me at the tap of a finger hurts every time, but I still put myself through it daily. I go through the other checks: his mum's page, his friends', desperate for a hint or sign of the life he is living. The one he felt the need to remortgage our home in order to fund. Just like every other day, there's no new information to glean. I fling my phone on the sofa and kneel down to clear up the broken glass.

I know that I should start thinking about legal action. Speak with the police or, at the very least, a lawyer. There's also a niggle that my indiscreet estate agent might gossip, and other people – my sister and mother – will start asking questions about it all. Everyone already knows my marriage ended with a text message; imagine the humiliation if they discover Sean remortgaged our house behind my back, too? I need to come up with answers – even if they're lies – and getting to the bottom of what happened will help me do that. But opening myself up to legal scrutiny while I'm trying to pull off a fake pregnancy feels like a terrible idea . . . and I want to believe there's an innocent explanation for Sean's actions.

I find myself face to face with Kurt, the only bump of the seven still compressed and wrinkly within his shrink wrap. My No Going Back Bump. With Gretl, Marta and even Brigitta, I have a chance to 'terminate' the pregnancy; a woman's right to choose extends to those of us pretending. However, once we pass that threshold into Kurt, I'll reach the point at which women aren't allowed to terminate. Once I strap him to me, there's no get-out, which is why I've felt his presence in my living room all week.

Our stand-off is interrupted by the doorbell. Expecting it to be the postman with a book I've ordered on pregnancy, I fling the door open, safe in the knowledge that Alf is usually so distracted by my chest, he won't clock a tiny bump under my dress. But it isn't Alf with my book. It's a birdlike woman in her sixties, barefoot, with jeans rolled up and a military-style tweed blazer. She marches straight past me and heads into the kitchen.

I'm so relieved she hasn't noticed the Austrian choir of baby bumps lining the hallway, I don't take in everything she says. Something about how my house is just like hers but in mirror form. She looks at me, expectant.

'So, where is it?' she asks.

'Where's what?'

'The stopcock.' She rolls her eyes. 'The thing you use to stop the water.'

I steal a glance at the bumps. 'It might be better if I show you in your house.' I take her out of the back door and she charges off round the side and over to the next-door property. I follow, flinging Gretl into the bin as I go. In hindsight, I wish I'd selected the one allotted to paper and cardboard and not food waste.

The water falling from the hole in the woman's ceiling has created two inches worth on the floor. I navigate to the airing cupboard in the back bedroom to turn off the supply.

'Thank fuck for that,' the woman says as the steady flow switches to a drip. She offers me her hand. 'I'm Trish and I need a coffee.'

I shake it begrudgingly. 'Well, it won't be very relaxing given your living room is semi-submerged in water.'

Trish assesses me, no doubt working out if I'm slow on the uptake or just pretending I haven't realised she is inviting herself over. Flood or no flood, I'd much rather she had a coffee at her house, and me at mine. However, my wet feet inform me I'm bound by neighbourly duty. I tell her to give me five minutes to have a quick clear-up before running back to mine, scooping Gretl out of the bin as I go. I fling open the living-room cupboard and pile the bumps on top of one another like an amateur game of Tetris, slamming the door on them before they can topple out.

I examine my living-room invader through the serving hatch as I froth the milk. Trish paces around, her phone sandwiched between her shoulder and face while she writes a number down on the back of her hand. I can tell she's charming her landlord, a cantankerous man named Jeff or Bob – I can never remember which. He sent me an email a few days ago to say he'd found a new tenant for a few months, and to look after her as she's new to the island. I had no intention whatsoever of agreeing to that, so I let him know that – given the lack of rental properties for locals on the island – his poor decision lacked community spirit, deleted his initial message and forgot all about it. But here she is, most inconveniently in my living room.

I step in with the drinks just as she hangs up and parks herself . . . in Sean's gaming chair?!

After an awkward pause, she points to the coffees. 'Is one of those mine?' Her face brightens when she notices the professional finish on the top of the milk. I pass one to her but remain in the middle of the room like a redundant nutter.

Her choosing to sit in the gaming chair of all places has really thrown me . . . all I can think is my husband has swapped bodies with a nosy baby boomer.

Trish takes in the broken wedding photo on the side and a box of Sean's stuff I packed up this morning. Her eyes then flick to the sofa I was expecting her to sit on, eyebrows raised. I whip around. Liesl – the biggest bump of the seven, who I thought I'd stuffed into the cupboard with the others – is actually monopolising the seat where I left her last night, still wrapped up in the zip-up hoody of Sean's I dressed her in after I'd had a few wines and was feeling lonely. Yeah . . . not a high point.

I can feel my jaw tighten under my grimace.

'Should we have offered that a coffee, too?' asks Trish, not unkindly.

'It's a "her",' I say without thinking. Trish's eyebrows tremble with the effort to raise even higher than they already are.

There's no getting around it: with that faux outie bellybutton in full view, it is undeniably a fake pregnancy bump. I consider my options: I can tell her I'm an actor preparing for a role where I will be playing a pregnant woman . . . or that I have purchased the bump out of extreme empathy for a pregnant friend to live the experience alongside her . . . or I could say that Liesl is an ergonomic cushion, my only friend, a cuddly container for a family member's ashes—

'Are you faking a pregnancy?'

'No,' I reply, just as Friedrich, Louisa, Kurt, Brigitta, Marta and a rubbish-stained Gretl tumble out of the cupboard and onto the floor by her feet.

So long . . .

She takes a big sip of coffee.

Farewell . . .

She swallows.

Auf wiedersehen . . .

The gaming chair squeaks as she rests back, glancing up

at the framed *Alien* movie poster on the wall. 'If you tell me you're doing this to win some Minecraft-playing, generic film taste, awful fashion sense man back, I'm going to be very, very—'

'I just want the time off work!'

I seem to have taken to shrieking revelations of late.

Trish delights in it; she nods emphatically when I tell her how expensive it is to travel during the school holidays and rolls her eyes when I describe my teacher colleagues constantly on maternity leave and me left behind to deal with all the shit. Her bottom lip juts out when I confide that – without this – I'll never be able to get away and actually make something of my life. 'Have you and I not suffered at the hands of the patriarchy too? Why must we also endure a matriarchy deficit?!'

I have to tone it down after that as I worry she might be tempted to accompany me on my sabbatical.

I clear my throat and sit up a bit straighter. 'Anyway, Trish, what do you do?'

She pauses for a moment and rubs some non-existent coffee from the side of her mouth while she looks around the room. I panic, thinking perhaps I've misread this situation and she'll storm out of here in disgust. But then she turns to me and smiles.

'I'm a doctor. Specialise in obstetrics.'

Chapter Seven

'Your advantage is that pregnancy symptoms affect everyone differently, so you can pick and choose what works for you,' Trish says.

We're finishing our second bottle of wine by this point. I have Friedrich strapped to me, splashing the occasional spot of red wine on him as I attempt to balance my wine glass on the shelf the bump creates. Trish is on the sofa, her arm around Liesl like they're old pals catching up after years apart. Sean's hoody is discarded on the floor.

'The most sensible thing for you to do is stick to the truth as closely as possible, whenever possible. In the first trimester, it's common to suffer from fatigue, mood swings and morning sickness. Moodiness seems to be your default, so lean into that, I'd say.'

Trish picks up an ormer shell from the side; its iridescent interior winks in the light. 'What are you going to do once the leave is up and you have to return sans bébé?' she asks.

I glance through to the kitchen at the fridge photo of Dad in Edinburgh and feel the corner of my lips turn upwards. 'Easy. I'm just never going to come back.'

Trish shoves the shell back on the shelf the wrong way

up so that the grey, rough side makes a scratching sound on the wood. She tucks her bare feet under herself. 'But won't people be upset? Family, friends?'

I snort. Even if I left tomorrow, my family wouldn't miss me. Not emotionally anyway. They might be annoyed there's no one here to mend clothes and be a back-up to pick the boys up from football when my mum's not around, but that's all. I'll just head off at the start of my leave with a vague communication that I've decided to relocate for a bit and leave it at that. They'll assume I'm being my usual antisocial self, and I can easily brush off any attempts to reconnect in the unlikely event there will be any.

The school will be even easier to handle. I'll maintain light, professional comms throughout my leave and then, when they ask about my return to work, I can spin them a line about having fallen in love with where I am and hand in my notice while I'm still on leave. I've double-checked my contract, and I wouldn't have to pay anything back. A clean break and all above board, meaning I can get a new teaching job in Edinburgh.

I look up at Trish. 'You don't need to worry about any of that.'

She glances at Sean's discarded hoody. 'What about the, er . . . well, the husband?'

I shrug. 'The husband's gone.'

Her cheeks flush, possibly worried she shouldn't have brought that up. 'And have you considered the moral implications of faking this pregnancy?'

I'm preoccupied with the thought she probably hasn't rinsed her feet since paddling through her flooded living room. 'Defrauding the state is a victimless crime, don't you think?' I say, trying not to let myself fixate on what mucky remnants of Bob/Jeff's old carpet may now be seeping into Big Blue, my beloved sofa.

'I don't know how it washes in Guernsey, but in the UK, taxpayers really don't love people stealing their money.'

'Yes, but people hardly pay any tax over here.' Trish gives me a doubtful look. 'OK, so it's a bit . . . questionable, but it's my lemon drizzle. My matriarchy deficit—'

'Yes, yes, not all that again. You had me at "I just want the time off work!"' She shrieks this (a poor imitation), and pours us a fresh glass of red from the wine bottle she just plucked from the rack.

'If it's too much for you to reconcile with, you don't have to help,' I say. 'We can finish this bottle of Barolo I was saving for Christmas Day that you very rudely just helped yourself to, and pretend like none of this ever happened.'

She just laughs this off and leans in to observe my face, like a scientist inspecting some mould in a petri dish. 'It would be good if we could get you a bit more . . . glowy. We'll also need to decide what we'll say when people ask who the father is . . .'

Trish's use of the word 'we' sobers me. Signing a form is one thing. I don't want or need an accomplice. It's stressful enough having to go through this solo, bringing someone else in on it feels reckless. Both for her and me.

She takes her feet off the sofa and hooks her toes onto the edge of the coffee table instead. I exhale at this slight improvement in grubby foot placement. I can't remember the last time someone other than me or Sean passed the threshold of our cottage, and now I know why.

When she finally leaves, a plan agreed for her to come by with the maternity form tomorrow after her shift, I collapse into bed and fall straight to sleep.

The following evening, Trish knocks on my door as planned – medical bag in hand and hospital lanyard around her neck. Before I have time to even say hello, she bundles herself inside.

'Come on, let's get this over with,' she says, beelining for the dining-room table and pulling a piece of paper and pen from her bag.

'How was your first day?' I ask, still standing in the hallway with the door open.

The pen drops out of her hand and rolls onto the floor. 'Bollocks.' She kneels to grab it. 'Oh fine, fine. I mean, people aren't usually that friendly to locums but I had a very warm welcome, given I'm only here a few months.'

'Guernsey,' I say. Trish sighs in frustration. 'You don't seem very happy about it?' I press.

'No. It was nice in that respect, but we had a very poorly newborn. He pulled through, thank God.' She rests back on her heels where she's kneeling and dabs her eyes with a tissue from her sleeve. 'Sorry, it's been . . . but all OK now.'

I move towards the table to look closer at the unsigned medical form that will legitimise my lie.

'Anyway, enough about that!' Trish sits at the table and poises her pen above the paper, her hand trembling.

'Are you OK?' I ask.

'Yep,' she says, pen still hovered above the paper.

'Would you like a cup of tea?'

'No, no.' She still doesn't move . . . like she's willing for her hand to write, but her body is struggling to comply. She sighs and sits back in the chair. The furrow of her brow creates a double speech mark in the middle of her forehead. 'I'm sorry. I've had more time to reflect on this in the cold, sober light of day and . . .'

Feeling very much like I might be on the verge of losing my doctor, I pull the opposite chair out and sit down, placing my palms on the table. 'This goes without saying, but you have my word I won't tell a soul about your involvement, even if I get caught.'

Trish pulls her medical bag onto her lap and clutches it to herself. It's a beautiful soft burgundy leather with the initials 'P. P.' on it. Dr Patricia Pepper, I deduce from her lanyard. I wonder if this bag was a gift and if so, who gave it to her? She fiddles with the gold-plated clasp. 'What if you change your mind?'

I snort. 'About telling people you're involved? I can't see why I would ever have a reason to—'

'No, about the pregnancy?'

I glance at the bumps, lined up in size order in the hallway. 'I won't change my mind.'

'Even if your husband wants to get back together?' she presses.

I feel my cheeks flare at the mention of Sean and look down at my hands. I've taken to wearing one of my granny's costume jewellery rings on my wedding finger, which feels odd, but not as strange as having nothing on it at all. I fiddle with the giant amethyst-style gemstone. 'Sean doesn't want to get back together and even if he did . . . I don't think we could.' I look around the living room and wonder again what on earth possessed him to remortgage this house without telling me. Revenge for me not wanting a child? Maybe. Gambling debts? I hope not. A new start with someone else? My stomach does a tumble-turn at the thought of that. I stand up and head to the kitchen to put the kettle on, trying not to let that horrible thought percolate.

When I come back in, Trish is still where I left her, staring at the form. I lay the tea tray down, having put the milk on separately as I believe it's disrespectful to assume people take their tea the same as me.

Trish picks up the jug. 'Is this . . . cream?'

'No, Guernsey milk is just far superior.'

Trish nods in concession and goes for a little splash so that the swirling brown liquid of hers is a Pantone match to mine.

I sit back down and look across to her, willing her with my mind to sign the bloody thing.

She takes a sip and relaxes her shoulders, which had previously been up by her silver stud earrings. 'I do want to, you know . . . help you. I'd just like to be sure we agree on all the ground rules. To make sure I'm taking a punt on the right horse so to speak.'

'OK . . .' I say, determined to show my thoroughbred credentials. 'In the very unlikely event that I chicken out, I'm allowed to "terminate" the pregnancy up until the usual point a woman can do that.'

'Twenty-three weeks, six days,' she says quickly.

'Yes.' I glance at Kurt. 'But after that, there's no going back. Either, option one, I come clean about the fake pregnancy, leaving you out of it; or, option two, I leave the island and never come back.'

There's a pause. She worries her hospital lanyard in between her hands. 'There would be a third option, of course,' she says. I study her fidgeting hands and wonder about her day. A little boy nearly lost, the prospect of breaking the news to grieving parents. How many times has she had to do that in her life? I think I understand what's bothering her.

I sit back. 'No way.' She raises her eyebrows, questioning. 'I mean it. Options one and two, people will think of me what they think of me, but at least that's on me. Pretending I have lost the baby is an absolute no-go as far as I'm concerned. You have my word on that one.'

She lets out a breath. 'In that case, you have a deal.' She grabs the pen, her hand much steadier now, but before she scribbles her signature, she looks up at me, her glasses balanced on her nose. 'Choosing to not have children is a privilege too, you know. So many people who would love to have them can't. And I don't just mean couples who can't conceive. People who, due to circumstances out of their control . . .' She clears her throat, doctorial again. 'I urge you to remember that as you embark on this.'

'I will,' I say. And I mean it.

I take a big gulp of tea while her signature scratches the paper. 'Do you mind me asking why on earth you're helping me?'

The down-light of the lampshade above exaggerates the lines in Trish's face as she considers my question. 'It's good for the soul to jump aboard a hare-brained scheme every now and again,' she replies, handing me the form.

I decide to let this absolute bullshit answer fly. Now I have the signed document Trish's role in this is over.

I am an exceptional phaser-outer of parasitical people. Ruthless. Since Saturday night, Trish has attempted to contact me multiple times, all combatted with cut-throat precision.

The trick is not to ignore or say no, but to delay. Treat your social life how an executive assistant might manage the busy diary of a CEO who doesn't want to take a meeting. Make a plan with the person (because people love putting things in the diary, a trait I detest), then, closer to the time, send sincere apologies – please can we reschedule? And push it back one month minimum, six weeks if you have the nerve. Keep doing this and, eventually, the desire to meet fizzles out without it ever hitting their consciousness that you never wanted to have coffee with them in the first place.

Safe in the knowledge Trish will soon give up trying to encroach on my life, I can focus on the next terrifying job at hand. The first time wearing Gretl in public. I was going to wait longer, but Julie rattled me when I went to present her with the signed maternity form earlier in the week, which, as expected, she snatched hungrily from my hand.

'Dr Patricia Pepper?! Never heard of her,' she'd said, disappointed.

'She's new to the island. Contracting at the hospital for a bit,' I'd replied.

'Oh . . .' Julie had spread the form on her desk with the palm of her hand, and I became irritated when a tiny edge of it collected some ink from the open end of a pen. The extreme Christian vitriol and manic sofa-scrubbing that went into obtaining that document!

'I can't wait until the cat's out of the bag,' Julie went on, 'and I'm obviously showing a load of self-restraint by not asking who the dad is . . .' Not gleaning a response from me, she'd appraised my stomach. 'Still not showing. Won't be long!'

So, this weekend is the trial run for Gretl and me: a trip to the garage on the Braye Road. It's a nostalgic homage to the first time I was allowed to leave the house on my own, aged seven, and my dad let me buy a newspaper from there. The mixture of freedom and adrenaline I felt whizzing down there on my bike, out in the wild for the first time. I could have done anything: knocked for a pal, headed down to the beach, befriended a dolphin and asked her to swim me to the mainland. Of course, the trust placed in me to do this most grown-up of errands kept me on a clear path – in, out and straight home again.

I feel that same adrenaline today as I head out of my house, my smallest bump strapped to me. I suppose Gretl does, in many ways, represent freedom . . . or at least a pathway to it.

My heart beats faster as I pass one of my neighbours, a balding man in a festive jumper walking a pug. Normally, I don't see the point in wishing a good morning to anyone because I don't give a stuff whether they have a good, average or terrible morning. Today, however, I am a pregnant woman. I whack on a huge smile.

'Lovely day, eh?'

The man jumps out of his skin; my exclamation at least twenty decibels above the desired volume required to come across as jovial, unthreatening, and not hiding a fake baby bump under my dress. I clock my maniacal grin in a car window reflection. I'm so hyped up and tense that I don't seem to be able to readjust my jaw muscles into anything resembling normal.

He mumbles, 'Yes, it is,' and scurries away.

I take some deep breaths and remind myself that the

chances of anyone noticing my bump are non-existent because of the huge smock I have selected to wear for this first outing. Baby steps.

When I arrive at the garage, I pretend to peruse the newspapers. For nostalgic reasons, I have already preselected the *Sun*. A publication I detest, but it's the one I bought for my dad twenty-eight years ago. As I reach down to pick up the paper from the row of piles at the foot of the magazine rack, my foot slips on a rogue magazine insert that has fallen on the floor. Try as I might, I can't stop myself from toppling forward, and I end up sandwiched between the row of newspapers and the wall. I clamber out as gracefully as I can manage, but my smock still rides up to reveal my neat bump poking out.

'Er . . . Barri, are you OK?' Yolande stands above me, sporting a similar-shaped smock, staring at my stomach. Thank God I had the foresight to disguise Gretl under a pair of one hundred denier tights pulled up to my bosom. I pull my smock back down. I can feel that maniacal grimace on my face again. She stares at my stomach, no doubt trying to work out whether she saw a baby bump or an extravagant breakfast.

To disguise the situation, I grab some sanitary pads from the opposite shelf. Quick thinking indeed! Confident I have averted the crisis, I tell her I'm in a hurry and head towards the counter. She stares at what I'm holding, her mouth curling upwards into a salacious smile and I realise my error. Incontinence pads. No doubt stockpiling them for after the birth of the baby I am now unequivocally carrying.

I drop the *Sun* and incontinence pads on the ground (a pleasing mise en scène!) and leg it home, only mildly impinged by Gretl. When I get there, I lean back against the wall in the hallway, nearly snapping my ankle on a haphazardly discarded shoe in the process.

It just had to be Yolande! She'll have called my sister already to fill her in, not only on the hilarity of witnessing my tumble into the tabloids but to question whether there's a chance I'm up the duff. As soon as Lara hangs up the phone, she'll be on to my mum to quiz her. Yolande, meanwhile, will have WhatsApped Julie 'Any chance Barri is preg?!' and I can just see Julie's hairy-tashed smile as she sends the two eyes emoji. Her way of saying, *I can't tell you, but I'm telling you* . . . *YES!* From there, Yolande just needs to call my sister again.

My phone pings.

> **Mum:** YOUR PREGNANT I CANT BELIEVE IT COME ROUND NOW WHOS THE DAD

My mum only texts in shouty capitals without using punctuation, giving the disconcerting impression she's permanently furious with you.

> THANK YOU FOR THE FLOWERS THEY ARE VERY NICE
>
> CAN YOU PICK UP A FEW BITS FROM TOWN FOR ME TA
>
> ANSWER YOUR BLONEY PHONE YOUR DAD DIED

Pausing Operation Phase-Out, I hammer on Trish's door, desperate for a crash course on how to pretend to be pregnant now my research window has been obliterated. No response. I run round to the back garden and peer into the window of her kitchen. Remnants of breakfast, a mug, an open book on the counter, but no pregnancy expert.

SEE YOU HERE IN HALF AN HOUR OR WE ARE COMING THERE

Chapter Eight

'One thing that can always be said about the Roussel women. We know how to birth!' Mum steers me into the kitchen. Roussel is her maiden name. She loves referring to me in that context . . . as if her separation from Dad reverted me from Brown to Roussel too.

'Did they mention whether you have an unusually long vagina?' asks Lara as she fills the kettle. Given her long, lean back and long, lean legs, I suppose it figures Lara's vag is also of that persuasion.

'Many Roussel women have long vaginas and yet we still know how to birth!' Mum adds.

Overheating from stress, I fan myself with a magazine, which reads as a hormonal moment. They guide me into the living room, mute the TV – much to the annoyance of Luke and Harry, who are cross-legged on the floor enjoying a cartoon – and sit me in Mum's favourite chair – feet up on the footstool no less – while a decaf tea is brewed. The forced decaffeination of all hot beverages consumed in public is unfortunate, but I haven't had this much fuss from Mum since I was seven years old and slid down a slide not knowing someone had placed a drain gutter up it, slicing both inner thighs on the sharp plastic. Which, on reflection, could have resulted in *no* vagina.

A piece of dyed red straw flies into the window and is pinned there momentarily by the wind before flying off again. This year, Mum's 'Spice Crows' made the front page of the *Press* so she's refused to remove them from her driveway despite the scarecrow festival having been and gone months ago. They've disintegrated so much over the past weeks that only half of Ginger Crow in a very faded Guernsey flag dress (my mum – a proud Guern – couldn't bring herself to use the Union Jack) remains.

Lara eyes me, suspicious. 'The baby's definitely not Sean's?'

I glance at her. 'How could it be? I've not seen him in over six months, remember.'

She puts her hands on her hips. 'You never know with him, he might have snuck back over.'

'Without the island's top investigative journalist getting wind of it?' She doesn't react, just continues to study me. 'Well, he didn't,' I add.

My mum hands me a mug. I take a sip and make a satisfied sound to signify that the interrogation is over, but alas, Lara isn't finished with me. 'How did you select him, then?' she asks.

'Eh?' I turn the TV volume back up a bit, drawing a nod of approval from Harry.

'The donor!'

'Oh. Yes.'

The bloody sperm donor. On my panicked cycle over here, I couldn't for the life of me remember whether Trish said sperm donor was a good or bad choice for the father, so when they asked me the inevitable question within three seconds of arrival,

I just went with it. Now I'm fifteen minutes in, I recall Trish's red wine lips advising against it – 'It sounds like the simple option, but it will only make things more complicated.' I see what she meant. Although getting pregnant by a nameless visitor to the island would have resulted in conservative Guernsey judgement, a one-night stand is a concept most people understand without needing to do a deep-dive into the ins and outs.

'Yes, how *does* all that spermy stuff work?' pipes up Mum, as she perches herself on the arm of the sofa, hands clasped around her mug.

'Oh, you know. It's like shopping but instead of groceries it's . . . semen,' I say, hoping that will be the end of it.

'So they give you a shopping basket, do they?' Mum asks.

'No, it's not like literal shopping.'

'Oh. Online is it?' Mum rolls her eyes. 'I hate shopping online. I like to see all the things and feel them. Though with sperm, I suppose you'd rather not, you know. Look at it and touch it . . .'

'Go on, tell us about the donor.' My sister examines me like I'm an exhibit in a circus of curiosities. Even Harry and Luke are paying attention.

'Well . . .' I scan my eyes over Mum's bookshelf for inspiration. 'He's half-American, half-Italian. Glasses. Bald head but he can pull it off bald.'

'How do you know he can pull it off?' Lara folds her arms. 'They don't let you see photos of donors.'

'Oh, yeah, I know . . . That bit I assumed because, well . . . Mediterranean men can pull off baldness better than anyone, eh?'

Lara doesn't look convinced but luckily Luke pipes up. 'Like Pep Guardiola!'

'Yes. Pep Guardiola,' I agree, despite having no idea who that is. I glance at the book again. 'It did say on the website profile thingy that he's an actor . . .'

'Oh yes. Out of work actors are always desperate for money,' Mum chimes in. 'I bet they get paid a pretty penny for that sperm.'

'I'm not sure.' I grab a cushion, thump it flatter, and hold it against myself, trying to ignore the narrowing of my sister's eyes. 'But he's intelligent,' I add. 'Degree level. He's written books and can cook too . . . Loves it. Can't get enough of it. Or so it said on his profile.'

'Lovely!' Mum clasps her hands together and tucks them under her chin.

Lara turns her head pointedly between Mum and me like she's watching a repulsive tennis match. She fixes on me. 'Are you seriously expecting us to believe you've done a full one eighty on the whole pregnancy thing?'

I shrug. 'I changed my mind.'

'I knew you would,' Mum says as she pulls a drooping sock back up over her ankle. 'Women always do in the end.'

My insides clench at that but I say nothing.

Lara takes a sip of her coffee. 'There's a rumour going around that Sean remortgaged your house behind your back.'

'Lara!' Mum smacks my sister on the arm.

A bit of tea slops down my front. 'Where did you hear that?'

'Oh, one of my colleagues goes to some CrossFit class with your estate agent.' I mentally curse that woman again. 'You didn't tell us you were planning on selling up?'

I feel my cheeks redden. 'Well, it's what you do, isn't it? When . . . when a marriage ends. You sell the house.'

For a moment, I think Lara's going to take pity on me. She draws the window blind to stop the sun from dazzling her and turns back towards me for round two. 'It costs thousands for sperm donation. IVF.'

This wrong-foots me. 'I . . . used my half of the remortgage money.'

'He paid you, then?'

I nod, thumping the cushion again, resolute that I would rather double down on lies than deal with the shame of them knowing the truth about the remortgage. 'It is my money after all.'

'And the baby's definitely not his?'

'No!'

Lara leans on the sill, arms folded. 'What clinic did you go to?'

'I can't see why that's any of your business.'

'It just seems a bit too . . . convenient to me.'

I increase the intensity of my magazine fanning. 'I went to a private place on the mainland.' Her eyebrow flies up in disbelief. 'When I . . . when I went to London for that training course.' Off her doubtful look, I reiterate again. 'It's not Sean's!'

'And you just changed your mind?'

'Yes. You were right. Mum was right. I suddenly felt . . . broody and with the marriage ending and Sean leaving it made me realise it's what I really wanted.' My insides feel like a pan on a rapid boil as the lies spill out, but I do my best to appear calm by taking a slow sip of tea.

Lara studies me for an excruciating amount of time but finally sniffs and drops her shoulders in concession. 'Well, Sean's going to be devastated.'

When she announced her pregnancy, I didn't irritate her

with a barrage of opinions, bring up estranged lovers or chastise her for her terrible life choice; I left her to her own judgement-free devices.

I tuck a bit of loose frizz back into my bun. 'Please don't tell Sean.'

'Oh my God, as if I ever even talk to him . . . but he will find out.' She readjusts a copper milk can on the windowsill. 'For some reason, he's got a load of friends over here, despite him being a prick.'

I don't rise to the bait.

Lara takes a seat back on the sofa and we all watch Luke and Harry's cartoon for a bit.

Lara glances down at my bump and shakes her head. 'That donor could have any kind of genetic flaws.'

'You didn't take that into consideration with your selection of a husband,' I counter, looking at Harry in apology. 'Unless you sent Dave's full bloodwork to the lab prior to agreeing to procreate with him?'

Lara whisks the boys off in a strop after that, and for once Mum seems happy to be left with me for company. I consider asking her why Lara's so upset, but I leave it. Dad was the one who went in for the deep and meaningfuls.

Towards the end of my visit, Mum takes my empty mug from me. 'Well, I think the donor sounds wonderful. Bald, glasses, American–Italian, loves food.' Her brow furrows. 'Hang on . . .' She picks the very book I used for inspiration off the shelf. 'He sounds just like Stanley Tucci!' My heart races, worried I've been caught in my lie, but Mum just gawks at the cover. 'That man can even make gluten sound sexy.'

* * *

Instead of going home after Mum's, I take myself to the west of the island, where the sunset streaks over the bay as if the sky has been set to the grill function. I treat myself to some chips and sit on the sea wall to devour them. It's bracing in the cold and the tangy taste of vinegar helps me focus my mind.

Spending the afternoon lying to my family was exhausting. Each fib felt like a thread being fed into an over-ambitious tapestry I don't have the skills to complete. I know there's still time to tug the yarn back out, but soon there will be so many loops and twists, pulling will only make those knots tighter and the final result will be a scraggy, tangled mess.

A golden Labrador skips in and out of the sea as the owner enjoys a cigarette, scuffing the sand around with her foot as she puffs. She waves a greeting to a fellow dog walker and they strike up a conversation as the latter's jet-black Scottie dog joins the Labrador in the water.

Pulling off a fake pregnancy on a small island like Guernsey has its obvious risks, but at least people here take you at face value. My late granny and her contemporaries living through the German occupation had to believe that they would be liberated. Faith in the world and the unwavering trust of the people in it runs through the very fabric of what it means to be from here. And here I am exploiting it. Even if I lived in a cynical place, when someone has a visible bump and a signed maternity form, who would question it?

A rev of an engine pulls my attention, and my heart falls into my stomach as I recognise Sean's beloved but bashed-up purple Mini Cooper pulling out onto the coastal road. The sight of it never fails to cause alarm, despite knowing his best friend, Ish, who wrote his car off a few months back – quite an achievement on an island where the maximum speed limit is thirty-five miles per hour – now uses it. Sean has a company car in the UK because he has to travel around so much to different places, and probably didn't want the Mini battery to die given I never drive it.

As Ish speeds past without seeing me, the purple of the car contrasting nicely with the blue of the postbox on this side of the road, I think about what my sister said – how it's only a matter of time before Sean finds out about the pregnancy. Even though this is my chance to throw some pain back towards him for everything, I don't want to. Especially when me not wanting children was the reason our marriage ended in the first place. It feels too spiteful.

A big part of me wants to quietly make my exit and put all this – the money, the heartbreak, the fictitious new girlfriend I've convinced myself he's building a new life with – behind me. But I can't just let Sean steal from me . . . if that's what he's done. What would Dad think about that? His hard-earned money gone to a man who abandoned our marriage the moment things didn't go his way.

'Look, they're blue here!' A pair of tourists in hiking boots pause their stomp to grab a photo of the postbox before carrying on again.

I compose an email to a lawyer at a firm in Town. I choose her because the bio says she moved here recently and so the chances of us having any mutual acquaintances are smaller. She responds quickly and offers me an appointment next week. Instead, I request a time in the New Year. This afternoon's sperm donor fiasco taught me that I need to focus my attention on getting this fake pregnancy right. The last thing I need is the added anxiety of serving Sean with legal papers. Besides, I want to give him a few more weeks to get back to me with an explanation because there still might be an innocent reason. If he doesn't provide one, I'll have to conclude that it's not a mix-up; that he's stolen from me intentionally.

As I pick up the final pieces of salt from the chip packet with my finger, I let the antsy thoughts float through the top of my head. Up and out to form a bright red helium balloon I don't want near my consciousness. A big bunch of balloons often follows me around like Eeyore's raincloud, brightly coloured to mask the reality within.

Chapter Nine

My family agreed to keep my pregnancy private for now. I hope it will buy me a bit more time until the news is made public . . . though with Yolande in the know, I'm sure the rumour mill has started. Over the past few days, I've noticed a few double-takes at my stomach from colleagues, but no one has said anything so far.

I've always found it fascinating that when they suspect someone is pregnant, people love playing detective – clocking the refusal of alcohol and the popping out for appointments – gossiping, asking others if they've noticed. When the person in question shares their news, the amateur sleuth takes complete pleasure in shouting, 'I knew it!' It may sound dark, but I'm willing for the day someone announces the no-drinking, vomiting and medical leave is because of a stomach tumour and for someone to pre-emptively shout, 'I knew it!' with glee before realising their terrible mistake.

I've grown used to wearing Gretl by the time we approach the final week of the Autumn term. Trish is still AWOL, which suits me fine, and I've used all my spare time for research. One thing I learned is why I got the due date so very wrong when I calculated it in my head. Pregnancy isn't exactly nine months; it's split into forty weeks. Absolute baffling minefield!

To avoid confusion, I write everything in my diary up to the due date: the pregnancy week I'm on and how big the baby is. Most importantly, I've marked down what bump I need to wear when. By the time I'm back in the New Year, I'll be at week fifteen and already on Marta! Maybe I'll bury Gretl ceremoniously in the garden . . . the idea of a confused future owner digging up all the discarded bumps and wondering what horror went on here amuses me.

I flick through the many daunting weeks and months ahead . . . the mixture of food items my imaginary foetus will be compared to for size would make a funky-tasting smoothie.

It is ironic that I am in the middle of discussing Arthur Miller's description of Willy Loman using 'little cruelties' towards his wife with my Year Elevens when Callum Le Brocq flings the door of my classroom open, smashing the handle into the adjacent wall. Actually, I would call his sudden appearance a humongous cruelty.

The young men and women of that persuasion swoon at his transformation from gobby clown to tall, brooding enigma like this is a makeover montage in a teeny-boppy movie. Callum would be that mysterious student a TV company making one of those fly-on-the-wall documentaries in a school would get all excited about. They'd push to focus on his story, to show the power of an unjaded teacher taking a chance on an irredeemable miscreant. But I'm not an unjaded teacher, and Callum can't feature in a fictitious documentary about this school – because he no longer attends it.

My usually focused class fidget as they assess the change to the socio-political situation within the room. How to behave now that Callum Le Brocq is here?! A few students giggle.

He plants himself in the seat next to me, removes his jacket in a performative manner to reveal the green Victor Hugo High School sweatshirt underneath and smirks across at Hunter Mason. It is as if I can see the literary talent evaporating out of Hunter's brain as he, delighted to be singled out, returns the look. The boardroom configuration of my classroom – where we all sit around the table – is usually my preferred set-up for Year Eleven classes as it gives the students agency to have a grown-up discussion. Had I known Callum would be in the lesson, I would never have opted for this non-hierarchical seating arrangement.

'What are we looking at, miss?' Callum asks.

Rather than question whether he is trespassing on school property and disrupt proceedings further, I present him with the play and turn it to the correct page. I pre-empt his request for a pen by sliding both a pencil and a pen towards him. This throws him for a nanosecond, giving me time to follow up with a pencil sharpener, a rubber and a highlighter.

He parries by pulling a compass out of his pocket. Its sharp metal point flashes as it catches the light.

Anything related to arithmetic gets my head in a twist at the best of times, but a mathematical implement inside my literary habitat is alarming. He drops it onto the desk with a clunk. We all eye it nervously, reassuring ourselves that Callum is way too smart to stab someone with it . . . in plain sight.

I rub my bump reflexively – amazing how quickly that

has become a habit. Of course, none of the students are remotely aware I might be pregnant, too wrapped up in the trials and tribulations of teenage angst. But Callum clocks it. Of course he does.

I struggle to find enthusiasm for the lesson again, but luckily one student, no doubt to make her hands look supple and alluring for Callum Le Brocq, applies some moisturising cream and her neighbour, who suffers from a severe nut allergy, goes into anaphylaxis. I am occupied for the rest of the lesson administering the EpiPen and liaising with the paramedics.

Even in the chaos, I feel Callum's presence leave the room. I look up to see the door swinging on its hinges. He has thieved all my loaned stationery. The compass, however, remains balanced across the top of my pen pot.

As I approach Julie's office, he's already there, waiting for me. I try to ignore him as I knock on her door.

'Congratulations, miss.'

'Thank you, Callum.'

I hurry into the office and shut the door in his smug face. The light from Julie's laptop illuminates a cold sore on her upper lip. It glistens with whatever oily cream she has applied to it.

'Since when is un-expelling someone a thing?' I ask.

'Let me expl—'

'Back in my classroom without any warning. And in my condition!' Remarkable how precious I already feel after a few Sunday afternoons spent in my mum's one comfy chair.

Julie leans back in her seat. 'Callum is a very bright boy. He just needs an excellent teacher to encourage him.'

'The ceiling still has fire-tinge!'

'Lottie Le Page set fire to her own hair, apparently.'

'The world's vainest teenager? Pull the other one, Julie.'

'TikTok trend.' Off my incredulous look, Julie holds her hands up. 'If Lottie's saying she made it up, we have to let him back.'

'But . . . what about all the other stuff Callum's done? The stealing, the vandalism, the time he sold cannabis to Tim Bell.'

Julie sits up straight and turns her attention back to her typing. 'Tim is a totally excellent teacher with a promising career ahead of him. It's best for all involved that that one never gets out.'

'So we're welcoming him back to Year Eleven with open arms?'

'Correct.'

The cold sore has a pockmarked texture that makes me think of the surface of the moon. It would be immensely satisfying to watch a slow-motion video of a facialist scraping it off with a dermaplaning tool.

I lean on Julie's desk, forcing her to meet my eye. 'I think Suzie should have him.'

'I don't agree.'

'She's Head of Key Stage Four.' And Julie's ride-or-die best friend.

Julie closes her laptop and rests her chin on her fist. 'Barri, when we become teachers, we take an oath to children. All children, no matter what their background, how difficult their behaviour is, or whether or not they like us.'

I cross my arms. 'We don't take an oath.'

'It's a metaphorical oath. Anyway, how are you feeling? Keeping your folic acid up?'

I turn on my heel and storm out of there without responding, passing Callum, who is now snogging the face off Lottie Le Page. Convenient. In fairness, the pixie cut suits her. I make a mental note to look up whether that TikTok trend actually exists as I storm into the staffroom, hoping to find it empty. I stop in my tracks.

My colleagues are gathered, excited grins on their faces as they cup mismatched steaming mugs of tea. A 'congratulations' banner with a stork holding a sling in its beak is on the wall. There's a cake, various bowls of cheap party snacks, hideous napkins with rows of mini babies in nappies printed on them. *Unbelievable.*

I rip the banner off the wall, not caring that my rough grab tears it in half. 'There is a way to go about these things and this generic offering is not it!' I stamp on the stork for good measure. I gesture to the mugs of tea: 'This has been made with limescale-infused kettle water – look at the scum!' I snatch Tim Bell's mug out of his hand and tip the contents down the sink, splashing him in the process. 'Completely inappropriate for the welcoming of a foetus.' I pick up the sickly-sweet cake they have bought, which is half-pink, half-blue. My hand gets covered in the buttercream as I brandish it at them, making the icing mix to a purple. 'I don't want to have a gendered baby before it has even left my vagina.'

I fling the cake back on the table, the icing ruined. Good! As I lick my fingers in defiance, I notice that everyone is looking behind me, making apologetic faces. Suzie Martel must have been there the whole time. She rubs a perfectly formed bump, not a dissimilar size from mine.

'But . . . you only just bloody had one,' is all I can think to say as my colleagues scowl at me for shitting all over the lovely thing they had planned for my more popular colleague.

Suzie laughs it off. 'Oh come on everyone, let's make this a joint celebration for both of us . . . Barri's pregnant too!'

As one, they shout, 'I knew it!'

'Actually, it's a stomach tumour,' I say, leaving it three beats too long before telling them that I'm kidding, it's a baby.

It takes a while for the party atmosphere to return.

Chapter Ten

Suzie Martel being pregnant at the same time as me is an eventuality I hadn't considered. Initially, I couldn't work out if it was good because I'd have someone to compare myself to, or bad because everyone would compare us to each other. However, when she starts acting like my mentor – a spiritual sensei for the pregnant Barri – I conclude it's a nightmare.

A few days after the surprise staffroom party, she invites herself into my classroom before registration, leaning on the doorframe, her hands cupped around a mug. After a barrage of unsolicited advice, where I pretend to listen but am actually distracted by her barrels of blow-dried shiny waves wigwagging from side to side, I'm pulled out of my hypnosis when she perches on the end of my desk. 'I hope you don't mind me not telling you when you told me . . . I didn't feel comfortable sharing it until I was over twelve weeks,' she says, sipping her tea as if this is a casual Saturday morning and not the start of a working day. She chuckles. 'It's funny to think that we both have little kiwi-sized nuggets of joy growing inside us at almost exactly the same rate. The English department's gonna be in real trouble without us!'

Fully in the knowledge that I didn't miss Suzie one iota last year, I'm irritated that the lowering of standards because of my absence will also be accredited to her.

'Oh my God, what happens if they become best friends . . . or fall in love?!'

I get a bit pale then and escape into the toilet because I feel like I might vomit at the thought of even an imaginary child of mine befriending any of her offspring.

I spend lunch over at the library catching up on some marking. There's a stupid Christmas gift exchange going on in the staffroom that I'm avoiding. Last year, they roped me into it and I received a tiny clock shaped like a cat. I was flummoxed by this so-called present. At no point have I ever expressed a liking for cats or indicated that it would be a good idea to purchase me something quite so hideous.

When I'd agreed to partake in the secret Father Christmas event – I will not humour this 'Santa' Americanism, despite the alliteration – I'd expected everyone to commit to the spirit of it. But whoever had pulled my name out of the hat had headed straight to Creaseys and purchased the first thing that cost them exactly ten pounds. Not a natural present buyer myself, I'd thought long and hard about what to get Julie, and in the end I'd even gone over budget with a two-for-one offer on Lemsip.

Sean found the cat clock hilarious. He put it on the shelf in our kitchen and we got into the habit of tapping its head and saying goodbye to it every time we left the house. One of those silly in-jokes all couples have. It's now in the kitchen drawer so I don't have to look at it.

When I arrive back after lunch, there's a see-through purple plastic water bottle on my desk. It looks like a smaller version of one of those giant vessels you screw into the top of a water cooler but with a handle built into the side of it. There are various slices of chopped-up fruit floating on top of the water like Lucky Charms – lemons, raspberries, blueberries. A Post-it reads:

Drink for two – it will help with the morning sickness. Merry Xmas, love S xx

An English teacher who abbreviates Christmas. Just the beginning of my quibbles with this 'gift'. I picture the smug expression on Suzie's symmetrical face as she drove to the shop during her lunch break to select this hideous receptacle, chopping up fruit in the staffroom and filling it up. I would prefer her energy to be channelled into raising the standards of her work. Though, as it happens, I am a little parched.

It's a struggle to lift it to my lips without getting a hernia. How a five-foot twig like Suzie lugged it all the way up here from the staffroom, I'll never know. A particularly sharp slice of lemon whacks me in the face as I drink.

'That's very un-you, miss,' Callum says, just as an unexpected piece of raspberry passes into my mouth and goes down the wrong way. Some water dribbles down my chin as I splutter.

The smell of biscuity fake tan and over-sprayed Lynx deodorant foreshadows the imminent arrival of the rest of Callum's form group. As they file in, I protest through my coughs. It materialises that one of my colleagues went home unwell over lunch. No doubt an infection contracted from the communal bowl of nuts at the staffroom baby celebration the other day. I avoided eating anything from there after Julie rummaged her unwashed hand in it to scrabble for the last cashew.

I look through my emails and spot an apologetic note sent to me from Julie not two minutes ago to tell me the group was headed in my direction and would I mind giving up my free period to cover. Yes, I bloody would!

PSHE is the most pointless lesson imaginable. The curriculum is so over-saturated with cotton-wool-wrapped nonsense that does the kids no favours when they have to venture into the real world. The last time I covered this lesson, I got in trouble for discussing a rape case at a boarding school in which the lads accused got off despite video evidence. The students deeply impressed me with how insightful they were in their discussion of the topic. How was I supposed to know that they were all due to go on a trip over to the UK to visit the Mary Rose, and would be so concerned by England being such a lawless place that they would be too terrified to get off the plane in case they got attacked while embarking on a guided schools tour of a Tudor warship? Overactive imaginations cultivated by being mollycoddled.

My Year Elevens stare up at me as we go through the dull and unimaginative factsheet the teacher I'm covering for emailed through: 'How to stay safe online'. Everyone is paying attention apart from Callum, who is at the back of the room wearing a huge pair of headphones. Rather than sit at a desk, he's perched himself between two rows of books on the back windowsill. It doesn't look very comfortable, but the very act of separating himself from his peers communicates to me he is not one of them, nor should I try to make him one.

'Quick show of hands if there is anything on this sheet that is new information to you,' I say. No hands go up. 'Who agrees that the remainder of the lesson would be better spent watching earnest influencers on TikTok explaining what drink to order to communicate to a barman you've been kidnapped?'

All the hands go up . . . apart from Callum, who is bobbing along to whatever music he's listening to.

'Well, get to it, then,' I say, as I pretend to proceed with some casual marking to disguise how much of a rockstar I feel to these students at this precise moment.

After fifteen minutes, I ask them about the videos they've been watching: a young woman who spends her time styling awful outfits, no doubt sent to her by companies exploiting cheap labour in factories; someone who mocks people who show off their wealth in delightful, tongue-in-cheek observations; and a naive influencer making a show of paying for a stranger's shopping and it backfiring horribly.

We have an interesting debate about the themes these videos throw up and the students love being given the opportunity to interrogate some of their favourite TikTokers and the messages they send out to the world.

Slipknot blasts out from Callum's phone. I pause for a moment to appreciate what a bloody good drummer Joey Jordison was – may he rest in peace – before I muster the energy to engage. I head towards Callum's windowsill throne, take his phone and pause the music. I consider confiscating it, but the lad looks so alarmed, I decide I might curry more favour by returning it to him. He takes it and puts it in his pocket. Progress.

I ask the students if they could go back in time, would

they destroy social media? Some interesting views here that lead to a discussion around technology and how it connects us but also removes us. I point them towards the excellent short story by E. M. Forster, 'The Machine Stops', to reinforce the point that we were concerned with isolation from technology even before it had an impact and yet here we are, making the mistakes we feared we would.

'Like the way we know global warming is happening and the adults are just letting it,' a student says.

'Exactly,' I reply.

'Are you worried for your baby, miss?' one girl asks. 'About the world it's being born into?'

I pause for a moment. 'You heard the news, then?' A knowing smirk passes between them . . . I'm not sure why. I take a sip from my huge water vessel to buy myself some time. I hadn't considered that I might have to discuss my 'pregnancy' with the students . . .

'If any of you had children, wouldn't you be worried for them?' I ask instead.

'Yes,' replies a gob on legs called Nikita. 'That's why I want to be a DINK.'

DINK, I learn, stands for Double Income No Kids. The flipping of the narrative by these Gen Zedders to make child-free by choice an aspiration is genius, but the cynical side of me wonders how long it will take for social pressures to grind this lot down and they go from proudly pronouncing, 'I want to be a DINK,' to sitting in the corner of a room, rocking back and forth and wondering why no one will believe them when they say they don't want children.

I'm so irritated DINKs came up *after* I faked a pregnancy. I'd have relished this conversation. Instead, I find myself defending my fake choices because anything else would raise suspicion.

'I just got to the point where I didn't want to wait too long and then regret it,' I say, trying to ignore their eye-rolls and disappointment. I used to be a DINK . . . and now I'm a SIFK. Single Income Fake Kid.

The sound of a video plays from the back of the room. A male voice impersonates a woman, shrill and annoying. I can't make out what they're saying, but my students are now on the brink of hysteria.

'Well, I have to say, I'm pleased you've finally decided to engage with the TikTok exercise,' I say to Callum. I head towards him. 'Let's have a look.' Callum smirks. It's his personal TikTok account. In the video, he has fashioned a red wig out of what could either be an orange fishing net or satsuma bags tied together. He's wearing a generic polka-dot top and a pop of red lipstick.

I ignore their sniggers as I scroll through video after video of Callum impersonating me in the classroom. Chastising someone for not being able to spell onomatopoeia (parrots only eat in autumn). Getting annoyed when students question whether the writer really made the sky dark to reflect the inner emotions of the character, or was it just night-time? (Valid point, but not something that earns one a level nine at GCSE.) And the kicker: me making a big deal about being the cool teacher. Allowing the students to sit around the table to make them feel like equals but then not letting any of them speak; how I occasionally let them bring a hot drink into the lesson on a cold day and then expect them to ignore the way I patronise them with my opinions. Desperate for them to love me but unable to move my ego out of my own way. Here I was thinking they saw me as a rockstar when all along I've been as much of a joke to them as I am to my contemporaries.

The students are all studying me to see how I'm going to react to this.

'It's a passable pastiche, if a little mannered,' I say. 'And I like to think I apply a better red lip than the one you've administered.' I can feel inexplicable tears stab my eyes. I cannot let them see me get upset, so I dismiss them five minutes early.

'A Christmas present from me to you, or maybe it's me trying to buy popularity!' Once they've all left, Callum smirking as he goes, I lock myself in a cubicle in the staff toilet, sit on the seat with my head in my hands and take some calming breaths.

The portrayal of me being patronising, dictatorial and dismissive of their genuine feelings is a gut punch. But the thing that has thrown me the most is the pillow Callum had tied to his stomach with a belt. A fake pregnancy bump.

Chapter Eleven

On my cycle home, I go the scenic route to try to calm my nerves. There's one lane in particular where all the houses go to town on their Christmas lights, and they morph into lightsaber streaks as I whizz past.

How else was Callum supposed to impersonate his pregnant teacher other than strap that cushion to himself? If he had even the tiniest suspicion that I'm faking the pregnancy, he'd have given me some kind of sign by now. He's smart, but he's also an adolescent. Not someone who holds his cards close to his chest when he has the upper hand. They were just cruel, semi-funny videos of a teen mocking a teacher. I can't imagine many people other than his classmates have even watched them.

As I take a detour because another bloody road is up – that's the Vale for you – I spy some condiments for sale on a wooden shelf outside a farmhouse. I pull over, deciding to treat myself to a Christmas chutney. As I post the money into the honesty jar, there is a movement in the corner of my eye.

I duck behind the wall before Callum sees me. He looks shifty as he sneaks up the path of the adjacent house – a huge new-build with incredible floor-to-ceiling windows. He glances around before forcing the sliding door open and slipping inside. I weigh up being a diligent member of the public against the hassle it will cause by incurring further wrath from Callum. I'm not proud of it, but I head home.

When I pull up at Mon Petit Rocher, I notice Trish's living-room light is on for the first time in weeks. Reminding myself about Operation Phase-Out, I head straight to my front door. But, as I do, I sneak a glance through her window. She looks miserable – slumped on the sofa, scrolling on her iPad.

In my hurry to get inside before Trish sees me, I stub my toe on a humongous box on my doorstep. Another Post-it with swirly handwriting tells me this is Suzie again.

We over-ordered, thought I'd offload! Merry Xmas again, love S xx

I bend down to look. Nappies. Brilliant. I shove the box into my hallway with my foot – why is everything she gifts me oversized?! – as I head inside, whipping Gretl off and sighing out the relief.

I pull some festive cheese out of my fridge and create a board with grapes and some of my new chutney. God, Sean would have loved this cheeseboard. The huge black hole of my first solo Christmas opens up before me.

I eye up a bottle of red from the rack and clock the empty space where my Christmas Barolo was. It would be useful to have a reassuring sounding board after my tumultuous last week of term. What's one more evening?

I send a text to Trish.

Even her knock sounds sad.

* * *

Trish's is a face that has spent a lifetime feeling things wholeheartedly. The full spectrum of laughter, fury, and everything else in between. Her facial muscles perform a sun salutation, forehead to chin as I fill her in on all my recent mishaps – Stanley Tucci sperm donor, incontinence pads, Suzie Martel's ruined party – and show her a couple of Callum's TikTok videos.

'You have to hand it to him. The kid has captured you to perfection,' she says, wiping the tears of laughter from her cheeks.

'Well, I'm glad it seems to have cheered you up.' She stops laughing. An awkward pause. I leave the gap for her to fill.

She looks down at the cushion she's clutching to herself. 'I took the job at the hospital here to get some time away from the UK. My wife . . . my wife died earlier this year. It was her birthday the other week. I wanted to go back to . . .' She bursts into tears. I grab some toilet roll from the loo. Unless afflicted with a cold, the idea of having a box of tissues on the side purely to blow one's nose feels like an extravagance.

I sit beside her on Big Blue, handing her the toilet paper. 'What was she like, your wife?'

Trish smiles. 'Lil? Brutal, abrasive. An absolute chaotic nightmare half the time. But her soul . . . I know it sounds cheesy, but it shined.' She pulls out her iPad and shows me a photo of her and a woman with brown curly hair and hazel eyes. They're on a beach holiday. Trish is leaning back onto Lil as they share a sun lounger and they are howling with laughter. In between Trish's legs, leaning back onto her is a girl of about five or six, eyes identical to Trish's wife's.

'Ripley. Lil's from a previous relationship.' Trish looks at me, sad again. 'I don't get to see her much any more. She lives with the biological dad . . . He and I . . . we don't see eye to eye on a lot of things.'

As an afflicted individual myself, I always feel for children with unconventional names. The Beyoncés, Sunshine-Rainbows and Hugh Cumbers of this world. The worst I have ever heard is a poor girl in Year Seven with the unfortunate name Beberly. Apparently, her mum had spent her life mishearing the name Beverly. I suppose it's not dissimilar to the mindboggling day I realised that stationery and stationary have different spellings but, unlike poor Beberly's mum, I chose to course-correct going forward. Beberly, like her mother, isn't the brightest button in the box, but she's popular, kind and full of enthusiasm. Exactly as you'd expect . . . Beberly's bubbly.

Trish and I camp out on the sofa for the rest of the evening and – despite having watched it too many times – I put on *Alien* in honour of Lil's obvious penchant for the film, having named her child after the main character.

During one of the quieter sections, I glance at Trish, who has nodded off. I take the opportunity to do a Sean search. These have increased in frequency due to my building paranoia he is a) gambling, b) under the threat of loan sharks, c) embarking on a new life with another woman, or – my latest insane rumination – d) dead.

Despite promising myself I'd put it out of my head until my – now fast approaching – appointment with the lawyer, I've spent a lot of time going over those final months leading up to our marriage ending. Anything that might hint at something else causing him distress in addition to me not wanting a baby. His stress levels were very high, but he'd been on the road more. Pressure to meet sales targets, especially with businesses cutting budgets in a difficult economy. But I'm wondering more and more whether he'd got himself into some kind of financial difficulty that he couldn't face telling me about, which is what triggered him to remortgage.

We prided ourselves on having our own independent lives, often commenting how smug we felt that we didn't need to be joined at the hip like other couples. But that also meant I couldn't always get a read of him. He wasn't exactly a steady ship when it came to mood and sometimes an innocent question would be met with irritation and I felt like I was prying when I shouldn't be.

I screw my eyes closed, trying to obliterate the pain of his abandonment, the deceit, the radio silence, but it's hard to do that when those feelings are also fused to the happy times, the love and the best-friendship.

Sean and I first met in the library at Southampton university after I'd deferred my Edinburgh place too many times and then failed to get back in. He was working for the student union at the time and his office was just off the main reading room where I used to like to sit and write my essays. Going to uni at the age of twenty-four put me in a strange no-man's-land between childhood and adulthood and so rather than attempt to befriend people five years younger than me – which at that age is a lifetime – I leaned into my work.

It was a pleasant spot there; the sun shone in through the window, and I enjoyed being among the tatty spines of the huge reference books that, Google not quite being the powerhouse it is now, people actually used to use.

As the days went on, I also enjoyed the proximity to him.

He was handsome, but it was also his magnetism . . . I'd observe him coming and going with his colleagues and other students and it was like everyone wanted to be in his orbit. People like him have always fascinated me, I suppose because they possess a skill I don't.

One day, he took his coffee break at my table to read the sports section of a newspaper. I carried on with my work, conflicted by the fact someone I admired was nearby but that he was breaking the rules by consuming a hot drink by the books. When he left to get back to his work, I realised I'd not taken a proper breath since he sat down.

To my delight, his coffee at my table grew into a daily routine. I'd sneak looks up at him, focused on his newspaper. The Thermos fascinated me. To twenty-four-year-old me, it was the embodiment of someone having their shit together. This man took the time to wake up early to brew coffee so that his future self could enjoy it later in the day. Mindboggling forward-planning. This was pre-Nespresso machines. Did he make it with a jar of gravy-like granules, those sachets premixed with milk powder and syrup, or was he a cafetiere man? I decided on the latter. That man looked like quality mattered to him.

Which is why I was astonished when he noticed me.

One day, when he pulled his Thermos out of his bag, he had an extra cup. He filled it up and slid it over. We enjoyed our java in silence, him smiling, and me trying to wrestle with the discomfort I felt in breaking the rules. This went on for a few days; sharing the coffee became the new routine, never speaking to each other, just enjoying the peaceful company and a shared drink. Delicious cafetiere coffee, just as I'd guessed. Until one morning, he slid over his newspaper.

Scribbled by the crossword (where I tried not to focus on the fact he had misspelt 'mischief') was 'What's your name?'

And for the first time in my life, I was afforded the opportunity, upon introduction, to allow my name to be read first before it was sounded out loud.

Barri.

He read it, smiling. It is lovely when it's written down.

Although communicating by note suited me well, I nodded at his next written offering of 'coffee outside lib?' He led me to a pub across the road from campus known predominantly for live music, and not the kind I would choose for a day date. I wondered if this was all some kind of wind-up. But it turned out that, in the day, it operated as a community meeting place/coffee bar and in the upstairs function room they played reruns of *Friends*.

We selected bean-deprived beanbags and while, in the background, Joey pranced around in every item of clothing in Chandler's wardrobe, I just sat there and let Sean's words wash over me. No obligation to put on a pretence or say something interesting. Just listening, sometimes not even that. I realised how tiring and effortful every interaction is for me. With him, I could just exist.

He was so generous with thoughtful gifts – a personalised bookmark, a vase I'd mentioned in passing that I liked, which suddenly appeared in my room. He would tell me how much he cared about me all the time and it felt so good. I'd been starved of that since my dad died. Even latterly, Sean had a tendency to charge in with a big, romantic gesture – a RIB boat ride at sunset with champagne that left me with Bridget Jones-style windswept hair, which we'd then laugh about.

Although I loved all this, it was overwhelming too. He'd

either be dialled up to eleven or fiercely private and impossible to penetrate.

Like now.

Nothing new on his Facebook, but when I click on his mum, Kerry's, I sit up. There's a new profile picture of her and Sean beaming at the camera. I search for clues in the photo for anything that might tell me if it's new or old, but it's just them in the doorway of her house. I sigh in frustration and am about to move on to his company LinkedIn – a new low-point addition to my daily mining for information – when I spot that the picture has a couple of comments. I tap to expand and can't believe my luck when it lets me read them! One of her friends has written 'lovely photo x' and Kerry has replied, 'Thank you. It's so lovely having him back home for good!'

'You should get rid of this,' Trish says. I jolt and lock my phone screen, not having noticed she'd woken up.

'Get rid of what?'

She studies me as I fidget to the side to shove my phone in my pocket. 'This.' She taps Sean's gaming chair with her foot.

She's right. Sean's not gone into hiding from loan sharks or lying dead in a ditch. He's just back home in Crawley with his mum – who I didn't know he was even that close to – *for good*.

Trish stands to help as I heave the hefty chair through the front door and – with more difficulty than I'd envisaged – we finally get it through the doorway and shove it onto the grass in front of the house.

'With any luck, someone will just steal it,' Trish says, breathless.

'You still have a lot to learn about Guernsey,' I reply, as we head back inside to finish the film. 'I could leave ten grand in cash outside and it would still be there a week later.'

'So you're the only thief on the island,' she says, nudging me. I'm aware she's joking but it hurts more than I'd care to admit.

Later that night, I have a particularly vivid dream in which I am sitting in a cafe enjoying a latte when my stomach splits open and a furry kiwi bursts out through the chasm, exposing my lie to the world. I wake up in a panic and can't get back to sleep for the rest of the night.

Chapter Twelve

Town is full of busy shoppers snapping up bargains in the January sales. I hear remnants of festive playlists floating towards me from the shops as I cycle along the seafront. It's remarkable how depressing Christmas songs are in January. The Victor Hugo statue that sits atop the Victor Hugo bench has a soggy and precariously close-to-breaking Christmas-cracker hat on his head. An undignified vision indeed for the island's most famous literary immigrant.

The overcast weather gives both sky and sea a dirty dish-water undertone.

It's Marta's first outing today, so I expect the kiwi dream – which, since Trish's 'thief' comment before Christmas, has become a recurring nightmare – to feature an avocado tonight instead. I'm hoping the variation in fruit bursting through my stomach will provide some respite from the horror.

The sleep deprivation hasn't helped my overactive imagination either. I spent my first Christmas alone, picturing Sean and his mum sitting around an ostentatious tree with an abundance of extravagant gifts under it. Louis Vuitton handbags, posh scented candles and that perfume that costs about two hundred quid per spritz – all paid for with my money.

But in my heart, I know he wouldn't do anything this duplicitous without an excellent reason. If I can get to the bottom of how he's done it, maybe it will help me to understand why.

The lawyer's office is in a brand-new building further along from Town than I thought, meaning I'm now running late. Assuming this initial coffee chat is a freebie, I want to get my money's worth before I have to pay legal fees.

I prop my bike against some railings and bound up the stairs. I can smell the fresh paint of the shiny new building as I charge through the open doorway . . . which is not an open doorway, but a huge pane of perfectly clean, newly fitted glass. Luckily, Marta cushions the impact and I avoid any nasty facial injuries. Unluckily, I am travelling at such a speed that I rebound off the glass and tumble backwards down the eight or nine steps leading up to the building.

When I open my eyes, the concerned face of the moustached building security guard peers over me, eyes wide.

'I'm fine, I'm fine. Please don't make a fuss,' I say. I wiggle my joints. My head is throbbing and my coccyx feels a bit bruised, but I don't seem to have broken anything.

The security guard turns to a woman running down the steps towards us. She has a tight bun on top of her head, and the sound of her courts clip-clop on the stone. 'She just bounced!' he says. He examines my face. 'I thought your nose would be broken for sure?'

'My large stomach took the impact,' I reply.

The two of them look at me, and then at my stomach . . . and then back at my face in confusion.

I pat my hand on my midriff. 'Where's Marta!?' I look around me, frantic.

'Who is Marta? A kid?' asks the security guard. 'Marta! Marta!'

Somewhere in between saving my face from breakage and my plummet to the ground, Marta has become detached and now seems to have disappeared into thin air! I do a fuzzy-headed risk assessment. I can't stay out here in full view of everyone. What if someone I know passes by and intervenes? The security guard and Bunhead are still yelling for Marta.

'Can you stop shouting and let me think?' They stop yelling and stare at me, wide-eyed, and awaiting instruction.

Better to get inside and then work out where my bump went once these two have calmed down.

As I stand, the dramatic pair recoil in horror.

It is then that I realise Marta has not disappeared into thin air at all but swivelled round to my back like an annoying skirt that won't stay in the right place. These two idiots now think they visibly flinched at a person with some kind of back growth, rather than an insane woman who believes she can pull off a fake pregnancy.

As they help me hobble inside, Bunhead informs me she is the building manager. She is apologetic at her reaction to my physical appearance and clearly terrified I'm going to take out some kind of discrimination or personal injury claim, or both. My only concern is reassuring them I'm fine so that I can get out of here as fast as I can to return Marta to her rightful position. However, I do pause to suggest they get some stickers on that pristine glass door.

'Hmmm . . . I'm not sure the architect will be happy with that,' Bunhead says. Before I can respond in irritation, my lawyer comes into the foyer to find out where I am. Bunhead has a discreet word with her, and despite my protestations,

I am whisked through a concealed door behind the reception desk and led to a suite of glass-lined meeting rooms.

'Is it part of your company ethos to only have invisible doors or something?' I ask.

'You're sure we shouldn't call an ambulance? It sounds like it was a pretty nasty fall.' My lawyer is doing her best to not stare at me as I struggle into the chair with Marta on my back.

'No, I'm honestly fine.'

She doesn't look convinced but pulls out some documents from a folder on the table. She's a lot younger-looking and more glamorous than I thought she'd be based on her telephone voice, which made me imagine a mousy, middle-aged person in an ill-fitting trouser suit.

'I've been doing some digging.' She gives me a sympathetic look. 'It turns out that your mortgage never was a joint one; it was only ever in the name of Sean Baxter.'

I sit up taller. 'That's impossible.'

The documents she presents me with are not the ones I signed for our joint mortgage application and I waste no time in telling her this.

'Who was responsible for making the payments?' she asks.

'We have a joint bank account and everything goes out of there,' I say, flummoxed. I open the banking app on my phone and, after a few attempts, apologising for my absolute idiocy with technology, I manage to log in. I ignore how severely overdrawn it is and show her one of the regular mortgage payments that came out at the start of the month. 'See. HSBC mortgage payment!'

'Hmm . . . do you mind if I take a look?' She notes the account information for the transfer on her notepad and then turns her laptop screen around so I can see it and logs into a banking app I'm not familiar with.

'This is a personal cash account of mine that I use.' She scrolls up to the top to conceal the balance but I clock it, doing my best to conceal my jealousy that she has eight grand just sitting there. 'I like this account because the payments are super safe. It's almost impossible to transfer money to the wrong person.' She clicks on a payment transfer button, enters the details of the account my mortgage payments go into and selects 'business' for the account type.

She enters a transfer of five pounds and the details she jotted down. An alert flashes up: 'Are you sure this is a business account?' She then selects 'personal', enters 'Sean Baxter' instead of 'HSBC', clicks 'confirm' and it goes to the next step, after which she cancels the transaction, her point made. 'The mortgage payment you see in your app, "HSBC mortgage payment", is just the reference name that the person who set up the transfer used. I think your husband probably relied on the fact that you aren't very tech-savvy. All those payments have been going into a personal account belonging to him.'

I grab my phone and look for the email he sent me five and a bit years ago with the deposit transfer details. I compare them to the bank account information the lawyer jotted down. It's a match. The fifty thousand pounds I inherited when my dad died transferred straight over to Sean's secret account. I sit back in my chair, remembering at the last moment that Marta the Bump is currently Marta the Hump and slide onto the floor with a thud.

It is a struggle to get back up again.

Chapter Thirteen

The moment I step out of the lawyer's office, I dash into an alleyway and swing my bump back into the right position. I squat down to ease the shakiness in my legs, moving my knees out wide to accommodate Marta. The hip-opening position feels both torturous and satisfying. I pull out my phone, my hand trembling as I dial Sean's number. It rings out. I try calling on WhatsApp instead. Nothing. I take a few deep breaths. Sean has been duping me this whole time. Not just a couple of months, but since the day we bought our home together over five years ago, a couple of months before our wedding. Why do that unless he knew all along he was going to steal it? And what happened a few months ago that made him want to cash in?

'Barri, are you . . . pissing in the street?'

My sister, laden with shopping, regards me in my floor squat.

'Of course not.' I stand with effort and move to pass her, but she blocks me, bags down, arms folded.

'We were disappointed not to see you on Christmas Day. I hand-rolled you a cracker.'

'I'm sure my lack of attendance was a tremendous loss to

you all.' I'm confused why it's a surprise to my sister that I didn't go round for Christmas. I never go there – Sean and I always spent it just the two of us and I certainly didn't accept the invite this year either.

'What's wrong with you?' she asks. 'You look all . . . clammy.'

'Oh, you know. The usual.'

Lara follows my line of vision to the lawyer's office. She narrows her eyes, takes a sharp breath in to speak but pauses, releases the breath and turns her head back to me. 'I've got some good herbal tea I can give you when you come round later.' Off my confusion: 'Luke's birthday.'

'But I came last year!'

Lara picks up her shopping bags and straightens up. 'You only have two nephews, Barri. It's fine to make it clear to me you don't give a fuck about them, but try to make an effort to pretend to them.' She marches off.

When one is not a member of that particular church, the football section of a sports shop is an intimidating place to be. Added to this, Sean's best mate, Ish, is the manager and I'd like to avoid bumping into him at this present time. I lurk in the alley nearby until I see him leave to head out for his break, the keys to Sean's Mini jangling in his hand. He always goes home for lunch to hang out with his two-year-old while his girlfriend makes him bland high-protein salads. She banged on about her unwavering commitment to his 'gains' for an unnecessary amount of time the last time I saw her and the way she blathers on, I'm confident he'll be the full hour.

I stand in the middle of the football kits, turning slowly

on the spot in the hope the perfect present comes to me by osmosis. In previous years, poor Luke has received some shockers from me. Mostly down to prolonged shopping trips with Sean complaining about how long it's taking me when I'm not even that keen on the kid, resulting in me panic buying items such as hair gel contained within a cricket ball, a high-visibility tabard and a tube of shuttlecocks.

After a lot of dithering and a move over to the less scary general sports section, I decide on a tennis ball caddy and some sweatbands. What's the point in spending even more time here when whatever I choose will be crap, anyway?

As I head over to the till, I notice Callum, in the shop tracksuit uniform, sorting through some stock. He looks up, appraising me coolly. 'Do you . . . need help?'

'No,' I say, 'I've been looking for a gift for my ten-year-old nephew but I'm sorted now.'

Callum looks at the items in my basket. 'Tennis fan, is he?'

'Well . . . no, he likes football really. Manchester City. But he already has the home and the away shirts plus this other random third one.' I recall Dave complaining about how expensive they were when I went to drop Luke off at his work a few weeks back. One of those moans that was really a brag to show off how his children want for nothing.

Callum raises his eyebrows. 'Lucky kid.'

'Is there a special kit for when they play at the Wembley or something?' I ask, hoping he'll be impressed I've used the word 'Wembley' in a sentence.

Callum smirks – 'No, miss' – and turns his attention towards some clothes rails.

I assume that this is the end of our interaction and head

towards the till with my substandard items, trying to reassure myself that Luke might take up tennis and become the next Rafael Nadal, when a half-zip, long-sleeved top and shorts are pressed into my line of vision.

'Man City training kit,' Callum explains, his head turned away from me like he wishes he wasn't helping. When I don't take it from him, he pushes it into my hands. 'Trust me.'

The top looks nice and practical, good for those biting Saturday mornings Luke spends out on the pitch and I like the fact that it will zip up to his chin to keep him warm. The shorts are shorts but they match the top and even I know that's good.

I look inside my basket at the items Luke will be indifferent to and then at Callum, who has the exact style, haircut and demeanour of the footballers my nephew worships. 'Thank you, Callum, ring them up.' My eyes water at the cost, but I remind myself about the years of Brylcreem and shuttle-cocks.

Callum seems happy with his sale and I panic he's upsold me something awful purely for the commission, but I reassure myself that a training kit does sound like a legitimate thing a footballer would have. Like a barrister doesn't wear their wig when they're in the office or an actor their costume prior to the dress rehearsal, it makes complete sense that footballers wouldn't wear their match gear in training. A footballer needs the ritualistic donning of the armour before a battle as much as anyone else.

I keep a firm eye on Callum while he handles my credit card.

'I'm not going to nick it, miss.'

'I was thinking nothing of the sort.' Not a lie. I was making sure he doesn't clone it somehow. Who knows what tricks and tips he collected during his time in the UK?

'Are you and your dad back at the States houses in St Martin's?' I ask.

Callum stuffs the top into a carrier bag, ruining the neat folding he just did. 'Yeah, why?'

'No reason. Just thought I saw you up in the Vale the other day.'

'Well, it wasn't me.'

He gets all flustered after that, which is exacerbated by the credit card machine running out of receipt paper. I want the receipt to make sure Callum legitimately rung it all through and insist on him providing me with one, which is my right as a customer.

Still, I feel like a pedant.

Chapter Fourteen

I always get a small pang of envy when I pull up to my sister's traditional Guernsey farmhouse with its arched front door, slate grey roof and beautiful burnt-orange, grey and pink walls of Guernsey granite – all different shapes and sizes – that gives it that unique, rustic feel; cosy and unassuming despite its generous size.

I spy the original stone witches' seat jutting out the side of the exterior wall. It's a Guernsey folklore thing, built into old houses to provide a resting place for witches passing over on their broomsticks. The idea being that this would deter a witch from deciding to have a rest inside the islander's home instead. When he learned about them, Sean became obsessed with the idea of getting a fake one added to Mon Petit Rocher's chimney but I managed to veto the idiocy – I'd want an original one or none at all. Luckily, I was backed up by the exorbitant quotes from all the local building firms.

I push open the door. 'All right, Barri, how's the screenplay?' Dave doesn't wait for an answer as he passes me, hands and arms full of beer bottles. Instead, he turns to his mate and fills him in on how he's now an adviser to Netflix.

Lara takes my coat and attempts to hang it on a

precariously full hook. 'You know, if you have more research to do on that, I could help you.'

Classic Lara, offering unsolicited advice on something she knows nothing about. 'It's fine. Dave had the expertise I needed.'

'No, I mean how to research in general.' Lara gives up trying to balance my coat on the hook and opts to hang the hood over the end of the banister instead. 'I can give you pointers on where to look.'

I let out a sharp breath through my nose. 'What was the article of yours I read in the *Press* yesterday? "Couple Who Honeymooned in Guernsey Back to Celebrate their Diamond Anniversary". Required a lot of research, did it?'

She bites her lip. 'We all have to write filler. But I've actually just been working on a really interesting story.' She folds her arms and leans against the wall. 'About a fraudster in Alderney.'

I look at her, my interest piqued. 'Oh yeah?'

Her face flushes, like she's a child too shy to tell me what she did at school today. 'This nurse falsified medical records to make out she was using more morphine than she was and then sold the extra on the internet. One of the broadsheets rang the news desk, asked someone local to report on the court case. I've been working it up into a story.'

She looks at me, expectant – but I'm not sure what for. I rummage around in my bag for my water bottle. 'Is it really that bad?' I ask. 'Nurses are chronically underpaid . . . and it's just the insurance companies footing the bill at the end of the day.' I locate the water and take a swig.

Lara shrugs. 'The taxpayer will suffer in the long run. The legal bills, not to mention her stay in prison.'

I choke on my water. 'Prison? For a bit of skimming the cream off the top?!'

Lara arabesques into the downstairs toilet and out again, passing me some loo roll to wipe the dribble running down my chin. 'She's a public employee in a responsible position,' she says. 'Of course she got prison time.'

I lower myself onto the hallway ottoman.

Lara studies her fingernails. 'Anyway, if you wanted . . . if you wanted to come over one evening, I could show you how I—'

'No, no. It's nice of you to offer, but I prefer to do my research solo.' I wrestle my shoe off with the toe of the other.

'Oh.' For a moment she looks disappointed, but then one of her friends calls her over and she dashes off.

I call after her, 'Hang on. How long did the nurse go down for?' but she's already forgotten I exist.

I take a few calming breaths. I knew if I got caught I'd probably lose my job. But a court case? Articles in national newspapers? A prison sentence?! Until this moment, it seemed unlikely that someone like me with no previous convictions would get jail time but if it's already happened to someone else in the Channel Islands, and for what could arguably be seen as a lesser crime . . .

'Barri!' My mum beckons me over, desperate to show off her pregnant daughter to her friends.

All the more reason to not get caught. I try to put the unease to one side for now and head on into the birthday party.

Lara's dark wooden beams, pristine surfaces and sofa cushions so plump it is as if they have been injected with dermal filler are a far cry from the modest place we lived in as teenagers. However, her house feels a lot smaller this afternoon because of the sheer number of guests here. There are children *everywhere*. Running around, skidding on the wooden floors in their socks. After half an hour, I've already had my fill of unsolicited baby advice from the various parents in the room.

I've observed that mums seem to be evenly divided into phases corresponding to how old their children are. It goes like this:

Newborn to two years: I'm so tired and will never finish a cup of tea again.

Two to three years: I can't even shower alone, but I'll probably have another one.

Four to eleven years: Thank God for school but school holidays are a nightmare.

Moan, moan, moan.

If I were to decide to run a marathon, I wouldn't make my struggles known to other marathon runners out of fear of derailing them. I wouldn't constantly complain about how hard it is, how tired I am and how no one who isn't training for one could ever understand. If I did so, I would fully anticipate that people would roll their eyes and say: 'It was your choice; what did you expect?!' If a child-free person dares to make this point to complaining parents of pre-teens, they will annihilate you in one breath . . . and encourage you to have a child yourself in the next.

I fell foul to this once at Harry and Luke's school fete. Lara had been called on a breaking story at the last minute – some drug bust, which turned out to be a teenager with a tiny bit of weed in her pocket that she accidentally dropped into the guitar case of a busker when she meant to give coins. Unluckily for her, the busker was this smug know-it-all musician who wrote about it in her blog. The only reader of said blog – her mum who also happens to be senior at Guernsey police.

And so I got a desperate call . . . could I please man the treasure hunt stall? It involved a tray of sand that people could scoop and sieve to find a coin. Stupid six-year-olds were paying twenty pence to find the two-pence pieces I had hidden, convinced they were winning. That the money was going towards the school seemed like a ruse to me – these children had not been educated well enough to do basic maths and, as a result, were making a loss every go, meaning the school was profiting from their own incompetence.

Although a part of me enjoyed the power of running such a racket, school fetes are also hotbeds for boring people. The particular group I was forced to be near, one of whom was jiggling the ugliest baby I had ever seen, was moaning about the difficulties of child-rearing. No longer able to cope with the incessant complaints, and irritated that a precocious seven-year-old had just won the only one-pound coin in my treasure pit, I turned to them. 'You all knew having children was hard; it's actually quite irritating to everyone else that you now complain about it.'

Did they consider this feedback with an iota of humility? No. They launched into a tirade about how it wasn't a fair statement, how I didn't understand. Children are worth all the effort. It's just important to vent about feelings with people who get it. I examined the group, wondering where the heads-down, getting-on-with-it marathon runners were.

'You'll get it one day when you have kids,' said one of them.

'I don't want children.'

Although I was met with a couple of 'fair enough' nods, the ringleaders told me I was wrong despite not ten seconds ago bemoaning how awful it is. I half wonder whether this is some kind of trap; parents decide their lives are so miserable that they are desperate to inflict it on everyone else. But it won't work. In my experience, people who don't want kids have often thought it through much more carefully than those who have them.

Later that day, the lady with the ugly baby asked me to hold it for her, which I imagined was a trick to fire up my ovaries. She was gone for such a long time, I became concerned people would mistake her unfortunate-looking child for mine. In the end, after one particularly sympathetic look, I resorted to covering the baby's head with the cloth thing meant for wiping up the sick. The baby fell asleep. On her return, the woman was stunned I had handled the baby and the treasure hunt stall with no issues whatsoever.

'You're a natural,' she said.

'You might wish to allow your child to wear make-up sooner than is societally expected,' I replied.

A balloon pops, pulling me out of my thoughts. The offending toddler bursts into tears, and its mother, one of the worst moaners, brings the crying tot into the kitchen and sits it on the worktop.

'Babies are lovely, though . . .' she says to me while she comforts the crying toddler with one hand and stops her older child from smacking Harry over the head with a plastic sword with the other. Harry, who has the air of a Buddhist monk today, doesn't even flinch. 'The smell, the feel, the cuddles.'

My sister's kitchen is like a B&Q advert, with the most

impractical worktops known to man. They pick up every fleck, smudge and mark going. Forensic schools should use this material as textbook examples for collecting perfect fingerprints. Lara, who opts to keep her home as forensically clean as a science lab herself, never stops buffing away at the surfaces. Today, she works doubly hard on account of all the sticky sweetie fingers touching them. She looks like the wax-on-wax-offing Karate Kid.

Moany Mother places the placated toddler back on the floor and moves her hand towards my baby-less stomach. I move faster than Mr Miyagi at the dojo. I snatch the cloth out of my sister's hand and buff, blocking Moany Mother's hand with an aggressive outward defence move.

The mother yelps in pain and buggers off to the garden in a strop. My sister purses her lips at me and goes after the woman to explain I'm not a 'toucher' and to apologise for my inappropriate behaviour. They park themselves in a heated outside area for the adults to sit, drink wine and ignore their offspring.

In a world where we are expected to hug strangers all the time, I have invested a lot of effort into cultivating the perfect anti-cuddle so that when people fling themselves uninvited around me, they think twice about doing it ever again.

The idea came to me after Dad died. I took a job in the darkened basement office of a fiduciary . . . I'm still not sure what that is other than it makes rich people richer. After a few days there, miserable while I tried not to imagine who was occupying my abandoned university room in Edinburgh – a clearing student perhaps, no doubt a svelte weasel upgrade with a winning personality – I became irked to observe that all the smokers got cigarette breaks within their core hours.

The non-smokers were instructed to 'Man the phones, will you?' like we were Blitz-spirited workers in Winston Churchill's underground cabinet war rooms. All the while, our charred-lunged contemporaries made a break for sunlight, taking up to ten minutes each time! On behalf of the clean-lunged downtrodden, I made a valid request for us to be given an equal number of fresh air breaks. Equal rights for equal work! The manager waggled his nicotine-stained finger at me and said I had to 'suck it up and take a vitamin D pill.'

Sticking my head above the parapet made me first in line when they did a round of redundancies a few months later (it wasn't because I still didn't know what a fiduciary was).

After springing redundancy on me out of the blue, the boss, who I had long suspected to be a bit of a perve, demanded a hug 'to make you feel better'. I was shell-shocked and preoccupied with the question of how on earth I was going to get myself out of bed if I didn't have a reason to. When he flung himself towards me, grabbing a bit of side boob in the process, my body kicked into anti-hug survival mode. I transformed into a clawing, rigor mortis alien, digging my rigid fingers into his back so that he yelped in pain. I accompanied this with a noise that, before I had perfected it into the sinister rasp it is today, was a mix between a death rattle and Donald Duck. I made this sound in his ear, extra spittle supplied courtesy of my livid salivary glands. The man jumped back in disgust and ran to the nearest meeting room, shrieking at his assistant to get him a tissue. She fetched it for him, demonstrating a disappointing lack of solidarity.

I've been cultivating that cuddle ever since and I've been

reliably informed it's a disturbing experience. It is a constant challenge being a non-hugger in a world where hugging is now the social bloody norm.

Picturing the prison bars closing in around me, I spend the next few hours dodging flat palms like a high-stakes episode of *Takeshi's Castle* and I find the buffing cloth a good technique for deflecting bump-touchers. Irritated that I'm using the wrong cloth to buff the wrong surface, my sister demands that I pass some sandwiches around instead, shoving two heavy plates into each hand.

I am exposed. Vulnerable.

At that very moment, one of Mum's friends spies my unprotected stomach, and her hand moves towards it. With no free arm to block, I assess the room like Jason Bourne. I spy Harry peering into the fridge, shunt him gently to one side, and shove my stomach in there to protect it from the encroaching hand. This stops the woman in her tracks.

'I never thought "bun-in-the-oven" meant my stomach would feel like an actual furnace,' I say.

The woman waits patiently.

After an arm-tremblingly long stand-off, she realises I have no intention of removing my stomach from this fridge with her in the vicinity and buggers off. Poor Marta is freezing cold. As I shake out my aching biceps, I wonder whether I'd have done any damage had it been a real baby I stuck in there.

After a lifetime, all the guests leave and it is just the immediate family left. I'm ready to go home myself, but I'm so exhausted, I take a quick seat in an armchair. I'm handed a steaming mug of tea and a piece of birthday cake balanced on some polka-dot kitchen roll and, before I know it, the rest of the family joins me where I'm seated. Mum and Lara on the sofa, Dave, Luke and Harry on giant bean bags. This is the longest I've stayed at any family occasion in recent years. Normally I'm whisked off by Sean, who would have reached saturation point by now. I remember last year on Harry's birthday expressing a wish to stay, but Sean wanted to go to the pub with Ish, who is joined at the hip with his girlfriend. In addition to constantly waxing lyrical about her boyfriend's muscles and going on and on about her son – who that night had gone for a sleepover at his grandparents' – the girl is an absolute drain. Never asks a single question, so I had to put on my best Michael Parkinson interview act while Sean got more and more drunk with his mate.

We are to watch Luke open his presents. I am flabbergasted at the generosity of his friends and the quality of the gifts bestowed upon him and I conclude that my eldest nephew at the age of ten has achieved something I never have: popularity.

Dave reads the label of my gift.

Dear Luke, Happy Birthday. Regards, Auntie Barri.

He mutters, 'This will be good, eh Luke?!' before resting back in his beanbag with a smirk.

Luke feels the parcel with apprehension. I spotted some football-patterned ribbon that matched the paper in the card shop. I used it to embellish the wrapping and I think, on reflection, it was worth the extra £1.99.

I can see him psyching himself up to mask the obvious disappointment he's about to feel, exacerbated by the need to work extra hard to give real-time feedback now I'm here to witness him open a present for the first time in his life. Usually, his mum sends me a general 'thank you for the gift' text message as she did for the staplers I gave the boys for Christmas.

My heart is racing. The only person I've watched open a gift I've bought them in recent years is Sean, who hates surprises so much that he always knows what he's getting.

The pressure of having to feign delight is weighing on Luke's shoulders. Being ten has its burdens. His mum gives him an encouraging smile. For the first time, I see the resemblance he has to my side of the family because his false grimace is identical to the one I adopt when I'm panicking. He unties the ribbon, and picks at the Sellotape, delaying the inevitable. Everyone braces as he rips.

His jaw hits the floor when he sees the contents. He lifts the top against himself like a bride pulling her new dress out of a box. He runs his hand over the shorts, feeling the material. Either Luke is the best actor known to man, or he is genuinely thrilled. To my surprise, he comes over to me, arms stretched wide. He halts, remembering the alien cuddle bestowed on him the last time he tried that, traumatising him aged three, and holds out his hand instead, which I take firmly and shake.

'Thank you so much, Auntie Barri . . . I love them.'

'You're welcome, Luke.'

My sister squeezes my arm and, for once, I don't recoil at the touch.

By the time I leave, it's late. We enjoyed a buffet of all the leftover party food and played a game called Who's in the Bag in which you have to describe famous people without saying their names. I was terrible at it and they were all falling about laughing at me when I couldn't think how to describe Shrek and so I just screwed up my face and stayed like that for the full thirty seconds. Lara, who they teamed me with for maximum laughs, flung a cushion at me in mock annoyance, spilling wine all down herself in the process. She was laughing so much, she didn't even seem to care that there was a red stain on her pristine white top. She seemed appreciative when I offered to treat it with some Vanish at home.

I'm by the front door, coat half on, when I become distracted by a message from Suzie Martel. It irks me that she's used my number for a personal communication when I only provided it for work-related emergencies. There's a link to an antenatal taster class. Her message reads: Obvs early to start full classes but this will be a good intro to breathwork. I'm going if you fancy it? S xx

What is the meaning of this?! I type a hurried message to Trish to see if she thinks this is something I have to take part in. I'm so distracted, I don't notice little Harry come into the hallway. It's only when I go to zip up my coat that I realise he is standing there, hand on my bump, his eyes wide at the feel of the swell of my stomach.

'I felt it kick, Auntie Barri,' he says, in complete wonderment.

The minute Lara's front door closes behind me, I'm sick in the hedge. Why did it have to be Harry with his little face? It's that same ick-feeling I got when the students talked about my pregnancy. Lying to innocent minds. Though also, thank Christ it *was* Harry and not someone who could tell it's not a real bump.

I message my sister to apologise for throwing up in her front garden. I'm still feeling nauseous and so I decide to wheel Melva along the road for a bit.

'Barri, hang on!' Lara runs after me in her slippers. She holds out a box of tea. 'I swore by this for the morning sickness.'

Today has been a barrage of anxiety, too much social interaction and . . . undeserved kindness. I feel so overwhelmed all of a sudden, I can't bring myself to even touch the box Lara's holding out to me. Instead, I lift up the cover on the bike basket and she pops it in.

'Thank you,' I say, hopping onto Melva.

'Cheerie.'

I pause for a second, wrong-footed by Lara's use of Dad's sign-off. She's studying me, perhaps wondering whether she should have said it or not.

I take a breath. 'Cheerie.' I push off, desperate to get home.

I feel her gaze on my back until I turn the corner of her road, where I have to pull over to throw up again. I wonder whether that ginger tea also works for guilt sickness.

Chapter Fifteen

'Is it called *anti*-natal because no one wants to go?' I ask Trish the following Saturday as we head towards the church hall where the session is taking place.

'Much better to hide in plain sight,' Trish replies, pushing me towards the door to join all the actual pregnant people waiting in the corridor.

I look back at her. 'You make me sound like a sexual predator.'

I insisted Trish accompany me given that being partner-less might expose me to bump touching – something I'm especially nervous about since Luke's party. Harry's face as he looked up at me with his hand on my bump has haunted me in recent days despite my best efforts to push the thought into a helium balloon above my head. But every day, the guilt has eased a little bit and I'm now almost back to my base level.

I glance down at the burgundy medical bag swinging at Trish's side. 'Are you going to be like Monica in that episode of *Friends* when she goes to the beginners' cooking class and then spends the whole time showing off?'

Trish lifts up the flap of the bag. Stitched to the lining is an embroidered child's drawing. I assume a recreation of one Ripley drew: her, Lil and Trish. Pointy stick fingers holding hands in a triangle formation. 'It was a special gift and I like having it with me.'

I grimace. 'Well, now I feel terrible.'

'Good. Come on!' Trish marches off before I can pry further.

I think back to what she said when she signed the medical form about how not wanting children is a privilege. For her, as a step-parent to Ripley, it must be especially raw. Ripley's biological dad has managed to block in-person contact as far as I know. She doesn't like talking about it but it must be a big reason why she's taken the job over here. The empty house back home too much to cope with. She puts on a brave face but the separation must be unbearable.

Suzie leans against the wall in chic athleisure, rummaging through a large tote shoulder bag and pulling out various Tupperware. There is swirly writing on the side of the tote that says 'Lattes and Pilates', indicating that the tote and I have 50 per cent in common but that I now dislike the bag's owner even more.

'Why is Suzie even here when she's already had three kids?'

'Maybe it's for you,' Trish replies, ignoring my doubtful look, and choosing to wave back at Suzie when I don't.

I'm taken aback by the sheer handsomeness of Suzie's husband, Xavier. His suave beige suede shirt is pleasing on the biceps and he has that tall, wide rugby player physique that I am biologically programmed to swoon over. Positive even Trish will be turned, I cast a look at her but she's far more enamoured with Suzie, who I suppose is equally beautiful and glowing with pregnancy.

'I've heard so much about you,' she tells Suzie.

'All good, I hope.' Suzie beams. Trish beams back, but her silence is deafening. The woman has got to learn to blag better.

I help myself to a carrot stick from Suzie's Tupperware – crudités for the four of us with a home-made aubergine hummus dip. There aren't any chairs or tables in the corridor so she balances the tubs on her upturned palms and we stand in an awkward circle around them, unable to stop eating the moreish gunge.

'This is delicious,' I say somewhat begrudgingly. 'And I'm not sure I've said it yet, thank you so much for this.' I hold up my water bottle, which I now can't seem to go anywhere without. 'Smaller lemons next time, though, you nearly gave me a lip piercing.'

Suzie laughs. Xavier turns to her and says, 'Yep, she's just as funny as you said she is.'

That's me, a tragic source of entertainment for attractive, well-adjusted, happy people.

'I can't believe I'm missing the first ormering tide of the year for this nonsense,' I mutter to Trish through gritted teeth as we're beckoned inside the hall.

'Becoming a fake parent takes sacrifice,' she responds, smiling as she takes in the warm, well-presented room with yoga mats and sausage-shaped cushions laid out in a circle.

We are invited to choose a space that 'feels like home', and I consider asking whether I could choose my actual home, rather than remain here among this nonsense.

All the mums-to-be eye each other. Our fellow marathon runners, united only by biology, geography and – for one of us – duplicity. A few familiar faces in the crowd – because

Guernsey – but mostly strangers, which serves as a relief. There's one young woman of about twenty-one fiddling with a wedding band. Got to be God Squad. She places herself on a mat, pulling her husband to sit behind her as she leans back against him. Despite this being a much more comfortable position for her, they both grin like competition winners, stroking each other and using 'boo' as a term of endearment. Despite not being asked to remove our shoes, they are both barefoot. The husband's feet are hairy and Hobbit-like. I decide to pull Trish away from the original mat we were headed towards to sit on the opposite side of the room.

The woman leading the session wears black parachute pants and a wraparound fitted top that accentuates a cracking bosom. I always think it's strange that women don't acknowledge other women's breasts. Men are so obvious about having a good look, but we pretend we haven't noticed when someone has an impressive pair. As someone who doesn't have a bad set myself, I often notice other women staring at them and I will them to comment so I can be unfazed by it. Usually, they clock me noticing them looking and they say, 'Nice top.'

Trish nudges me. The woman leading the session is looking right at me, having asked me a question I didn't hear. I am still looking at her breasts. Everyone is staring at me, staring at her.

'Nice tits,' I say. Fuck. 'Top, I mean TOP!'

Trish lets out a high yelp and scampers out of the room. Everyone now thinks that my life partner is devastated about my perving on the teacher when, in reality, she's crying with laughter in the toilets. God Squad Wife doesn't even try to disguise her disgust at the lesbians causing disruption to her wholesome day. Xavier is doing his best not to laugh, but the tears brimming in his beautiful eyes are visible from here.

I wait for as long as I dare before excusing myself to locate Trish. I find her in the toilets, holding a sheet of toilet roll against her eyes to blot her mascara. 'Best Saturday morning I've had in months,' she says.

'Will you please compose yourself and come back in there with me immediately? We're doing some kind of hideous hippy dippy breathing exercise and I'm worried Marta's Velcro won't hold.'

We breathe in for four, out for four, and then build it up in increments of two to sixteen counts and back down again. I would have found it relaxing apart from the fact that I was forced to sit with my back up against Trish, who insisted on breathing out on an 'F', which, given the gap in her front teeth, created an awful amount of spittle that landed on the back of my neck.

'Must you make that sound?!'

'There has been a lot of research into the amount of extra control one has breathing out on a voiceless labiodental fricative,' she replies, no intention of course-correcting.

By the end of the session, the instructor is sitting on the mat next to me (having pointedly flung on a sweatshirt), glasses on, taking copious notes as Trish takes her through the finer points of pregnancy yoga to aid sleep in the second trimester.

People are lapping it up like she is some kind of guru, here to make the process of pushing a melon-sized object out of our vaginas not only enjoyable but desirable. When she described how one of her patients managed to 'just breathe her baby out', God Squad Wife actually cried warm, emotional tears, her husband smiling behind her, no doubt confident that their lifetime of prayers to the baby Jesus will send them the same luck, and his wife's newly de-virgined vagina won't be ripped from front to back by a humongous hairy baby head.

I wait as Trish handles all the questions in the world from the room of anxious soon-to-be parents, dishing out hospital information leaflets from her bag and recommending various sleep aids and giant inflatable balls. Finally, she heads over to me, looking exhilarated and happy for the first time in days.

'Having fun, were you?'

'I was, actually, yes.'

'I can't wait to get home and take this bloody thing off,' I say, rubbing Marta.

'Well, you're going to have to wait. I've told Suzie and her hubby we'll go to them for lunch,' she says.

'You did WHAT?!'

Trish pats me in a patronising manner and heads out of the hall.

I imagined Suzie's house to be a generic affair. Live Laugh Love and the like. It's more curated than that, with weighty copper-coloured pots and pans, Art Deco tiles, and an intuitive cutlery-drawer-to-kettle proximity set-up. There is a delightful floral stained-glass window above the sink that projects rainbows of light onto the stone floor, and massive patio doors that lead out from the kitchen to a beautiful garden with a large wooden eco pod building at the bottom. We make our way down there and spend the first five minutes taking in the spectacular view in silence. Despite humans being unequivocal about the blueness of the sea, it is tourmaline green today. The day is as clear as any I've seen, and France looms in the far distance. The biting cold is made palatable by the heavy Fair Isle blankets and wood burner on offer.

'We're very lucky,' Suzie says. I note that she apologises frequently for her affluence and I decide she probably hasn't always had money.

Trish and I are seated in aesthetically pleasing chairs that look like they've been designed by a suspension bridge engineer. Xavier lowers a tray of coffee mugs – complete with chocolate-dipped madeleines that Suzie baked this morning – onto the expensive-looking stone coffee table. Suzie breaks up some of the cake and places it in front of her one-year-old, who, just like me, is chubbily delighted with the sweet treat. I too am tempted to clap my hands with glee, but I'm constrained by the awkward feeling that I am compromising my professional relationship with a colleague by being in her family home.

Their older children, who were at some kind of birthday party this morning, are still wearing their princess paraphernalia with warm, colourful coats on top. They sit nicely inside a tepee on the lawn, joylessly tucking into madeleines and orange squash. Like a dystopian John Lewis advert.

'Did you lace these with Ritalin or something?' I ask.

Suzie and Xavier laugh. 'This is eerily well behaved for them. They must be detecting the ferocious discipline of Barri Brown,' Xavier says.

Suzie nudges him, perhaps worried I might be offended. There is a moment of awkward silence before Trish pipes up to ask about where they got their mugs. They inform us it was the Etsy shop belonging to a contestant from a TV pottery programme and that the style is Japanese/Scandinavian fusion.

'Japandi,' Suzie says. I was just thinking how bloody pretentious that sounds when she adds, 'Pretentious, I know. I just like 'em.'

As someone who is also very particular about my drinking receptacles, I can see why Suzie favours these. They are nicely weighted with a porridgy colouring, slightly rough to the touch and the kind of ceramic that almost sings as you swipe your finger across it. They have a neat little groove for a thumb in the exact place you would want to put your thumb, which until this moment isn't a feature I realised was missing from any of the mugs I have used in the past. I wonder how I will ever enjoy a hot beverage again without a convenient little groove in which to rest my most dextrous digit.

Xavier shows Trish around the garden, and she humours him by stopping to admire all the places where the flowers, herbs, fruit and vegetables will be once he's got round to planting them. Suzie tells me about her childhood growing up in Milton Keynes and reassures me it's surprisingly green there. Her estuary accent coats everything she says in warmth.

'Do you miss it?' I ask.

'I miss the anonymity. It all gets a bit much over here sometimes, doesn't it?' She looks out at the view. 'But it's a beautiful island. We're well lucky.' She takes a sip of her coffee. The ceramic sings again when she moves it away from her lips. She smiles at me.

A sudden knot in my stomach as I imagine the flurry of messages between Suzie and Julie after this. 'You'll never guess who came to mine for lunch!!' and then some back and forth about how out of place and awkward I looked parked inside her suspension bridge chairs that were designed solely for svelte weasel bottoms. I think again about the way she nudged her husband earlier.

I stand up as abruptly as one can from a reclined, springy chair and accidentally knock the coffee tray with my knee. One of the mugs falls off, hits the metal corner of the wood burner and breaks. And, for some bloody unknown reason, I start to cry. Suzie reassures me she can always buy another mug. But I'm sobbing now.

'I don't know what's wrong with me. This is all . . . it's out of character. I just . . .'

Suzie reassures me it's hormones and I deduce that my body is having some kind of visceral reaction to the intimacy or the hoodwinkery or – I don't know.

I sprint away from their beautiful home, past the dystopian kids, the stained-glass window and the well-placed cutlery drawer and out onto the road, leaving a very confused Trish behind. I head down the hill as fast as I can, and attempt to turn onto a cliff path, but not before circumnavigating a Range Rover trying to turn round in the road. I must look like a lunatic as I yell, 'That car's too big for the island!' through the windscreen at the flustered driver, tears pouring down my cheeks. I hit the cliff path, follow the uneven mud around a bend and trip on a rock jutting up. I grab a bit of hedge to stop myself from falling and curse in pain as my hand encloses a thorny branch.

I pause for a moment as I feel my body going into panic mode and allow the biting January air to do its job of focusing my mind. The bright sun illuminates a cluster of rocks in the sea below, white-speckled with seagulls. Across the cove, a solitary dog walker circumnavigates the cliff path. I watch her march on round the bend, ball-throwing caddy swinging at her side, and wait for her to reappear again when the path juts back out.

One of the cottages on the cliffside is burning a log fire. The whips of smoke create long, thin spectres gravitating to the sky. I hear my dad's voice. *Don't sweat it, Baz. The smoke goes up the chimney just the same.* I take a seat on a wooden bench that looks out over the sea and let the unexpected presence of him sit with me a while. It's funny how it is with the dead. Sometimes they rug-pull you with sadness, but at other times it's as if they are extending fingertips towards you. You pause there for as long as possible, basking in that moment of nearly touching and know you're not alone.

I arrive back at mine about an hour later expecting to find Trish buzzing around my doorstep, but she's nowhere to be seen. I picture her at Suzie's making apologies on my behalf and them all having a good laugh at my erratic behaviour.

Later that evening, I hear knocking on my door. I don't answer and run myself a bath instead, tucking into a bottle of Rioja. I decide to cheer myself up by doing some more research into my trip. I find an amazing ranch just outside of Nashville where you can get cheap bed and board in exchange for helping out with the horses. I used to ride when I was younger and I love the idea of trying it again. I fill in the contact form on the website to ask about availability.

I'm going to spend a good three months exploring some of America's southern states before moving on to Edinburgh to settle, find a place and hunt for a new job. I've decided to do some tutoring to begin with until I'm ready to hand in my notice at my current school. I think I can just about afford it all if I budget well, though I could really do with a little financial buffer in addition to the maternity pay. I try Sean's number again. It doesn't even connect this time. He's blocked me.

I click into my emails and find a chaser from the lawyer about next steps, suggesting I report Sean to the police as a first port of call. But, in reality, it feels like the only viable 'next steps' are pulling off the pregnancy and getting out of here. I can't afford a legal case, nor do I wish to be pulled back to the island in a year's time to face him in court after having left for good to have a non-existent baby. At this point, I have to accept that I may never find out why Sean's done this to me, and, worse still, I may never see any of my dad's money again.

Chapter Sixteen

I feel an instant calm wash over me as I arrive at Belle Greve at daybreak the following morning. The long expanse of seaweed glistens in rows along the beach, making it look like nature is paving my way to the ormers. I take a big breath in and allow the jetpack blow of the wind to obliterate my cobwebs. This is where I should have been yesterday, not that bloody antenatal class.

We are permitted to search for the prized molluscs between January and April every year, only at low tide on days of each full moon and each new moon and the two days immediately following. We must *never* ormer at night.

I know it sounds like random logic invented by an enthusiastic fantasy screenwriter, but these are the genuine guidelines laid out on the fishing and aquaculture page of the States of Guernsey website. The penalty for being found guilty of a breach of any of the regulations could be six months' imprisonment. Believe me, the rules are much more sensible than leaving stagnant water in kettles; they protect the delicate ecosystem and enable the ormers to breed and grow.

The twenty or so days of the year when one may look for

these gorgeous shell-encased snacks are the finest of days; wellies submerged in rock pools, ready to discover a coveted and delicious prize that can be slow-cooked into a pleasing stew, or, in danger of sounding like a TV chef on that awful Saturday-morning cooking programme, flash-pan-fried in a big nub of Guernsey butter.

There is no one else on the beach yet – my preferred scenario. I'm tempted to rip Marta off and leave her on the sand, but it's far too risky. Instead, I approach my favourite assortment of rock pools. I select my first stone with care. This is not a job to be rushed. Each sea boulder is an opportunity, an expectation. I make my choice, anticipating the feeling of resistance as I turn the rock – like a pirate, lifting the lid of a newly discovered, much coveted and rarely opened treasure chest. But this one lifts easily, the loot non-existent.

I survey the scene. Each rock looks wrong, misplaced; as if they have already been disturbed. Inside a pool I have yet to step into, the sand whirls from the flurry of previous activity. A bashed-in crab is splayed across a rock like a corpse discarded out in the open by a reckless serial killer – if only I could interview it to find out what went on here.

All calm gone from the situation, I move from one rock to another, turning, turning, turning. Not a single ormer underneath any of them. Not even baby ones.

I wade towards the family cricking nook. In thirty years of ormering, this nook has never failed me. I reach my hand inside, feel for the third nubbin, and sweep upwards in a seventy-five-degree arc. My armpit develops a seawater sweat patch as I reach further and further inside, scrabbling at nothing.

It is time to face the facts. Someone has been here under cover of darkness and illegally stolen all the sweet mollusc supper for themselves.

Sea Fisheries Pierre's office is along the harbour, just beyond where the boats take the day trippers over to the surrounding islands. Despite the biting weather, there is a small queue of eager sightseers in bright waterproofs waiting to board the milk boat to Herm, the paradise island that lies a twenty-minute ferry ride from St Peter Port.

Pierre is inside his portacabin office on his laptop with his dad, Jean, leaning over him. They are chalk and cheese – Jean in a smart burgundy Guernsey jumper, which offsets his bright white Captain Birdseye beard. Pierre wears shorts and a tatty, neckline-chewed T-shirt despite the biting January cold.

'That's a boy racer boat,' Jean says, pointing at the screen. 'You don't want people to think you're flash, eh?'

Pierre smiles, still looking at the screen. 'I don't care what people think.'

Not wanting to interrupt the father–son moment but aware I have the weight of the Guernsey ormer ecosystem on my shoulders, I knock on the open door.

It's irritating to constantly bump into people you once went to school with. No planned reunions where one can handpick the most fantastic outfit that flatters and have one's make-up done at Charlotte Tilbury. Nope. In Guernsey, every day is a school bloody reunion. Though the way Pierre is gawking at me, I must look especially rough. I smooth my frizzy hair with my hands and, as I look down at my faded khaki waders, I notice how taut they are across my bump.

As Pierre stands, he smacks his head on the lampshade hanging from the ceiling. He was always taller than everyone else our age and constantly outgrowing his trousers, meaning he was often referred to as 'ankle basher' by our classmates. He's now six foot six at least. His bright green eyes grin down at me from under the peak of the faded blue baseball cap he often wears, his too-long curly brown hair tufting out at the sides.

I know for a fact that if I were ever to wear a Croc, I too would never wish to put on any other shoe, which is why I will never allow one to grace my foot. Anyone who hasn't resisted that temptation is lacking in fortitude, in my opinion. Pierre's are bright yellow, and don't get me started on the mismatched socks – one a thick sports and the other a thin trainer. Visual difference aside, every step must be a torture of different textures.

'Good to see you, Barri. How you doing?' he asks.

'No time for pleasantries, Pierre.' I fill them in on what went down at the beach.

'We'd better get to some of the other spots and see if it's the same there,' Jean says to Pierre, pulling on his coat. As Pierre's predecessor, Jean doesn't seem to have accepted the fact that he retired two years ago. I miss seeing him as I come off the beach, there for one of his spot checks. Quietly impressed with my haul while he measured each ormer to ensure it was the permitted minimum of eighty millimetres. Pierre is far friendlier during bucket inspections and never thorough with mine, choosing to chat away instead. When I asked him why he wasn't inspecting my ormers properly once, he just said, 'You always were a stickler for the rules, even at school, eh?'

I notice him clocking my bump. He reddens and says nothing. As I leave, they promise to keep me updated. I have no time to lose. I head straight to Lara's.

'Oh God, is it Mum? Or the baby? What's happened?!' Lara, dressing-gowned and sleep-ruffled, stares at me in alarm. In hindsight, I suppose it is unusual that I've turned up here unannounced first thing on a Sunday morning.

'It's much more serious than that,' I say as I charge past her, not having time to remove my wellies.

As I fill her in on the ormering-thief story as it unfolded, Lara gets more and more fidgety. When I finish, I look at her expectantly, but it's like she's not even listening any more.

'Well . . .' I say.

'Well, what?!' she asks.

'Don't you think that this is exactly the kind of thing that you, as a member of the press, should be interested in?' I am baffled that I need to spell this out for her. 'It's a scoop!'

She sighs and begins pulling bowls and boxes of cereal out of the cupboard, laying them out on the shiny marble island. '"Local Woman Goes Ormering But Doesn't Find Any". It's hardly a story, Barri. We had a police officer accidentally taser themself yesterday when they were meant to be breaking up a fight in a pub. You see the difference?'

'But . . . someone is breaking the rules. It's illegal.'

'Don't you think you might have just had an unlucky day?'

'There weren't even any in the family cricking nook!'

Lara does a micro-pause as if suspended in time, before fussing with her dressing-gown cord. After a lot of huffing and sighing, she tugs the knot around her waist, so tight I'm concerned she won't be able to breathe. 'He showed you it, then,' she says, finally.

'Eh?'

'Dad. He showed you where it is. The nook.'

I snort. Of all the things for Lara to get a bee in her bonnet about.

She flings the door of the dishwasher open. Water from the still-wet dishes splashes all over the floor as she puts things away, not making any effort whatsoever to be quiet. The sound of footsteps above. Lara tuts, as if it is my action that has woken someone up and not the aggressive clatter of cutlery into the drawer.

'Who were you planning to pass it on to?'

'Eh?'

'Before you decided to have a baby – after years of snide, judgemental remarks and disinterest I might add – who were you going to tell about the location of the family cricking nook?'

We are silent as we stew over the answer. *The secret would have died with me.*

I pull my stool in a bit, making a horrible scraping sound on the floor. 'I don't know what all the fuss is about when you don't care about ormering anyway.'

She sits back down, clutching a serving bowl to her chest, making her dressing gown damp from the water residue. 'My boys aren't good enough to know, is that it?'

'There's nothing there to show them because there is a thief at large stealing all the ormers!'

A sleepy-headed Harry comes in and pours himself some cereal. It would take nothing for me to say, 'Hey Harry, how do you fancy coming ormering with me next time I go?

I can show you where the family cricking nook is,' but I'm so pissed off that Lara doesn't care about the thief, I don't want to extend that olive branch.

My fortitude wanes when, on my way out, Lara hands me some more of the teabags she gave me last week after Luke's party and a carrier bag full of baby things, including a beautiful blanket our granny knitted when Luke was born, but I stick to my guns. If she's not willing to show an interest in my hobbies, I shan't extend the same courtesy to her children.

Chapter Seventeen

'DON'T TOUCH ME!' I moderate my tone. 'Please.' The well-meaning but highly irritating waitress whose palm is hovering near my swollen solar plexus retracts it. The lethargy and trajectory of the retreating hand make it look like a prize trundling along the conveyor belt of that nineties TV game show. What was it called? TV . . . cuddly toy . . . obtrusive lady's annoying hand. I think I might have baby brain, which is . . . ironic.

Brigitta is strapped to me as of today. A big step up from Marta, as no amount of clothing will disguise my pregnancy any more. I'm also patently aware that I am now one bump away from my no-going-back bump Kurt, who I still haven't dared to unwrap.

But Brigitta's weight on my stomach feels comforting somehow. Like she's a pigtailed prepubescent girl who is yet to discover that the world can be a scary place. My diary tells me that today – week nineteen – my fictional foetus is the size of a mango and, next week, it will be a bell pepper – which confused me, because aren't mangos bigger than bell peppers?

Wounded by my outburst, the waitress shuffles off to fetch

my latte and I settle into reading today's *Press*, hoping one of Lara's colleagues (all of whom I have emailed multiple times over the past few weeks) might finally have the sense to cover the story of the ormer thief, even if she won't.

'Police Officer Tasers Themselves . . . Again', 'Woman Pulled Over by Dog While Walking It' and 'Local Man Steals Sea Bass from Guernsey Aquarium and Enters It into a Fishing Competition' are the headlines of the day. Furious that the theft of one measly and common breed of fish from captivity has provoked a headline over multiple molluscs being poached prematurely, thus putting the ecosystem in danger, makes my blood boil. Though I suppose the moral outrage of the man having won the eight-hundred-pound prize for first place in the competition gives the story a tabloid angle. That he was discovered because someone 'recognised the fish' throws up the image of a *Usual Suspects*-style police line-up. A plaice, rainbow trout, sea bass and an eel, all swimming on the spot while an emotional witness in a darkened room points towards the sea bass through the mirror glass.

I decide to browse some flights to Nashville instead but I nearly drop my phone. They are now twice the price compared to last time I looked! I don't have time to fret any further because my attention is pulled towards some laughter outside. Trish and Suzie pass the window, coffees in hand. I duck down behind a menu and watch them carry on up the street. Suzie laughs and puts her arm through Trish's as the latter finishes the punchline of a story. Bezzy mates, then. A pang of alarm that Trish might spill about my pregnancy, but I reassure myself that she too could get in serious trouble if the truth came out, having been the one to sign the medical form. She wouldn't put her neck on the line if she didn't intend to keep the secret, and she certainly wouldn't want to end up with her mugshot on the front page of the *Press* like Mr Sea Bass Thief here.

Since I learned there's a high chance I'll end up in prison if I get caught, I've spent some considerable time wondering how I'd fare behind bars. Second-hand spice inhalation, awful food, a spartan library full of discarded romance novels and driving theory test manuals. I'd be a loner . . . until perhaps an older, sexual-orientationally ambiguous woman named something like Viv, in for murdering her abusive husband, will attempt to take me under her wing. I'll join her prison commune of women who have been driven to crime by men, like an incarcerated Greenham Common. I suppose that wouldn't be too bad.

I finish my drink, abandoning the little heart-shaped chocolate that accompanied it, which I assume is in aid of Valentine's Day next week . . . not that Sean and I ever went in for that nonsense, but it stings all the same. I tip the waitress a little too much on account of my earlier outburst and continue up towards the school. As I head towards a shortcut through the back door of the canteen, I encounter Callum sitting on some piled-up paving slabs. I was hoping English lessons might get easier with him since our interaction at AllStar Sports and they did . . . because he stopped bothering to turn up at all. This lack of attendance irks me, not only because it is a legal requirement that he attend school but also because he's reading a book, so he must have a mild interest in literature at the very least.

It is very telling that he makes more of an effort to cover up the book than conceal the vape he's puffing on. I sneak a glance at the cover as he shoves the small paperback into his pocket – *The Machine Stops and Other Stories* by E. M. Forster.

I recall the passing comment I made about this short story in the PSHE lesson I had to cover with Callum's tutor group before Christmas. It hadn't occurred to me he might actually have been listening. I cast my mind back to secondary school and can't think of a single time I did more than the bare minimum that was required of me. I was an uncurious robot automaton, memorising whatever it was my teacher said about *The Merchant of Venice* so I could regurgitate it and pass it off as my own opinion in my exam. And here he was, reading around a topic.

'Put the vape away, Callum, and I'll pretend I haven't seen it . . . Come on, it's not good for me to be breathing that stuff in.' I rub my bump. He stuffs it in his pocket and stares at my stomach as if he can see through to my empty womb.

I shift my weight from side to side, to get some heat into my feet.

'You had any cravings yet, miss?'

Every single person who knows you are pregnant without fail asks you if you have any cravings. I have done my best to be as imaginative as I can . . . for my amusement to begin with until I realised that it's a useful technique to manipulate people into bringing you things you need.

When Julie asked me the other day, my blood sugar felt low, so I said, 'Jelly babies,' and a packet appeared in the staffroom. A few days after that, I ended up with some custard creams gifted by a begrudging Yolande when I clocked she was eating them just as the school receptionist asked me. Yesterday, I got in a spot of bother when I didn't have time to get to the shops, and was thrilled when a bottle of Persil was left on my desk by a bemused Tim Bell after telling him I had a craving for laundry detergent. Clean pants for Barri!

'I don't know if we'd call it "a craving", but I'd like my student to return to his lessons.'

Callum shrugs.

'What are you reading?' I ask.

'A book.'

'Great. You know where there are plenty of those?' I nod my head towards the school building. 'In English classrooms.'

'I don't like the teacher.'

'Why's that then?'

He meets my eye. 'She's a receipt-demanding mentalist who loves the sound of her own voice.'

I bite my tongue at the urge to reiterate yet again that it was my right as a customer to demand that receipt. How was it my problem that they had run out of rolls and he had to wander up and down the arcade to the neighbouring shops on the scrounge for a new one? The fact it took a while for him to get hold of one is more of a poor reflection on his ability to charm than my stubbornness as a paying customer.

Callum looks tired today. I wonder if he ever goes to bed at a reasonable time or if he's out partying with his mates every night.

'I'd appreciate it if you would start coming back to my lessons and I promise to not be a receipt-demanding mentalist . . . can't change the loving-the-sound-of-my-own-voice thing as that's kind of bedded in by this point.'

Callum shrugs again, pulls out his vape, and clicks it several times before it switches on. He puffs while looking at my bump pointedly. This lack of care about my unborn fake foetus irks me. 'I know it was you the other week up in the Vale,' I say, fanning the steam away from my face, getting a whiff of blueberry in the process. 'I saw you going into a house. What were you doing?'

He pauses, mid-puff. 'Why you so obsessed with me, miss? You stalking me or something?'

A pull in my stomach again as – over Callum's shoulder – I spot Ish revving down the adjacent road in Sean's Mini. I then register what Callum just said to me and whip my head back towards him. 'Just come back to your English lessons or I'll put you on report.'

I charge into the school, letting the door slam behind me.

I rummage around in the kitchen drawer until my finger connects with the metal loop I'm after and head on into Town.

Despite it being a disgusting metallic purple that should pop against the sea of conventionally coloured cars, it takes me a good hour to locate Sean's Mini by pacing around all the various parking spots and pressing the 'unlock' button on the key fob. Eventually, I hear the welcome *beep beep* from behind a van on Albert Pier and find the car tucked in on the wonk beside a row of motorbikes. All parking in Guernsey is done via a cardboard clock. You set it to the time you arrive, and display it on your dashboard so the warden can tell whether you've outstayed your welcome or not. All very dignified.

It irks me that there isn't a parking clock in sight. Ish – like Sean – seems to think the rules don't apply to him, and he's probably well aware that I'm the one who'll end up picking up the fine given the car is in my name and the ticket will arrive at my house and not his. It makes me feel much less guilty about what I'm about to do.

It takes me a while to get used to the clutch after not having driven for so many years, but, after a few bunny hops through the car park and a couple of hairy moments on tight bends in the lanes, I'm feeling pretty confident again by the time I've got it to Mick's – an old mate of Dad's from his mechanic days – at his garage on Route de Carteret.

This Mini was initially a gift from Sean to me for my birthday, but after a few days, it became apparent that he was besotted with it and he gradually took it as his own. I didn't mind one iota; I didn't have the heart to say but I much preferred getting around on my trusty Melva.

'The purple's a bit . . . unique.' Mick walks around the Mini while I wrestle Melva out of the back.

'I know,' I say. 'My husband absolutely loves it. We joke that he should've married this car instead of me.' I feel a squeeze of hurt in my stomach – that gag isn't as offhand to deliver post-break-up. I picture my dad grinning down at my gumption and sigh out the sadness.

Mick points out the various bumps, scrapes and the rust underneath and I reiterate that – despite being the registered keeper – this was predominantly my husband's vehicle.

'What will he think of you selling it, eh?' Mick asks, wiping oil off his hands after closing the bonnet.

Knowing Mick is a connection to Dad emboldens me to come out with a bit of truth for once. I smile at him. 'Trust me, he deserves this.'

Mick pats me on the back in a paternal way that makes

my eyes sting. 'It's pretty beat-up and the colour is . . . Reckon I can stretch to two thousand two hundred?'

It's not in any way a life-changing sum, but it will cover the cost of my Nashville flights and – if I can hold my nerve to get a cheaper fare – it may even leave me a little buffer. I nod. 'That will do me.'

I take great pleasure in messaging Ish to tell him the car is no longer under his stewardship. The worst thing that could happen is Sean will ring me in a rage, and perhaps then I can challenge him on the house and finally get to the bottom of what the hell happened to our marriage.

After a week of lugging Brigitta around and constant phone-checking for calls or messages from Sean that don't materialise, the weekend cannot come soon enough. I can eat unpasteurised cheese and drink caffeine without scrutiny. I'm sick to the back teeth of people telling me how big I am, how small I am, giving me their predictions over whether it's a boy or a girl. It is like my pregnancy is now the only thing that defines me. Like I am not a human being that exists beyond being pregnant. I'm irritable and fed up and emotional and then . . . Of course, I come on my period.

With a complete lack of same-day grocery delivery available on the island, I am at a loss as to how I can get hold of some tampons without having to leave the house to buy some. With a quarter of a roll of toilet paper left, the idea of spending the weekend squatting over some Tupperware in front of Netflix isn't something I can get on board with, and even I can't go for more than one hour in the bath.

I briefly workshop the idea of texting Tim Bell 'Have cravings for Lil-lets', but even he would know that this request in pregnancy would be biologically impossible. And then my eye catches the box of nappies Suzie dropped round . . .

I weigh up the extreme need I have for a lazy, bump-free weekend against the requirement to conduct myself in a sane and sanitary manner.

I rip open the box, plunge my hand into the neatly packed nappies and pull one out. It has a picture of a yellow rubber duck on one side. After a quick deduction that this bit must be the front, no doubt intended to cheer up the poor bastard tasked with swapping this one out with a poo-filled one, I step my feet through the elasticated holes of the nappy and pull it up, where it meets the barrier of my calves. I chuckle at my stupidity as I bunny-hop around the house, trying to locate some scissors to fashion a sanitary pad out of the between-the-legs bit instead, splashes of blood landing on the carpet as I go.

I am midway through struggling to free my feet from the nappy holes when the shape of a figure looms through the frosted glass of my front door. I freeze. Just the postman, I tell myself, as the letterbox moves.

Where the letters should be: a pair of eyes. They widen in alarm as they take in the scene. Me frozen, balanced on one leg, the nappy, the scissors, the blood and – most upsetting of all – my full-frontal vagina. The Unmade Bed art installation taken to the next level in my hallway exclusively for me and this lucky solo spectator.

Trish says nothing, closes the letterbox, and waits for me to sort myself out. I open the door. She's come from work, still wearing her navy scrubs with a pink long-sleeved top underneath, hospital lanyard round her neck. She hands me a bottle of red and heads off. She returns ten minutes later with a bumper box of sanitary products, some Hobnobs and a bottle of white ('I thought it might be more palatable after all the . . .').

We stand in my kitchen as I open the wine, an unspoken pact made that we will never speak of this again. She bends to wipe away some blood from the floor with a piece of kitchen roll before washing her hands like a surgeon about to perform a triple heart bypass. The scrubs she's wearing only add to the effect.

'Have you had a good few weeks?' I ask.

'Not really. My mate's been ignoring me.'

I think about all the messages and the many knocks on the door, pelting past her on Melva on my way to work. 'I was—'

She rests her forearms on the worktop. 'We're all anti-social fuck-ups, Barri, most of us just don't show that on the outside.'

'You've got a new friend now.'

She rolls her eyes. 'Suzie's really nice. If you gave her a chance, you'd see that.'

'She's boring. She and her cackling bunch of teacher witches.' I laugh, having repeated how Sean used to refer to Julie, Suzie and Yolande whenever I mentioned them. Trish gives me a weird look but doesn't say anything.

As I spot-clean my carpet, I fill her in on the ormer situation and I'm pleased she shows more interest in the thief than my sister did.

'It's funny that you care so much, though, given you're never coming back here,' she says.

'It's the ecosystem!'

Trish takes a sip of wine and fiddles with my keys in the bowl on the sideboard. 'How come you didn't just sell this place? Surely it would have been easier than faking a pregnancy.'

'Sean and I remortgaged recently.'

She looks up at me then, eyes narrowing. 'Did you? Where's that money then?'

I scrub harder on the carpet despite the stain having gone. 'Why are you so interested?'

'Because I care about you and . . . I have a feeling there's something you haven't told me.'

I pull off my rubber gloves and slap them into my cleaning caddy. 'Well, there isn't.'

I can't put my finger on why I don't want to tell Trish the truth. She definitely wouldn't gossip or judge me for it. Maybe it's that – despite what he's done – I don't want her to think badly of Sean. Some kind of embedded loyalty to him and our marriage. Trish and I pretend like we are having a nice time for the rest of the day, but there is a definite charge of tension emitting from her.

As Trish dozes off on Big Blue, I eye the ormer shell on the sideboard and decide to message Pierre for an update. He replies almost instantly suggesting I meet him later. As much as I would prefer for him to lay the facts out over WhatsApp to avoid having to a) go out with Brigitta unnecessarily and b) interact with someone socially when I can't be bothered, his 'some evidence you have to see' sways me.

Chapter Eighteen

Pierre waves to me as he strides towards the pub. He has a gilet over the same outfit he was sporting the other day, except he's wearing a different pair of odd socks and – thankfully – trainers instead of Crocs. Awful bright orange running trainers with soles that look like they have been made out of foamy test tubes, mind you, but an improvement nonetheless.

Sean was always very well dressed. Some days, smart with a tweed jacket, fitted shirt and a trilby, and others, a crisp white T-shirt, blue jeans and some fancy trainers he spent hours bidding for on eBay. I always thought we must have looked like an odd pair with him all on trend and me very conventional in a generic stripy T-shirt and jeans combo or an M&S polka-dot smock dress.

We tried going clothes shopping together only once a few years back. He spent the best part of an afternoon convincing me to try on a denim all-in-one. I wasn't opposed to some kind of jumpsuit but had envisaged a romper or perhaps a bright-coloured dungaree. The one he insisted would look fantastic on me was a figure-hugging faded black denim number with a zip up the front. After a lot of encouragement, he sent me off into the changing rooms while he waited on a pouffe outside.

When I couldn't get it over my hips, the assistant kindly grabbed me the next size up to avoid me having to go back out. Sean had smirked when he saw the size I picked off the rail and I didn't want the cheeky sod to know he was right.

When I put it on, I didn't think it looked that bad. It had a tie belt bit that went around my waist that seemed to do the job of pulling me in. The zip took a bit of work, but I eventually managed to get it done up over my boobs and I thought that, on balance, it did a good job of streamlining my shape. It had some cool fringing at the back of it that made it feel less catsuity and more 'cool chick at festival'. I was overheated from the exertion of getting it on, so the kind shop assistant fanned me with the cardboard lid of a shoebox. I could tell by the look on her face she thought I looked pretty good too. She nipped out and returned with a green scarf that she tied in my hair with a bow at the top.

'Super cute – the colour is so nice with your hair,' she said.

I felt OK stepping out to show Sean, who was now standing, chatting with one of his gym class buddies. A pang of anxiety at feeling so exposed in front of someone I didn't know that well. I nearly headed back into the changing room without saying anything until the assistant piped up, 'Well, what do we think?'

I could tell that Sean wasn't sure by the way he spent an excruciating amount of time appraising me. Affronted that her work hadn't provoked a better reaction, the assistant went to fetch some cowboy boots with a perfect chunky mid-heel height. My heart leapt at the sight of them; I'd always wanted a pair. I thought they finished off the look, but Sean had lost interest by this point and became distracted by his phone.

The assistant smiled at me. 'Men, eh?'

I bought the outfit anyway and decided to wear it out to the pub that night, but when I got home, I couldn't get the scarf to sit the way the girl in the shop had.

Sean came into the bedroom looking dapper as usual in jeans, a shirt, and some new Chelsea boots he'd bought that day. 'Come on Barri, it's only the pub quiz.'

'I'm ready!'

The bow wasn't perfect, but I felt pretty good. I'd also gone for a nice bold lip, which I thought elevated the outfit further. 'What do you think?'

'To be honest, it's not very you . . . but it's not up to me, as long as you feel good,' he said.

I assessed myself in the mirror again, this time trying to view myself through Sean's eyes. It did all look a bit try-hard.

'I'll take it all back, I think.'

'Yeah, I reckon.'

It's all still sitting in the bag at the bottom of my wardrobe.

I amuse myself by imagining the very tall Pierre in my denim jumpsuit but decide it would be an improvement on his current garbs.

'Aren't you freezing?' I ask him, wrapping my coat around me, making a mental note that I might need to invest in a larger one.

'I don't feel the cold.' He holds up a manila folder. 'I can't wait to show you what I've found so far.' We head inside the pub, where it looks like Cupid has projectile-vomited love hearts across the entire space. The chalkboard reads: *'Valentine's Weekend: 2-4-1 meals and back-to-back love songs!'*

'Since when is Valentine's Weekend even a thing?' I ask, as the very tall Pierre bats an assault of helium heart balloons out of his face.

'I dunno.' He manages to break free, losing his baseball cap in the process. He bends to retrieve it, shoves it back on his messy-haired head and grins. 'What you having?'

'A large glass of Rioja, please.' Pierre gives me an odd look, hesitates, but heads to the bar. I smooth my hair down again and make another mental note to purchase that high-protein shampoo Trish recommended for pregnancy glossiness.

Pierre has put together an investigation that wouldn't look out of place in a high-end detective show. He shows me a picture of the corkboard in his office – photos and maps of the different ormering spots with pins and bits of string. Inside the file on the table are number plates, lists of regular ormerers, even a few visitor records from the hotels. I spy a photo of me cycling along on Melva. Pierre looks into his beer.

'They say to keep an eye most on people who insert themselves into the investigation . . .' He pulls out some more photos. 'This is what I wanted to show you.'

'How in the world did you get hold of CCTV footage?' I ask, staring at a grainy picture of a shifty-looking hooded figure walking along the seafront.

'Less said about that the better, eh?'

I trace the CCTV stills along with my finger, like a picture story: the figure shielding itself from a car driving through a puddle, putting on some wellies, heading off down the slipway . . . the mystery mollusc pilferer.

'That's where we lost him.'

'Do we even know it's a "him"?' The image is so blurry, it could be any adult on the island.

'Well, women don't tend to be criminals, eh?' he says, smiling. I take a big gulp of wine.

I don't realise my absolute idiocy until I am halfway into my second glass of Rioja, bobbing my head along to R. Kelly's 'Ignition'. Controversial, I know, and hardly a 'love song'. It's the 'Mama' line teamed with a body roll I struggle to achieve with the impingement of Brigitta that makes me realise my error. I spit the red wine back out into the glass and stare at Pierre, who is trying his best to talk over the music, posing his theory that the phantom ormerer is part of some wider shellfish smuggling racket.

'Why the hell did you buy me this?!'

He laughs. 'I guess technically it's your round, but it all comes out in the wash.'

'No, Pierre. I'm pregnant.' I shunt the glass towards him. 'I can't be drinking this.'

'You asked for red wine,' he says, wiping the splashes of liquid with his beermat.

'I forgot. Shit!'

'I wouldn't worry, Barri. My sister was at least six months pregnant before she found out. She'd been on a work ski trip the week before and got twatted every night. My niece turned out fine.'

'Ally in year seven? Blonde plaits?'

Pierre smiles. 'Yeah, that's the one. Little monkey's always—'

'Can't even conjugate a basic verb clause!'

I think I hear him muttering, 'Neither can I,' as I storm out, barging past the waitress bringing us our microwaved jacket potatoes.

Confident that Pierre hasn't followed me out of the pub, I switch to a brisk walk. I'm so annoyed with myself for the slip-up that I push to the front of the taxi queue.

'Oh, bot I say, eh?' The thick-accented old Guernsey girl whose car I'm about to pinch clutches her handbag strap as if she is going to smack me with it. I reference my bump, which makes her stop – no doubt pondering if pregnant trumps age in this situation. I'm about to jump in the car when my phone rings.

'Barri, bit of an odd one.' Julie hacks away at her cough for another thirty seconds or so before continuing. 'Callum Le Brocq has got himself into a bit of bother with the police. They can't get hold of Social. His dad's away working, they can't reach his grandfather and so they called . . . the school.'

She means they called her and I can see where this is going already. I help the old lady into my taxi – which was her taxi all along – as Julie blathers on. 'In all honesty, I'm feeling pretty awful. Think it might be a chest infection . . .' I hear the sound of adult laughter in the background. A nasty illness when it suits her. '. . . And Suzie's at her sister's wedding . . .' she adds as she moves into a quieter room to disguise the sound of the dinner party happening in the background of wherever she is.

I pace around the taxi rank, feeling springy all of a sudden. 'So, if I go and bail him out, would we say that I am doing that in my capacity as Deputy Head of Key Stage Four?' I ask.

'That role doesn't exist.'

'Interim?'

'You can be Acting Deputy Head of Year Eleven *for one night only*.'

Whenever I hear 'custody suite', 'custody desk', or 'custody sergeant', I picture rooms, tables and people absolutely covered in custard.

A round-faced police officer in her mid-forties mans the desk. Neither she nor the desk is custardy, much to my disappointment. She watches me with smug amusement as I waddle in, getting Brigitta caught on the heavy door as it swings back towards me.

'I'm here to collect Callum Le Brocq.'

She examines me, dubious. 'You his parent or guardian?'

'I'm his head of year at school.' *Oh yeah!*

'Lucky you.'

The PC's patronising air makes me dislike her immediately. I have to stop myself from brushing away the remnants of whatever pastry product she scoffed before I came in. The greasy flakes scattered on her bosom as well as the surrounding desk are interspersed with the occasional glob of herby meat, suggesting sausage roll.

'Is he in trouble?' I ask.

'This is Callum Le Brocq we're talking about. He's practically got his own wing at this station, madam.'

Don't get me wrong, Callum is a troublemaker. But him having his 'own wing' is more because of the low crime rate on the island as opposed to him being a notorious criminal. I'm about to take great pleasure in voicing this when they bring a mute Callum out, wearing his sports shop uniform, and sit him in reception while I sign some paperwork. He does not appear happy to see me, but the mucky look he gives this PC at the desk indicates he shares my disdain for her.

'Serious this time, though, eh?' The police officer adds. 'Nicking money out of someone's wallet at AllStar Sports, weren't you, Le Brocq?'

I wait for a punchy retort from Callum but, for once, the kid looks visibly chastised. The PC notices this too and chuckles. I turn to her. 'Wow, an actual robbery to investigate. That must be exciting for you!'

The police here are sensitive about how relatively easy their job is. Especially since the recruitment video they made depicting high-speed chases, explosions and armed raids went viral, opening them up to ridicule when the national press compared them to *Hot Fuzz*.

Her cheeks redden. 'Second one actually . . . if you count the greenhouse glass going missing down at Icart.'

'And how many murders?' I ask.

'None . . .' she says.

'Don't be downhearted. There was that tasering . . . but actually, I'm not sure we should count that, given it was a police officer doing it to themselves . . . twice! I mean, really, how stupid can you—'

The PC rubs her arm reflexively and, when she realises I've clocked this, fiddles with some paperwork. I lean in towards her. 'Maybe they put the police officer in question on desk duty . . . PC Pluckrose,' I add, reading the name scrawled on the top of her clipboard.

She bristles and fiddles with her paperwork some more. 'I'm on an extremely important case, actually, madam.'

'Come on, Callum, the PC has important work to do filing her report on . . . a lost purse with nothing inside it but a Costa voucher card with one pound ninety-nine left on it that Mrs Ida Le Tissier would very much like back.' A teacher's ability to read upside down does come in handy from time to time.

We step outside into the chilly night, both of us laughing.

'That was brutal, miss!'

I feel my cheeks glow red, a bit guilty for my harsh takedown.

'Well, see ya.' Callum moves to head off.

'You fancy some chips?' I call after him. I'm starving from my aborted jacket potato and I can definitely make this snack reimbursable by the school if it is under the guise of Callum needing to eat. He looks over his shoulder, eager to make an exit, but then his stomach rumbles.

We sit at the bus terminus eating in silence. It's quite a rowdy Saturday night and some karaoke music from a nearby bar carries over on the breeze. Someone murdering Shirley Bassey. Sacrilege. Callum shudders too and for a moment I wonder whether he's a fan, but he's shivering.

'Where's your coat?'

He shoves a chip in his mouth. 'Forgot it at AllStar's.'

'You *left* it at AllStar's?'

'Actually, I got dragged from AllStar's by the police and no one bothered to ask me if I had a coat or not.' Callum's eyes brim. 'They wouldn't listen to me when I told them . . . I was putting it back.' He takes in a few quick gasps of air. 'Lost . . . my . . . job . . .'

His eyes grow wide in desperation as the panic gets the

better of him. He wraps his arms around himself in an attempt to apply pressure but it doesn't seem to be working.

'Can you . . .' He signals towards his arms with his head. 'Please.'

The look of sheer panic on his face forces me to act. I grab him from the side, round the shoulders and chest and squeeze him tightly. We stay like that for a while until Callum's breathing calms and he pulls away. 'What the hell is that?' he asks.

'What?'

'That sound you're making in my ear – it's creepy as fuck.' I fill him in on my alien anti-cuddle strategy. 'That's a lot of effort to go to to avoid human touch, miss. You're like the character in that book you made us read.'

I decide now is not the time to point out that I didn't *make* them read it. 'Did you like it?'

'Yeah. It was creepy and sad. Still feels like a future we're all heading towards but could prevent.'

Callum has finished his chips and is eyeing up mine. Despite still being hungry, I hand the packet to him.

The foghorn sounds. There must be some sea mist about to roll in, but no sign of it yet in St Peter Port. I can still see the distant boat lights twinkling through the darkness.

'How come you got to the police station so quick?' he asks, munching on the chunkiest, most succulent, vinegar-soaked chip I was saving for last.

'I was already in Town. There's someone been stealing ormers and . . . oh ormers are these mollusc—'

'I know what ormers are, miss. I'm not thick.'

'Sorry. I know you're not.' The foghorn blows again as if highlighting my faux pas. 'That pressure hug thing works wonders,' I say.

Callum smiles. 'Yeah, learned it from my stepmum. She did some reading up on it and that when I started feeling a bit . . . you know . . . aggy in the head.'

'She sounds kind.'

'She was.' He looks down at his empty chip packet. I remind myself how young he is, despite carrying himself like he's older.

I think of how I can resolve a small part of this, but dare I open that can of worms . . . ?

'Come on,' I say, pulling out my phone.

'Shit, Barri. I had no idea.' Sean's mate Ish stares at my bump in transfixed horror.

'You're about the last person on the island to find out, then,' I say. I enjoy the shock and panic for a little longer before putting him out of his misery. 'No, I haven't told Sean. No, it's not his. Sperm donor.'

Callum's eyebrows raise, both at my openness and my forced familiarity with his ex-boss.

Ish keeps staring at me as he turns the key and pulls up the shutters of AllStar Sports. His huge shoulder and bicep muscles struggle under the seams of his leather jacket.

In no time at all, Ish is in and out with Callum's coat and the shutters are back down. I watch him stride away. 'How is he?!' I call after him, immediately regretting the desperation in my voice. Callum gives me a look of undiluted pity.

Ish stops, turns back and shrugs. 'Pissed off you've taken the car off me but, other than that, he's great.'

'Could you tell him to—'

'No.' Ish strides off again, pulling his phone out to make the call to Sean.

'Well, that's that, then,' I say as we head away from AllStar, Callum's coat in my hand.

We wait in silence at the taxi rank while I obsess over how Sean is going to take the news that I'm pregnant . . . It dawns on me that I may never find out.

Callum breaks the silence. 'Your ex. You're well shot of him, miss.'

'You knew him?'

He looks up the street, waving at a taxi that's headed in our direction. 'Just seen him about is all.'

'Sean's a gregarious character, which from a distance could be an off-putting characteristic. But everyone loves him when they know him,' I say. 'Anyway, enough about all that.'

The taxi pulls in. I hand Callum some cash and then realise I'm still clutching his coat to me. 'Sorry,' I say, handing it to him and opening the taxi door. 'Come back to my class.'

'OK.' Callum goes to get into the car but stops and turns back to me. 'Cheers, yeah.'

As he turns his coat over to shove it in the taxi, an ormer shell clatters to the floor. It's the way he grabs at it, scrabbling to stuff it back into his pocket without me seeing . . .

'It's you,' I say.

He stops scrabbling. 'What?'

'You're the ormer thief!'

Callum stands up tall. 'I'm not a thief,' he says through gritted teeth.

I take a step to block him from getting in the taxi. 'Then why do you have that?'

'It's none of your fucking business actually, miss.'

I think about the figure in the CCTV walking along the front. Something in the gait . . . and then remember that I only saw photos, so how could I possibly know how the person walked? My mind has gone there because I wanted it to.

I hold my hands up. 'I'm sorry. You're right. I shouldn't jump to—'

'Fuck you.'

Callum pushes past me, gets in the cab and slams the door in my face.

'Get a receipt!' I yell through the window. He looks head-on, ignoring me. The car pulls off.

'I NEED A RECEIPT TO BE REIMBURSED!'

Chapter Nineteen

About three weeks after my run-in with Callum, I'm woken abruptly by someone standing over my bed. I yell out in horror before remembering I hung Kurt on the back of the door, ready for his inaugural wear today . . . I would have preferred the axe-wielding nutter. The dressing gown on the hook underneath has wrapped itself around him as if he donned it on purpose during the night to add a sense of drama to the occasion. Admittedly, this would have been more impressive were it a plush red velvet gown rather than the dowdy off-white towelling robe it is. But, still, I get it, Kurt; you're ready for your debut.

Despite the gravity from being suspended on a coat hook all night, Kurt's round shape has remained solid. A small downward curved crease in the middle of his plumpest part gives him the haughty air of an arrogant high school jock. I think of the more awkward students I teach, with their pomegranate acne and angle-poise posture. Kurt is not one of those. From this angle, the smooth texture of his material looks like creamy, alabaster skin. He is strong, chiselled and glossy – a caricature football jock in an American TV show. He's a Big Name on Campus.

To delay the inevitable, I spoon my coffee beans one by one into the machine, squeeze out the toothpaste slither by slither and shower until the hot water runs out.

This makes me late and so I end up putting Kurt on in a rush, without ceremony.

'Jesus Christ, you're heavy,' I say, looking at him in the full-length mirror in my bedroom. There is an extra band of Velcro and a few more ties than Brigitta had for added security, which takes a bit of getting used to, but, having listened acutely to every aeroplane safety demonstration, I adopt the life jacket technique and fasten him securely.

I pull on a new balloon-sleeved dress I picked up in Town at the weekend. It's a beautiful apple green that I wish wasn't a maternity dress – it would look lovely during my trip to Nashville, paired with an offensively fabulous cowboy hat and sunglasses combo. I take a step back to examine the ensemble.

The beauty of the dress is eclipsed by Kurt. He is the hero here; calm and in control, whereas I am the wimpy sidekick in the sidecar, hands tight over my eyes as we speed through a tiny gap between two lorries.

In this next phase of pregnancy, if I want out, I have to come clean or leave. Those are the choices. As of today, either I am getting off this island or I'm headed to prison, where I don't think they will let me wear a dress, a hat or sunglasses . . . or ride in imaginary sidecars.

I take a few calming breaths and step outside into the welcome March sunshine.

The morning goes without a hitch, so I'm feeling completely calm by the time I head in to cover Year Seven Food Technology during my free period. I tend to mind less about stepping in to teach this lesson, as it often involves the opportunity to eat various delicious food items the kids have brought in.

After I have sated my savoury tastes (cheese, olives, Parma ham), I move on to sweets. I waddle around, trying a few mixtures from bowls, lingering to take a second spoonful of salted caramel from one particularly delicious concoction.

The student who made the caramel seems affronted by the attention I'm giving her bowl. She drags it away from my side of the counter, covering it with a plate. But when she turns her back to help her classmate fan a sponge cake with a chopping board, I take the opportunity to get thirds. As I lean over the counter to lift the plate and pilfer another spoonful of mixture, I hear a ripping sound coming from my stomach. I look down.

Shit.

I try to regain my balance by circling my arms, but Kurt's heavier weight forces me to continue my trajectory across the worktop towards the salted caramel, meaning there is nothing I can do to stop the six-inch chef's knife from spearing my abdomen.

I fling my caramel spoon to the side and use my hands to push back off the counter, but it's too late. The knife has plunged in so deep that it stays where it is, impaled in my bump – so far in I can barely see the blade. The ripping sound was my gorgeous apple green dress, which now has a frayed slit up my front.

I look around the room. Thankfully, all the students are focused on their cookery . . . until I clock poor, sweet, bubbly Beberly. She stares at the knife jutting out of my pregnant bump in complete, silent horror; *The Scream* for the Alpha generation.

I bundle her into the store cupboard under the guise of needing help to carry a box and remove the knife in a nonchalant manner that indicates fatally stabbing your own foetus is no more strange than brushing one's hair or blinking.

'I wouldn't mention this to anyone as it's common knowledge and people might think you're completely thick for not knowing,' I say after having explained to her naive, sweet little face that it's a miracle of pregnancy: you can skewer yourself and your unborn child and come out completely unscathed. 'Something to do with a fattier fascia,' I add, which I think sounds scientific.

She thanks me for saving her from the embarrassment and returns to baking her biscuits, all the while gaping in open-mouthed wonder at the marvel of the female body.

I sincerely hope this doesn't have future negative repercussions for her.

On my lunch break, I head home to get changed. With Kurt in tow, it's only a matter of time before I have to stop cycling and surrender myself to the Guernsey bus system. I cast my lovely new dress to the side to fix later. There's a large, knife-shaped hole in Kurt too, where his arrogant sneer once was. I apologise to him as I shove the foam back in, which feels weirdly invasive. I pop on a new vest, dress and cardigan, and head back to work.

I'm on my way to the staffroom, almost strutting with the arrogance of blagging my way out of that one, when I pass PC Pluckrose, clearly no longer on desk duty, stalking the school corridor with an excitable black Labrador and a very hyped-up Julie in tow. Up ahead, I spy Callum darting into a row of lockers, his head turned towards them in horror. I look back at the PC and Julie but they are too busy in conversation to have noticed him.

Callum hasn't said a word to me since I accused him of being the ormer thief despite my best efforts to engage with him in lessons. I speed up my pace and poke my head around the side of the lockers. He stops; a rabbit in the headlights.

'What are you doing?' I ask. His eyes dart behind me at PC Pluckrose and the sniffer dog, who are still heading in our direction. Callum is breathing heavily, his forehead sweaty from panic.

'Please tell me you aren't carrying any illegal substances,' I say.

Callum stares at me for a moment as if making a judgement call. He glances back around at the ever-encroaching sniffer dog. He pulls a bag of powder out of his trouser pocket and frantically tries to rip the lockers open. None of them budge. He checks for gaps in which to stuff the packet, but the lockers are too tight to the wall and floor to hide anything.

Maybe it's because I feel so bad about accusing him of being the ormer thief, the thrill of blagging poor sweet Beberly, or maybe after years of being a stickler, I'm becoming addicted to breaking rules . . . I grab the bag.

'Run!' I hiss.

Callum doesn't need telling twice.

Just as the PC, sniffer dog and my boss are about to come around the corner, I pull up my dress and shove the drugs inside Kurt's knife hole.

Chapter Twenty

The dog goes berserk immediately. It tugs on the lead, desperate to approach.

PC Pluckrose scrutinises me. 'Was that Callum Le Brocq I saw legging it just then?' She checks all the places Callum did when he was looking for somewhere to stash the stuff.

'Yes. Late for his French lesson,' I say. Julie eyes me, doubtful. 'He loves French,' I add. My voice is at least two tones higher than usual and I have a horrible dry feeling in my throat, like someone has sucked all the moisture off my vocal cords with the Kärcher tool I use to dry my shower screen.

PC Pluckrose releases the dog from her grasp. It jumps up to my stomach, pounding its nose against my bump wherein lies several . . . bumps. I bat it off, which I hope just looks like a pregnant woman protecting herself.

PC Pluckrose eyes me. 'Are you carrying any illegal substances?'

'Me?!' I say.

'Barri?!' Julie snorts.

PC Pluckrose scrutinises me again. Recognition dawns. Her lips turn upwards into a sinister smile.

In hindsight, my cheekiness at the police station feels misguided.

Inside the sick bay room, Julie left waiting outside, the dog bounces at my stomach again.

'Can you tell it not to please?'

'Empty your pockets, then.' PC Pluckrose makes this demand as if I should be familiar with the stop and search process. She searches my armpits, pats down my arms and legs. Nothing. Convinced that's that, I head towards the door.

'Take your dress off now, please, madam.'

'You can't be—'

Her dead eyes tell me everything I need to know.

As I take off my cardigan, it occurs to me that I have spent a lot of time pondering how I might be discovered faking this pregnancy, but not one scenario involved me also being in possession of Class A drugs. How many extra years in prison would that be?!

Trying to stop my fingers from trembling, I unbutton the front of my dress, smoothing my vest down over Kurt as I go, attempting to channel his unflappable, borderline psychopathic energy.

PC Pluckrose seems embarrassed by the intimacy of my half-nakedness. I guess strip searches aren't a regular part of her day either. I look down – Kurt's seam is visible through the vest but, other than that, it looks like a pregnant tummy . . . as long as no one looks too closely. I slip the straps of my vest off carefully and pull it down below my boobs so that it still covers the bump. Desperate times. I whip off my bra.

PC Pluckrose is stunned I have pre-empted her and she

gawks at me as I jiggle my bosoms at her. I lift one breast and then the other to prove I'm not concealing anything underneath them. Eyes averted, she passes my bra to me.

'Put it back on, please.' Her tone is imploring with a smidgeon of disgust. No 'nice tits' from her, then. I pull my vest back up over my bra and place the straps back on my shoulders, willing her not to ask me to remove the vest completely.

She looks down at my stomach with more trepidation than she did at my breasts. Maybe it's the light, but the seam of the bump looks more prominent now. Under Kurt, my stomach feels like a washing machine on an aggressive spin cycle.

'Do you have any children?' I ask, hoping that she isn't equipped to spot the difference.

'God no . . . and don't you dare tell me I'll change my mind—'

'This was the worst decision I've ever made,' I say, bile rising.

Please don't make me take my vest off. Please don't make me take my vest off.

She softens and looks at my bump again. I make a point of shivering so she'll take pity on the cold pregnant lady.

'Do you mind if I . . . just give it a quick feel?' She looks like she wants to do this about as much as I want her to.

'Be my guest,' I say.

She does a quick, awkward skim of the bump to ensure there aren't any drugs under my vest. That stupid joke about what police officers say to their belly buttons whirls around my head. After what feels like an excruciating amount of time, PC Pluckrose sighs and ruffles the fur on top of the dog's head. 'You daft little thing.' She turns to me. 'He's still in training. Got excited at the airport the other day. Turned out it was just a kid bringing a Big Mac over from the mainland.'

The dog is still eyeing me with a terrifying intensity for such a cute animal. I hurriedly put my dress back on. I spot Kurt's tie cords poking out beneath my vest. They must have come undone at some point during all my stressing and undressing. I shove them down my pants, pull my dress over, and breathe. It's over.

Do you know what the most humbling sound is following the glory of having stripped in front of a police officer while sporting a fake pregnancy bump, several grams of ketamine, and not getting caught?

The sound of a rubber glove smacking against a wrist.

'Just a quick internal and I'll be happy,' PC Pluckrose says, as she moves towards me, her hands held up like a surgeon about to approach the operating table.

Not in any way sure this is the official procedure for internal examinations, even in Guernsey, I'm nervous that my protesting might result in another strip inspection from someone more capable than this PC. In the interest of this being over, I decide to acquiesce. Just as my hands move towards my dress to lift it up, she bursts into laughter. 'I'm *joking*!'

Feeling like I might pass out, I sink down onto the sick bed.

PC Pluckrose removes her gloves and chucks them in the bin. 'The look on your face.' She chuckles, no doubt thrilled at her revenge following my takedown the other week at the police station. 'No one in their right mind wants to shove their fingers inside someone else in the line of duty. What do you think we are, the Met?'

And on that inappropriate nugget, she departs.

Chapter Twenty-One

My mum kept Dad's ashes in the airing cupboard after he died. Although my parents were separated by that point, legally, the decision about what to do with them was left to her. It distressed me. Him trapped in an airtight urn in that stifling cupboard. I used to lie awake at night, imagining the particles of him vibrating in the heat, unable to settle or rest.

'They say to not make any rash decisions for at least a year,' Mum said when she caught me trying to sneak the urn out of the house. It had been months, and I had given up begging her to let me hold on to him for safekeeping.

After that, every time I went there for Sunday lunch, I would sneak up, grab a handful of Dad, and shove him into my pocket. I'd then head to Belle Greve and scatter a bit of him in the cricking nook, in a rock pool, on the sand . . .

It made me think of the way they got rid of the dirt from the tunnel in *The Great Escape*, by scattering it bit by bit in the yard through their trouser legs, which I think would have pleased him. His final Great Escape. I haven't been able to bring myself to wash that pair of jeans in case there are any bits of him still in the pockets.

Over time, I got pretty much all of him to Belle Greve

without my mum noticing. I had a plan to refill the urn with sand so she'd never know, but before I had the opportunity, out of the blue one Sunday, she put down her knife and fork, looked at my sister and me and said, 'I checked in on your father this morning. I'm sorry to say he's evaporated,' before helping herself to another Yorkshire pudding.

I don't know what reaction she wanted, but we just sort of accepted it and carried on with our roast beef. I like to think she was comforted by our indifference somehow, even if she never showed it.

Mum always acted like the hard-done-by parent – as if Dad being better at it reflected poorly on Lara and me rather than on her. She wanted something from me that I couldn't give her because she'd done nothing to deserve it. Not because she's cruel, but because the emotional tools required to be the kind of mum you see in storybooks – the ones that give and expect nothing in return – aren't in her arsenal. But that was OK, because Dad's toolkit had a bumper triple layer.

Over the years, I watched my sister try and fail to get what she needed from our mother. Whereas my feelings have turned to indifference, Lara still carries a hope that one day Mum might take an actual interest in her beyond the superficial chit-chat, cups of tea and the odd hint about a granny annexe. I suppose, of the two of us, I fared better because, despite us losing him when we did, Dad was always enough for me.

I'm not sure what pulls me to Belle Greve tonight, but I feel calmer as soon as I step onto the sand. I stand for a moment, allowing the light from the almost-full moon to cover me like a balm.

I always felt like Dad wanted me to be more rebellious.

When I was a teenager, he'd suggest I dye my hair blue, ride a motorbike, or make a half-serious joke about getting a tattoo of something monstrous. He'd have feigned anger (to placate my mum, who hates tattoos), but deep down, he'd have been proud to have an unconventional daughter. I pat Kurt. Well, Dad, you got what you wanted.

I ponder what he would advise me to do about Sean and the money. Head to Crawley, find Sean and demand he explain the deception, demand my share back, maybe even involve the police? Or stay fully focused on the fake pregnancy to give myself the best possible chance of getting away with it? He'd hate to think I'd been deceived by someone in such a calculated way but, on reflection, I think he'd agree that I'm better to cut my losses and make sure I get my clean break without getting caught.

One thing's for sure: he'd have found my actions leading up to the strip search today unnecessary and reckless. The first thing I did after I left that first aid room was flush the ketamine down the toilet. Next, I sat on the loo seat and screamed into Kurt, who was a surprisingly effective vocal mute. I felt so jumpy still that I decided to leave Melva and walk. But instead of heading home, I went the opposite way. I trudged for hours, turning everything over in my head, trying to calm myself down from the adrenaline until I ended up here.

No cars pass along the seafront tonight; it feels like the rest of the island is tucked up in their beds apart from me. I can pretend I'm on my own solitary rock in the English Channel. Perfection.

The tide is on the turn from low to high, ruining signs of its own journey out with every wave that comes back in. I step barefoot into the freezing water and allow my feet to become buried in the sand as the waves gather. For the first time in my adult life, I howl at the moon gutturally. I don't care it's not a full one; I just feel like doing it.

This is exactly where I am and what I am doing when I come face to face with Callum, bucket in hand as he skulks around a cluster of rocks, flabbergasted to find his pregnant English teacher paddling in the dark, making disturbing noises while staring at him with such livid rage, she is vibrating. A good amount of ormers in that bucket. He doesn't even attempt to conceal it; he just grins at me.

'What does it feel like being Callum Le Brocq?' I ask, the rage burning through me.

He shrugs. 'What do you mean?'

'Doing reckless thing after reckless thing and just . . . getting away with it?'

'I don't—'

'No thought for how your actions might affect others, or indeed sabotage entire ecosystems.'

He says nothing, just smirks like he doesn't care.

I point my finger at him. 'Have you got any idea what I risked today? For *you*?' My emphasis on the word 'you' appears to touch a nerve. The smirk disappears.

'You snatched it off me—'

'If they'd found those drugs, that would have been it for me. Prison.'

He laughs. 'I doubt you'd have gone to prison for—'

'Oh, I would. An adult – a *school teacher* – with no pity sob story to feed a judge like you have.' He gives a single irritating, entitled shrug. 'Why on earth did you have it in the first place?'

'I wasn't dealing it or anything, miss. I was just holding on to it for someone.'

Guernsey isn't exactly a breeding ground for drugs cartels and his expression does appear to be genuine, but I look down at that bucket of ormers and feel my fury bubble up again.

'I'm sick of it, Callum. You use your capable brain and shit home life to manipulate people into helping you. Well, I'm not helping you get away with anything else. Not this time.' I pull my phone out of my pocket. Dial nine-nine—

'No, miss, please don't.'

'Guess you'll be doing your GCSEs behind bars.'

'No!' He grabs my phone off me before I can dial the final nine. 'I'll tell them you hid the drugs!'

'Oh, there's no way they'll believe that after the rigorous search I was subjected to today.'

He turns his head up to face the sky. 'Please don't call the police. I'm sorry, all right.'

I shake my head. 'I don't want to hear it. Find another teacher to latch on to. If you ever get back into school, that is.'

Frustrated tears brim in his eyes. My head tells me to stop talking, but I'm too enraged. 'You're . . . you're like this . . . parasite.' I try to pull my phone back, but he will not let go of it. 'Stealing things. Playing on people's empathy. A drain!' We struggle in a tug of war like two smugglers fighting over a gold coin.

In the tussle, the bucket of ormers goes flying, scattering them into the sea. Callum cries out, furious his night of illegal activity has been for nothing. I howl at the moon again. Victorious!

Emboldened by the wolf howl and the freed ormers, I gear up for a mic drop moment.

'There is only so long you can continue to do something really stupid without getting caught, Callum. And today is your reckoning.' I make a sudden snatch for the phone.

SPLASH.

Normally the sound of a splash is cause for joy – a diver jumping in off the rocks, dolphins leaping out of the sea, ormers being returned to the ocean. But not in this moment. Because in this moment, the splash we hear isn't the phone I just successfully commandeered from Callum. It is the sound my fake bump makes as it falls off my body and into the sea.

I never did reattach those extra tie cords properly after they came loose during the strip search. Teamed with the sudden lunge for the phone, well . . . Kurt did a mic drop of his very own.

Chapter Twenty-Two

Kurt bobs between us. Little bubbles effervesce as he ingests the water. The area around his knife hole is particularly lively as it gulps the liquid in. *Glug, glug, glug.*

He made quite an impact when he hit the sea. Callum takes a moment to wipe the water from his face. I just let mine run down my cheeks. The extra ties I shoved down my pants instead of reattaching taunt me as they snake in the water.

I consider leaning into the tragicness, telling him I am so damaged by the breakdown of my marriage – make up some lie about my desperation to have a child. Instead, the truth tumbles out. The injustice, the frustrations. I bring up the patriarchy because all roads lead there and I take a moment to chastise him for rolling his eyes. I tell him about my plan to visit Nashville, my road trip, and then how I'll start a new life in Edinburgh; the place my dad always dreamed I'd live. And then I talk about Sean. Not just that he left. I tell him about the money. How every penny I ever owned got stolen from under my nose. The money my lovely, kind, hilarious father earned working as a mechanic. The job he died at – far too soon.

In hindsight, I have huge regrets over opening up about the period nappy episode. Even so, it all comes crashing out of my brain and into the sea to join Kurt and this fifteen-year-old little shit who is staring at me with an unreadable expression on his face.

A discarded ormer floats past us, making its escape. I don't blame it. This is the world's most uninviting beach party.

Callum computes the situation: the hypocrisy, the deceit, the disgust (period nappy). I try to think how I would feel if I were him. A teacher who had just berated me for being irresponsible with the law and whose own irresponsibility spilled out of her literal stomach in front of him.

When I finish my monologue, he takes his time to process the leverage he now possesses. An office junior who has caught a desperate superior insider trading and now wields all the power. He looks at me. 'OK, then,' he says.

I tilt my head, waiting for more. There is nothing more. 'OK?'

'Miss, it's fucking tapped, but I appreciate the fact you didn't bullshit me by making out you have some kind of psychological disorder or something. And I respect it in a weird way. Like, you're doing it for all the washed-up old people who didn't do the same old boring shit everyone else did just because . . . that's what everyone else does.'

I let the 'washed-up old people' bit go because the sentiment is there.

He looks down at Kurt. 'And you saved my arse earlier when you shoved them drugs in the knife hole. It was pretty thick of you, miss, but it was also pretty . . . sick of you.'

I wiggle my now numb toes, creating mini sandstorms under the water. 'So that's it?' I ask.

'Yeah.'

'Well, that's—'

He looks up at me. 'I'll be wanting 50 per cent of the money obviously.'

Obviously.

Chapter Twenty-Three

I try to scoop Kurt out of the sea, but he's too heavy from where the foam has ingested all the water. Callum grabs the other side to help. He hangs between us like a limp child who has requested a few too many goes of One, Two, Three, Wee.

We struggle out of the sea towards the beach.

A colossal shift in power took place between us this evening. Although we both technically have leverage over each other, it's obvious I have more to lose than he does. A teenager illegally poaching an obscure mollusc will not grab the *Daily Mail*'s attention in the same way a secondary school teacher pretending to be pregnant would.

I side-eye his smirking face. 'You do realise that maternity pay isn't dished out in one lump sum at the start, don't you?'

'Oh.' He looks down momentarily and then snaps his focus back to me. 'So, what *do* you get?'

'Just my salary for a few months and then half my salary for a few more months.'

'Fine, I'll take 50 per cent of that then.'

'Huh?' I scoop my head towards him in a way that would rival Scooby-Doo. 'I can't give you 50 per cent. I need that money to leave!' His expression doesn't shift. 'It's a completely unreasonable ask,' I add. When he rolls his eyes, I raise my voice. 'I'm the one doing all the hard bloody work!'

He sighs and looks at me like I'm his younger sibling. 'We both know you're gonna have to let me blackmail you, miss.'

'You could just not let me let you?'

He laughs.

I tilt my head to the side. 'What about the fact that I saved you from getting arrested today . . .?'

Callum brings his lips up to his nose as he considers this. 'OK, make me a what's it called? A counter-offer thing. What's it worth for me not to spill the tea on you?'

'I'll give you 5 per cent of my full salary for three months.'

He turns his back on me and strides up the beach, leaving me struggling under the full weight of Kurt. 'OK, 7 per cent.' He quickens his pace. 'All right, 10!'

He stops. Turns, and walks back towards me, shark-like. 'Twenty per cent of your maternity salary paid monthly into a bank account of my choosing every month for six months. My final offer.' He takes out his phone. 'Or I'll take a photo of you right now and post it on Snapchat.'

I really don't want to give this bloody kid 20 per cent of my money. I don't want to give him 0.0001 per cent of my money. But what choice do I have? I clench my fists. 'OK. But you have to promise you'll step in to help me if I get into any situations at school.' My bottom lip juts out in despair.

Callum puts his arm round my shoulder. 'Just see it as an investment in a lifestyle, miss . . . AKA avoiding prison.' He grins at me like a competition winner.

I jiggle Kurt. 'Can you help me get the rest of this water out.'

We squeeze the foam in silence for a few beats, giving me time to get more and more irritated about the events of the past ten minutes. 'I knew you were the ormer thief,' I mutter. 'You will do whatever it takes to get under my skin, even sabotaging my obscure hobby.'

Callum stops squeezing water. 'Like my ormering has anything to do with you, you narcissist.'

'You stole them from my cricking nook.'

'It's *my* cricking nook.'

'You've always had a vendetta against— Careful, you're going to get him sandy.' Callum has dropped his side of Kurt and is shaking his hands out to relieve the ache from the wringing.

'Him? Oh, miss. Please don't tell me you treat it like an actual person.'

I lay Kurt down on the beach. 'Of course I don't. I simply named all the bumps, for ease.' I perch on a rock to let my breathing calm. 'So why are you ormering all the bloody time if it's not to piss me off?'

He shrugs. 'Why do *you* do it?'

'I enjoy it. It calms me, connects me . . .'

'Well, there you go. Why would I be any different?'

'Because you're a teenager on the brink of a Criminal Behaviour Order.' I shudder as I attach a freezing-cold Kurt back to my stomach, picking off a slimy bit of seaweed. 'And it doesn't explain why you're breaking the law to do it.'

He studies me, brow furrowed. 'I've never had a vendetta against you, miss. You're, like, the only half-decent teacher.'

'Your half-decent, soon-to-be impoverished teacher,' I say, shivering from the cold to highlight my point.

Callum doesn't notice. He's too busy rubbing his hands together like a villain in a kids' film who has just opened the vault of a bank and discovered a room full of gold. The rubbing stops when I tell him my take-home salary.

'No wonder you turned to crime.'

I'm affronted by this, but I suppose on an island with a high concentration of millionaires, my salary would be considered sub-par.

When we're back up at the top, Callum heads towards a moped. Teenagers over here are allowed to ride these on a provisional licence from the age of fourteen, but I'm surprised he can afford one.

'Drugs, isn't it, miss,' he says, as if reading my thoughts. Off my horror, he laughs. 'I told you, I'm not into that. Seriously, I'm not. I just . . . borrowed it.'

'By "borrow" . . .?'

'Do you want a lift or not?'

Riding on the back of a student's probably stolen moped, while pregnant, and at 11.30 p.m., is a terrible idea. So, naturally, I hop on.

As we wend along the lane towards mine, I consider the past twenty-four hours. I've had worse in my life, but this has got to be up there. And yet, somehow, despite feeling like I've been dragged through hell, I also feel . . . emboldened?

The feeling disappears when we pull up in front of Mon Petit Rocher to find Sean sitting on the lawn in his discarded gaming chair.

Chapter Twenty-Four

Sean remains seated, scrolling on his phone as I wrestle my way off the moped. Flustered, pregnant and mortified to be in the company of a fifteen-year-old at a quarter to midnight. Instead of scooting away, which was my hope, Callum climbs off the bike with more decorum than I did and watches on, arms folded as I approach Sean.

A horrible thought that he's already let himself into our house and seen the bumps jolts me, but I reassure myself that, if that was the case, he wouldn't be sat out here waiting in the cold. Perhaps it's out of respect for my space since the separation, which strikes me as very considerate.

It might sound stupid, but it's as if a coveted celebrity has materialised on my front lawn, higher definition than I could ever have imagined. He looks good. Shorter hair, a well-groomed beard and a dark green puffa coat I haven't seen before. I smooth my hair down and wait for him to look at me.

When he's on form, Sean is a social heavy lifter. One of those people who can befriend instantly. We would go on a little holiday and, by the first evening, he would be on first-name terms with the landlord of the pub. I, on the other hand, would be as lovely as possible ordering my Rioja and be met with a lukewarm reception and left to my own devices after making payment. It's quite a skill, and perfect for the sales job he does now. I loved hearing him on the phone talking with his clients. He remembered all the details – their nicknames, who their kids were, what their favourite drink was.

At one point, he was headhunted for a lucrative job raising capital for one of the financial firms over here looking to secure investors for a health tech fund. It fit his skills and expertise perfectly, but he said he liked what he was doing too much. I never believed him on that score. He was irritable and snappy when he'd had an unsuccessful trip, especially latterly. I thought getting to travel business class, staying in five-star hotels on roadshows across different continents and charming investors would have been much more appealing. Sean is also an awful driver so I preferred the idea of him being chauffeur-driven rather than hurtling up and down the M1 at night in all weathers.

After encouraging him a couple of times to go for the job, he stormed out to the pub and didn't come back that night, despite my countless messages . . . When you've had someone you love drop dead on you, it makes you somewhat paranoid you're the angel of death and more people in your proximity will meet that fate. When he came home the next day, silent and huffy, I didn't mention it again. He carried on spending weeks at a time in the UK and returning each time more agitated and preoccupied.

Sean's rage was something to be aware of, navigated and respected. He was never physical with me, not ever. But it was omnipresent. I imagine it not as a monstrous creature but more like living under the constant scrutiny of a diligent Ofsted inspector – a tall, balding man with a slight stoop and a stern expression. Mr Sniveley. Silently judging, making notes. Every slip-up, a scratch of pencil to paper. Always there to provide a state of edginess.

The feeling of Mr Sniveley was there from the moment Sean and I moved in together, but I can't determine when this figure – summoned from the depths of my overactive imagination – started to manifest in human form. Maybe he appeared gradually like the Cheshire Cat, but instead of eyes and a menacing grin, it was his long, pointy nose and skeletal fingers pinching the pencil hovering in mid-air.

Mr Sniveley was most satisfied when Sean and I were in our default, which was a perfectly ordinary life of pub, Sean playing video games and me marking on the sofa. No external forces rocking the equilibrium. Not an awful life at all. Every couple of weeks, Sean would head off on a work trip, but Mr Sniveley stayed behind. Watching, always watching, pencil poised.

The day Sean left me for good, Mr Sniveley remained; determined to be conscientious. But as the days rolled on, he lost his life's purpose. He became dishevelled and unfocused. He grew a beard. Until one day, he didn't bother turning up at all. I can see him now, though, just beyond Sean's right shoulder, pristine and clean-shaven, delighted to be back in the office but displeased with me. He takes in my sandy feet and inappropriate teenage companion, just as Sean does. There's a wet patch soaking through my dress from Kurt's dunk in the sea. All Sean can see is the bump.

'You're pregnant, then.'

I don't think this requires a response. Nor can I form one

iota of intelligible sentence in my head because Sean looks so hurt to be confronted with what he thinks is the truth. I did want a baby, just not with him.

He indicates a hire car parked haphazardly on the road, the H on the bonnet as conspicuous as possible to let locals know to give the tourists a bit of leeway on the idiosyncratic Guernsey roads.

'Ish said you took the Mini back. Where is it?'

'I sold it.'

The news at the loss of his beloved car causes Sean to turn his head towards the sky, fists clenched. 'Fuck!' He points a finger at me. 'I want the money for it.'

Callum snorts at the hypocrisy.

Sean glares at him. 'Who's the kid?'

'This is my student, Callum. Callum, this is—'

'I know who he is,' Callum says.

Sean stands. 'Yeah, who's that then?'

Callum appears to be doing some kind of calculation. I widen my eyes at him, willing him not to provoke. Eventually, he replies: 'You're that prick who stole all her money.'

Sean looks at me, then back to Callum, trying to decide whether to address the 'prick' insult or turn to me and handle the whole stealing my dead dad's money and throwing me into financial ruin thing.

'Barri, can I have a word?' Sean gives me that wounded puppy look and I hate myself for wanting nothing more than to barnacle myself to him like a limpet.

I put my hand on Kurt. 'It's late. I need to go to bed.'

'Good idea.' Sean heads with me towards the house. 'You'll have to let us in, I left my keys in Crawley.' He turns to Callum. 'Night, kid.'

'No, I don't . . .' I look at Sean, mustering the courage. Sniveley scrutinises. 'I don't want you to come in.'

'It's my fucking house!' A light in the upstairs room of one of our neighbour's houses switches on. I glance at Trish's. Darkness.

'Keep your voice down,' I say. 'Why are you back here?'

He points at my stomach. 'Because I heard about this monstrosity, and decided I'd come back to see for myself.' I take a few steps back from him. His face softens. He sighs, moves towards me and takes my hand. 'Bazza, I can explain about the money. I promise. But this –' he looks down at my bump – 'this is a big thing you're doing. You're going to want help.'

What does that mean? That he wants to get back together?! I meet his eye. His expression has such sincerity, I'm almost taken in, but I remind myself that he left me, blocked me, took the money . . . and that the baby he wants to 'help' with doesn't actually exist.

'Go on, then,' I say.

He frowns. 'Go on what?'

'Explain about the money.'

He glances at Callum. 'I don't want an audience. If we could just go in—'

I let go of his hands and step back. 'No. I don't want you to—'

'It's not really your choice, is it?' His spittle attacks my face like little darts.

'Get away from her.' Callum fronts up to him.

'Chill out, dude, this has got nothing to do with you.'

'She said she don't want you here, *dude*.'

Callum holds his position, eye to eye with Sean. Although

the former is a head taller, Sean is fuller in the shoulders; a brawler's build.

After an excruciating pause, Sean strides off, jumps into the hire car and screeches away, knocking over Callum's moped. Callum grimaces at the sight but doesn't say anything. He looks at me. 'You OK, miss?'

As he pulls me into the boa constrictor hug, this time Callum makes the sound of the rasping alien along with me.

Chapter Twenty-Five

Sniveley snuck into my house while I was panicking on my lawn. I find him in the living room inspecting the bumps with a look of disdain on his face. They (and I) are a bitter disappointment. I scoop them all up and carry them to my bed, tucking them under the duvet to shield them from his scrutiny.

I prepare to activate my robot vacuum cleaner, Gilby. He's not one of the expensive ones that you can program to know every inch of your house. This one sweeps about haphazardly, pivoting every time he reaches a hard surface – no logic to the random movements. I have to conduct a pre-robot triage before I switch him on. I move around the house now, lifting all wires and phone chargers to stop him from becoming entangled. This negates the point of having an automaton housework assistant, but if you leave him to zoom around for long enough, he gets good coverage.

Whenever I whip out my James Dyson to conduct an effective manual vacuum, I can't bring myself to look at Gilby sitting there in his little base, primed and ready to help me. Like a puppy observing an owner packing a suitcase and knowing in his heart that he won't be going too. I've taken to covering him with a cushion to spare his feelings whenever a faster hoover is needed.

As soon as I press the button, he whizzes into action; the gentle suction sound provides the white noise needed to mask the busy thoughts hurtling through my head. I had high hopes he'd ingest Sniveley and the essay he is writing, but Gilby heads straight for the stairs, repeatedly butting the bottom step. Good call, Gilbs. I pick him up and carry him to my bedroom, closing the door in Sniveley's face. I fall asleep with the bumps in the bed around me, and Gilby whizzing on the ground around us.

I was a bed-wetter until the age of about eight, which I learned recently is a sign of being a psychopath. I was relieved to hear that this is often teamed with the torture of animals or setting fire to things, neither of which is my wont.

But the bed-wetting was chronic. Almost nightly. My poor dad used to have to pick me up out of bed and place me on the toilet every night before he went to sleep to avoid having to change more sheets.

The trickiest thing to navigate was sleepovers. I was invited to my first one when I was seven. It was a huge deal to me. As an eccentric child, making friends wasn't the most natural thing in the world and I was desperate to go . . . but the bed-wettings.

Dad and I worked up a strategy. No liquids after 4.30 p.m. and a safety wee just as I felt I was drifting off. By the time the day came around, I had had a dry run for two consecutive weeks and was confident I had won The Battle of the Bladder.

But with sleepovers come fun things like hot chocolates

and fizzy drinks. I couldn't turn down a cherry Panda Pop. I wanted to be part of it – to share in the sugar highs and the artificially pink tongues. When we agreed to go to sleep, I was full of worry. The house was quiet, and I was too nervous to go to the bathroom for my safety wee, in case it might wake someone up. Instead, I made a pact with myself that I would stay awake all night. But of course, I didn't, and of course I woke up to the feeling of warm liquid seeping through my pyjamas.

I looked around the room – my contemporaries, dry and asleep in their beds – and felt such shame that my own body was intent on humiliating me. I crept downstairs and used the house phone to ring my dad and whispered to him in panicked floods of tears.

Where I had become complacent about winning the battle, my father was ready for the war. He had called up my friend's mum and explained the situation. She was very understanding and had placed a bin bag under the sheet on my mattress. Dad had purchased a matching sleeping bag and PJs, which were hidden under my friend's bed.

'All you have to do is whip everything off the bed and shove it in your bag, replace it with the new stuff. Job's a good'un Baz. No one will ever know.' A few hours later, my friends woke up. All of us were dry, giggling, our tongues still pink. I felt invincible.

But for some reason or other – possibly because she underestimated her own daughter's capacity for cruelty – my friend's mother told my friend and swore her to secrecy, which worked about as well as the time Lara found out about Father Christmas, promised Mum she'd not say a word and then announced it in show and tell.

It all came to a head when my story, 'The Dull Star', impressed my teacher so much, she suggested I read a section out in assembly. When my turn came to read, I opened the exercise book to find my story ripped out and replaced with a poem. Misreading my demeanour as nerves, the well-meaning teacher running the assembly, who was none the wiser, stepped in to read out a poem about a little girl called Barri who wet the bed because she wanted to stay like a baby.

Due to small island ridicule, this fable followed me to secondary school. I just thank my lucky stars that the only form of online bullying was people updating their MSN Messenger status to 'Barri is a baby bed-wetter'.

In adulthood, my brain does this rather clever thing whereby, if I need the toilet in real life but I'm still asleep, I dream about needing to go but I can never actually find a toilet. Or, if I do, it is in such a public place, I can't bring myself to go. The last time this happened, the toilet was in my old university library. No cubicle walls, just a loo in the middle surrounded by book stacks and students typing away, Sean drinking his coffee in the corner looking right at me. Dream Barri can't bring herself to go and so real-life Barri wakes up with a screaming bladder but a bone-dry bed.

It is, therefore, alarming to wake up and find I am lying in a wet patch this morning. My relief is palpable when I realise it is because I fell asleep with all the bumps in my bed, including Kurt, his sea-sodden material soaking into my mattress. I laugh out loud in relief and give him a salty squeeze.

At some point in the night, Gilby ran out of juice, and is in the middle of the room, mid-task as if suspended in time.

The tracks of the pathways he has taken are visible on the carpet; chaotic but clean. I put him back in his charging point with a *bleep*.

I look at my phone. Nothing from Sean as yet. Sniveley is still here, of course; bolt upright at the dining-room table, scribbling away. He goes upstairs to my bedroom, nods in approval at the hoovered floor, spots the wet patch, pushes his glasses up the bridge of his nose and makes a stern note.

I think about a journalist discovering the bed-wetting titbit when working on a news article about me and using it to shape a story about who I am in the media, framing me as a potential psychopath for faking a pregnancy. Is what I'm doing psychopathic? I don't think so . . . But then again, that is what a psychopath would say.

'Baby Sham,' says Trish from the stool opposite me in her kitchen. 'That's what the podcast about you would be called.'

I take a sip of coffee. 'Yes, that's good . . . though podcasts about female criminals are always a bit more . . . sincere, aren't they? You know, "conning", "scamming", "getting lured into a cult".'

'Usually with some kind of over-earnest BBC journalist taking the story oh-so seriously.' Although she's joshing along, there is something about Trish's mood that tells me she's on edge. She can't quite meet my eye in the irritatingly earnest way she normally does.

I knocked on her door this morning, brandishing some pastries before filling her in on my day of hell yesterday. Trish didn't find Callum discovering the truth anywhere near as hilarious as the drugs search, where – when I told her about Pluckrose's prank on me – she made a witty remark about being violated by the long arm of the law. Callum has rattled her. So much that, when I get to the point in the story where he dropped me home on his moped, I decide to omit the estranged-husband-on-lawn situation to avoid causing further stress.

Her uneaten pain aux raisins remains in front of her. The way the fruit has been scattered in the pastry without any attention to even spacing means two raisins look like a pair of beady eyes boring into me. I will Trish to bite into it to shatter the illusion but when I look up at her again, I jump at the similarity of her piercing black pupils to the shrivelled fruit.

'It's unfair really,' I say, aware I'm over-compensating for the awkwardness. 'Master male criminals are painted as loveable rogues by comedians talking in Guy Ritchie-esque accents accompanied by powerful music. The podcasts about women are rarely badass. They have string synth and focus on . . . psychology.'

'Would you like it if someone made a podcast about you?' Trish asks, like a host of the latter.

I think back to the words I used to convince Trish to help me in the first place. *Must we also endure a matriarchy deficit?* How easily this could be spun – journalists and podcasters and vigilante crime TikTokers concluding I did all this because I secretly wanted a baby. I'm sure that's what my sister will think – that I was so alone and incapable of nurturing another human that I faked it to feel normal and happy. And I won't be able to defend it because no one has ever believed me when I've told them I don't want a baby in the past, so why would they believe it now when I've spent however many months pretending? God, I'd *hate* to have a podcast. However, I can't help wondering how they would cover the bump splash. Maybe an added sound effect. I must be grinning at the thought because Trish takes a pointed sip of coffee, eyebrows raised.

I put my mug down. 'Right. What is it?'

'You're quite pumped up.'

'It's been a very stressful twenty-four hours.'

'But you don't seem stressed . . .' She appraises me like she's giving a diagnosis. 'You're hyper.'

'I dodged a bullet, Trish!'

'Did you?' she says, leaning toward me. 'Because as far as I can see, that gun is still pointed at you. I can practically see the red dot on your forehead.'

I snort. 'Stop being so dramatic.'

Trish presses a flake of pastry on the plate with her finger, which makes it stick, but she doesn't eat it. Just stares at it balanced on her pointer. 'And if I looked in the mirror, maybe I could see a red dot on my forehead too.'

The image of Trish sitting upright in her Edinburgh tweed reading a book, all the while a red light scanning over her, makes me chuckle.

'Did you mention me?' she asks.

I meet her eye. 'When?'

'When you were telling this reckless teenager with a penchant for rule-breaking every detail. Did you tell him I signed your form?'

Ah. The rub. I give her a bared-teeth look that feels like that grimace emoji.

'Right.'

'I wasn't thinking . . . it was . . .' I move my hand towards her on the counter, placing it near her plate.

She glances at her hospital lanyard hanging over the top edge of the corkboard. 'I could be struck off for this.'

'Trish, please don't worry. It will be fine. It will. I'll say I faked the form if anyone asks. Forged your signature.'

She takes a deep breath like she's gauging whether I'm stable enough for this next bit.

'You need to start taking this more seriously, Barri. There are only so many near misses until you get caught. You'll lose everything. And so will I.'

I retract my hand. 'Why are you *really* helping me?' I ask. 'I'm happy to be a distraction from the grief, Trish, but it doesn't give you the right to dictate—'

'Because I want you to bloody well get away with it! And . . . you're not going to like me saying it –' another exhale – 'I have a feeling that there's more to you and Sean than you're letting on.' Her voice gets louder as I turn away from her to look out the window. 'That he's dealt you a shitty hand and . . . well, you deserve to be happy and far away from here before he comes back.'

I whip my head back towards her. 'He turned up last night out of the blue,' I say, more to wound than because I want her to know. I'm not proud of it, but I'm irked with her and I know Sean's reappearance will exacerbate her paranoia about being implicated in the pregnancy lie.

Trish stands abruptly, knocking her plate and sending the pain aux raisins flying across the table. She rushes through to her lounge window and looks out as if he might be there right now watching the house. She starts pacing her living room and I follow, one step behind her, the fury rising.

'You have no right whatsoever to cast aspersions on my marriage . . .'

'What did he say when he saw you?'

'. . . we broke up because he wanted a baby and I didn't and that was that.'

'Is he back for good, or . . . does he want to get back together? Do *you* want to get back together?'

'There was nothing sinister or whatever it is you're insinuating. We were bloody happy, Trish.'

She stops. Looks at me. 'Is that right?'

'Yes!'

'Then why don't you have any other friends on this whole island?'

I throw my hands up in exasperation. 'Because we didn't need anyone else!'

She lets out a hiss through her teeth.

'We didn't,' I reiterate. 'We were happy until I fucked it up.'

'What did he say about the pregnancy?'

'He was angry, obviously, but I managed to use the money thing to my advantage—'

She narrows her eyes. 'What money thing?'

'Why are you so bloody interested in Sean, anyway?'

I'm desperate to go home. I want a shower and I want to try to compute all the things without nosy neighbours giving me unsolicited advice. I grab my keys and head for the door.

'Don't do that bloody thing, Barri.' Trish stands at the window, looking out like the dramatic wife of a troubled detective in a crime drama.

'What thing?'

'That thing you do when you feel uncomfortable and go off-grid.'

'I wasn't . . .'

She turns to face me. 'A little bit of truth. A little bit of intimacy and – *poof!* She's off.'

I clench my fists, my keys jabbing my palm. Everything in my body compels me to storm out. I'm furious with her for saying stuff about Sean when she doesn't even know the man. I ignore the gnawing thought that questions whether I really know him either.

I don't want to prove her right so I sit with her, watching Saturday-morning television. Someone with an irritating personality cooks dishes no one watching can be arsed to make and they sit and drink wine that sounds delicious but no one watching can be arsed to go out and buy. I can hear Trish huffing and puffing beside me like a defunct steam iron. She mutes the TV. 'What else aren't you telling me? This money thing.'

I shrug.

She unmutes the TV and we carry on pretending to watch it.

'I don't get you, Barri,' she says after a moment, not taking her eyes off the screen. 'It's like . . . it's like you're intent to live on your own bloody island despite the fact it's miserable there.'

I smile. 'Would we call it "Barri Island?"'

She can't help but laugh, and the mood relaxes.

As I put my coat on, a plan agreed for a pub tea later in the week, I look at her. There is nothing but openness there but I can't bear the smug satisfaction if I tell her about the money. She's got a warped enough view of my marriage as it is.

She fixes me with a resolute look. 'You need to start taking this all more seriously, Barri. Focus on the job at hand, which is getting away from here and not looking back. That means keeping your head down. No gallant rescues from the police and no more bloody moped rides from teenagers. And, for God's sake, keep that manipulative, conniving arsehole at arm's length.'

'Callum?'

She leaves it a beat, her eyes narrowing. 'Yes . . .'

Chapter Twenty-Six

I had to suspend Kurt on the towel rail in my bathroom so he would dry out in time for school. He looks like a strung-up hostage undergoing interrogation. Pointless, as he already gave up my biggest secret in the sea with no persuasion, didn't you, Kurt . . . DIDN'T YOU?

I untie him from the rail and strap him on extra tight, reminding myself about Trish's words. Head down, and focus on the job at hand.

I had multiple missed calls and messages from Sean over the weekend. I replied once to say that I needed a full explanation about the house being in his name and the recent remortgage. He said he'd had to go to back to England again for work but he'll be over again soon and wants to talk about it 'face to face'. I managed to resist the urge to tell him that I thought text message was his preferred method of communication for the important conversations.

After that, it was a barrage of messages about my pregnancy and how hurt he is about it, all of which I ignored. One, because I'm so annoyed that he still hasn't given me any answers about the house and two, well . . . because I'm not actually pregnant. I also had an offer from Ish's girlfriend to meet for a catch-up coffee, which I declined, telling her that even in normal circumstances, this would be unpalatable. Sean may be back on the scene, he may even want to get back together, but I can't let him derail me.

To keep my head in the game, I printed out a few more photos of famous Edinburgh landmarks – the castle, Arthur's Seat, a topless hunk wearing a kilt – and stuck them to my fridge. I have no idea what I will be able to afford American-road-trip-wise since Callum's bloody blackmail so, for now, I've added a magnet of some cowboy boots I found in the kitchen drawer. I bought it last year from a market stall during Seafront Sunday, where the entire front in Town is closed to make way for local businesses to sell their wares. Something about the tackiness of it appealed to me, but the pink stars on the spurs made it a bit girly for Sean's taste so we didn't have it on show in the end. But it is now – pride of place. A trip to Nashville is still doable, even with Callum's cut. One of the airlines has a sale next week, so I'm holding my nerve in the hope I can get a good deal on flights.

When she popped in for a coffee yesterday, Trish called the display my 'manifestation fridge' and every time she passed it, she touched a different picture and muttered, 'Manifest, manifest,' in the breathy voice of a fortune teller, which I'll admit was amusing the first few times but became tiresome after that.

A sensible pregnant woman by this point would stop cycling to work and so, with regret, I have left Melva in my hallway to take the bus.

Despite having to leave much earlier, I enjoy the journey as we sweep through the lanes. It's a joy to see the signs of spring creeping in, from the daffodils lining the banks beside the road, the pinks in the hanging baskets, as well as mottles of yellow and purple joining the green foliage on the distant cliffsides.

The bus driver is a master of spatial awareness, navigating the tightest of corners, a mere sheet of paper away from scraping into the stone wall that lines the road.

He is one of those people who seems to know everyone. He waves and shouts hellos through the window, has bite-sized conversations with pedestrians in paused traffic. He even stops the bus at one point and gets out to high-five the poo cart driver heading off to pump out the sewage cesspits. The irresponsibility of the latter (delaying his passengers/ high-five hygiene) doesn't even irritate me because the man is joy personified.

I can't imagine being capable of walking around and spreading that much happiness everywhere I go. People's worlds being brightened by my presence. I imagine myself skipping around doing the same thing. Islanders recoiling from my grimace, moving to the other side of the road to avoid my attempted warm hello. Children crying when I brandish my knuckles towards them for an unreciprocated fist bump.

The bus is running earlier than expected, so I get off a couple of stops before mine to take a detour to my favourite coffee shop before heading to Julie's stupid Huddle.

The way this island can stun you with the sideways glance of its beauty is something I'll miss for ever. I pause, resting my hands on the cold metal of the harbour railings, and look over at Herm and the surrounding islands, clear as a high-definition photograph today against the orderly blue around them. I turn my head left, closing my eyes in the brightness and picture particles of Dad on Belle Greve reflecting powerful golden rays back up towards the sky.

I'm about to leave the cafe with my latte when I come face to face with my lawyer. No doubt here to use up some of that eight grands' worth of dosh sitting in her account. She double-takes when she sees my bump, having not been aware of my pregnancy when I met her in her office with Marta on my back, not two months ago.

'Oh, hello.' I keep my back angled towards the door so she doesn't see my lack of hump. 'I'm in a bit of a hurry – I know I owe you a response to your email . . . I've been, erm . . . busy.'

'So I see. Congratulations.' She looks at my bump again, brow furrowed at the sheer growth between the last time I saw her and now.

'It's twins,' I say, a little louder than intended.

I didn't spot Yolande at the time. No doubt her structured outfit made her blend in behind a sodding lampshade or something. My sister texts me almost immediately. Yolande messaged. I can't believe you're having twins and you didn't tell us!!! That's IVF for you!

I send Trish a panicked message looking for some counsel. Her reply is quick.

Trish Pepper (Neighbour): This is exactly the opposite of keeping your head down!

Me: I know, but I didn't have a choice! I'm sorry! Should I tell them I was joking? Or go along with it?

Please say joking . . .

> **Trish Pepper (Neighbour):** You have to go along with it now . . .

> **Mum:** OH MY GOD IM SO HAPPY WE NEARLY HAVE A FIVE A SIDE FOOTBALL TEAM IF THEYRE BOYS

I don't have the energy to respond.

At Huddle, Yolande looks at me, all smug in the knowledge that she got the inside scoop. It occurs to me not for the first time that her penchant for indiscretion is in no way compatible with her being school counsellor . . . though I can't say I've ever noticed her gossiping about the students, and there's always a long queue of them outside her office, suggesting she is competent at her job. Perhaps it's like when people have to be super organised for work but are then pure chaos in their personal life as a result. Her need to be discreet about the students means she finds it impossible to not gossip in every other situation.

'It was none of your business to tell my sister,' I say to her.

'She's my best friend!'

We both know she sounds like a petulant child. She'll be racked with guilt all day now – not because she feels bad for me, but because she needs reassurance to make herself feel better about her indiscretion. I'm happy to leave her squirming.

During Huddle, I'm asked to cover another PSHE lesson because Suzie's one-year-old has sodding chicken pox.

'Don't worry,' Julie says through a blocked nose. 'There's an external guest to talk to them about sexual health. You can just sit there and put your feet up, *twin mum!*' Yuck.

When I get to the classroom, Callum is there ahead of the rest of his form. I pull him to one side while the sexual health lady sets up.

'It's twins now,' I say.

He looks at me, all bleary-eyed and confused. 'Eh?'

I hold my stomach aggressively towards him. 'Twins!'

The Sex Lady looks up, alarmed. *Head down, Barri.*

'Why does it matter, me knowing if it's twins or not?' he asks, leaning back on the windowsill.

'I feel like we need a free exchange of information or something.'

'This isn't Interpol, miss.'

I take in his bloodshot eyes. 'You look knackered.'

'Big weekend partying.'

'Well, you need to stop all that.'

'You worried I'll get drunk and spill the tea?'

'No. You've got your English mock next week. Have you done a single practice essay?'

He snorts.

'What's so funny?' I ask, already exasperated with how this day is going.

'I was just, er . . . it's funny you nagging me about school work when there's this, like, massive secret I'm helping you keep . . .' He beckons me towards him, and I have to put my hand on the wall to steady myself with the weight of Kurt. 'I've actually been thinking, miss, that the eighty-twenty split isn't going to work for me any more.' He pokes my bump with his pen. 'Boop!'

I stand up, stepping back. 'Don't do that.'

'Trouble is, I don't feel incentivised,' he adds.

'This isn't a bloody pay review.'

Callum holds his hands up in defence. 'I don't think you've been completely honest with me about the financials . . .'

'No, that's genuinely all I earn as a —'

'Sean was pretty pissed off about you selling his car the other night. How much did you get for it? At least two grand I reckon . . .'

I turn away from him and head towards the classroom, not willing to even entertain the notion that my Nashville flight money is going anywhere near this kid's bank account.

'You have way more to lose than me, eh? And with your wanker husband back on the scene, I'm worried I'll accidentally let something slip.'

This is a low blow, even from Callum. I turn back towards him, studying his face for any sign of guilt but I just see a blank expression, like those faces make-up artists use to sketch their designs onto. I point a finger towards him. 'I'm the best chance you have of getting a bloody GCSE. How will that work for you if I'm behind bars breathing in second-hand spice in an iron-clad cell?'

'Guernsey prison's meant to be all right. They have Xboxes.'

I look him dead in the eye. 'If the truth comes out, you'll get nothing at all. Neither of us will. So you may feel like you're in control here, Callum, but the fact is, you're not.'

The rest of the form arrives before he can respond, but he looks . . . not pissed off, more resolute.

The Sex Lady does an informative presentation (if a little disgusting) about sexual health. It involves telling a fictitious story using various members of the class who she makes stand in a line. She pours each of them a little see-through cup of white liquid and assigns them a character. As the story unfolds, they are asked to mix and redistribute the liquid in their cups whenever their characters have unprotected sex. I don't find the hetero-normative skew of the tale very inclusive but on the whole, the visual is effective, especially at the end when she uses a pipette to drop some liquid into their little cups, leaving all the characters who contracted an STI with bright blue fluid.

The students are in high spirits by the end of the demonstration, titillated because patient zero was played by the least likely fifteen-year-old on the island to want to have intercourse with anyone with a vagina.

At the end of the lesson, Sex Lady opens it up to a wider discussion. We move on to the topic of pregnancy and abortion. Sex Lady explains people can terminate a pregnancy until twenty-three weeks and six days. Someone turns to me and asks, 'How many weeks are you, miss?'

'Twenty-four-and-a-bit,' I reply. Some of the students make 'Ooooooh, bad luck' sounds. 'No going back now, miss.'

Sex Lady pipes up. 'Yes. If I were to cut Ms Brown open and pull out her baby, the chances are it would be able to survive.'

Jesus, that took a turn. I'm watching the back of Callum's head. The lad doesn't flinch. He just turns and looks at me, a neutral expression on his face. Some students laugh, and some are grossed out by the gratuitously violent imagery. I give Sex Lady a 'can we tone this down' look but she's enjoying the showboating too much. I imagine it's a downfall of a job where you have to talk about sex with teenagers;

it blurs the boundaries of what's actually appropriate to talk about with them.

I decide not to correct her that it's twins. Twice the babies equals twice the lie to my students.

Sex Lady continues. 'I was actually listening to a podcast recently where they talked about a woman doing that. She pretended she was pregnant by wearing these fake bumps and then, at month nine, she went to visit a friend who was at the same stage as her but actually pregnant. She cut the baby out of her friend, leaving her for dead, and stole the baby.'

'Noooo! That is soooo baaaad!' say the students.

I should intervene, chastise this woman for being too graphic with impressionable minds, but I am having an internal meltdown. This brief mention of faking a pregnancy feels more exposing than the strip search. I can feel all their eyes on me, wondering if my bump really contains a baby. In reality, it is only Callum who is wide awake now and eyeing me, expectant. I'm floundering.

'What happened?' says another student.

'She got the death penalty,' says the bloodthirsty Sex Lady.

More exclamations from the room.

'Bit insensitive, all this, eh? With miss being pregnant and everything,' Callum says.

The teenagers who are that way inclined swoon at Callum's maturity. I wonder whether I should consider a modification to the money split . . . 78:22 should do it.

'If she really is pregnant, that is . . .' Callum adds.

My heart falls into my babyless stomach. There is the longest pause imaginable where the entire class turn to appraise my bump. I put my hand to Kurt as if to block their X-ray eyes from seeing the empty-wombed truth.

Callum laughs to break it. The students laugh. I grimace-laugh.

While Sex Lady moves on to the condom application demonstration, I have to step outside for some corridor air. I stay there until the end of the lesson.

As the class files out past me, Callum makes a money gesture with his hand as he mutters, 'That was close for comfort, eh, miss? I'll still be taking my cut of your salary as agreed, plus a two-grand lump sum paid in full on the first day of your maternity leave.'

When I get home after work in a state of high agitation, there's a parcel outside my house. I assume Suzie again, but when I take it inside and open the box, the card says:

Just a few bits for some self-care as you're carrying two!
Love Lara, Dave and the boys xxxx

There's a beautiful hamper of locally made food products – honey, cheese, posh teabags and a few chutneys as well as a hand-painted plate with an ormer on it by a local ceramics person I love, and a matching tea towel.

I lean back against the sofa. This is so typical of Lara – the extravagant OTT gesture. But deep down, I know the irritation I'm feeling towards her is guilt that she's gone to all this trouble when it's all a lie. I clutch the tea towel to myself and text her to say thank you.

It was a struggle to get to sleep last night, but I drifted off eventually. I had a nightmare about Lara and Mum searching for my babies. 'Baby one, baby two!' they were shouting and shouting on repeat. Callum was there, and I was begging him to help me, but he wouldn't. He just stood, mute and robotic. My sister shook me at one point: 'Why aren't you worried about where they are?!'

My agitation over Callum hasn't improved this morning. I woke in a tossed and turned duvet with a dried patch of dribble beneath the right side of my mouth. Not only have I lost my Nashville flights fund, Callum could keep upping his cut of my salary, making everything I've gone through be all for nothing. Or worse, he could blab if a better offer comes along. A newspaper or something. It irks me even more that the little shit is profiting from finding out about my secret as a result of his own ormer-thieving criminality. Callum Le Brocq on top again.

I spend the morning at school avoiding Callum, even looking up his timetable and taking intentionally long routes round the school to steer clear of him. I needn't have worried. He hasn't even bloody well bothered to come in today apparently.

I am so swept up in my thoughts, I don't notice Suzie standing in the corridor when I'm on the way to the staffroom. Our bumps almost collide, but I stop myself just in time. She looks pale and drawn. We've not interacted much since I legged it from her house, so every instinct tells me to pretend I haven't noticed. 'Are you OK?' I ask.

'There's some complications . . . with the pregnancy.' She looks like she's about to cry so I guide her into the staff toilets. 'The doctors said I need to take it really easy, so I'm going on leave a bit earlier than planned to rest up. End of next week.' She rubs her arms even though the radiator beside us is blasting heat. 'It's a worry, you know. And then with the other kids and that . . .' I don't feel that usual pang of annoyance at the kid moan. 'We don't really have family help. Mine are back in the UK and Xavier's aren't interested . . . I mean, who cares about baby number four? It's just old news, isn't it? People just assume that you're fine and you don't need help. It's all well and good putting them in nursery, getting childminders, but it's the bedtimes, the meals. The washing pile is so big they made a fort out of it.'

'That's fun,' I say.

She shakes her head. 'In the garden. In the rain. With the clean pile I'd just folded.' I picture Suzie's muddy John Lewis advert children in their muddy John Lewis advert wellies, draping muddy John Lewis advert clothes over the climbing frame.

'Ah . . .'

'Xav's doing his best, but his job's stressful. He's got to go to Helsinki tomorrow.' She bursts into tears, burying her face in a wedge of blue paper towels that must feel abrasive on her very well-taken-care-of face.

I contemplate slipping out, but as I turn, I clock the water bottle she gave me poking out of my bag. I take a deep breath.

'Suzie,' I say. 'You live in a beautiful home with lovely children. You've got a delightful life.'

She smiles at me politely. 'Yeah, that's what matters, I know.'

'Fuck that!' She raises an eyebrow, and I marvel at the smoothness of her forehead. 'I can tell from your estuary accent and past mentions of an upbringing in Milton Keynes that you're not what I would refer to as "a posho" so what

I'm going to say to you isn't going to be easy to hear.' I take her hands and look at her blotchy, teary face. 'Do what rich people do –' I lean in to whisper – 'outsource the dirty work.'

She laughs. 'You're right. I'm minted, aren't I?'

'Yes. Pay someone else to do the sodding washing.'

As I listened to Suzie reeling off her problems, it struck me that no one has ever confided in me like that before. Anecdotes I collect and retell in my head are often out of mockery. It's rather refreshing to have a kinder one. I allow myself to sit in the warmth of it for the rest of the day.

The solution to my Callum predicament presents itself to me in an unexpected form when I step off the bus after work.

Pierre's old-school safari-style Jeep is parked outside my house. My heart drops a bit when I realise he's been beavering away at hunting down the ormer thief while I've known his identity for days. I recall our last meeting and my sudden storming out of the pub and prepare myself for an awkwardness, but it doesn't come.

'I've left you so many messages,' he says, taking a sip from a massive reusable coffee cup. It has ComplyHi written on the side of it. A freebie of some sort, I guess.

I pull out my phone, scrolling past the multiple messages from Sean, the most recent one being: COME ON BAZ, STOP IGNORING ME!! I CAN EXPLAIN ABOUT THE MONEY!!! I ignore that for now and click on the three unread messages from Pierre, one of them just a question mark.

'"So many messages" is a bit of an exaggeration,' I say.

I take in Pierre's outfit today. Some running shorts and a gilet on its own, no T-shirt beneath it. A laptop, no case, is tucked beneath one arm. I barely note his surprisingly muscular calves due to the hideous lime-green Crocs on his feet. These are worse than the yellow ones.

Pierre puts on a mock American accent. 'Our man is gonna strike tonight.' He switches back to his regular Guernsey lilt. 'Little bugger always changes his spot but I've picked up on a pattern, eh?' He rests his laptop on the bonnet and opens it. 'See, it looks like it's random, but it isn't.'

I join him in leaning over the computer, using the bumper of the car as a shelf for Kurt to take the weight off my back. I take in the multi-column, multi-row spreadsheet with its colour codes, drop downs and mathematical formulas. 'Are you some kind of secret genius or something?'

Pierre's cheeks redden. 'No, no, it's a simple model.' He brushes imaginary hair out of his eyes, a tic I recall him having at school whenever he got an answer correct in maths. He pulls a piece of paper from his pocket, unfolds a rudimentary sketched map of Guernsey and points to an area he's circled, marked 'Lihou Island'. 'That's where we'll nab the bugger.'

The answer has been staring me in the face all along. Pierre needs to catch Callum red-handed. The teenager will be so embroiled in legal trouble that he won't have time to come for me and my money. I trace my finger over the circled spot on Pierre's map. 'How sure are you that he'll be there?'

'I'm positive. You and me are going tonight.' Pierre shuts his laptop with purpose, folds his little map up and plunges it into his gilet pocket. I'm relieved to spy the seam of a vest beneath it. It was an alarming thought that anyone might wear a gilet over their naked torso. 'Low tide's just after 1 a.m., so I'll pick you up at 12.30,' he adds.

As much as I would love to be there to watch Callum

being apprehended, I don't want anything to suggest I'm involved in his capture in case he becomes loose-lipped about my secret. Pierre seems disappointed when I tell him I can't come, but promises to keep me posted with live updates.

Comeuppance will finally come to Callum Le Brocq.

Chapter Twenty-Seven

'Why are we relying on the Excel modelling capabilities of a fisherman?' Trish asks after I fill her in on the Callum arrest plan.

Before I can respond, she heads off towards her car. Her keys are poised in her hand, but instead of unlocking the thing, she pauses to scan the mid-evening darkness.

'Hurry up, it's freezing.' I wrap my coat around myself. 'What are you looking for?'

'Nothing.'

Trish has tied a scarf around her hair, which admittedly looks chic against her elfin features, but teamed with the tweed, it's giving Queen driving around Balmoral, not two mates off for a casual tea at the pub.

'A pubby tea . . .' I say into the silence as we reverse out of her driveway.

We turn onto the road with the huge house I saw Callum sneaking into. 'Pull over a sec,' I say. The trees lining the lane are blowing around like over-zealous background artists wailing in a panicked crowd scene.

'I thought you were giving Callum a wide berth until he gets arrested,' Trish says.

'Just for a sec, I want to see if he's here again . . . find out what he's up to.' I peer towards the house. There's a light on towards the back but no sign of activity.

'Why does it matter?'

'Because you've put some doubt in my head now! What happens if Pierre's spreadsheet is wrong? We need to gather some extra ammunition. Switch your lights off, Columbo,' I say.

She obliges but looks behind us. 'I don't know . . . cars whip round that bend . . . it's probably better to switch them back on.'

'They don't whip round the bend.'

'Only because whenever you come here, you're slowing everyone down by cycling at five miles an hour. It's treacherous. Lethal!'

'Fine, put them on.'

As she does so, the headlights illuminate the face of a man standing opposite the car, staring into the windscreen. We both shriek.

It is an elderly man of about eighty. The whites of his eyes glow in the headlamps like lychees.

'He seems a bit dazed and confused,' I say. Trish remains in the car, still spooked. I look at her expectantly.

'What?'

'You're the medical professional . . .'

Trish gets out and starts speaking to the man. He puts his hands over his ears.

'I don't think he likes you shouting,' I say through the wound-down window.

'It's too windy not to shout.'

Trish guides the old man into the back of her car and gets

back into the driver's seat. He seems happy with this arrangement.

I don't know what it is about old people and seatbelts, but they get to a certain age and can no longer operate them. Until her mid-nineties, my granny could bake a mean lemon drizzle, send me a text, she could even ride a bike, but sit her in a bloody car and ask her to slot a silver buckle into a perfectly shaped plastic hole and she went to pieces. We spend about ten minutes trying to help the old man do his belt up, it retracting like a hoover plug every time it gets close, until finally, he is strapped in.

It is only when we are also buckled in ourselves that we realise we only pulled him into the car to have a bloody conversation and all the seatbelt nonsense was pointless.

I turn to look at the man, who seems ever so happy with the expectation of an adventure. 'What's your name?'

'Cedric,' he says. He points at my bump. 'Good name.'

'Where do you live, Cedric?' Trish tries.

'Drive,' he says.

'I guess that means he'll show us?' Trish says to me.

'What about pubby tea?'

She side-eyes me as she pulls off. 'It's your fault we stopped.'

Cedric takes us out of the Vale, to the Bridge and along the front in Town. He points out Herm, Castle Cornet and the bathing pools as we travel up towards St Martin's.

'Do you think he actually knows where he's going?' Trish whispers to me.

'Seems to.'

I lose my conviction when we circumnavigate the south and head towards the west coast.

'Lihou Island,' he says, pointing at a few blinking lights in the darkness.

'What is this, a bloody guided tour?' I say. I look at my watch – 8 p.m. In five hours, the low tide will have revealed the causeway leading to the little island. I imagine Pierre striding over in his Crocs, the sound of rubber splashing in puddles of seawater, ready to catch Callum red-handed.

Trish appears to be having a lovely time, confessing that she hasn't seen much of the island.

'You can't exactly see much of it in this weather,' I say as sheets of rain cascade diagonally across the road in front of us.

Cedric winds his window down once we hit the coastal road by my favourite beach, Cobo. I've got many fond memories rock-pooling here as a child, Lara and me catching shrimps in our nets and peering into the castle-shaped plastic bucket to see how many we'd caught. This beach is also perfect for an evening swim on the high tide while the sun sets above. None of that today, though – the wind is blowing directly into the bay, showering Cedric in rain. I gaze jealously at all the people in The Rockmount enjoying a pubby tea as we pass.

As we continue round, the rain pelts even harder into Cedric's open window. His laugh is so infectious, I decide to stop being such a killjoy and wind my window down too, breathing in the sea air against the onslaught of water.

By the time we have circumnavigated the north tip and have pulled up back where we started, we are all drenched and shivering. Trish grabs a blanket from the boot and wraps it round Cedric. 'We really need to get you home now, otherwise we're going to have to call the police.'

'Home.' Cedric points at the house I saw Callum sneaking into. I take in Cedric's well-fitting but weather-worn suit. He looks smart and well taken care of, but incongruous next to the modern, glass-fronted architect's dream opposite.

Trish and I exchange a look. 'Come on then, Cedric.'

We guide him out of the car and knock on the enormous front door, which pivots open on an axis in the middle, meaning when Callum answers, he can only see Cedric and Trish as the other half of the door conceals me.

'Gramps! Thank God! You're soaking. Give me a sec, yeah,' he says to Trish. As Callum takes Cedric away to warm up, Trish and I take in the surroundings of the enormous mansion. A few empty cans of beans on the side and a line of ormer shells. It's clean, but there's no furniture in the vast open-plan space. The outside decking in the garden beyond looks incomplete – there is a cement mixer but no tools, as if the building people paused halfway through the job.

'That was Callum,' I whisper to Trish. 'He didn't see me . . . should I go and make myself known do you think?' I indicate upstairs. She nods. I head up the glass staircase designed to look as if it is floating. I feel like Indiana Jones in *The Last Crusade* when he steps out onto that invisible bridge.

The upstairs floor hasn't been surfaced yet; it's rough beneath my boots. Every bedroom I look in is enormous, but none of them are carpeted or furnished. One has an empty room with some plumbing I'm assuming will be a plush ensuite. At the end of the corridor in the smallest of the bedrooms, I spy Callum through the slightly open doorway. He is kneeling by his grandad, helping him put a pyjama shirt on. Two lilos are side by side with sleeping bags laid out neatly on top. A small plug-in heater on the floor beside them blows warm air onto Cedric's shivering body. They talk in low voices, animated and laughing. Perhaps discussing the adventure Cedric has just been on. I feel like an intruder, so I head straight back downstairs. I grimace at Trish. 'I think they're squatting.'

I don't know what I imagined to find here – a group of teenagers partying; some stolen copper wire; a farm of cannabis under the heat of a hundred lightbulbs. Not a young lad and his grandad living in an ill-equipped mansion house.

Callum comes downstairs beaming at Trish. 'Thank you so m—' He stops when he clocks me.

This time it's Callum's turn to let the truth come tumbling out.

Chapter Twenty-Eight

'You say anything about this to anyone, I'll tell them you're faking the pregnancy,' Callum says as he finishes his story. He stabs his finger at Trish. 'And I bet you're that doctor she told me about. The one who helped her.'

Trish gives me a pissed-off look but I ignore that and head over to the kitchen, where the buzzing of the fridge-freezer reverberates through the spartan ground floor. I wrench open the door, which is suctioned with all the power of the American Dream.

The sight of the frozen ormers floors me. The desperation and stress that went into filling this space. And for me to assume he was stealing them to spite me . . . I turn to Callum. 'I'm assuming you've tried other things from his childhood . . . something that wouldn't send you to prison if they found a freezer full of them? Liquorice Allsorts, perhaps?'

'Ormers are the only thing that work . . . it's like the taste just makes him breathe easier or something.' Callum looks upwards as if he can see his gramps through the ceiling.

I'd love to say I'm surprised that the two of them managed to slip through the net over in England. But an NHS and social care system in absolute pieces after a pandemic, a parent who had given up on life beyond booze and Paddy Power. I'd have done a runner back to the safety of Guernsey with my most treasured family member too. But none of the services over here are aware that Cedric needs support. And Callum needs help too. He's only fifteen for God's sake.

I turn back to him. 'What about your stepmum?' I ask, recalling the kind strategy she armed him with for coping with his anxiety.

The guttural sound Callum lets out skewers my chest. I want to do something but I don't seem to be able to move. Trish strides over and puts an arm around him. He buries his head in her shoulder. It hits me what a lucky child her stepdaughter Ripley must have been to have had Trish in her life.

After he's calmed down, Callum looks at me. 'She left. Took my stepsister. Got fed up with my dad's drunken temper. Flips faster than a Guess Who piece.'

'Did she not tell you where she was going?'

He lifts his head up to the ceiling as if the tilt will steer the tears back into his eye sockets. 'She didn't even say goodbye.' Trish and I must both look horrified because when he looks back at us, he laughs. 'Biology at the end of the day, isn't it, miss?' Trish bristles at this but doesn't say anything.

Callum walks over to the patio window and looks out into the darkness. 'Never made me feel anything other than hers . . . until the day she fucked off.'

The freezer gives a pert *beep* to warn us the door is still open. I close it and wipe away a smudge on the handle with my sleeve.

'Aren't you worried the developer will turn off the electricity?' Trish asks.

Callum sighs and presses his fingers against his forehead as if he's trying to find an off-switch for his brain. I give Trish a why-the-hell-did-you-ask-that look. She grimaces back at me in apology.

I picture Callum's contemporaries arriving home, dumping their school bags, grabbing a snack from the fridge and slumping on the sofa. The minute Callum steps through this ostentatious door, he must be in firefighting mode. Is the freezer still on? Is Gramps OK? Are we safe?

No wonder the kid wanted the money. My assumption that I have so much more to lose than he does was a naive one.

'We have to tell someone,' Trish says. Neither of us could settle once we got back from Callum's so, despite the rain, we donned our waterproofs and came out for a power walk around the block to burn some nervous energy. We speak in curt whispers as we pass a quiet row of cottages with an eclectic mix of names. Ma Chérie, Sea Folly, Elvis . . . In the front garden of the latter, a hedge shaped like the singer's famous quiff, which I assume is intentional. 'It's irresponsible not to say anything,' Trish adds like I didn't hear her the first time.

'He has us over a barrel on the whole pregnancy thing, though.'

'Yes. Thank you for that.' Trish side-eyes me. 'It was a really shitty move . . . You looked me in the eye and promised you wouldn't . . . you know. Bring me into it.'

We turn back onto our street. 'I really am sorry. It was an unforgivable—'

I stop suddenly, put my arm out to halt Trish. A hire

car – the same one Sean was driving last time he turned up – is pulling up outside my house.

'What is it?' Trish asks, on high alert. I pull her into a driveway and we duck behind a hedge.

'Sean.'

We watch through the bushes as he climbs out of the car and clambers towards my house. Part of me wants to march over there and demand our 'face-to-face conversation' once and for all but he's giving off a hyped-up almost aggressive energy that makes me pause. He looks up at the house, takes in the darkness, and puts his hands on either side of his face to look through the window. Next, he heads towards the front door and is reaching into his pocket – I assume because he brought his keys with him from the UK this time.

'Please tell me the bumps are hidden away,' Trish whispers. I nod, thinking that I should consider changing the locks.

He's about to open the door when his mobile rings. We both duck down lower as he gets back into his car having agreed to meet someone – probably Ish by the pally tone – and pulls off.

Once I'm satisfied he's gone, I move to continue up the road when Trish grasps both my upper arms in a clamp-like grip. 'No one hides from their husband unless there's more to the story than him leaving because he didn't want to have a baby.' I don't respond so she shakes me. 'What the fuck really happened, Barri? Come on. You owe it to me.'

I sigh. 'He stole all my money. Put my house in his name and remortgaged it behind my back. He still hasn't told me why and I want to know but I've also got a lot on –' I gesture to my bump – 'which makes it all a bit complicated.'

We start walking again as Trish computes this. 'You can

never get back with him in that case.' I refuse to look at her but I can tell by the tone of her voice that she's smiling.

I pull my hood tight around my face as the rain gets heavier. 'There's no need to sound happy about it. It was my dead dad's money.' This was not the reaction I was expecting from my predictable neighbour. Sympathy and compassion, yes . . . not something that borders on, what . . . relief?

'Sorry, of course. No. It's just with him coming back, I thought there was a chance you might want to get back together with him which given –' she indicates Kurt – 'would be . . . but he's stolen from you, that can never happen.' While she continues to bang on about how I must feel like I'll never be able to forgive Sean, the weight I thought might lift feels like it's quivering above me, ready to come crashing down again.

She turns to me, eyes bright. 'Are you going to go to the police?'

'Just leave it, will you?' I snap.

'Sorry.' After a beat, she nudges me gently. 'I wish you'd told me sooner. That's a big thing to be walking around with.'

'I haven't even told you the worst bit. He's been lying to me our entire marriage.' She freezes like she's bracing herself for impact. 'He put the house in his name over five years ago. Like he knew he might need the money one day. Why the hell would he do that?'

The thoughts in Trish's head reflect on her face beneath the street lamp like a sped-up projector – so quick I don't have time to register what emotions they are. Nor do I have a chance to ask her because her stomach rumbles and she says, 'We missed our pubby tea. Shame we couldn't have brought back some of Callum's ormers. I'm desperate to try—'

'Shit,' I say. 'I forgot to warn Callum about Pierre being on to him.'

'Oh for . . . How did you forget that?'

I think about Callum's dispassionate tone as he described his dad's drunken temper . . . what was that turn of phrase he used? 'Flips faster than a Guess Who piece'. I look up at the sky. 'I don't know, Trish, maybe I was distracted by the harrowing story he told us. What's the time?'

Trish looks at her watch. 'Just before midnight.' She bites her lip. 'Maybe Pierre's wrong.'

Off my doubtful look, she whips my phone out of my jacket pocket and thrusts it towards me. 'Call Callum. Tell him not to go this evening.'

'I don't have his number, do I?'

Trish stops walking suddenly, meaning I charge on for about five steps before realising. I turn and head back towards her. She fiddles with a toggle on her raincoat. 'I feel awful about this suggestion, but maybe it's for the best if Callum does get caught. It'll alert the authorities that he's living without a capable guardian and then we wouldn't have to intervene at all.'

I'd be lying if I said I'm not tempted. It would make everything less complicated for me in an already messy situation. But I think again about Callum's stepmum fleeing without saying goodbye. That's what upset me the most. How he said she never made him feel anything other than hers until the day she left him; in that moment, the animalistic urge to protect her own biological cub outweighed her responsibility as a grown woman to look after him.

Trish is still staring at me, waiting for an answer. I wipe a spike of wet hair from my face.

'No, we can't let him get caught. If Callum is headed for Lihou, I'm going to have to divert Pierre.'

Chapter Twenty-Nine

'How many coffees have you had?' I ask Pierre as he jitters away behind the wheel of the boat.

He laughs. 'I dunno. I feel pumped!'

I take that tatty ComplyHi coffee cup out of his hand and tip the contents over the side. I observe the wonky, dank grooves of various teeth marks around the rim and consider tossing it away too, but I'm doing enough damage to the environment this evening by enabling Callum's illegal ormering.

'Barri, that had about five quid's worth of creatine in it!'

'You put creatine in your coffee?'

'It makes you strong.'

'Only if you actually go to the gym.' Pierre looks wounded at this. For someone who wears intentionally holey shoes, he is very easily offended.

The boat makes light work of the waves on our way over to Herm, one of the small islands across from St Peter Port. I rest my hand on the side and move it again immediately as it connects with the remnants of water from the storm. The weather flash-mobs in extremes here. Thunder to calm, fog to blazing sun. The temperature has dropped but the sea is like a millpond now.

'Bloody good luck you overheard those people chatting in the pub, eh?' Pierre says, smiling.

'Yeah . . .'

'Mates of the ormer thief, I guess.'

I rummage in my bag for my scarf. 'Yes . . . or maybe friends of friends?'

'I wonder how he knew we were on to him?'

'Oh, they said something about someone seeing "Lihou" written down on your desk when they popped into your office when you weren't there . . .' Pierre looks puzzled at this. 'No, it might have been your corkboard?' This gets a nod of agreement. 'With Lihou circled? No, underlined? Yeah. That was it. It was loud in the pub, so . . .'

'So he switched his pattern. Well, we're one step ahead of him now, thanks to you!'

I grimace at the warm smile he gives me. 'Of course, it might not be Herm . . . as I say, it was very loud in the pub . . . I bloody love boats!'

Pierre grins, not noticing my unsubtle subject change. 'I know it's bad luck to change the name and that, but *Lynn III* really doesn't do it for me, eh?'

'I also worry about what happened to *Lynn I* and *Lynn II*,' I reply.

It's a gorgeous boat, not at all ostentatious – compact, speedy and ergonomic . . . if a boat can be ergonomic – with a lovely aqua-blue stripe across the side. The inside is gleaming, and everything has its place. Lights where you need to see to make a cup of tea, leather couches upon which to lollop in the sun. Even a pull-down screen to project movies onto when bunking down for the night. I think about the colourful-bottomed fishing boat I've always wanted. 'Sea

Bob is a good name for a boat,' I say. 'Though, from first-hand experience, having a name that doesn't match your aesthetic can be a burden.'

Pierre looks at me. 'Oh, you can pull off Barri all right. I can't imagine anyone else being able to.'

I tug at my scarf to loosen it.

'Speaking of that . . .' Pierre glances sideways at me. 'I have actually always wondered . . .'

'Why I'm called Barri when the rest of my family have ordinary names?'

'Well . . . yes . . .'

I slump back on the side of the boat and fiddle with a piece of rope that dangles between two brass fixings. 'When my mum was eight months pregnant with me, my parents decided to leave Lara with my Granny and have a little holiday in Sark before I was born.' I gesture in the rough direction of Sark. 'They were having a horse and cart ride round the island when Mum went into labour.' Pierre's eyebrows raise. I nod. 'I know. The driver pulled over, helped deliver me there and then.'

'Impressive.'

'The poor woman didn't have a choice, Mum was lying on the floor of the carriage, legs akimbo, insisting that she help. Mum's quite old school. Wanted a woman at the business end of things.'

'Fair enough.' Pierre takes his cap off and fluffs his hair before replacing it.

'When the driver said she didn't know anything about babies and was squeamish at the sight of blood, Mum got all accusatory. Pointed out that it was the jiggle of the carriage that brought on the labour so she was obligated to help.'

'That's quite the claim.'

'Wendy can be very persuasive.' I tuck some fly away hair behind my ear. 'Once the deed was done – all quite straight-forward, thankfully – and we were about to get on the boat ambulance thingy back to Guernsey with me in a bundle of clean blankets, the bloody ones discarded on the side, I think the reality of what just happened hit the horse and cart driver. She came over all pale and passed out, hitting her head on a fishing crate.'

Pierre breathes some air through his teeth in a grimace.

I fiddle with the rope again. 'Luckily her top hat cushioned the blow so it avoided any head injuries but the medical team insisted she come back to Guernsey with us to be checked out at the hospital . . . which probably added to her trauma to be honest.'

Pierre steers the boat between some buoys. 'You can't try to un-see the things when the things you've seen are still in front of you.'

'Exactly. My dad was so grateful for her help and mortified that we'd caused her such distress. He told her they'd name me after her as a thank-you.'

Pierre smiles. 'And she was called Barri.'

'No. She was called Florence.'

He tilts his head to the side, confused.

I shrug. 'There was a Florence at my mum's school and she hated her. Refused to honour it.'

'Wow.'

'I know.' I rest my hands on the plinth thing the boat wheel's attached to and face Pierre. 'Imagine the audacity of looking at poor Florence – who at that point was hyperventilating into a paper bag, her smart uniform covered in both your blood, and the birthing fluid of your second born – and saying, "No, we shan't name our child this delightful name as a thank-you for delivering our baby into the world because when I was seven, a kid called Florence graffitied my pencil case."'

Pierre laughs and gives the top of my arm a playful nudge. 'So, come on then, why Barri?'

I clear my throat and look behind him. 'Is there any more tea in that Thermos?'

Pierre grins, waiting for the resolution. I sigh and turn my face to the sky. 'After a lot of wrangling while Florence listed every important female in her life and my mum ruled out each name for petty reason after petty reason, they moved on to the names of important *men* in Florence's life.'

Pierre's forehead wrinkles. 'Her . . . dad was called Barry?'

I sigh. 'The horse.'

'The horse?!' Pierre claps his hands together. 'They named you after the horse?!'

'Dad described it as an "alleluia moment". He and Mum both looked down at me and the name just felt right apparently. They agreed to switch the 'y' with an 'i' to make it read more like a girl's name and there you have it. Destined for people to yell, "Oi, Manilow!" after me for ever more.'

'What an origin story!'

I point my finger at him. 'You cannot tell a soul . . . if my students find out.'

Pierre pretends to zip up his mouth and lock it. 'Your secret's safe with me.'

I pour us both some tea and we are silent for a bit, watching the waves part as the boat cuts through the water. I try to ignore the way Pierre's mouth is curled upwards into a smile as he thinks about the horse.

As we get nearer to land, Pierre pulls out a pair of small black binoculars with a tinted green lens.

'Are they . . . night-vision goggles?' I take them from his hand, studying them.

'It's the best way of being able to see what's happening out there.'

I hold them up to him. 'Did you buy them specially?'

He shrugs. 'No.'

'So you already had them knocking around? What on earth for, Pierre?'

He can't suppress his grin. 'No, I . . . OK, I bought them.' The schoolboy excitement is so adorable, I can't bring myself to mock him further. I lift them to my eyes and look towards Herm.

Through the glasses, the island is disconcertingly green, the lights from the tavern near the harbour and the adjacent posh (ish) hotel positively neon. Herm has no street lights, no cars apart from the odd quad bike, or the tractors pulling trailers of luggage up to the campsite at the top of the hill. The day trippers leave on the last boat and just the residents – the permanent and temporary – are left on their very own Kirrin Island.

A young couple cuddle up on the sea wall, wrapped in duvet coats, their Twiglet legs dangling over the edge as they stare up at the stars. I lower the binoculars and look up. The sky is breath-taking, with galaxies of golden orbs spread across it like the inside of an Aero bar.

We veer around to Shell Beach – a long stretch of white sand that, in the summer, wouldn't look out of place on a Caribbean island. It's a very low tide, so we moor up far out and head towards shore in a motorised dinghy. I rest back on the rubbery edge and look upwards.

'Sky's a beaut tonight!' Pierre says.

'Did you used to come and camp when you were little?' I ask.

'No. We stayed on Dad's boat, though.' He tilts his head. 'Used to come the same week as you, I think.'

'Really?' I don't recall seeing Pierre here at all. 'I loved being here at night,' I continue. 'I'd spend hours lying on the harbour wall, just looking at all these stars. I invented an entire opus in my head about one star in particular that could only ever be seen on Herm as the light everywhere else was too bright.'

'What was it called? The story . . .'

'"The Dull Star". Very original, I know.'

'Where is it, then?' he asks.

'I think she's . . . there.' He cuts the engine and lies his head back, trying to follow my finger point. 'She was sad because no one could see her. She didn't gleam as brightly as the others. And then one day a little girl does spot her and they become friends.'

'How did they talk if the star was all the way up there?'

'Telepathy. Silly really.'

'No. I like it.'

We stay lying like that for a moment. The boat bobs up and down in a comforting rocking motion. It's such a still night and this side of the island is deserted. Just Pierre's loud breathing in and out through his nostrils.

'You sound like you're doing antenatal breathing,' I say, immediately regretting the direction I've steered the conversation in.

He chuckles, nods to Kurt. 'Do you know the gender?'

'According to my diary, they're a pair of courgettes.'

He laughs again. 'You're brave doing it on your own. I could never . . .'

'Ah, women on the whole are superior to men. I don't anticipate having any issues.' I smile at him to show I'm joking. 'Do you want children?'

His face drops. I hate myself for asking him this detestable question. In the end, he just says, 'Maybe you and your husband will . . . you know . . . Maybe you'll work things out. Do you think?'

'Oh, I think that ship has sailed. Probably on the *Lynn II*.'

Pierre sits up and prepares to restart the engine. 'I knew Sean a bit, you know.'

'Everyone knows everyone here, I suppose, eh?' I smile. My Guernsey 'eh' doesn't come out very often. Pierre fires up the engine again as we head to shore. I catch the aromatic smell of oil that always makes me think of Dad.

'Well, thank you for a fun excursion,' I say to a despondent Pierre when he pulls up outside mine. We spent a good hour lurking in wait on Shell Beach for the non-existent ormer thief, me full of guilt as I watched Pierre go from excited to frustrated to downright disappointed, before we called it quits and headed back to Guernsey.

He opens the passenger door for me as I struggle out of the Jeep. He eyes Kurt. 'I'm sorry I took you on a wild goose chase.'

'I'm the one with the dodgy intel. Still, it was fun. I got to go on a boat and you got to use your creepy stalker goggles.'

He smiles and neighs, mock-trotting into his car. I laugh, shaking my head.

He turns the car around in the road while I rummage for my keys. When he's facing his required direction of travel, he pulls up again by the kerb.

'Night then,' I say to him through the open window. He says nothing. Just sort of looks at me.

My cheeks flush, and I drop my keys. There's an awkward moment where I want to bend down to retrieve them, but he hops out, insisting he does it. He continues to hold them as I take them, meaning we are connected for a moment by the keys. For some bizarre reason, it makes me think of Benjamin Franklin.

'Night then,' I say again, and head towards my house, my keys tinkling in my hand.

'She was just further away.'

I stop and look back at him. 'Who was?'

'The dull star. She gleamed as bright as the others.'

The battered Jeep's suspension bounces as he jumps back inside and drives away.

Chapter Thirty

I arrive at school early the following morning and I'm stunned to find Sean sitting in the staffroom having a cup of tea with Yolande and Julie, who are lapping up some story about a run-in he had with a fellow passenger on a flight. Sniveley is there too, gazing at Sean like a fanboy who has spotted his favourite pop star. Suzie has distanced herself from the group and is head down, doing some marking at my favourite table, rubbing her bump absentmindedly.

I watch Sean from the doorway wondering if he'll detect my presence . . . He should just sort of feel me being here, no? But he carries on holding court.

As a couple, we wore our independence from each other like a badge of honour and I wonder if that distance is the reason he doesn't detect me in this moment. I remember Lara commenting on it once: 'Aren't you worried about where he goes and what he's doing?' At the time, I said no, but maybe my commitment to respecting his privacy is what enabled his secrecy. Maybe I need to face up to the fact that our whole marriage has been a sham so he could scam me out of my money and disappear. But if that's the case, why is he back?

Objectively, the name Sean suits him. It belongs to a charmer, a chancer. He has the vibe of an enigmatic drummer in a successful rock band. Oozing cool and not caring whether anyone knows who he is. Is that right? Because the man I'm looking at now cares about people seeing him. Knowing him. It defines him as a person, even if he is trying to convey the very opposite.

Yolande waves at me, alerting him to my presence. I redden and go to join Suzie.

I assume rather than know that Trish confided the full sordid remortgaging shitshow to her. The fact that she isn't over there sitting with him tells me whose side she's on. I think about what she said the other day about how no one ever makes a fuss about the fourth baby and an idea begins to form. I make a mental note to speak about it with Julie later. Talk of the devil – her laughter at Sean's story punchline reverberates through the room.

I take out some marking and join Suzie in the solitude, trying to pretend that the complete stranger who was once my best friend isn't in the vicinity.

After about five minutes, he saunters over to us and hands me a letter. 'I came by this morning to drop this off and Julie offered me a brew and so . . . read it, will you?' He gives me that look again . . . the one that makes me want to lock into him like a rollercoaster shoulder brace. I remind myself that this is typical Sean, insisting on a face-to-face chat but now capsizing my expectations by producing a letter. And, of course, he didn't post this at my house the other night, but instead came into my place of work. A performative gesture for the benefit of my colleagues. Everyone stares at me as he leaves. I give it a few beats for the conversation in the room to pick back up and place the letter on the table between Suzie and me.

'Do you . . . want to discuss that?' she asks.
'How are you feeling today?'
'Better thanks.' She does look better. More colour. 'We found someone to do the washing, and she's gonna cook up a few lasagnes and things for us and bring 'em round for the freezer.' She side-eyes me, smiling. 'I feel like the poshest woman alive, but I'll get over it, I guess.'
'I'm pleased to hear it.'

I touch the edge of the letter, terrified of its contents. Either it contains brutal truths or pleas to reunite and I'm not sure I have the fortitude to withstand either. I slide it over to Suzie. 'How would you feel about reading this and giving me a precis?'

She doesn't look pleased at the idea, but takes pity on the vulnerability I've shown in asking her. She opens it and I pretend to carry on with some marking but, of course, I can't concentrate on anything other than her. When she's finished, she looks at me. 'So he's very . . . erm . . . It's hard to be . . . because I'm so . . .'

An idea strikes. She picks up her pen and proceeds to mark it up as if it is a student's work. She spends a good deal of time making purple scratches, circles and comments.

She slides it over to me.

I have underestimated Suzie's literary proficiency.

Hi¹ Barri,
(I'm) sorry if ²(my) leaving this letter for you at school

---

1 Inappropriate use of informal salutation
2 Try to avoid passive-aggressive assumptions

has made you annoyed.³ (I) ~~just~~ couldn't go on without addressing the issues that have been existing in our marriage for a while.⁴ ⁵(I) know (I) shouldn't have left Guernsey the way (I) did. You ~~just~~ have this habit of being so negative and shooting (me) down all the time, and it's ~~really~~ hard for (me) to be around. (I) feel like for the last year we were together, (I've) been living in this ~~really~~ hostile environment where (I) have to tread on eggshells. (I'm) airing this out loud⁶ now because (I) have to let you know how (I've) been feeling.

    The baby thing⁷ is something (I'm) finding hard to get (my) head around. You were always ~~so~~ adamant⁸ you didn't want one and so it was ~~really~~ upsetting for (me) to find out you were pregnant. It made (me) feel ~~completely~~ shit⁹ because it was like¹⁰ she wants a baby but not with (me).

    (I)¹¹ hope you understand why (I) was upset. (I) feel¹²

---

3 'caused you discomfort'
4 Clunky sentence
5 New paragraph here
6 You are articulating this in written form
7 Too informal
8 Good word, well done!
9 Try to find better words to articulate your feelings other than swear words, not appropriate in this setting
10 Avoid
11 Try to avoid all sentences beginning with 'I'
12 Try to avoid over-use of 'I feel' / 'I think'

like you will because you're ~~such~~ a good person underneath all that toughness.

(I) never intended to go behind your back with the house. If you'd asked (me) about it without getting all hysterical[13] (I'd) have explained that you were still ~~so~~ upset about your dad and grieving. It had put such a downer on our wedding plans as it was,[14] and (I) ~~really~~ didn't want to bother you with the mortgage and all that boring stuff when all (I) ~~really~~ wanted was for you to focus on getting your head better so we could enjoy our marriage. Because when it's good, it's great, right, Baz.[15] So that was all it was. (I) put the house in (my) name to make it easy for you.[16]

(I) feel like you jumped to the conclusion that (I) had stolen the money for (my) own gain and that was ~~pretty~~[17] hurtful. We need to have a grown-up[18] conversation so (I) can explain it all and make you see that (I) only ever had our best interests in mind.

(I'm) not proud of it but (I) lost my head[19] a bit about the you not wanting a baby thing and (I) did the remortgage to piss you off (I) think.[20] You know (I'm) a

---

13 *Barri being hysterical doesn't sound realistic to me – gaslighting?*
14 *Gaslighting?*
15 *This should be a question mark*
16 *For whom?*
17 *Something is either hurtful or it isn't*
18 *Accusatory tone here*
19 *Colloquial*
20 *'I think'? Inadequate and lacking an apology*

hot head sometimes. (I've) still got the money and want to talk about it. (I) also have some exciting news to tell that (I) hope you'll think is good and will show you how much our marriage means to (me).

(I) think²¹ (I) will be able to treat that baby just like it's (mine) and then one day (my) biggest wish is for it to have a brother or sister that is (mine).

(I'm) here whenever you're ready to talk.

I love you, Baz.

S

P.S. When you rocked up on that moped with that student, (I) found it really weird. What were you doing with him?²²

---

21 Avoid 'I think' – makes you sound unsure
22 ?? Mrs Martel would also like to know the answer to this!

*Summary from Mrs Martel: Childish tone. Too much use of 'I' and 'me'. This letter is not impactful. Skirting around an apology is not the same as apologising.

I finish reviewing Suzie's humorous and brutal marking-up. 'Thank you for making this experience, if not enjoyable, then palatable.'

'He knows it's twins now by the way . . . Yolande told him before you came in.'

I close my eyes. 'Of course she did.'

She gives my arm a reassuring squeeze. 'Hang in there, hon.'

It irks me that Yolande continues to be so reckless with my private information. Still, Sean knowing it's twins doesn't really change anything. Despite the awful letter, I can't help feeling a softening that he does want to get back together. It feels good to know he hasn't been out there in the world having a great time and not missing me at all. And he has explained about the money . . . if it was all connected to my dad's death and shielding me so I could grieve, maybe it was innocent after all. And then the remortgage recently was just his hot-headedness taking over . . .

'Can we discuss the student on the moped?' Suzie asks.

'Oh. Yes. It was Callum Le Brocq. It's a long story, but I bumped into him in Town and he gave me a lift back as I was feeling a bit under the weather. I appreciate it's strange but . . .'

'Is he OK?'

'Callum?' I gather up my marking. 'He's fine. Just stressed about his exams like every other teenager.'

Later that day, I knock on Julie's office door. She's at her desk, looking stressed. Having been on a roll with consoling my colleagues of late, I decide to risk an 'Are you OK?'

She spouts off a monologue about how they have bought a property in Cornwall but their new neighbours haven't been at all welcoming. All she's doing is buying up all their land so she can have an investment for her firstborn. She calls him that. 'My firstborn'. Julie is so of the heir and the spare mentality, she has several photos of her eldest on her desk and no one else, despite having three other children. I hope for their sake her husband is better equipped for the modern world.

'And then one hick kicked some mud, and it went all over Hugo's mustard trousers. I've honestly never seen him so angry. He threatened to get his shotgun, which was, of course, a joke, but they called the police on us anyway.'

I have no idea what on earth to say to all that, so I just come out with, 'I think we should throw Suzie a baby shower.'

Her mouth drops open in astonishment to begin with, but her expression gets warmer as I explain that Suzie's always so kind to everyone; she deserves a bit of a fuss even though it's not her first, second or third rodeo.

Julie may not be my cup of tea, but I'm heartened when she shows such delight at my suggestion. 'Exciting! Let us know once you've chosen a date and time and we'll all be there.' She turns her attention to her computer.

This dismissal wrong-foots me. I came in to make the suggestion, expecting Julie to jump on it and launch into organisation mode, taking all the glory for herself. I don't know the first thing about throwing a baby shower; I've never even been to one.

It hits me that if I wasn't leaving the island in a few months, this gesture might have solidified a genuine friendship with Suzie. I think back to how much derision I used to throw at her despite her constant kindness. It will be good to do one lovely thing for her before I leave. It will be nice to have the memory even if I no longer have the friendship.

I head into Town after work and pop into the party shop. I examine rows of banners and balloons with storks holding knapsacks and cutesy slogans like 'Welcome, Baby'.

What is that about? The way people refer to a baby as just 'Baby'. 'Is Baby kicking?' 'Does Baby have hiccoughs?' An optician doesn't refer to your eyes – which are similarly connected to a person by a cord – in the same way, do they? 'How have Eyes been feeling?' 'Can Eyes read the top line?'

'Bit early for all this, eh?' I nearly jump out of my skin. Lara stands behind me, peering over my shoulder.

'What are you doing here?' I ask, as if bumping into someone on this tiny island is some kind of coincidence.

She holds up a wedding anniversary card. 'Fifteen years this Friday.'

'That's a big milestone, congratulations.'

She studies me, looking for sarcasm where there is none. 'Thanks,' she says. 'What are you doing?'

I grimace.

You know how they say that people become immune to violent sex because of the amount of porn they watch? Due to the number of baby scans that had been thrust in my face against my will over the years – either in person or on social media – when my own sister told me she was pregnant for the first time, my reaction was far from enthusiastic.

We were sitting in my favourite window seat in the cafe looking out to the harbour when she slid it across to me. An unsolicited scan pic. I rolled my eyes before I even processed what it was. I've never forgotten the look of hurt on her face. In my heart, I was delighted for her. She'd always wanted to have a family, and they'd been trying for a while. I was determined to make it up to her, and become a supportive sister and a brilliant auntie, but I just couldn't get out of my head how I wasn't up to the challenge of it. It's like I was frozen by the responsibility. And so, rather than stepping up to help, I stepped away.

Lara's generosity of spirit in this card shop, therefore, when I tell her I am responsible for organising Suzie's baby shower when I didn't even bother turning up to hers is commendable. We go back to that same cafe where she slid the photo across to me. She pulls out her laptop, which is contained within a chic millennial-pink case, and in no time, I have invites, a special WhatsApp group, decorations, and I've even messaged Suzie's husband to see if we can sneak her sister over so she can attend the party.

It's fun. Lara talks me through one game called 'labour or porn', where several images of women either in the throes of orgasm or the pain of childbirth are displayed and we have to guess which is which. We laugh because in all the porn ones, the women have perfect skin and make-up and in the labour ones, they all look rough as hell.

'Do we have to play games at all?' I ask.

'You're the organiser. It's up to you.'

I make the executive decision that games are unnecessary, as is my view in life, not just baby showers.

I have one nice idea I'm rather proud of. Lara points out Suzie will already have a lot of items to use from the older children, not to mention the fact that they want for nothing in that household. I suggest that instead, we curate a library, not just for the baby, but a collection of books for all the stages of childhood that the older ones can enjoy too. Everyone can buy a childhood book they love and write a note in it saying why they love it. 'You can never have too many books.'

Lara loves it. We add it to the WhatsApp group and my phone goes berserk with heart, book and thumbs-up emojis.

'Who's Trish, by the way?' Lara asks when Trish puts a thumbs-up on the library message.

'Oh, yes. She's Suzie's friend . . . and my neighbour. She's a doctor contracting at the hospital. And she's my friend too, I suppose.'

Lara pops her credit card on the silver dish to pay the bill. 'You know, I can't remember the last time I came over to your place.'

'Must have been just after we moved in,' I reply, recalling how Sean gave me a lecture on how our house was not a thoroughfare and that the family should wait to be invited instead of turning up out of the blue. The latter being a weird Guernsey thing, apparently.

She smiles. 'I bet you've got shelves full of books.'

Later that evening, I take out a beautiful collection of classics I got from my granny when I finished my GCSEs. The covers are embossed in a thick, textured material in various jewel tones. I run my hand over *Pride and Prejudice* before placing it on the bookshelf that previously held all of Sean's DVDs and comic book action figures.

I have stacked it horizontally on top of a couple of other different coloured ones for a pleasing aesthetic. My ormer shell is beside the pile. I pick it up and feel the roughness in my hand before turning it over to let the iridescence catch in the light.

I message my sister. I'm sorry I wasn't there for you more. I should have been a better auntie. As an afterthought, I add, And a better sister.

My heart pounds as I watch the 'typing' symbol appear.

You're here now. Xx

The reply sends a chill down me, like my blood has turned to liquid nitrogen. But no sooner does the horrible thought enter my head, I let it float right out of it again to form a millennial-pink helium balloon above me.

Chapter Thirty-One

I turn up at Lara's at 6 a.m. the following Saturday sporting Louisa, who is a monster. I feel twice the size I did the last time I saw my sister and I'm sure she's going to notice the sudden increase in mass.

Instead, she opens the door and speaks over her shoulder about how excited the boys are. After a few beats waiting on the doorstep, I realise she was expecting me to just follow her inside.

Harry and Luke are waiting in the kitchen wearing their wetsuits. 'They aren't allowed to wear those,' I say to Lara, who I note is still in her pyjamas, causing me a pang of irritation that we will be delayed waiting for her.

'Well, that's stupid,' she replies.

My phone rings: Sean. Lara looks at it, her eyes widening with concern. I press the reject button. 'Not wearing wetsuits deters people from diving,' I say. My sister watches me put my phone back in my pocket with relieved satisfaction. I appraise the boys. 'As you're minors and I'm pals with Sea Fisheries Pierre, I think you'll be OK . . . but keep those heads out of the water at all times.'

Lara leans against the door, cupping her mug of coffee.

She might like some of Suzie's Japandi mugs for her birthday . . . It strikes me that I don't know her postcode . . . I should note down her full address before I leave Guernsey.

'Pierre, eh? Le Lacheur? From school?' She peers at me above her steaming mug, all feigned innocence. Perhaps I should get her a voucher for a barista course instead. That claggy milk belongs in the bin.

'Why aren't you ready?' I ask.

'I thought you might want to have a special auntie day. Just the three of you.' I commend Harry for whooping. Luke is less enthused. 'As long as you're feeling up to it, that is . . .' she says, eyeing my bump.

'I'm not an invalid, Lara.'

'Well, in that case, it's going to be hot later. You could go to the beach afterwards,' she provokes.

'What a brilliant idea! Come on, you two.' I brandish the new ormering hooks I've bought for the boys at her like Captain Hook. 'I'll try not to impale your children.'

Our morning is fruitful. The boys love turning the rocks and using the hooks to remove the ormers. Luke especially adheres to the rules . . . at times with megalomaniacal rigour. I had to break up an argument between the two of them when Luke held the measuring tool up to an ormer Harry found and insisted it was a millimetre too small when it wasn't.

I describe how Dad used to pretend to trip but catch himself from falling just in time to make me laugh and then I make a show of doing the same thing, causing them to burst into hysterics as I repeatedly pretend to nearly trip up and stagger through the water with a Buster Keaton deadpan.

When the sun is shining enough to give us the warmth to

move deeper into the water I decide it's time to show them the family cricking nook. Just like Papa did for my dad when my mum wasn't fussed about knowing, despite it being her family legacy, and then my dad did for me, I show the boys how to follow the cluster of rocks round and which building on the front to keep in their eyeline.

The boys' careful footsteps create giggles of water around us as we move. 'The location of this nook is top secret,' I say. 'Passed through the family for generations.' They shield their eyes as the sun catches on the rocks like a mirror signal. 'You aren't to tell anyone apart from your own children.'

'We aren't your kids,' says Luke.

'This is a one-time exception.'

'I don't want to have children,' Harry says, his eyes still squinting in the sun. 'I want to be a loner like you.'

Luke and I laugh. 'You do you, Hazza.' He looks at me, caught off guard by my adoption of his pet name. 'Right,' I say, also surprised by this slip. 'Reach in here. You'll have to go quite far . . .'

It's thrilling to watch Harry's eyes widen with excitement as his hand closes around the shell. Luke hooks it out; the biggest ormer of the lot.

'A gift from your grandpa,' I say.

Harry yells at the sky, 'Cheers, Grandpa Brown!' The sound reverberates around the rocks, rousing a few seagulls from their resting places.

As we walk back up the beach, carrying our bucket of fifteen ormers, we pass a woman in her early forties reclined in a deckchair, reading the newspaper. This is a rogue beach for relaxing when there are many more picturesque offerings, but each to their own.

'You were making a lot of noise with your children,' she says, not looking up from her newspaper.

I glance at Luke and Harry, who are several paces behind, writing their names in the sand with their feet, their faces flushed from the fresh sea air. 'They were just excited. It's their first time ormering,' I say. 'And they aren't my children. I'm their—'

She looks at my bump in pure disgust. 'It's the people with the offspring's world and the rest of us just live in it.'

'I . . . I . . .' I blow a raspberry at her and stride up the beach. Yes, I wanted to drop to my knees and worship at her altar, but this soulmate of a woman also irked me. Of all the children to target with her disdain, my nephews are the least deserving. But I couldn't say that . . . it's like when people say, 'But you'd love *my* cat,' when I tell them I'm more of a dog person.

'Did you just spit at that lady, miss?' Callum is waiting for us at the top of the beach.

'Pipe down, Le Brocq.' I hand him the bucket of our legally obtained ormers – like we are executing the world's lamest drug deal – and a shopping bag of toiletries I picked up for him. All the while, Luke stares at Callum as if he's a god. 'Is he your friend?' he asks.

'This is Callum, he's in Year Eleven at my school. I said he could have our ormers to cook his gramps a stew.'

Harry taps Callum on the arm. Callum bends his head down towards him. 'They're from our grandpa for your grandpa.'

The heat in my heart is cooled by that cryogenic chill from before. I look at Callum. 'You're still coming over for revision next week? And we can discuss . . . everything.'

Callum flicks a speck of sand from the rim of the bucket. 'Yes, miss.'

We have been eggshelling each other for a while under the breezy guise of me providing provisions like he's a hapless student in university halls when we both know we have to resolve his living situation soon. One that ideally doesn't lead him to expose me as a fraudster in the process.

'Come on, you two, I need some breakfast.' We wave Callum off and take the bus to Cobo, where I treat the boys to a bacon sandwich at the kiosk there, the brightly coloured inflatables on offer directly in our line of vision. A rainbow of smiley-faced animals poised to sweep an unsupervised sprog out to sea on a retreating tide. I buy the boys a red plastic flyaway football instead before leading them onto the beach, power walking to secure us a top-notch spot despite not many people being here yet. I like to be away from the constant chatter and traffic of the slipway and directly beneath the sea wall so I can rest my back against the warm granite.

For early April it's a hot day and, as the tide creeps in, I can feel my body yearning to swim, but I have to make do with watching Harry and Luke playing volleyball in the sea instead. I settle back against the wall with my Thermos, trying not to pay attention to the melancholy that has been creeping up on me all morning.

A figure blocks the sun from my face. 'All right, Barri!?'

I jolt, spilling coffee over my bump. I leave it a few beats too long before reacting to the supposed burning I should be feeling and let out an unconvincing, 'Ahhh!' Pierre doesn't seem to notice, too busy drinking in the beauty of the day.

As torsos go, Pierre's is adequate. Quite sculpted, really.

Surprisingly so. 'Good swim?' I ask, trying not to stare at the beads of salty water trickling down his skin.

'Lovely, eh? You weren't tempted?'

I pat Louisa. 'Yes, but not up to it at the moment.'

He circles his arms like an athlete. They have striped tan lines from where he has worn various T-shirts in the sun . . . a bit like that Mr Men character with all the bandages. He plonks himself next to me on my rug, catching me off guard. The hair on his wet arms feels like static against my dry skin. I make a point of wiping some sand from my leg so I can shuffle myself away from him slightly and pour him some coffee from my Thermos.

Pierre has this unique ability to give you his full and undivided attention when you are talking to him. It is empowering that he doesn't look around, grasping for a subject change or someone better to talk to. I find myself confiding in him about discovering Callum's living situation and how I don't know what to do.

'It sounds like a difficult situation, but it can't stay how it is,' he says. 'He absolutely should not go back to his dad, though . . .'

I can't help but wonder what Sean might say if I confided in him about this. I like to think he would be concerned and show an interest but I decide he'd probably just roll his eyes and tell me it's not my problem to get involved and that Callum should be sent back to live with his dad.

'Isn't some kind of family better than nothing?' I ask.

The places on Pierre's arms and chest that were specked with water before have become white and powdery from the salt sticking to his skin. 'Not everyone is cut out to be a parent,' he says, brushing the salt off as if reading my mind.

'Yeah, that's one of the reasons I never wanted a baby.' I realise what I have said only after the words have left my mouth. Pierre stops brushing.

'Barri, I have no doubt whatsoever that you will be a fantastic mother. You shouldn't doubt that.'

I scan the horizon to see what Luke and Harry are up to. Jumping off rocks with some friends they've bumped into.

Pierre fiddles with a tassel on the edge of the rug with his fingers. 'I was a dad once . . .'

My heart stops in my chest like a specimen suspended inside a bell jar. '. . . My daughter Margot died three days after she was born. My wife and I were both so devastated by it, there wasn't room for anything else. We separated a couple of years ago. No one's fault, of course. Not the best time, but, hey, I get to sit back and be a parent vicariously through other people . . . if they'll let me, that is.' He smiles at me, a flash of sadness and then it's gone again like island weather.

There was once a baby in existence that, even for a short time, had this man for a father. The destiny of a lifetime of happiness ahead taken away from both of them. The injustice of it is too much to bear. I stand up abruptly. 'Those two are too far out. Better get them back.' I waddle towards the sea.

As I watch Luke and Harry swim towards me, I can feel Pierre's eyes, but I can't bring myself to turn and look at him.

It takes me an age to get to sleep that night, plagued by the guilt at how I responded to Pierre's story. I must have just drifted off though, because I'm woken by my landline phone. I look at my radio clock: 2 a.m. Never a good sign.

I jump out of bed and run down the hallway to answer. My sister's voice. 'Barri, thank God. Can you get over here?'

I clutch the receiver tighter to my ear. 'What's happened?'

'It's Dave. He's in hospital. Can you get here, please?'

The line goes dead.

When I arrive at my sister's, she sprints past me, leaving the front door wide open, jumps into her car and screeches away before I can ask any questions. Harry and Luke, who must have woken up in the commotion, stand at the bottom of the stairs, looking at me bleary-eyed.

'What's happened, Auntie Barri?' Luke asks.

I'm not sure what Lara would want me to say . . . I opt for the truth. 'I don't have all the facts at the moment, but your dad has had to go to the hospital and your mum's gone to visit him. So I'm here with you for now.' I take in their worried faces and pray to God Dave's OK.

'Do either of you feel like getting back into bed and seeing if you can get some sleep?' Harry looks to his big brother, who shakes his head. He mirrors.

'Well, I happen to be a grand master hot chocolatier. In fact, I'd say it's a crime neither of you have ever had an Auntie Barri hot chocolate.'

Everything in my gut tells me I shouldn't be doing this – bonding more with my nephews. My day yesterday was lovely but it made me realise that I need to start phasing everyone out to minimise hurt feelings further along the line. But I've got no idea what's happened to Dave. If this is their last night of being Luke and Harry before they are Luke and Harry with the dead dad, I'm going to make it a good one.

As I stir the milk pan, the chocolate melting into the

liquid, I turn to them. Their mouths are brown from helping themselves to the extra bits of chocolate we smashed with the rolling pin. 'The only thing that would make this midnight drink even better is an equally good snack to feast on . . .' I hand Luke the spoon to stir the milk and pass Harry my phone. 'You can be DJ!' Harry squeals with delight and scrolls through Spotify, selecting some singer I don't know the name of, but I've definitely heard her song via my students.

I dance from cupboard to cupboard, encouraging the boys to participate in our kitchen disco. I don't find any promising food items, but when I lift the lid of the breadbin to reveal some brioche, I shake it above my head like it's a World Cup trophy. The boys' laughter feels like a drug. 'We can have French toast!' I'm not sure they even know what that is, but they cheer anyway.

I'm woken by the sound of a front door closing and realise I'm not in my house but on my sister's sofa. I wriggle my fingers to get rid of pins and needles. Luke is fast asleep on my arm. Harry is scrunched up in a ball beside me, his head on my lap, nestled up against Louisa.

My sister walks into this scene and, despite her pallid appearance, smiles at us. I gently lift Harry's head off my lap and cover them both with a blanket before I follow Lara into the kitchen.

It looks like a bomb has hit it with mixing bowls, drops of chocolate on the floor and an eggy burger flipper dripping onto the worktop, but Lara doesn't flinch. She just sits on the stool and bursts into tears.

I dash up to her and wrap her into a hug, using every

ounce of mental strength to not make the alien sound. I don't see the point in skirting around the topic. 'Is Dave dead?'

Despite the tears, she laughs. 'No.' She lets out a huge breath. 'The stupid idiot had too many after they won the five-a-side. Fell off the harbour wall into a boat. Concussion and a broken arm. For a horrible moment, they thought it was much worse as he did this weird thing with his body that suggested a serious brain injury.' She lifts her arms up into a disturbing zombie-like pose to punctuate the point. 'Thought they'd have to fly him to Southampton in the air ambulance, but when he came round it wasn't as serious as they thought, thank God.'

I pick up a mixing bowl and open the dishwasher. Lara holds up a hand. 'You don't have to—' She stops when she clocks my 'don't argue' look.

After I've packed everything away, I locate a cafetiere and scoop some heaped spoonfuls of coffee into it. Lara sighs again. 'Jesus, it's been a night. Thank you for coming so quickly. I honestly don't know what I'd have done . . .'

'You couldn't get hold of Mum, I'm guessing?' I fill the kettle with water.

'I called you, little sis. No one else.'

I stop the tap and stand there for a moment. I turn to smile at her. I can't for the life of me remember the last time Lara called me 'little sis'. It feels like a warm bubble bath.

Lara places her hand on her chest. 'The shock. You'd think after Dad, I'd have been more ready for it, but it still hit me like a two-tonne truck.'

'You hardly ever mention Dad,' I say, stopping the tap from dripping with my finger.

'I do with other people.' She pulls her hair up into a messy bun, gripping it with a hair claw clip she's plucked from the side. 'The two of you were always such a unit, I feel like I'm invading your grief or something.'

I turn to her. 'You wouldn't be at all.'

She pauses for a moment and smiles. 'I ran into Doctor Green the other day in Town.'

'Bloody hell, he's still alive, is he?'

'Just, eh? We only chatted briefly in passing. I told him again how much it meant to us that he came to the funeral.'

The memory comes back as clear as the glass I just washed. I'd spent the funeral service sat next to Mum, who – despite having been separated from Dad for four years by that point – was sobbing beside me, the feathers of her black fascinator quivering with every whimper. I couldn't concentrate on the eulogy because of her constant sniffs, so I handed her my packet of tissues. Rather than take one, she grabbed the entire packet and clutched onto it, not blowing her nose, meaning the rustle of the plastic added to the noise.

After the service, I hid around the side of the building for a few moments of calm before we had to get in the car to the crematorium. I felt like the gingerbread-man-shaped sewing set my granny gave me when I was five – just about stitched together into something that resembled the rudimentary shape of a human.

And that's when Doctor Green came out of the side door to light up a cigarette. He winked at me, holding up the packet. 'Only have half of one occasionally.'

I gave him what must have been a very weak smile and he came to lean against the wall next to me. 'You know, your father was the only patient I've ever had who would come into my office and be more concerned with how *I* was.'

I laughed at that. It almost ached because I hadn't smiled properly in so long. Dr Green held up his cigarette. 'He's the one who made me cut down in the end. Gave me such a lecture once during one of his appointments, I couldn't face telling him I was still on ten a day when he came by next.'

I shielded my eyes from the sun with my hand to study Dr Green. 'Seriously?'

'Yep. I was so sad to hear he'd . . .' Doctor Green stubbed out his cigarette on the wall and took out a handkerchief to polish his glasses. 'The week after he died, he was due to come in for an appointment. I couldn't bring myself to schedule another one over it, so I kept it in the diary, made myself a cup of tea, and I sat there for the full slot, just thinking.' He put on his flat cap and turned to me. 'He really made his mark, did Derek Brown.' And with that, he walked away.

I relay the story to Lara, who bursts into tears. I hand her a bit of kitchen roll for her blotchy eyes and move over to the basin, where I squeeze the dishcloth and hang it over the side. 'I'm sorry you felt like you were invading my grief.'

'Not to begin with . . . I guess . . .' She clears her throat. 'It was when you met Sean, he made me feel like he had it all covered . . . there wasn't room for me as well.'

I fuss with some drying-up. 'Yeah. He got a bit protective maybe . . .'

She spins the cafetiere plunger on its metal bar. 'Seen much of him since he got back?'

'Not really. I mean, he says he wants to get back together but I'm trying not to . . . you know, let him back into my head. But let's not talk about it.'

She tilts her head to the side. 'No. You're right. That's never been our happy convo.'

She presses down on the lid of the hot chocolate tin to click it into place. 'Looks like Luke and Hazza were well looked after last night. They love hanging out with their Auntie Barri, you know. Kept saying that they can't wait to show your twins the family cricking nook when they're old enough, which I thought was the cutest!' She claps her hands together. 'It's made me realise how excited I am to be an auntie. There's something really special about it, I think. Different from a mum, but the same if that makes sense.'

I turn away to face the sink. I don't want Lara to see the tears pouring down my face.

Chapter Thirty-Two

I plonk a bottle of wine on Trish's breakfast bar.

Trish presses the button on her iPad to check the time. 'Bit early for that, isn't it?' she says. The photo of her, Lil and Ripley laughing on the sun lounger stares back at me from the lock screen. It feels like a taunt. I turn the iPad over and meet Trish's eye.

'I can't go through with this any more.' This is not a cosy living-room conversation. This is a full glass of red wine, leaning on a kitchen island situation. I go to the cupboard and take out two wine glasses.

'There isn't a way out now, you're well beyond the threshold.'

When I can't meet Trish's eye, she twigs that I mean the unthinkable. Her expression darkens. 'You said you'd never do that.'

I rummage in her draws for a corkscrew. 'Maybe there's a way of doing it without upsetting people?' Trish snorts at this. 'I'd need some kind of medical document for school ... they will probably insist on giving me some time off and—'

'You knew when you went past twenty-four weeks that that was it.'

'I know, but—'

She folds her arms. 'I'm not doing it, Barri. It's abhorrent.'

I slam the corkscrew on the counter. 'I know!'

She softens . . . I think because she's never seen me cry before. 'What's triggered this?'

'I don't know . . .' I attack the cork with a firm twist. 'It was a weird day yesterday, I think. With Harry and Luke. Then my sister this morning. Lovely but . . . God, and Pierre told me something so devastating, and I guess . . .'

'You like Pierre.'

I wrench the cork out of the bottle. 'Yes. As a mate. I mean, what's not to like? The man lives in a state of pure and uncompromising joy.'

I pour the wine. Trish takes a sip and grimaces, spitting it back out again. 'Vile!'

I take a big gulp of the rank wine, the thick sugary taste clagging in my mouth. 'I didn't think I deserved anything better.'

She snatches my glass, pours it away and selects a bottle of Argentinian Malbec from her wine rack. 'I won't be pulled into your disgusting wine penance by proxy.' She pours us both a fresh glass, which is a more appealing rich red colour. 'The thing is . . .' She catches a drip of wine with her finger and licks it. 'If you're happy to hear what I think?'

'Please!'

'You're not going to tell people the babies have died. Even if you think you can, I don't believe you're capable of it, which is the only reason I agreed to help you in the first place.'

I think of Pierre on Cobo and take a gulp of wine, the welcome peppery tannins hitting the back of my nose as I swallow. 'You're right. I can't do that.'

'So your choices are these. Either you come clean to everyone, which will make them all hate you and make you miserable for upsetting them, and jobless, financially insolvent and potentially heading to prison. Or you carry on with the plan. Bugger off, see Nashville, move to Edinburgh and don't look back.'

I rest my forearms on the counter and lay my head on top. I can feel the edge of sunburn on my hairline where I must have missed the cream. I let out a frustrated sigh. 'I've really fucked this up. I thought leaving would be the easiest bit, but how am I supposed to just walk out on them now? When they're all so excited and . . . well . . . happy.'

'What would your dad say about it?'

'That's the question I've been asking myself this whole bloody time,' I say into the counter, contemplating whether to elaborate. I sigh out, drum my fingers on the worktop and lift my head up to look at her. 'The thing with my dad . . . he was an absolute legend but if I'm being completely objective about it, his moral compass was a little bit . . . skew-whiff.'

Trish narrows her eyes. 'Are we talking occasionally ate a grape on his way round the supermarket or armed robbery?'

I screw up my face. 'Somewhere in the middle?' I drum the counter again. 'It's hard not to make it sound . . . My dad, he wasn't born and bred in Guernsey; he's from Bromley originally. As a teenager, he fell in with some pretty questionable characters, which happens.'

Trish nods. 'It does.'

'But he met Mum, went straight and moved over here to settle down.' I take a big gulp of wine. 'He built up a good career in finance, and he was generally happy I think, but

I'm not convinced the domestic reality of his life here lived up to what he hoped . . . My mum is . . . and the slower pace didn't always suit him. I think he missed a bit of the thrill.' I top us both up. 'He wasn't a bank robber, though.'

Trish takes a sip of wine and smiles. 'Well, that's good.'

'He just provided *hypothetical* advice to a select few of his former associates on how it might be possible to wash stolen money through various channels to clean it up.'

'Nothing serious at all in the grand scheme—'

'But then when it became apparent that he, in his offshore location, could potentially be the best man on the ground to put that advice into practice . . .' I shrug. 'It was a stupid one-time lapse in judgement on his part. But he got caught and ended up doing a two-stretch for money laundering.'

Trish blows air out through pursed lips. 'That is . . . a lot.'

'Yeah.'

'I can't imagine your mum was very happy.'

'Wendy Brown reverted to Roussel overnight and then we never spoke about it again to anyone. The island's best kept secret.'

Trish glances at Louisa. 'Until now.'

'We lost the house. It was an absolute mess.' I take another sip of wine. 'When he was let out, Dad couldn't go back into finance for obvious reasons. He ended up working as a mechanic – a friend of a friend sorted him out – and he became the go-to guy on the island for all fancy car repair needs. It helped he had plenty of pals with expensive cars from his previous job and they all came to him and told their mates to do the same.'

Trish holds her glass up to cheers mine. 'A lesson in resilience.'

I don't reciprocate. 'The last conversation we ever had was him all excited to be staying late to fix someone's Ferrari after they offered to pay him double. He was separated from Mum, so there was no one to notice he hadn't come home. I got up, ate my breakfast, and went to school with no idea that he was lying dead in a pool of oil on the floor. Brain aneurism.'

Trish places her hand on mine. 'I'm so sorry, Barri.'

Afterwards, I imagined Dad up in heaven watching me going about my business – the Barri before she was Barri with a dead dad. It must have been quite nice seeing me in that oblivious state. Like when you see someone you know in the wild and they haven't seen you . . . you feel like you're watching them in their own habitat. *That is who they are when they aren't with me.*

Of course, it's occurred to me over these past few months that I have inherited more of his thrill-seeker side than I would care to admit. But I don't enjoy telling people about this part of him because my father wasn't a criminal to me. He was my champion. The man who took me ormering, and saved me from bed-wetting embarrassment, and told me I was 'a smasher' when I didn't feel like one.

'But what would he think about what you're doing?' Trish asks.

I rest my head on my forearms again. What *would* he think? He was all about sticking it to the man, taking arms against the establishment. He'd have called it a 'Pregnancy Heist'. He wouldn't love the whole deceiving my loved ones. But, in fairness to me, before I started all this, I didn't have any of those.

I lift my head up. My eyes are woozy from staring at the pattern on the countertop. 'I think he would say I'm in too deep, to carry on with the plan and bugger off into the sunset without getting caught.'

'Well, there you go,' says Trish. 'Sounds like a good, solid, pragmatic man despite his . . . mistakes.'

'He was.' I dab at the tears on my cheeks with the heel of my hand.

She puts her arm around me, squeezing me to punctuate each important word in her speech. 'It's natural to have a wobble, but that's it now. You need to focus on the job in hand, which is to see this through to the end, secure your maternity leave and get away from him.'

I wriggle out of her grip. 'Him?'

'What?'

'You said "get away from *him*"?'

'Well, I meant *here* . . .' She takes a long sip of wine. 'But yes, him too . . .'

'There's an explanation about the money.'

Her razor eyes meet mine. 'You've spoken?'

'He gave me a letter.' She goes to speak, but I interrupt. 'I don't want your input. OK? I know I need to keep him at arm's length. But for the record, you're wrong about him.'

'Fine. But you should probably keep *everyone* at arm's length. Not just him. Your sister, the boys, Pierre. It's kindness in the long run if you start to . . . detach.'

Chapter Thirty-Three

I chuckle to myself as I finish cutting out the final triangle of material. Non-fake-pregnant Barri would BAULK at this. Handcrafting bunting for a baby shower?! Not only am I doing it, I am *enjoying* it! I haven't forgotten Trish's advice the other day, I just don't see the harm in showing my face at Suzie's next month considering I've put in all the work. Just a quick stop by on the day. An aloof hello to my sister and off again.

The sewing also distracts my brain from the guilt over all the ignored calls and texts from Lara since our heart-to-heart the other day. I have to remind myself that it's a kindness to detach in the long run. Things will go back to how they used to be before I faked the pregnancy, meaning when I leave they won't even miss me.

I have a collection of undrunk mugs of coffee gathered around me and I'm enjoying the sewing too much to attempt to make another, despite my body's tug for caffeine. However, my deep concentration is obliterated by a sound I haven't heard in a very long time. Someone else's key in the lock and the creak of the front door opening. I stand in a panic at this unwanted invasion. Several pieces of handstitched patchwork triangles fall to the ground. The random assortment of letters from the 'Happy Baby Shower, Suzie' I was planning have fallen to spell out 'PAY UP BABY'. A fitting message to greet Sean as he steps into my living room.

'You really shouldn't be—' He has a huge, fresh cut on his cheekbone. 'What happened?!' The stain he has across his face from attempting to wipe the blood away looks like when the *MasterChef* contestants do an artistic smudge of puree on a plate.

He looks at me; a lost child. 'I rang the doorbell, but you didn't answer.' Slurry words. I can't tell whether this is out of concussion or alcohol . . . or both. 'I used my key.'

'I didn't hear the doorbell.' I grab the first aid kit from under the sink and a bag of peas from the freezer. Every rational thought tells me to hand it all to him to sort himself out, but I fall into the familiar rhythm of our marriage.

I pull out some antiseptic wipes, gauze, dressing and tape, aware that my nursing, along with the remnants of various crafts around us, depicts a wholesome scene. Sniveley is delighted.

It is only when I lean towards Sean to wipe his cut without impingement that I realise I'm not wearing Louisa, who is tossing back and forth in my washing machine after losing a bet with Trish that I could hold and consume a whole plate of roast dinner on my bump without spilling it. Sean seems too wrapped up in his self-pity to notice. I stand to rectify the situation, but he grabs my forearm.

'I'm so sorry for what I did, Bazza. I just love you so much.' Definitely drunk. As he sobs into his hands, I use the opportunity to dash into my bedroom. I have the choice between the two lads. Kurt or Friedrich. I opt for familiarity and strap Kurt on, my finger catching in the knife hole. This anchors me. I head back to the living room. He's over by the table now, taking in the sewing. 'Never had you down as a crafter.'

'What happened to you?'

I loathe the look he gives me; like a little boy wanting praise for riding no-handed on a scooter for a millisecond.

'I went ormering,' he says. 'Wanted to catch some for you . . . but I slipped.' He gives me this infuriating look; the pretence of a reluctant hero, but underneath, he's desperate for glory. I don't react or respond. He rubs his cut, creating another red smudge on his face. 'This could be a really serious injury.'

'I think you're drunk and you'll be fine.'

He is incredulous for a moment, realises there's no way out and gives me a winning smile. 'May have gone for a few drinks beforehand!'

His teeth have a texture to them close up . . . I've not noticed it before, sort of mottled but translucent. I feel like I can see the shadow of his tongue behind them.

He lurches towards me and plants a clumsy kiss on my unsuspecting mouth. Our teeth clonk. My white ones colliding with his mottled. Even though I recoil, I can still taste the cider he drank earlier. Second-hand, it is not a refreshing treat. The sweetness of it makes me gag.

'What the fuck is wrong with you?' he slurs; a spiteful inebriate.

'I feel a bit sick.'

'You're my wife.' He hurtles the word 'wife' at me like a win-hungry Wimbledon tennis champ serving his sixteenth ace of the match. 'You're my *wife*.'

He fiddles with a piece of pastel yellow bunting on the table. I try my best to not fixate on the bloody fingerprint it leaves.

As he tells me how everything is my fault – how boring life with me was; how I never wanted to be sexy for him, make an effort with how I look – all I can fixate on is his fingers as they continue to fiddle with my carefully stitched triangle. I imagine the blood particles seeping into the soft cotton fibres: iron and cells and whatever else blood is made of . . . plasma? The stain of this man.

He's still talking. Banging on now about how, despite my culpability in all this, he was wrong to have left me how he did. How he should have stayed so we could 'hash it out'.

I'm about to tell him, 'Go on, start hashing,' but instead I watch in horror as his hands move from the bloodied triangle towards the pure ivory ribbon. I spent a long time choosing that ribbon. The perfect colour to offset the yellow. I loved the sheen of it, the luxe way it reflected the light, unlike its cheaper contemporaries. Most of all, I liked the little beads dotted along it – like oyster pearls. Twelve pounds that roll of ribbon cost me! I knew it was extravagant to buy it, but I imagined all the triangles attached to it so neatly, the zig-zag stitch I'd use on the sewing machine, the pearls reflecting in the light. I picture Suzie smiling as she runs her hands along the little beads. Maybe she'll hang my bunting in the baby's room somewhere or keep it inside a little scrapbook. That's what women like her do, isn't it? Treasured maternal sentiments in floral boxes kept among hats, scarves and shoes in their wardrobes.

One damaged triangle is irritating enough, but the idea of Sean's DNA being anywhere near Suzie's beautiful ribbon is too much to bear. I snatch it away from him, coil it back up around its reel, and clutch it to my chest.

'What the fuck is wrong with you?' That snide smile again. Through Sean's teeth, instead of the shadow of his tongue, I imagine a serpent, its fangs bloodthirsty. 'This is all for you, isn't it? Sewing decorations for your own pathetic little party because no one else would bother to throw you one. Barri no mates.' He cackles at his weak joke.

I don't want to tell him this is for my friend, or that these past few months have been the most delightful of my life. That the thrill of it all – the pregnancy heist – was eclipsed by the warm balm of kindness and water bottles and hot chocolates and stars gleaming. I don't say it. Not just because I don't want Sean to have any part of it, but because I don't want to admit it out loud to myself.

I think of the character in E. M. Forster's 'The Machine Stops'. That blob of a woman living isolated in the room by herself. Incapable of functioning without a machine telling her what to do, feeding her, sustaining her. No friends, no conversation, no free thought. 'You shouldn't have gone ormering today,' I say. 'It's against the rules.'

Sean stands and moves towards me, a look I haven't seen before across his face.

'Where's my money?' I ask. I'm not sticking to the script of our marriage. Sean is the one who sets the tempo, decides when the big conversations happen. I imagine the wiring of his brain beginning to sizzle, the red flash of an alert that I choose to ignore. 'You said that you'd explain if I gave you the chance. Well, here it is.'

Sniveley rises to his feet in slow motion, sensing it too. He doesn't want this . . . he gives me a warning look, a subtle shake of the head. The little cruelties are OK. The jellyfish stings. But this is bordering on something more. I know now isn't the right time. I should wait until Sean's sober and in a better frame of mind to talk but I'm so enraged by how belittling he's being. The anger with myself at the realisation I am wrong about him. It has always been like this.

'You don't have it, do you? Because if you did, you'd come in here all smug, find a way of making it look like a gift.' I meet his eye. 'Because that's what you do, isn't it? You lie and bully and then twist it to make it feel like a present.'

I catch Sean's wrist just before his rage backhands across my face. The force of the smack that would have hit my cheekbone shudders through my whole skeleton.

We stay like that for a moment, eye to eye, my hand around his wrist as we both process what nearly just happened. The palm of my hand is in agony but I don't let go.

A flash of remorse registers on his face but then he pulls his arm away with such force, I stumble back and lose my footing. As my cheek connects with the edge of the table, my thoughts stop. I can hear my heart beating, the blood and energy raging its way towards my injured face, body in crisis mode. Those desperate gasps for air. As a child, I used to go into shock like this when I had an accident. Like the time I fell off my trike hurtling down the hill and split my chin open. My dad had to sit down in the middle of the path with me and shout, 'Breathe, Barri, breathe!' I feel that now, the shock at the injustice of it – not something I have a way of articulating or computing right now, but my body knows. It shows me. I just wish I had the comfort of a parent to make it better. *Breathe, Barri.*

Sean squats beside me. At first, I think he is reaching for the first aid kit, but instead, he snatches the ribbon. I grab at it desperately and wrap my fingers around some of the material. I yank a load back towards me as he pulls the plastic reel away. It unravels through our living room as he leaves our house. The Minotaur stealing the thread. It frictions through my fingers as he pulls it harder. Soon, it will stop spooling and we will be left with a tug of war.

I have some left, but every time I get a purchase, it is yanked again. Each pearl bead pops off one by one as it is tugged from my grip. POP. The beautiful ivory stained with blood. POP. Mine or his? Who knows. Mixed together. POP. His and hers.

I just about have time to look up and see the tail of it escape through the door before I fall forward on the ground, Kurt cushioning me. Once his car has screeched away, there is just the sound of the fallen pearls as they roll back and forth on the floor around me.

Chapter Thirty-Four

My head is in agony from sinuses flooded with salty, messy tears and the throbbing pain of newly bruised skin. I goaded him. I know I did. Even Sniveley warned me . . .

I look around for Sniveley now, but he's gone. Perhaps now rage has manifested in a physical act, my brain has made him redundant. No longer needed to be here as a warning now that my eyes are open to the reality of the threat. Well, that's something, at least. I hope he's retiring rather than finding a new role in a household somewhere else. I imagine Sniveleys across the world tormenting people. What would we call that collective noun? A slithering of Sniveleys? A schooling of Sniveleys? A scribbling, scratching, sardonic, shitty, sly, scathing of Sniveleys.

I hear a scooter hurtling towards the house, reminding me about the plan Callum and I had made to have a revision session today. The doorbell goes. I duck behind the sofa like I did one time at uni when I was feeling particularly lonely and agreed to have a pair of Mormons over for tea and then changed my mind when I saw their immaculate suited shadows through the window and couldn't bring myself to let them in. Maybe I was terrified I'd end up joining them, such was my desperation to have someone else take control of my life. On reflection, my penchant for rule-breaking would not have gone down well in that community.

'Miss! You hiding?' Damn. My position is in full view of the letterbox that Callum is peeping through. I think back to when Trish caught me with the newborn nappy around my ankle and can't help smiling. Which hurts my face. I grimace and get up to open the front door.

'What the fuck happened?' Callum surveys the scene as he walks into the living room – the blood-stained bunting triangle, the first aid kit, my shiner. He grabs the semi-defrosted frozen peas, wraps them up in a tea towel and applies the compress to my face.

There's no point lying. Callum can smell bullshit a mile off. Plus, there is something in the way he is handling this situation that makes me think this isn't the first bag of peas he's held to someone's face.

Water runs down my neck, making me shiver.

'Does he know? About the fake pregnancy?'

I shake my head no, which hurts.

'Hold still.' He places the hand not holding the peas on the other side of my head to stop me from moving it again.

It was a good question to lead with because the relief that Sean didn't discover my secret makes me feel better. 'We just argued about . . . I fell and . . . I provoked him.'

Callum opens his mouth to say something but pauses, thinking better of it. He feels so sorry for me, he doesn't even argue when I suggest he does a practice essay on *Death of a Salesman*, exam conditions, while I cook us some tea.

I set to work caramelising some onions with one hand, the peas held to my face with the other.

Cooking has always been therapeutic for me, even when I was younger. The gentle stirring of a sauce, feeling it thickening on the spoon. My absolute favourite part of a recipe was always caramelising onions. Not enough eighteen to twenty-one-year-olds know how to do it, in my humble opinion. The care and attention required means you can focus on nothing else. It's like meditation. If you allow your mind to wander, or become distracted by the television or your phone, you can accidentally let them burn. You have to stand there and believe in your heart that at some point, they will turn golden brown. They always do. It's like faith.

My university housemates weren't enamoured that I attempted to turn our shared kitchen into a sophisticated Parisian cuisine. They would bat away my strings of garlic and shove my shallots out the way while they overcooked their pasta and stirred in half a jar of pesto. To this day, the pop of a small jar of Sacla being opened transports me back to that kitchen. Bland and ill-equipped with cheap wooden spoons that had soaked up so much gunky food, they were never clean.

The thing that tipped my housemates over the edge was my – in hindsight far-from-considerate – decision to repurpose the airing cupboard into a meat-curing space. It irked me that my fellow house-dwellers insisted on air drying their garments there, even though there was a functioning tumble drier. I scooped up all the laundry – jumpers haphazardly strung across splintery beams of wood, odd socks wedged over pipes, camisoles suspended from nails – and shoved it all into the tumble dryer. Then I set about stringing up my meats.

It was unfortunate that the girl who discovered the scene

was a vegetarian. She flung the door open to collect her cashmere and met eyes with a hungry rat swinging off the bottom of a piece of chorizo, gnawing at it like a circus performer who had decided it was a better trick to eat the trapeze. On the shelf below, where I had dangled my prosciutto over the splintery wood slats, was a family of mice enjoying a banquet, unfazed to have their meal interrupted by a dramatic human.

Her scream reverberated through the house. Even the girl who spent all of her time alone in her bedroom listening to Evanescence came out to check what had happened.

There was a house meeting called where my affluent contemporaries three years my junior informed me through tears that silk camisoles and cashmere cannot be tumble-dried, unlike my synthetic Primark specials, and that suspending meat in an airing cupboard isn't appropriate behaviour in a house-share.

On reflection, I see their point. I now always air-dry my woollens.

I ceased all practices and prepared them an apologetic meal of pasta and pesto. They were unimpressed, said it tasted different. I told them well, of course it does; the pesto is home-made. They looked at me in complete disgust at this admission, as if I had somehow infected their spartan university experience with a tiny bit of grown-up decadence. I reminded them they were gathered around the table wearing approximately five hundred pounds' worth of collective cashmere. That was the first and last group meal we shared as a household.

That whole experience did mean that the Evanescence girl came out of her room and socialised with us for the first time. Her bravery in fending off the rat with that guitar-shaped burger flipper, and calling in the landlord to get the pest control people in, made her an instant favourite in the house.

Nisha, her name was. She and I became mates for a while, as you do in your early twenties when you are still figuring out the person you want to be and the people you'd like to have around you.

Nisha was funny – very funny – and had this ability to make me feel better without trying that hard. I think because she didn't change the subject when I was sad or struggling. She allowed me to sit there in my grief and come up for air in my own time.

'It's not that you're a sad person . . . you have a lot of joy in your life,' she said to me one day while we watched Marissa Cooper die in a car crash on *The O.C.* 'It may be weird and quirky joy but I'd definitely say that was your default. You're a weird, joyful person who *feels* sad because her dad died.'

Maybe she was sent to me by my dad. It sounds absurd, but it feels like she was just that – the perfect person to help me through that time. It's funny. If I'd been asked who that person was even a week ago, I'd have said Sean.

Sean didn't like Nisha . . . said she was controlling and becoming obsessed with me. When I moved in with him, Nisha and I had a huge argument about it – how I was making a rash decision, which solidified the whole controlling, obsessed narrative even more. We weren't friends after that, which is a regret.

I'm still caramelising the onions when the timer goes off ninety minutes later. Callum reads the final paragraph of his essay and makes a purposeful strike-through of a sentence before I snatch the paper from him. I nod towards the onions. He doesn't argue with me and stirs them while I sit down to read it. I feel my energy rise as I tick and comment my way through. Ten 'VGs' and one triple tick! My triple ticks are the Paul Hollywood handshake of the English department. Very few dished out, only when someone is deserving, demonstrating independent thought, not something regurgitated from me or Google or, God forbid, ChatGPT. I write the number nine at the end, circling it with satisfaction. I hand it to him and he stares at it like he can't believe it's really his to take.

'Callum, I'm so proud of you,' I say. I turn the onions off. 'Screw the onions. I'll put them in a quiche tomorrow. This calls for a treat.' I hold up the menu for the curry house. Callum is still staring at his essay.

'What's wrong?' I ask him.

He shrugs.

'Well, let's order our food . . . and then we . . . Well, we have to decide what we're going to do about your living situation.'

He looks dejected for a moment. Then, his eyes land on the perfect delaying tactic. Sean's Nintendo Switch. 'You ever played Super Mario Kart, miss?'

Ha! The assumption that I, Barri, would not be any good at Super Mario Kart. I am an expert at Super Mario Kart. If universities taught Super Mario Kart, they would be hard-pressed to find a better specialist. My whole thesis would be around how Bowser, on many levels, is a misunderstood creature who does not wish for annoying characters to turn up at his castle and race around his grounds. I, too, would jump in the first available vehicle and attempt to run them off the road.

I play badly for the first few games, selecting Princess Peach – the character Callum would assume I would choose as a naive thirty-something feminist. I land in lava, collide with every shell and drive in the wrong direction for a whole lap, pretending I haven't noticed, which causes him to chuckle to himself.

I broach the subject of his living situation again. He clams up and keeps his eyes fixed on Choco Island. 'OK,' I say. 'How about one more race and then we just discuss it for twenty minutes?'

'I just want to relax, miss.'

I breathe out in mock frustration, leave it a beat and then adopt an uncertain tone. 'We could do one more race and, if I win, we talk about it, and if you win, we don't?' I use an upward inflexion at the end to really hit home how unsure I am about this suggestion.

Callum laughs. 'Are you sure, miss?'

'I choose the characters. You choose the track?' That upward inflexion again.

He grins. 'Deal!'

I knew he would pick Rainbow Road. I've displayed no skill at keeping the car on the track – I'd have chosen it too. I decide to instil even more confidence in him by keeping the characters we've been playing with – me with Peach, him with Yoshi. He looks at me: *Are you sure?* I'm sure, kid.

He sits back on Big Blue, lolloped like an egotistical CEO at a mandatory compliance meeting. But by the time we hit halfway on the first lap, Callum is bolt upright. I navigate that track like I've been playing Mario Kart for years . . . which I have. Callum panics as I hurtle past him, whacking him with a green shell. He makes mistakes, grows frustrated. As I whizz over the finish line, he turns to me, furious.

'Miss, you hustled me.'

'Back in the day, we used to call that "schooling". Which, in this situation, could be seen as ironic. Because I'm your teacher.'

'Yes, miss, I get it.'

I flick the kettle on, explaining to Callum about the irritating water kettle politics of the school staffroom. Callum assesses my teabag collection, deliberating whether to risk an ambiguously named 'boost' tea flavoured with lavender and probiotics. He makes his choice – a calming chamomile.

We sit with our steaming mugs at my kitchen table. He runs his finger along a knife groove in the wood. Funny how things like that become unnoticeable after a while and how your attention can be brought back to them by an outside eye spotting the imperfection.

I explain to Callum that I appreciate I have been woefully unprofessional, allowing him to become part of the fake pregnancy situation and that I respect the fact that he hasn't told anyone about it. But in this situation, I am an adult and, more than that, I have a professional obligation to make sure he is kept safe. 'In honesty, I would rather everyone found out about me faking a pregnancy than me not telling anyone about your situation and then something terrible happening. So if the plan is still to tell everyone my secret if I intervene, it's incidental.'

'What's the options, though, miss? We report me and they'll send me back to my dad, which cannot happen.'

'I'm sure he misses you.'

Callum laughs. 'He doesn't.'

I remember meeting Callum's dad one parents' evening. The kind of man you look at and just know he would be well placed to manage a football team. Bona fide gravitas. I recall complimenting Callum's aptitude for English and noticing him almost bristle – as if the praise was an affront he couldn't handle. But when I pointed out that I wished his son would apply himself more, he became defensive and prickly. 'Did you not just say he's wicked at English?!' That isn't the behaviour of someone who doesn't care.

I relay this to Callum, who shrugs. 'That was then.'

I put plates in the oven to heat up in anticipation of our imminent curry arrival and then turn back to him. 'I'm going to tell you something about my family that no one knows other than my mum and sister. Which will surprise you for an island this small. My dad was—'

'A bank robber.'

This wrong-foots me. 'Well . . . he wasn't a robber . . .'

Callum shrugs. 'Semantics, miss.'

'He didn't rob . . . he—'

'Washed the dosh.'

I lean back on the counter, accidentally pressing the hob ignition button. 'How do you know that?'

'My grandad knew him.'

'Cedric?'

Callum smiles. 'Yeah. He told me all the stories. I think they were good mates back in the day. Said he was really upset when he went suddenly like that. That a man as smart as Derek Brown shouldn't have died in a second-rate garage in a pool of Lamborghini oil.' Callum clocks my discomfort. 'Sorry.'

'Oh God, don't worry. It was a long time ago.' I can hear the pitch of my voice two tones higher than it should be. 'And it was Ferrari oil.'

'I think most people know. He was pretty notorious,' Callum adds.

'Low level,' I counter.

'Nah, they reckon he got off lightly. There was a load more—'

'The point I'm making, Callum, is that people deal with a lot of shit and do bad things, but that doesn't mean that is solely who they are. My dad to you – and to other people, it seems – was a morally questionable man. To me, he was . . . he was wonderful.'

He tilts his head. 'All the time?'

'No one is wonderful all the time.' His eyes bore into me. Urgh. I sit back in my chair. 'OK. No. There were times when I hated him. When he was in prison, we had no money and we weren't allowed to tell people where he was. But now I see that although his morals were misplaced, his heart was always . . . kind.' I take a sip of tea. 'He went straight in the end, and grew a successful business.'

'Nah!' Callum laughs. 'He used to take the parts from them posh cars, replace them with cheap ones and sell them on eBay.'

'How do you know that?'

'How do you *not* know that, miss?'

I make up some squash in a jug Sean's mum made us for a wedding present. The ice I add tinkles against the porcelain. 'The point is there's always more to something than just the supposed facts.'

'What would your dad think about your bloke?' Callum asks.

'We're not talking about me.'

'We are.'

I don't respond; a skill I've cultivated as a teacher – if you leave enough space for them, they often fill it.

Callum sighs. 'My dad used to be all right. When I was a kid, he was fine. But he got more and more into his drinking, and now he works on the building sites, he spends all his time when he's not working standing outside the pub getting pissed with his mates and arguing about football. He didn't come home much.' Callum takes the cutlery out of my hand to set the table. 'I mean . . . everyone has a drink when they've had a stressful day, don't they? His life was especially shit so of course he drank loads to numb it. But if you think sending me home is the answer—'

'I'm not saying that—'

'Would living with my dad provide me with a better and safer situation than my current one, which is living with my gramps, who does care about me? And in a mansion? No.'

The doorbell goes and I leave the room briefly to collect our takeaway from the driver, a potential plan beginning to formulate in my head as I locate the cash to pay him.

We sort the curries, rice and sides out on the table in silence. An upturned lid leaves a turmeric-coloured stain on the wood, but it doesn't faze me.

'Miss, I think you mean well but sometimes, especially when it comes to dads, you find it hard to accept that yours wasn't up to scratch either.' On second thoughts, that stain could do with a scrub . . . Callum raises his voice so I can still hear him when I go to fetch the cloth. 'And so you prefer to defend all the shit ones. Your dad was a nice guy on the outside, but fundamentally, he prioritised the money and the thrill over you. Just like my dad does.'

I scrub the stain for a bit, decide it's not worth the effort and eat a spoonful of spicy jalfrezi instead, causing me to cough and splutter. Callum laughs as I stumble to the fridge to glug some milk from the carton.

'How come you're so good at Mario Kart?' he asks me. I know he feels bad about the nerve he just obliterated.

'I used to play it every night for a treat after I'd done my marking.'

'Didn't your husband mind?'

'To be honest, Callum, he was hardly here.' I rip up some naan bread and dip it in some saag aloo.

'Where was he?'

Fuck knows. Callum is looking at me weirdly all of a sudden. 'What?'

'I saw him once. In the UK.'

'Sean?'

'Yeah. At this service station I worked at.'

'Which one?'

'Pease Pottage near Gatwick.'

'What was he . . . No, hang on. We're talking about you.' I fiddle with the plastic lid of the rice, clicking it into place on the tub.

'It's OK. He was. Well, he was—'

'Here is my proposition.' I jab the table with my finger. 'Firstly. The drugs. Whatever you were doing with them—'

'They weren't even mine. Lottie asked me to . . .'

'Never lower your standards to impress anyone. Even when

the girl in question has cheekbones so defined she could use them as a butter knife.'

Callum smiles. 'Random, miss, but noted.'

I study him for shiftiness but find none, so continue. 'You have local residents' status, right? Lived here all your life up until you left in Year Ten?'

He nods. 'Yeah. Both parents born and bred as well. And grandparents.'

'A Guernsey donkey through and through, then.' He nods. 'Great. I'll speak with the school and put together a strong case for you to stay on the island. Child Protection aren't going to send you to your dad if we make it clear it will be detrimental to your education and wellbeing. I'm fairly sure they'll take your wishes into consideration too.

'Next, I'll speak with Trish. I'm hopeful you and your grandad can stay with her in the meantime and then we'll do everything we can to get you into a foster home and your gramps can go on a list for a place in a care home. It's not perfect, but it means you can do your exams and stay in Guernsey afterwards.'

'You'd do that for me, even though you have all this other shit going on?'

'Of course.' His eyes begin to water. 'Oh, Callum.'

'I'm not crying, it's the spiciness.' I hand him a piece of kitchen roll for the tears and the milk for the spice. He declines the milk because of my 'disgusting teacher germs', so I hand him a tub of yoghurt instead, which he wolfs down with his spoon, turning the contents of the pot red.

When we are back at the table, mental notes made to eat the jalfrezi in small doses, I raise the niggle in my brain. 'What were you going to say about seeing Sean in the UK?'

'Oh . . .' Callum smooths his hand over the top of his test paper and then picks at the edge. 'Nothing, miss. I just saw him through the window walking out with some sweets and then he drove off. Terrible driver.'

Chapter Thirty-Five

OK, so I should have checked with Trish about Callum and Cedric moving in *before* mentioning the idea to Callum. It just made the most sense to have them live with a responsible healthcare professional while keeping me close by to monitor revision practices. I also thought that they might give Trish's life a purpose when I leave.

'Charming!' she said when I explained all of this to her. 'And what if I have other plans?'

Despite being grumpy about it, I can tell Trish is fond of her new house guests. She pulled a few strings at the hospital and managed to source a bed for Cedric – one that raises up and down so he can get in and out more easily. We removed Sean's gaming chair from my front garden, dried it off and put it in Trish's office along with the Nintendo Switch and Mario Kart. I left a note for Callum stating that he could benefit from the practice. I also bought a tomato-shaped timer – the synonymous Pomodoro technique device for his revision – and left this for him on the desk in his new bedroom.

Transporting the ormers over from the mansion was a thrill. We packed them into my cool box and hid them under a blanket in the back of Trish's car. As we drove past the police station with a youth, a geriatric and a boot full of stolen shellfish, Trish and I argued over who should store them in their freezer. In the end, I agreed to put them in mine given I'd already dumped the youth and the geriatric on her.

After a few teething issues around Cedric's disturbing penchant for walking out of the house in the dead of night to hitchhike an island tour from friendly car drivers, all went swimmingly with him. I hooked him up at The Soup, and by all accounts (a shouty text from my mum), he is A LOVELY OLD BOY WHO HELPS HAND OUT THE BREAD ROLLS.

Callum has been a good house guest, apart from the fact that he is quite the lady magnet at school and he frequently wants to have girlfriends over to stay.

'I like to think of myself as a free spirit but I just don't enjoy the idea of two underage teenagers bonking on my spare bed . . .' Trish says to me after I witness the swift exit of one of Callum's beaus who sprinted away, not wanting to engage in a post-coital conversation with her dragon of an English teacher.

'. . . It's a Simba Hybrid mattress. It's very comfortable but . . .'

'Porous as fuck?'

'Porous as fuck.'

I laugh. Trish cries.

Keeping myself busy means I can ignore the giant helium balloon I have floating above my head. The pastel-yellow one with the ivory ribbon tied around the base. It inflates a bit more every time I decline a call from my sister or don't read a message from Pierre. During a brief lapse, I had a quick look at the Suzie baby shower WhatsApp group and noted that others have taken over the organising where I have been silent. It's probably for the best if I don't go at all.

I've started putting together lists of things I want to take with me when I leave and have purchased a large backpack that will hold all of my stuff. It took me a while to get over the confusion that they give you the size of these bags in litres on the website. *Litres?* How has this idiocy not been resolved in a marketing meeting by now? What am I supposed to do, melt down all my underpants and pour them into a measuring jug?

You can't fly heavily pregnant, so my boat to the UK is booked the day after I go on maternity leave. I'll travel with Louisa bump still on and then I'll dump her when I get to Poole, head to Heathrow, then fly to Nashville the following day. I finally got the deal I wanted on my flights, and I even discovered the details for a joint credit card I'd forgotten about when I was sorting through some documents and gifted myself all the Avios points – mostly Sean's – linked to it, giving me a top-notch discount on a fabulous convertible hire car. It's not the pink Chevrolet I envisaged, but it will still look cool as hell zooming along those dusty US roads.

I've had a lot of fun planning my road trip route once I've Nashvilled. Yes, I've decided that 'to Nashville' is a verb and it includes (but is not limited to) consuming a lot of liquor, listening to country music, purchasing a whopping cowboy hat and a toe-tapping visit to the Grand Ole Opry.

From Nashville, I'll head on to Dollywood and go on every ride, purchase some pink Dolly merch and eat all the junk food. Then on to the Smoky Mountains for a commercialisation detox. I'll do some hiking and general wholesome fresh air things for a few days. Next, I'll head to Memphis, pay a trip to Elvis in Graceland, and on through Mississippi, do a bayou swamp tour to spot some alligators and then head into New Orleans for more food, liquor and music. I'll finish up somewhere fun in Texas, hopefully via another ranch stay if time and budget allow. I might even write a blog along the way if I can think of a witty enough pseudonym.

I've been worried about running into or hearing from Sean, but neither has happened, thankfully. It's the Easter holidays, so I'm keeping my head down, not seeing anyone in the hope that the bruise fades before I have to return to school.

When she saw the mark on my face, Trish didn't conceal her incandescence. Even when I explained how it actually happened, she stormed about, adamant I should go to the police and lay claim to the house. But I explained that there's no point when I'm leaving anyway. That it's better to sever all ties than have anything that could pull me back here for a trial. Trish conceded but seemed frustrated by it . . . even more than I am, saying how unfair it is that he'll keep the house by default. But it's a price I'm willing to pay for the freedom of it all. My Great Pregnancy Heist.

One night over the holidays while Callum is out with a girlfriend and Cedric is watching *Coronation Street*, Trish joins me for some dinner at mine. I can tell she's preoccupied because she doesn't seem capable of following the conversation (me moaning about backpack litres). Eventually, she interrupts me.

'I'm in a custody battle for Ripley . . .' I put my fork

down mid-spaghetti twist. 'I haven't mentioned it until now because there's been a lot going on this end and also, well, I don't want Callum to hear about it given his own stepmum, you know . . . didn't want him.'

'Do you . . . do you have a chance of winning?'

She shakes her head. 'It's slim. I'm told the court will probably side with her biological dad. She lives with him and her nan, who was all right with me to begin with but he's spun some lies about me. Engineered it so I barely see Ripley except on the weekly FaceTime. I think he's hoping the bond will get weaker if he limits contact as much as possible.'

'Prick.'

'Yep.'

I take a sip of water. 'I think it's great you're fighting it but I'd be concerned about uprooting her and bringing her over here . . . won't that work against you?'

'Well . . . that's just it. That wouldn't be my plan.' She twiddles some pasta against a spoon, which is not the Italian way, but now isn't the time to be pedantic. 'I'd move back to where she is . . . This was only ever temporary, my stay over here. My contract at the hospital's up soon, and with you off . . . it's a natural end.'

'What about Callum?'

'Ripley has to be my priority.'

'I do understand.' I add another spoonful of parmesan to my plate but can't bring myself to eat more at present. I sit back in my chair, ready to articulate something that has been niggling for a while. 'It just seems so unfair that Callum doesn't get to be . . . he acts all grown up and independent but he's still so young. When I was fifteen, I was going to the beach, applying too much Body Shop tea tree to my acne and had a mild infatuation with Eminem.'

Trish laughs.

'I can't shake off the feeling that he's going to be forced to grow up more quickly than he should have to . . . does that make sense?'

Trish nods. 'Perhaps we should do a bit more to make Callum as prepared for adulthood as we can.'

'Hmmm . . . he doesn't respond well to being bossed around . . . but maybe we can do it without him noticing!' I go to my bureau and take out a notepad for us to make a list of nuggets of wisdom.

When I sit back at the table, Trish places her hand on top of mine. 'Thank you for understanding about the Ripley thing. Besides, it will be rubbish in Guernsey once my favourite cantankerous neighbour buggers off into the sunset.'

I hold my wine glass up for her to clink.

We set to work putting together a detailed programme of lessons for Callum – like an inverted finishing school. We teach him how to make a sofrito (me) – onions in cold oil always, garlic never – and the importance of changing one's sheets every week to avoid bed-bug infestations (Trish).

Callum is responsive, but when I interrupt him and his latest squeeze in the middle of a snog to show him how to iron a shirt, he becomes less willing.

It comes to a head when Trish, Callum, Cedric and I are eating dinner one night, discussing the amusing stories in the day's *Press* and, off the back of one article describing how a driver ignored a road closure sign and his car fell in a ditch, Trish comes out with, 'And, speaking of vehicles, when travelling on London's Underground, if one thinks they can smell urine or vomit, even the tiniest whiff, it most definitely is and it is strongly advised to change carriages.'

Callum slams his hand on the table. 'Right, that's it, you unsubtle pair of trollops. If you're so desperate to teach me life lessons, can you please just do it? And preferably not when I'm about to get my end away.'

While I show mock affront at being described as 'a trollop', and genuine disgust at 'end away', Trish puts her arm around him, laughing. He recoils a bit but doesn't shrug it off. They stay like that for a while and I hate myself for secretly hoping she loses the custody battle so this living arrangement can continue.

Chapter Thirty-Six

Callum flicks through the bundle of information I have put together for the hearing on Monday – reams of evidence to prove that remaining here is in his best interest. He stares at everything: position statements from all the heads of department, Julie and Suzie's letters of support. Tim Bell has written a poem, which frankly is a bit much, but I appreciate the effort. Even Yolande stepped up, providing us with some guidance on what to include, and liaised with the Committee for Health and Social Care to facilitate. She did it all with an air of superior smugness, of course, but it was helpful. I've also included Callum's excellent essay on *Death of a Salesman* written at my kitchen table as an example of his work. The only statement not in there yet is mine.

'Don't worry. I've got one to go in too,' I say when I clock his puzzlement. 'I know exactly what I want to say. I just haven't had a chance to put it down yet.' My phone pings. Another message from Lara requesting a meet-up with her and the boys. I turn my phone face down. 'Have you heard from your dad at all?' I ask.

Callum shakes his head. We had to inform his dad that Callum is back over here and wishes to remain in Guernsey.

In a way, it's good that we haven't heard a peep from him because it would be another hurdle if he demanded Callum come back, but I can't help thinking how sad it is that he doesn't seem to care.

Before I can think of what to say, there is a knock on the door. I shove Louisa on and head to answer it.

It is both wonderful and heart-wrenching to see Pierre there, the memory of his confided story and my guilt over having not responded to his messages since. He is clutching a toolbox. 'I saw Trish in Town and she mentioned in passing you're giving Callum some life lessons . . . she said you have it all covered, but I thought I could take him through some DIY fundamentals.' Pierre clocks the yellowing bruise on my face and his eyes narrow.

Callum comes up and shakes Pierre's hand like old friends reunited.

'Do you two know each other?'

'Callum sometimes hangs out at the gym I go to.'

I turn to Callum. 'Do you?' He shrugs. Pierre is red in the cheeks. 'Have you been running or something?' I ask him.

'No. It's just nice to see you.' He examines my bruise again.

Callum pulls the door wide. 'She's got terrible manners. Come in.'

Callum points out that every DIY hack is on either YouTube or TikTok, so instead they pull my coffee table towards the sofa and attempt to demonstrate some balances from this move-like-animals class at the gym. Callum is far better at it than Pierre and we have a good laugh when Pierre insists on doing this bear crawl movement with my mug of coffee balanced on his back.

'Sean used to go to that class,' I say, as I oversee an apologetic Pierre scrubbing the coffee stain from my carpet.

'Yeah, he did. I think I told you I knew him a bit . . . just to say hello to, really.' Pierre stands up. 'Right. Better head.'

He's done an excellent job of removing the stain, only a wet patch left that will dry in no time. He stops at the door and looks at me. Callum clears his throat and, for some reason, disappears into the kitchen. Pierre looks like he's going to say something, but instead, he puts his hand gently beside my bruised face and kisses me on the cheek. 'Night, Barri.'

I close the door and lean against it for a moment.

Callum comes back in, smirking.

'What?' I ask.

'You two. You're, like . . . completely in love.'

'Pierre and me?! We're just friends, united by our passion for the Sea Fisheries code. I nearly had a heart attack when he stood by the freezer. I felt like the ormers were calling to him: *We're in here, we're in here!*' Callum's doubtful expression compels me to reiterate, 'We are just friends!'

'If you tell me that, I'll believe you . . .' He smiles.

'There's no point in me forming any attachments anyway,' I say. 'I'll be gone soon.' And, because I'm an unstable mentalist, I burst into tears.

Callum grabs me a bunch of loo roll. 'You really need to buy a box of tissues.'

I slump onto Big Blue. 'I'm sorry. I don't know what's wrong with me at the moment.'

He disappears – I assume to escape my insanity – but returns with a cup of coffee. He hasn't done the milk at all well, but I appreciate the gesture. He collapses next to me and rests his arm along the back of the sofa. 'Do you know why I think you're sad?' he asks, dropping his head onto his arm as he looks at me. 'You did this whole pregnancy thing because you had every reason to get away and never come back. But all this stuff has forced you to, like, actually make some mates and now you're crying because deep down you're happy and it's all been built on a foundation of bullshit.'

The imaginary pastel-yellow balloon floating above my head squeaks under the struggle of the helium. 'Pierre was funny about Sean earlier. Did you notice?' I say, not caring how obvious my deflection is.

Callum sits up. 'Sean and the trainer at the gym used to bully him a bit. Take the piss and that.'

'That's just Sean's banter,' I say. The bruise on my face throbs in disagreement. 'Sean didn't recognise you the other day.'

'Puberty, isn't it, miss? And I don't think he pays much attention to people who don't, like, benefit him.' He fiddles with the tassel on a cushion. 'Did he ever tell you much about what he was up to? In the UK?'

'As much as anyone tells their partner about their day-to-day life,' I reply, getting up to tip out the disgusting coffee without Callum noticing.

This is a lie. Sean never liked to talk about his job in England. I just knew that he travelled a lot, visiting various hospitals. My phone buzzes. My sister again. I shove it in my pocket without reading it.

To begin with, when Sean went away for work, I would spend time with my family but that want to see them . . . or anyone, really, seemed to fall away. Sean isn't that close to his family either. I didn't meet his mum until just before the wedding five years ago. She seemed lovely to me, but he was prickly around her. She made us this beautiful ceramic jug as a wedding gift – something she'd been learning how to do in a pottery class. It's this beautiful, wide-bottomed, thin-topped affair with a very pleasing lip. A gorgeous ocean blue and when you pour water from it, it makes a satisfying *glug* sound.

When I opened the gift, I adored it. But as much as I told her again and again how much I liked it, Sean refused to engage. She was longing for him to smile, say thank you and hug her. I decided that there must be some kind of beef there and left it for him to tell me about it in his own time . . . which never happened. They must have patched things up though otherwise there's no way he'd have gone to live with her when he abandoned our marriage.

Callum seeing Sean out in the wild – two worlds colliding out of context – has set me on edge a bit. I feel weirdly jealous that he has this . . . I suppose *insight* into the part of Sean we didn't talk about.

As I tip the contents of the coffee mug out, I catch my blotchy, red eyes in the stainless-steel reflection of the kettle. A hot mess.

My phone vibrates. My sister . . . *again*. I come back to sit beside Callum and type a reply to Lara's Barri? Are you all right?? before deleting it. I fling my phone onto the adjacent armchair. When I look up, Callum is studying me.

'It was never part of the plan to . . . you know . . .' I sigh, thinking about Lara, the boys, Suzie, Pierre. 'They're going to be so hurt when I leave . . . it doesn't sit well.'

'I know, miss.'

I dab a piece of mascara gunk from the inner corner of

my eye with a bit of loo roll. Callum looks so concerned, I force a smile. 'Why did you ask about Sean in the UK?'

Callum is about to respond when Trish whirlwinds through the door, waving her iPad at us. 'My Wi-Fi's gone down, so I need to borrow yours. I'll be quick.' She charges towards the spare room. We hear the familiar sound of a FaceTime ring as she shuts the door behind her.

'What's all that about?' asks Callum.

'She speaks with Ripley every Saturday.'

'Ripley?' says Callum with more horror than is warranted.

'I know, awful name. Not her choice, though.'

Callum frowns, brow furrowed.

'Ripley. Her daughter,' I say. 'She might not have mentioned her to you because . . . well, she's her stepdaughter. Her wife's child from a previous relationship.'

'I knew she had a stepdaughter . . . but I didn't know her name.' Callum drums on the arm of the chair, wired suddenly, shaking his head as if trying to work something out.

'Her wife was a big fan of *Alien*, I guess,' I reply.

Callum stops percussing, looks at me, and then at the framed *Alien* movie poster on my wall. 'Sean's . . .' Callum says.

'God, you're right. How funny!' I take the poster off the wall. 'I don't know why this is still up. I should give it back to him. Good riddance. I hate that film.'

I know it's controversial to hate a film everyone loves, but Callum's shock is an overreaction. He's breathing heavily now, his head shaking slightly as if he is an overheating computer processor.

Trish comes out of the study, glowing. 'She's doing her Rainbow Promise tomorrow, so I gave her a pep talk. Though I feel bad for her as her dad's away and—'

Callum snatches Trish's iPad from her hand.

'Callum!'

Callum presses the button and stares at the wallpaper on her screen: The photo of Trish, her wife and Ripley on holiday.

'It's her,' he says. 'She's his. I saw them at the service station, heard him call her name . . .' He looks at Trish, eyes narrowed. '. . . But I didn't know . . .'

Trish's face loses all its colour. It's like a horror is playing out in front of her . . . well, between them both, actually, and I'm just not following. I look between them a few times while they have some kind of staring stand-off. I feel stupid . . . like I'm watching something with a simple plot, but I don't understand it.

'Don't, please,' Trish begs.

Callum points at Trish. 'She's not who she says she is.'

'I bloody well am,' Trish replies.

'OK, well, you haven't told her though, have you?'

I'm still feeling like I came to watch *Barbie,* but they've put on *Oppenheimer* by mistake. 'Told me what?'

Callum turns to me. 'That your wanker husband is her stepkid's . . . he's Ripley's dad.'

Chapter Thirty-Seven

My brain is on fire; synapses linking, loose connections soldered into place.

The Machine Starts.

I think about all the times Sean and I joked about his secret life with his other UK wife. Carrie, we called her. Barri and Carrie. We joked about all the things Carrie did better than me – she made better toast, made an effort with her appearance, managed the household expenses with the expertise of a tax lawyer, and walked around in pristine beige velour tracksuits like a boring but immaculate influencer selling a mundane life as aspirational.

All the time, there wasn't another wife, but another life.

Trish's iPad FaceTime goes again. I take it from Callum.

'Don't, Barri,' Trish begs.

I slide to answer. The voice on the screen is familiar but formal. 'I meant to ask you about the summer holidays, the lawyer said that—'

Sean's mum Kerry stops mid-sentence when she sees my face staring back at her. Eye to eye for the first time since our wedding. Kerry is surprised to see me, but she gathers herself.

'Barri!' And then with suspicion, 'I didn't know you knew Trish?'

'I know about Ripley,' I say. The shape of her name in my mouth cuts; the R, a rotary blade slicing through me.

'I wanted him to tell you, Barri.'

I think about the wedding, all the curt conversations behind closed doors. That was why everything was off that day. Not a family with old skeletons in the closet, but a teeny tiny new skeleton fusing inside another person. Now a fully formed human herself with Rainbow Promises to make.

And the irony is not lost that behind me is that beautiful jug Kerry made us for our wedding day, to celebrate my marriage to her son. The vows we made that warranted the crafting of that jug. I imagine the deceit and lies and guilt that got soaked into it as she spun it on the wheel. Seeping from her hands into a thing so beautiful with gorgeous glugging capabilities. I realise that's why Sean never wanted it in the first place. He knew the displeasure that osmosised into it. I can't bear the thought of the deception. It quickens like waters breaking.

I hang up and stare at Trish. 'This whole time, you . . . you kept this . . .'

'Barri,' Trish says. 'There are so many things to explain.'

I need to think about the chain of events before I hear Trish's. Carve out my own timeline here. But I also know in the back of my head that the minute I ended the call with Sean's mum, a frantic message would have been typed to him, letting him know what I know. A mother's son, no matter what he has done.

'Callum, I think you had better meet your grandad at the church.' He doesn't argue, just gives me a look that says, *I'm sorry I didn't tell you.* I squeeze his arm. 'It's OK.'

Trish and I head to the kitchen where all the brutal conversations happen. No glasses of good wine this time. I undo Louisa and wriggle her off so I can lock her away in the next room. I don't want her to hear it. Or maybe I don't want anything that links the camaraderie this woman and I once shared.

I go through the facts in my head. Trish moved in next door a few months after Sean left me. She befriended me, guided me, consoled me, made me feel . . . likeable. And the whole time, she had this colossal secret. A secret as big as mine. For some reason, I lead with the most un-urgent question imaginable. 'Are you not really an obstetrician?'

'No. I mean, yes. I am really. Genuinely, I'm an obstetrician,' she replies.

'You and Sean are working together? He knows about the fake pregnancy and you're using it to get the house?' I think about the two of them colluding, laughing at my expense, enjoying the perfect serendipity that I needed a medical professional to help me fake this. And there she was.

'No, Barri. I hate Sean. He doesn't know I'm here. Neither did his mum until . . . they think I live in Cornwall.' She rests her hand on top of mine on the worktop. 'In Polperro.'

'Why the fuck is that relevant?'

'I don't know. I thought you'd enjoy the specificity.'

I snatch my hand away from hers, leaving a greasy mark on the surface of the counter. I didn't realise I was sweating until then. Of course Barri Brown gets clammy with rage. She could never be dry in the face of betrayal. 'The only specificity I want is the truth.'

She nods, conceding. 'Sean had an affair with Lil before I met her. Started about six months before you got married.'

Given that there's now a five-year-old skipping about the

planet, this shouldn't be a shock, but hearing it out loud stings like a whip. 'So what's the money got to do with it all?' I ask.

'I didn't know about that until you told me, but I think . . .' She grimaces like I need to brace myself to hear this. 'I know there was a plan for him to leave you to be with her . . . before the two of you were married. She was skint and, with a baby on the way . . .'

'He was going to steal it from me.' I look through the window at the bright sunny day outside. Where's the thunder and lightning? Pathetic fallacies on demand should be the God-given right of English teachers everywhere.

'But then Lil saw sense, thank God.'

'How did he meet her?'

'Through work . . . she was a nurse. He'd come into her hospital to do a demo of some kind and they hit it off. He showered her with all these extravagant gifts and things, made her feel safe and loved, despite only seeing her when he was over there. But when she fell pregnant, he got more stressed out about what was going on. He became moody and controlling. Didn't like her seeing her friends. You know, red flags.' She gives me a concerned look, no doubt because I didn't spot the warning signs. 'She called it off, he married you, and visited Ripley whenever he could.' Trish smiles despite herself. 'I met Lil about a year and a half after all that and we were so happy.' She drops her head. 'And then she got ill last year. We got married shortly after that. We loved each other, but also, we thought I'd have a better chance of custody if it was made official . . . but he's so . . . wily.'

I lower myself onto a stool. There was a definite point last year when Sean's moodiness got even worse. The threat of Lil dying jeopardising his big secret. Maybe that's why he was suddenly so keen for us to have our own baby. A permanent tie between us would force me to stick with him when I found out about Ripley's existence.

Trish paces, hyped up now. 'When Lil died, he refused to let Ripley stay in her family home with me, and despite my having a strong claim, the courts decided she should go with him. He's her dad, I'm just the stepmum after all. He left you, moved in with his mum and brought Ripley there. Her whole world upended overnight.'

'But why remortgage?'

Trish shrugs. 'The legal fees for a start . . . his lawyers are top tier.' She lowers her head. 'He needs money in the bank too, to show he can support her, build a home. He probably . . . panicked a bit.'

I picture Sean swooping into Ripley's life every couple of weeks before Lil got ill. Fun Dad. Perhaps the twenty-four-seven reality of fatherhood made the idea of reuniting with me more appealing. It explains why he came back. Maybe he saw my pregnancy as an advantage because me doing that to him – getting pregnant with a child that isn't his – would soften the blow of his own betrayal?

She takes my hand again. 'I'm not going to tell anyone the truth, about the pregnancy, or—'

I snatch my hand away again. 'Is that a threat?' She looks genuinely hurt by my question.

'No, not at all. I'm really not.' Trish rests her head on her forearms. 'It was unbearable, Barri, keeping all this from you, but what choice did I have? Callum's story about his stepmum abandoning him – I wasn't going to let that be part of Ripley's narrative. I want to be her mum whether she came out of my womb or not.' She looks up at me. 'He's not cut out to be a dad. Especially not to a little girl.'

The defence of him tumbles out of my mouth like I'm on autopilot. 'Of course he's cut out to be a dad.'

Trish lets out a sigh of exasperation. 'He's a controlling, manipulative misogynist. Look what he did to you! Cheating, cutting you off from your family, making you think you didn't need friends, stealing your money behind your back, h-hitting you . . . or as good as hitting you, anyway.'

The realisation of it comes at me full force. Of course Sean doesn't have what it takes to be a good father. He's not even a good person. I've been completely blindsided by love . . . or what I thought was love.

'So why did you move to Guernsey if Ripley was over in the UK?'

She rests her hands on the edge of the worktop and leans back, turning her head to face the ground. 'I came here to get the dirt on him so I could have a stronger case for custody, all right?' She looks up at me. 'The job came up and then the house next door. It felt . . . he's the biological father. I needed something solid I could use to prove that I'd be better for her than he would. He said he had property here, a supportive wife. I needed to see whether that was true . . . and what kind of person you were. To vet you I suppose.' She sits down opposite me. 'And then I found out you were faking the pregnancy . . .'

The realisation smashes like an unreturnable cross-court volley. I lower my head. 'You were going to expose my lie to help you win the case.'

She pauses, tears brimming. Eventually, she nods. 'I was going to deny knowledge of the signed medical form – say you forged my signature. And it wouldn't have taken much to spin it to sound like Sean was involved with the fraud.'

She goes to the window; her shameful face reflects back at me in the glass. 'But I couldn't . . .' She turns to me and perches on the sill. 'I realised I couldn't and wouldn't exploit you. You . . . to be honest, you did help me through my grief and I realised that whatever happened with Ripley, I couldn't use you. I made myself a promise to get you through this idiotic plan. You deserve it. You deserve to be happy.'

'And it suited you for me to be out of the picture.'

If you told a child to draw a sad face, that is what Trish's looks like right now. Not a sun salutation any more. A hell valediction. She walks towards me. I back up against the fridge; its humming sounds like mockery.

'Sean stole from both of us. He wouldn't let me see Ripley at all when Lil died – I had to get a court order. It's so degrading when I know for a fact that if that kid fell over and she had the choice of getting comfort from me or him, she'd run to me. I only get to chat to her once a week on FaceTime through his twat of a mum.'

I move towards the breakfast bar and lean my forearms on it. 'She makes beautiful water jugs.'

'Doesn't make her not a twat though, does it? Everything's mediated through Kerry. I think they're hoping the less Ripley talks to me, the more she'll want to stay with them.' Trish pinches the bridge of her nose like she has a headache. 'Sean and I only met once before, briefly. I'm not sure he even looked at me properly . . . but I've been very careful since I heard he was back.'

The headscarf she's been wearing every time she leaves the sodding house. Trish once told me she didn't wish to have an online presence. Paranoid about some AI stealing her face and making her an extra in every Hollywood movie for ever more. I think back to the night we discussed it, laughing our heads off at the idea of her expressive little face being part of every Hollywood blockbuster ever made. In the background of huge movie franchises and Sundance Film Festival winners. Superimposed onto naked bodies and dead bodies, helmetless Stormtroopers, livid pitchfork carriers, and relaxed people in cafes drinking coffee. Like the expressive, visual version of the Wilhelm scream. But it was probably because she didn't want to be in photographs posted online. Anything that could link her to me.

She takes my hands, grasping them tightly as I try to snatch them away. 'Barri, help me, please. You can give a statement, tell the court what he's like.' I tug my hands free of her grip. She flings hers up in exasperation. 'Why didn't you want to have kids with him, then?' she asks. 'A part of you must have known.'

'I don't understand why people can't just accept that Sean or no Sean, I didn't want a fucking baby!' The eff of 'fuck' ejaculates over the counter, adding to the greasy clamminess. I wipe it with my elbow. 'Sorry.'

She sits on the stool opposite. 'No, I'm sorry. I'm so, so sorry. It has been such a burden and then seeing you carry your secret, knowing that every relationship you've built in the past few months has been based on a lie . . .'

I examine her, trying to work out if she is being genuine or presenting me with unsubtle subtext: you lied to everyone else, just like I lied to you. We're as bad as each other.

The words are left unspoken between us: the past few months have been based on a lie. Apart from our relationship. Mine and Trish's. That was the only bit of truth I had.

Chapter Thirty-Eight

My sister grasps my upper arms. 'Oh God, Barri, what is it? Are the babies OK? What's happened?'

I suppose it does come across as a little alarming that I've turned up here tear-sogged and out of the blue after weeks of ignoring all her texts and calls.

I know I've caught her at a terrible moment because I can see through the house to the garden, where Yolande and her husband are laughing with Dave around a barbecue. For once, Yolande is in a well-fitting dress and I nearly forget my woes in the relief that she is shaped like an actual human underneath it all.

Since last night, I've thought long and hard about what to do. As much as I didn't want to face the 'Well, really, what did you think he was doing when he was away all that time?' I have to confide in someone, and my go-to person just deceived me in the most hurtful way imaginable.

My sister pulls me into the first available room. The downstairs toilet. My bump nearly takes up the entire space, and I implore the world of karma to cut me some slack that Lara knows me well enough to not invade my personal space by touching it.

'Why are we in here?'

'I thought you wouldn't want to see Yolande and, well . . . she's not the most discreet person, is she?'

'I thought she was your bestie?!'

'God no.' Lara wipes away a mirror smudge with her sleeve. 'I'm trying to phase her out like your busy diary CEO thing.'

'Why is she in your back garden, then?'

'I forgot to reschedule her, didn't I?' She turns back towards me, leaning against the sink. Her legs are so long, the basin rests comfortably beneath her bum cheeks. 'At least she's not dressed like a fucking handmaid today. Scares the hell out of Harry – Luke told him the ghosts of five dead Victorian children live under that stupid oversized smock skirt she wears.'

I realise to my detriment that I have underestimated my sister's taste in people. I make a mental note to buy Luke a gothic novel for his next birthday to accompany the inevitable football-related gift. But then I remember I won't be here to see him open it.

Lara double-takes as she clocks the inconsistency of my face colour where my bruise hasn't healed. She switches the light on above us and cups my cheeks in horror. 'What happened!?' It is difficult at first. The sticky formality hasn't fully dissolved between us. But as she clutches my face, my bruise throbbing in solidarity, I tell her about Sean, the house, Ripley and Trish's betrayal.

The two of us stand in that toilet for so long, Dave comes to check Lara hasn't dropped dead. It's quite astonishing, the way she dismisses him – so direct, secure in the knowledge that whatever tone she uses to make him go away, he will still love her . . . because the partner she chose realises she has something else going on beyond the circle of his immediate world. After a marriage spent not treading on eggshells, but hovering above them, yet again, I find myself envying my sister. I wonder if the animosity that existed between us for so long isn't the narrative I've woven in my head, but something closer to what Trish said. That I have allowed myself to become isolated from her . . . it's not something I want to admit out loud. I am a strong person. Firm in my convictions. A formidable teacher and woman. It's embarrassing to think I've let someone walk over me so effectively while being oblivious to it.

I want to say something – to acknowledge that there's most definitely something in our relationship that I have messed up – but she's now ranting about police and lawyers and articles in newspapers.

'You aren't going to write about this. I'm not a way for you to finally get your opinion piece into some tabloid.'

'I'm more of a broadsheet writer actual—'

I hold my hand up. 'I came to you as my sister.'

'Think about the babies, Barri. If you don't want to go to the police for you, do it for them. Show them what a fighter their mama is.'

And I don't know if it is the closeness or the cheek holding or the disgusting use of the word 'mama' but it just comes out. 'I'm not going to be a mum, Lara.'

Lara looks down at my bump. She smiles. 'Whether you like it or not, you are.'

I want so badly to keep going. Tell her no, there are no babies. I've deceived you all and screwed it all up, but then we hear the sound of a car revving down the driveway.

Lara rises onto her tiptoes like a graceful ballerina to look out the window. 'It's Sean! For fuck's . . . how does he . . .?'

'There's only so many places . . .'

'Stay in here.' She charges out of the toilet.

I drag out the stool Lara keeps under her sink, left over from when the boys weren't able to reach the taps. I stand on it and peer out at Sean, feeling like a nearly caught adulterer looking for a safe exit. It isn't lost on me that I'm the adulteree and should not have to be the one hiding.

Lara's driveway is on a steep slope that begins at the top of the road and slants all the way down towards her house, lined by large, decorative chunks of Guernsey granite. Most guests park at the top and walk down rather than navigate it, but not Sean.

The impact of his sudden arrival is diminished by his Austin Powers-esque inability to reverse the hire car into the space available and I can't help enjoying the spectacle as he scuffs the side of it on a jutty-out piece of rock. There's no way he'll have taken out the extra liability on the car insurance. The satisfaction of watching him struggle and the apprehension over what is about to happen circle around each other like oil through vinegar.

When he clambers out, he's sweaty and agitated. My sister studies him, arms crossed, a vicious smile on her lips. I reason that Sean isn't stupid enough to reveal his true self to anyone but me. Not while there is an opportunity to wriggle out of the situation he finds himself in.

I think about the person Ripley might become under his guardianship. He will love her for sure, but I imagine a possessive love. A Daddy's Princess with high castle walls around her, just enough encouragement to do something with her life, but a conventional something. Nothing outrageous, no crazy dream-big goals. An agreeable, dutiful daughter, because God help her if she chooses to be anything else.

Ripley's life under the custody of Trish is one of laughter, warmth and endless possibility. A world not restricted by her bond to a parent. It wouldn't be a transactional love. She would have a safe place to escape to, a happy bolthole and it wouldn't matter if she did things that disappointed her dad because she would have a mum who backed her and encouraged her to be whoever she wanted to be. If Trish ever gets to be in Ripley's life.

The childproof window in Lara's downstairs loo only opens a crack so it is a weigh-up between watching them and not being able to hear much or holding my ear up to the window so I can get a sense of what's being said but not being able to see. I decide ear is more useful to me. I also reason that if Sean were to look in the direction of the toilet, an ear would be more easily mistakeable for the leaf of an exotic plant.

Sean has just finished a self-indulgent monologue because my sister sounds exhausted when she tells him I'm not here and to leave before she calls the police.

'You can't make me,' he says, still the toddler. 'What the fuck are you doing?!' I switch to watching through the small crack in the window. Lara is filming him on her phone. Sean is trying to regulate himself, all too aware that the filming has added another level of risk to his image. He holds his hands up in a conciliatory gesture and is just about to turn to leave when Dave comes out, looking for Lara. Dave's appearance seems to have empowered her further. I hold my ear to the window.

'You weren't cut out to be a husband and you're definitely not cut out to be a dad. Your daughter's better off without you and so are Barri's babies,' Lara says.

Sean yells, monster-like. I watch him launch towards Lara, but Dave intervenes using his good arm to hold Sean back. They start tussling instead, Dave's bad arm bouncing around precariously in its sling. No doubt summoned by the noise, Yolande's husband runs out to break them up.

I pass Luke and Harry in the hallway. They are holding hands, watching the events unfold with concern. Their eyes brighten when they see me.

'It's OK,' I say. 'Uncle Sean's a bit upset, but he'll be leaving soon. Go and play some football.' I give them both a reassuring pat on the head and go outside.

At school, we have this power of five thing for the Year Sevens and Eights. You hold up five fingers above your head and count them down silently: four, three, two, one. By one, they always stop what they are doing. Like they are programmed. Once the hormones kick in and they wise up to the fact they have autonomy, it stops working. I never use this method. I believe the students need not be patronised the minute they enter my classroom. This rabble of adults, however . . .

I move into the centre of the ruckus and hold my hand up – five fingers. The utter bemusement makes them all stop as I count down my fingers in slow motion.

'Barri.' Sean darts towards me. 'I . . . you have to give me time to explain.'

'What is there to explain?' says Lara. 'You're a thief, a cheat and a liar.'

Yolande's face is one of pure delight as she sniffs out some premium-rate gossip. She waves at someone behind me as if to say, hurry or you'll miss the fireworks. I turn. Suzie and Xavier, a bottle of wine and flowers in hand, are heading towards us. Xavier is holding Suzie's arm as they navigate the steep downward slope of the drive. They look surprised to see me here and eye Sean nervously. And then, from round the side of my sister's house, out lollops Pierre in actual clothes for a change. Chino shorts, T-shirt and deck shoes. An idiotic bucket hat with smiley faces on it, but still. No Crocs.

'OK, so this is really weird,' I say to no one in particular.

My sister looks sheepish now. No wonder she wanted me to stay in the toilet. She turns to me. 'We've all been worried about you. You've been cutting yourself off again, and we thought . . .' She eyes Sean. 'We suspected external forces were at play. So we all got chatting and . . . well, we decided we'd get together to work out how to, you know . . . so we invited everyone over to discuss it.'

Yolande's smug face drops. This is news to her too, having been an uncancelled guest.

'So . . . you're all here because you think I need some kind of . . . what? Help?'

Dave puts his arm around my sister and she wriggles into him. 'No, silly. We were just . . .'

And then Suzie, always the moral compass, comes out with it. 'Trish told me what happened between you yesterday . . . about her and . . . and so we thought we'd get together and strategise.'

Sean looks like a rabbit in between seven pairs of bright headlights.

I turn to my sister, who minutes ago in the bathroom

pretended the revelation of Sean being Ripley's dad was all news to her. She talks to my ear rather than meeting my eye. 'And the weather is so nice and Dave wanted to try out the new smoker. So we thought . . . why not make an afternoon of it?'

'An intervention barbecue?' I ask.

'More like the first meeting of Barri's support bubble,' adds Pierre.

I look around at my friends and family. Where I should be feeling irritation, instead, there is unadulterated affection for this gathering of folk around me. There isn't mockery or derision here. Just love . . .

Sean is trying to catch my eye. His expression says, *Come on Barri, don't fall for it. We laugh at these people. They are boring and tiresome. Not worth our time.* I meet his gaze. 'I don't want to see you again. Ever.' He goes to interrupt but I stop him, empowered by my witnesses. 'There's nothing you can say or do to change my mind so I think it's for the best that you go and leave me to enjoy this beautiful barbecue with my people.' I cringe inwardly at 'my people' as soon as the words leave my mouth but I style it out with a smile.

Pierre beams, my sister grows even taller, and Suzie, of course, is a beautiful crier.

Sean takes in this Barri love-fest in disgust, his chest heaving as he tries his best to suppress his rage.

'Your worst nightmare is happening right now, eh?' I say. 'You showed these people who you really are long before I ever saw it, but now I see it too.' I hold my stomach. 'And that's why I'm so relieved I'm not having these babies with you.'

He charges towards me, but Pierre – gentle, sweet Pierre – holds a forearm up to Sean's face, blocking his path. Blood bursts out of Sean's nose, little flecks of red spattering Lara's driveway. The others join Pierre, side by side like shieldless riot police. Pierre continues to hold his ground. 'You've lost, Sean. So I suggest you just . . . fuck off,' he says.

'Yes,' I say. 'Fuck off, Sean.'

It's like I'm the underdog hero of a sports movie and I have finally won the gold. My friends and family cheer. Harry jumps up and down. Doesn't quite crack a smile, but I know he feels it on the inside. Even Yolande looks happy for me.

Sean gets into his scratched hire car. The bright yellow sticker with the black H on the back, which signifies it's hired, should stand for 'humiliated!'. I focus on that sticker, trying my best to keep it together. The lights switch on as he starts the engine. He's leaving. I exhale, antenatal style, still fixating on that H.

By the time I realise the H is getting bigger, not smaller, it is too late. The engine roars as Sean attempts to ride the clutch to correct the failed handbrake start. But it's a pointless endeavour. The car rolls backwards towards me.

Chapter Thirty-Nine

The car hits me smack in the stomach, jamming me up against Dave's Range Rover. There is a collective gasp from everyone. Lara screams. They run towards me.

'I'm fine, I'm fine,' I say.

'But the babies!' yells Lara. She turns to Dave. 'Call an ambulance.'

Sean pulls forward, but not before the car does another accidental nudge backwards into my stomach. A collective sound of shock again as I'm rammed further against Dave's bumper.

As the car pulls forward off me, my stomach is no longer the round, pregnant shape it was before. The foam has burst out of Louisa's side, leaving a bumper-shaped hole. A chasm where a bomb just exploded.

They stare at me in fixated horror. Lara, Dave, Harry, Luke, Suzie, Xavier, Yolande, her husband and Pierre. Gorgeous, kind, brave Pierre.

Time's up, Barri, Louisa says.

I unstrap her from my belly and place her at the feet of my loved ones. A most unwanted sacrifice.

Sean's laugh is cruel. 'Oh. My. God!' Everyone else is silent.

I keep my gaze fixed on Louisa. Foam bursting through the seam. Better give that a good stitch-up. No, wait. That won't be necessary.

'Oh, Barri . . . what have you done?' As long as I live, I will never forget the hurt and disappointment in my sister's voice.

Sean clears his throat and opens the passenger door for me. I have every intention of sprinting past him, running away. He's a thief, a cheat and a liar . . . But, then again, so am I.

I get in beside him and I don't dare look back in the mirror as we drive away.

Chapter Forty

Everything feels like grief.

Including that moment when you wake up in bliss for a millisecond and can't remember the worst of it before realising your life will never be the same again.

When we left Lara's, Sean wouldn't let me out of his sight. I think I heard Trish's voice outside our house at one point . . . a heated discussion, Sean threatening lawyers and police. It didn't register. None of it.

Sean isn't here, but I can tell by the wrinkled bedding that he slept next to me. My bedside clock tells me it's gone two in the afternoon. Not good. I ease out of bed, my lower back bruised from Dave's bumper and my head throbbing from the hangover.

Last night, I worked my way through most of the alcohol cabinet – gin, vodka, Baileys, and even some Lithuanian mead I got given as a gift by the cleaner at school when I helped her with her English for a visa application. I seem to remember Sean giving me the drinks but I must have got carried away. There's a note on the sideboard.

You were a disgrace last night. Clear up before I get home.

I daren't even touch the paper because I don't want to believe that he's back. I've let him back.

Can a robot vacuum cleaner hoover up vomit? There is a lot on the floor in the middle of the living room. The stench of it . . . I look at Gilby, his green fully charged light blinks, compelling me to let him at it. But his compartment is so tiny, all the sicky chunks will be sucked up inside him and then I'll be left to clean the sick out of him, which will be worse than just cleaning it from the floor.

It always puzzles me that whether or not one has consumed sweetcorn in recent days, there always seems to be a chunk of the stuff in vomit. There's a piece right there submerged in the middle between two former carrots. I think of the Guernsey proverb my granny used to tell me: *'There is always a spike of corn lacking in the sheaf.'* Maybe this is where they go, those rogue missing spikes of corn. Here to remind us with every spew that we are lacking.

This bit has been down my oesophagus, bathed in stomach acid and was ready to go on its merry way to my bowels when the vodka and the gin and the Baileys and the Lithuanian mead had other ideas. It had to do the whole arduous journey again in reverse, and it's still in one piece after all of that. Whole and yellow. I envy it.

Fixating on sweetcorn spikes is a diversion tactic, of course, because I don't want to acknowledge the item next to the puddle of sick.

Callum's welfare dossier, spattered with carrot, corn, booze and bile.

Not only have I failed to finish my statement, I've missed the meeting entirely. I yell an expletive and stumble around the house looking for my phone, but it isn't anywhere. Then

I remember Sean took it off me last night. Said all the calls I was getting would be the police, the school, the press. Furious people. There will be gossip. News articles. Better I don't see any of it.

I grab my laptop instead, but no Wi-Fi. I go to inspect the router, but it's not there. Just the marks on the floor where it once was. Sean must have taken it with him. Screw it. I run over to Trish's and hammer on the door. No answer. I look through the window, but I can't see any sign of movement.

I trudge back to mine and opt for scooping the sick with rubber-gloved hands into a carrier bag and putting it in the outside bin. I clear the bottles, emptying them all and washing them out. This is what responsible people do. I scrub the sick patch and then let Gilby hoover it, using some old Shake 'n' Vac I keep in the cleaning caddy.

All the while, I'm turning it over in my head. Callum was counting on me. A fifteen-year-old lad. But the school will have stepped up. Like I have done a hundred times for other people when their children have broken arms or run a temperature or had a toothache. Someone will have been there to cover for me when my own childish behaviour took over.

But the more I think about it, the more it niggles that I have all the documents here. Why didn't I circulate a soft copy on email? Because, Barri, you were too concerned with finishing your statement, writing it in a tangible format, the joy you would get from seeing the impressed social worker flick through it all. A beautifully put-together presentation. Your ego got in the way.

Someone will have stepped in to help.

Sean gets home. The fake pregnancy is all anyone's talking

about. The *Daily Mail* has posted a nasty article calling me selfish and desperate. The thief exploiting the innocent taxpayer. The school has suspended me. None of my family wants to see me. It's important for me to know what is happening so I can face what I've done, but he'll shield me from the worst of it.

I go to bed. Wake up. Sean isn't here. He comes home. Fills me in on the horror.

REPEAT.

Sean has a new job. The one at the health tech fund. It means he will be in Guernsey much more. Better money, and he can be around for Ripley when she moves here permanently. Because he is going to get custody after what Trish did.

Of course, Ripley won't be moving in here. I am a liability. Sean has negotiated a relocation package, setting him and his daughter up in a new home until I can be trusted to act with decorum. He slags off Trish, calling her an abomination for trying to take his little girl away from him. I should tell him that Ripley would be lucky to have Trish in her life, but I don't dare. I just sit there and let him say what he wants.

Callum's hearing went fine, Sean says. Suzie, Julie, Yolande – the cackling bunch of teacher witches – stepped in to help. He's been fostered in Guernsey. It's a small reprieve, knowing he's been looked after, even if I have to live with the fact that I nearly screwed it up for him. Everyone knows Callum knew about the fake pregnancy, Sean tells me, and how I agreed to pay him off to keep quiet, and manipulated his situation to ensure I got away with the fraud. It's only a matter of time before the police come knocking.

Days and days pass.

MOTHERFAKER

I think of Callum often.

One day, as I head to the kitchen to make a cup of tea, something shiny catches my eye by the front door.

An empty ormer shell has been deposited through my letterbox. At first, I think it might be an act of solidarity from Callum, but as I turn it over in my hand, I notice the words etched into the pearlescent inside.

FUCK YOU MISS

Chapter Forty-One

I keep the ormer shell in my pocket as a reminder of what I've done. I feel its weight even when I'm sitting down, and nod in satisfaction every time I forget it's there, plunge my hand into the pocket, and the rough side scratches me. Good.

Liesl, Friedrich, Kurt, Brigitta, Marta and Gretl are in bin bags ready to go to the dump. After fearing him so much in the beginning, Kurt is the hardest to part from. Our tumultuous journey was a bonding exercise . . . I've finally befriended the popular kid. I think about Dave scooping up Louisa from his driveway, examining her material, the foam, and wondering whether she's recyclable. I wanted to ask Sean to fetch her so they can all be together in their final resting place, but I didn't.

I decide to add some more things to the rubbish, so I head up to my wardrobe. The apple-green maternity dress with the knife hole still in it goes straight on the pile, along with the books I ordered on pregnancy. I pick up the diary with all the pregnancy weeks, bumps and vegetables. I flick through it; no idea what date it is today . . . The imaginary foetus could be a butternut squash, cauliflower or lettuce for all I know. I think of my fellow marathon runners from the antenatal class and hope they're all doing well. Especially Suzie.

My hand lands on the bag with the black denim jumpsuit, my immaculate-soled cowboy boots, and the green headscarf I bought on that ill-fated shopping trip with Sean. I lay it out on my bed, boots at the bottom, headscarf at the top and jumpsuit in the middle. It doesn't look right, so I stuff the inside of the jumpsuit with random items of clothing I find. I want to shape a new Barri, the one who wore this outfit out to the pub. That decision might have been just enough to make her realise that even though she is a quirky entity, it doesn't mean she doesn't deserve more. *That* Barri wouldn't have made the mistakes I have. She'd have taken these boots to Nashville without betraying anyone.

As I reach into the wardrobe to find more clothes to stuff her with, I discover the unwashed pair of jeans I wore to transport Dad's ashes from Mum's airing cupboard to Belle Greve. I will the remnants of him inside the pockets to energise. Particles spinning to form the shape of the man they once were. Just then a gust of wind blows through the window, causing the curtain to parachute. What if that flurry collected the rest of him from Belle Greve and swooshed him all the way over here to join the bits of ash that have been hiding out in my wardrobe? I imagine them combining to form the shape of him sitting in the armchair in the corner, drinking a cup of tea out of his favourite 'Gone Ormering' mug. Derek Brown.

'I'm sorry, Dad.'

'I know you are, Bazza.' He'd take a sip of tea, his fingers stained with oil and grease. 'But this ain't the worst thing anyone has ever done. This ain't even the worst thing anyone in this family has done. Look at me.'

MOTHERFAKER

Dad's posthumous pep talk is interrupted by a knock at the door. I can't help thinking he's sent me a gift from beyond. The perfect person to scoop me up and repair me in this moment of need. I thump down the stairs, fling open the door and—

'Oh. It's you.'

PC Pluckrose stands with her default deadpan expression.

I wonder if she's also thinking about the time I waved my tits at her in a gratuitous fashion.

She looks at my flat stomach. 'Can I come in?'

PC Pluckrose examines my immaculate living room while I make the coffee. My hands shake so much as I froth the milk that the air hose keeps breaking the surface of the liquid, spitting foam at me. If she was here to arrest me, she'd have given me my rights on the doorstep. And she's not demanding I go to the station for an interview or anything. So . . . why is she here?

I come back into the living room with our mugs. 'Am I in trouble with the police?'

She purses her lips like she wants to say yes. 'No.' She leans back on Big Blue. 'If you'd got as far as claiming the maternity-leave money, that would be a different story, but even I can't arrest someone for sticking a cushion up their jumper for four and a half months. At the end of the day, it's just poorly judged clothing.'

'Oh,' I say. 'Why are you here, then?'

'The drug search thing . . .' We both shudder. '. . . I'm fairly sure now that you stashed some gear for Le Brocq.' I move to argue but she interrupts me. 'That's by the by now.' She looks down at her mug. 'I'm on a final warning with the whole double taser situation and then not even noticing a fake pregnancy bump . . . I'm . . . well . . .'

'Worried it won't look great from an optics standpoint?' I offer.

'Yep.' She takes a sip of her drink. 'Good coffee.'

'Thanks.'

'I mean . . . I get that in a few years' time it will be a funny story for dinner parties and that . . .'

'Oh, I very much doubt I'll be invited to a dinner party any time soon, or ever, given the circumstances . . .'

'. . . But I'm hoping maybe you can keep my name out of it?'

I study this strange, clammy woman with a stain on her top that I am sure is dried egg yolk. I'd bet money she bit into a bagel upside down. I imagine her cursing when she noticed the yellow had seeped through the hole. Colleagues clocking it and rolling their eyes.

I consider the fact that had this harmless PC been more competent, it's very likely that I would have been caught. And, besides, she was right. I was stashing the drugs. I smile at her as kindly as I can. 'PC Pluckrose, we can call it quits. I won't say a word.'

She smiles – 'Cheers. Nice one' – and plonks her mug on the coffee table *next* to the coaster.

As I show her out, she looks around the house. 'Immaculate.' Her tone is almost accusatory. Like she suspects I've cleaned up after a murder.

'Not much else to do at the moment.'

She bends down to tie her shoelace in the doorway, which irks me. I can't help wishing she'd waited until she was outside and I'd closed the door, as it means I have to wait here politely. This is exacerbated by one of the laces having formed a separate knot around itself, which she seems intent on untangling.

'Before I became a PC, I was a probation officer,' she says, doing the bunny-ear lace-tying method. 'Early twenties. Green as you like. You know who one of my first probationers was?' She looks up at me, smiling. 'Derek Brown.'

'You're kidding!'

'Charming man, actually. Shame some of that didn't rub off on you a bit more.' She stands up, folds her arms and leans on the doorframe, which bunches her padded police vest up around her face, puffing her cheeks up, cherub-like. 'It hit him hard, you know. Having to build himself up all over again when he got out.'

I'm stunned. It had never occurred to me before that Dad found anything in life hard. 'He always seemed so . . . solid.'

'To you, he did. But he wasn't. Not for a long time. But once he got over the fact that the fancy hot-shot job and the nice house weren't who he was any more, he stopped letting his ego get in the way of getting back out there, despite the shame he felt. And, over time, he got to learn who he was without all that facade. And he was all right in the end.' She pats the doorframe. 'For what it's worth . . . See ya.'

As I go to close the door on her, feeling like some of the heaviness has lifted, a dash of ivory catches my eye.

A strand of the gorgeous ribbon I bought for Suzie's bunting is caught on the wood of the door. It flutters in the wind like a piece of evidence at a crime scene. I shout after PC Pluckrose. 'What's the date today?'

She looks at her watch. 'Er . . . Saturday the second of May.'

There's still time.

Chapter Forty-Two

It's only 11 a.m. and Suzie's baby shower isn't until four. I use the next few hours to finish the bunting as best I can. It doesn't look quite as perfect without the ribbon running along the top but I make do by threading some brown string through the long side of the triangles instead. I take the pearls that popped off when Sean stole the ribbon and use a glue gun to stick one to each letter. The final effect is rustic, but not terrible. Even if Suzie flings it onto the wood burner of her eco pod, I hope she takes a moment to appreciate how much effort went into it.

I fish out the selection of books I chose for the baby. A few childhood classics and my all-time favourite, *Goodnight Mister Tom*. As an afterthought, I throw in my ancient and battered copy of E. M. Forster's *The Machine Stops and Other Stories*, as I don't think a child can ever be too young for a dash of dystopia.

While wrapping everything up, I go over the plan again. Go to the baby shower, apologise, find out where Callum is and apologise to him and then be back here before Sean even notices. Even if they don't accept it, at least I will have said what I need to and I can move on. Start anew like Dad did.

The only person I won't see today is Pierre, but I don't feel ready yet. The look on his face when he realised I'd been lying about the babies is impossible to get out of my head and I can't begin to imagine the pain it's caused him after everything he's been through. I refuse to let the shame float up into a helium balloon. I don't deserve the reprieve. Instead, it sits with me alongside the ormer shell in my pocket.

I jump on Melva for the first time in months. It feels fantastic riding her again, even if it is a lot tougher on my legs after so long not doing it. I navigate past a group I presume recently arrived via a cruise ship, marching along in their hats, shorts and walking boots. They are in for a treat; the bluebells will be out in full force.

I pull up outside Suzie's and sneak around the side of the house. Everyone is here – Lara, Suzie, Julie, Yolande, some more of our colleagues, and a few people I presume are her other friends. I recognise her sister from the silly picture she has on her WhatsApp profile, pulling a face inside one of those cut-out seaside things you put your head into. She looks better as a human than an octopus.

Whoever completed the organisation of the event has done a decent job. The balloon archway over the trestle table with the enormous pile of gifts and pastel cupcakes on it looks lovely. I don't approve of the literal Spotify playlist, though. 'Baby Love' blares out. But I'm not in a position to pick fault with anyone at the moment.

I decide to wait until Suzie has opened her presents and the novelty of the surprise has worn off a bit before I make my appearance. I remain hovered in the little passageway and peek out at them. Suzie looks wonderful in a floral dress that, on anyone else, would look like the doll-lady toilet roll holders my granny used to have. Her bump is Friedrich-sized. I go to touch mine and remember it isn't there any more. My courage wanes but I grip my fingers around the ormer shell in my pocket.

Suzie opens her final gift – some fancy pyjamas decorated with hand-illustrated stars and moon in a plush material and gives her sister a big hug. I locate my own sister in the crowd. She looks tired . . . and thinner, which doesn't look right on her at all, given she was already so slim. I notice she is on the periphery today, which is not her usual style.

Julie is still herself, however. She strides into the middle of the group, adopting her headmistress stance – a little wider than makes people comfortable. Her bow legs mirror the shape of the balloon arch. 'So,' she says, her voice sounding free of infection for once. 'Barri was the one who did most of the organising of this.' At the mention of me, Lara grows tense. Suzie's smile falters. A Lego brick of anticipation forms in my throat, waiting for the reveal of the gift we've put together. Julie continues, 'And she had this idea to do a sort of library thing . . . so there are some books and things for you too.' The women launch into chatter and tea drinking.

'No!' I stride out of my hiding place. 'You didn't explain it properly.' I turn to Suzie. 'The idea was that everyone chose a selection of their favourite books because you love reading so much and we wanted something the whole family can enjoy together. And your . . . well, the older ones can read to the baby and . . . You can all read together . . .' I trail off as I take in the collection of surprise and horror at my sudden appearance. Yolande has grabbed a cuddly toy hippopotamus and is clutching it to her as if it might come to life to defend her.

Julie is the first to speak. 'Barri, I really don't think it's appropriate for you to be here.'

I ignore her and approach Suzie, who is sitting in a chair beside the table, fanning herself with a greeting card. I give her the wrapped-up books and the bunting. She places the books on the table and holds the bunting up.

'I made it,' I tell her. I stitched the tiny piece of ivory ribbon I found on the doorframe onto the triangle with the 'S' for Suzie to give it some extra embellishment. She strokes it, feeling the luxe sheen, touches one of the pearls. 'I imagined you might have a keepsake box thing you might want to . . . but since I lied and manipulated you, you might not want a reminder . . . so you don't have to keep it in the box . . . assuming you have one. But I wanted you to have it, anyway.' I take her hand. A gasp from Yolande as if my criminality might rub off. I ignore her and squat down so my face is level with Suzie's. 'You showed me so much kindness.' I look around at the group. 'You all did. Well, not you, Yolande. But everyone else.' I turn to Lara now, who is studying me with a stern expression and tears in her eyes. 'What I did . . . I wanted to get away from here and start a new life where I could be . . . where no one would know me, or Sean. I'd lost everything. My marriage was over, all my money was gone. There was no way to . . . so the maternity leave felt like the only . . . I felt like I had nothing to lose. But that was before I knew how much I cared about you all. And then I didn't want to leave at all . . . but it was too late and I had to just keep lying.' I look at Lara who has occupied herself with picking some crumbs off the tablecloth. 'I don't expect you to forgive me. But I need you to know that I'm so sorry. I had no idea that what I was doing was going to hurt anyone because I didn't think . . . but I'm ready to face up to what I've done.' The warm reception I was hoping for doesn't materialise. Just silence, so I carry on. 'I need to see Callum. I let him down . . . badly. I need him to understand why. So if someone could tell me where he is . . . Sean mentioned something about a foster home in Town?'

Suzie stands up. It's a struggle. She grabs my arm. 'Barri, Callum got sent back to the UK.' She says this gently. Like a mother comforting a child with a grazed knee.

'But Sean said . . . he said that . . .'

Lara pipes up. 'Sean tracked Callum's dad down. Made this big thing about people who aren't blood relatives interfering with the custody of people's kids and that dads should stick together. Convinced him to claim what was his. He used the whole fake pregnancy deception. Said you and Trish weren't stable or responsible. The committee decided Callum had to go with his dad. Not enough money in the jar to put a minor in foster care here when they had a good alternative option.'

'But it wasn't a good option!' I shout. 'Didn't they listen to what Callum wanted?'

Suzie frowns and puts a hand on my arm. 'Callum didn't put up a fight at all when he realised you hadn't turned up. He just sat there and shrugged his shoulders whenever they asked him a question. Like he was resigned to it.'

I shake my head. 'It's all my fault.'

'I think you should go, Barri.' Yolande says. 'This is Suzie's day and you're making it about you.'

'No.' I humph down to the floor, cross my legs, my head in my hands. Instead of using her words, Yolande tries and fails to drag me away, once again showing how – in her personal life – she's incapable of demonstrating the attributes that make her capable at her day job. There's no denying she has the strength to pick me up – judging by her outfits, she probably spends her free time churning milk into butter, and all that winding has strengthened her biceps beyond belief. However, the embroidery on her A-line trad-wife skirt gets tangled in the adjacent holly bush and, in the end, she gives up, puts me back down and they all carry on with drinking their tea, admiring the muslin cloths and the party kind of happens around me, like I'm an ignored toddler having time out.

Eventually, Lara sighs and sits down opposite me, getting a grass stain on her pristine white jeans in the process. She huffs and crosses her legs too, lining her long shins up against my short ones. 'I think you should leave,' she says.

I put my forehead against Lara's like I used to when we were little girls playing secret messages on the beach. Heads touching to try to read each other's minds. Her thinking of ponies and unicorns and me of ormering hooks and existentialism. I expect her to recoil but she keeps her head against mine.

A propeller plane passes over the adjacent rooftops on its ascent from the airport. Unless there is fog – or the airline have had an absolute mare – the flights coming and going over here are as much an indicator of the time of day as a clock chiming on the hour, so I'm well aware that the one swooping above is the last to depart Guernsey today.

I cup Lara's cheeks like she did mine in the bathroom. 'I know I have no right asking this of you, but I need your help.'

Chapter Forty-Three

Lara puts in a call to Dave, who comes up with 'a plan'. Although I'm dubious that my brother-in-law is up to the task, I know now is not the time to voice it. We jump into Lara's car and head towards the harbour.

'Won't a ferry take ages?' I ask.

'Do you want our help or not?' The image of Sean's car reversing into my bump plays through my head. I should allow the frostiness; I'm lucky she's even entertaining this.

We don't turn to the ferry terminal as I'm expecting, but towards an area where some private boats are moored. Dave – who still has a cast on his arm but has lost the sling – Harry and Luke are there waiting for us in neon-orange life jackets. I think of the colour-coded calendar on my sister's fridge and how this must be disrupting their schedule. The boys don't seem to mind. Their hyper bodies bob up and down as we approach. Hovering behind them in shorts, a sky-blue vest and his yellow bloody Crocs is Pierre. I feel like someone has pulled a rug out from underneath my heart.

We step out of the car and he fusses with the ropes on the side of the boat rather than look at me. Before I can try to say something, Dave flings a life jacket around me, and I'm shepherded onto *Lynn III*.

Lara, Dave, Luke and Harry climb on too and join me at the table area near the back. Luke is in cricket whites, with a pad on one leg, one glove, and the red stain where he's rubbed the cricket ball against his thigh.

'He was about to go on to bat,' Dave says.

I look at Luke. 'Thank you . . . I didn't know you played cricket.'

'Yeah, I got into it after you bought me that hair gel in a cricket ball for Christmas.'

I recall choosing that gift in a desperate last-minute dash a few years back. I seem to remember teaming it with a couple of carabiner clips, imagining that a seven-year-old might enjoy hanging off them.

'The hair gel gave me this really, like, nasty allergic reaction but once I got better, Dad thought I should try cricket so I didn't get a silly fear or something.'

I nod my approval at Dave. Bad gift. Good parenting.

Harry squeals as the boat fires into action and, the minute we are out of the speed limit zone of the harbour, he squeals again as we go full throttle.

'Are we going all the way to England . . . on this?!'

Lara snorts at what I can only imagine is my stupidity.

'We're Jersey-bound,' Pierre says. He hasn't looked at me yet. I decide to stop asking questions and settle myself at the table as close to my sister as I dare. Luke and Harry are tasked with making everyone a cup of tea, and Dave tactfully takes the opportunity to go and quiz Pierre on *Lynn III*'s specifications.

Being on a boat suits Lara's aesthetic. Her hair is voluminous in the wind, but it blows in a way that looks chic, not scraggy like mine. The striped top she is wearing with the white jeans works well, as does the high-collared sweatshirt she grabbed from the car and draped over her shoulders. I look down at my tea-stained grey joggers and matching sweatshirt. Why did it not cross my mind to put on something more presentable for the baby shower? I must have looked deranged turning up like . . . like I'm wearing prison sweats.

'I really am sorry about everything,' I say, covering up the understatement I just made by fishing an elastic band out from my bag to tie my hair back because it keeps blowing over my face.

She sighs, and holds out a wrist with a hair bobble on it, which I tug off and use instead. 'I know you are.'

'I hope in the very least you contributed to all the articles. Made some dosh out of your first-hand experience.'

She looks at me, confused. 'What articles?'

'All the articles about me. The *Daily Mail*, *The Sun*, *This Morning* wanting me to go on . . . I've always felt like Alison Hammond and I would be trouble on a night out, so it's a shame I didn't go, but . . .' I let my weak joke trail off because she's shaking her head.

'Show me one article, Barri.'

'I don't have my phone. Sean took it the night you all—'

The way she squeezes her eyes in a pained way stops me mid-sentence. 'He has your . . .' She opens them again. 'Barri, there aren't any articles. We all kept it quiet. Even bloody Yolande when she realised it might reflect badly on the school, and by extension, her. Julie had to inform the police as a precaution but there are no charges or anything.' She hands me her phone. 'Look what he's been doing.'

I scroll through conversations between her and Sean, pretending to be me, telling her I don't want to see her. 'You really should have known it wasn't me from the overuse of exclamation marks,' I say, frustrated with myself that I so very easily let him deceive me again.

She pulls out a neatly folded tissue from her sleeve and dabs her eyes with it. 'What you did was abhorrent, and it's going to take me a while to get over it.' She sniffs. 'But I should have tried harder these past few weeks. I should never have let you . . . I was just so angry. And upset.' She grabs me into a possessive squeeze. 'No matter what happens – even if you lie and tell us you're having quin-bloody-tuplets next time – I'm never going to let Sean take you away from us again.'

I feel another Lego-sized lump in my throat. 'OK.'

She pulls me tighter. 'But also if you ever lie to me again, I will never forgive you.'

'OK.'

Her grip softens and we stay like that for a while. A big sister, hugging her little one.

When we arrive in Jersey, a chauffeur-driven Mercedes is waiting for us. Harry and Luke get in excitedly, but their dad pulls them back. 'Sorry you two, this is as far as we're going.' Off their disappointment, he adds, 'I've booked us a hotel and we'll go to the zoo tomorrow!' The boys cheer as they remove their life jackets and fling them back onto the boat.

I turn to Dave, guilty at how unkind I have been about him. *To* him at times. I signal the posh car. 'Dave Brookfield: the man to turn to in a crisis. How did you . . .?!'

'I've got some mates in high places,' he says as he pats Pierre on the back. Pierre gives a weak smile and gets in the car. He's coming with me. I don't know whether to be happy or dread the rest of this journey. I look back at my sister, Dave and the boys and without even thinking about it, I circle my arms around them all. As one, like the solid unit they are, they tense up their bodies and make my anti-cuddle alien sound. I laugh and join in, drawing confused looks from the passing people of Jersey.

As the car pulls away, Dave follows beside it to speak to me through the open window.

'That Netflix thing . . . is it real because I've been telling everyone and now I think I might have been taken for a mug . . .'

The sound of my 'I'm soooorrrrrry' reverberates through the car park as we drive off.

I smile nervously at Pierre, who still can't fully meet my eye. He and the chauffeur chat about the latter's family and how his son is neglecting his A Levels now he's got a girlfriend.

Pierre's ease and generosity of spirit with people is one of my favourite things about him. I think back to the night he and Callum did their animal movements in my living room. The silliness and laughter that was missing from my life until about five months ago when I made a stupid snap decision.

Please don't let it be too late for me to fix this.

We pull up at a private airfield where . . . a plane is waiting for us?! Pierre has put on a thin, teal-coloured hoody. The ends of the tassels that pull the hood tight have been chewed so much that they have separated into individual strands. I think about the boat, the posh car, that complicated Excel model.

'You're minted, aren't you?'

'Yep,' he says.

The two tattiest people in the British Isles clamber up the stairs onto the plush private aeroplane bound for England.

The jet takes off, affording us an incredible view of the sunset. A mixture of reds, pinks and yellows over the sea. The brightness is startling but I don't close the blind. Instead, I close my eyes and let the warmth bathe my face. When I open them, I catch Pierre watching me before he looks away.

The excitement of the rush to the plane has gone, and we are left with a feeling of discomfort between us. Many unspoken things. My hand brushes my pocket where the 'fuck you miss' ormer still is. I pull it out and use the sharp end of a safety pin I had knocking around in my handbag to add a comma before the 'miss'.

'One must always use correct grammar, especially when insulting someone,' I say as he watches me etch the comma. He laughs politely and looks out of the window. I decide it's now or never. 'I have a lot of regrets. And apologies and explanations,' I say, willing him to meet my eye. 'But I need you to know that your friendship has been . . . If you asked me if I would go back and make the decision to fake the pregnancy again, I would because I met you.'

Pierre keeps staring out the window. 'You already knew me.'

'Well, it made me see you, then.'

The demure cabin crew woman with a jaunty hat brings us some champagne, placing it in front of us. Is there anything sadder than a glass of champagne that doesn't feel worthy of being drunk? Pierre doesn't seem to have this quibble and takes a big glug from his. Mine remains there, bubbles fizzing upwards like helium balloons rising to a ceiling.

Pierre gives me a tight smile. 'You know, we probably would have reconnected anyway given Callum nicking the ormers was a separate thing entirely.'

'Shit, you're right,' I say. We both laugh. 'You knew it was Callum?'

'He fessed up before he left.' When Pierre looks me in the eye properly, it takes me by surprise so much my breath catches. 'I think I can get over most of it. It's a complicated thing, but I think . . . I need to know . . .' He takes a deep breath. 'What was the plan for after? When you came back from maternity leave. Were you going to tell everyone that the . . . that the babies had died?'

'No.' His eyes narrow, not believing. 'It was a rule from day one that I wouldn't do that. The plan was to relocate and cut ties with everyone completely. There was a point when I wanted to back out . . . when I realised I was making a mistake and I wanted it to stop but I never ever actually would have . . . I *couldn't* have.' Pierre says nothing, just takes another gulp of champagne. The glass looks flimsy in his giant hand. I touch the base of my own glass to steady myself. 'Having a termination or buggering off and never speaking to anyone again. That would have been on me – my decision, so people would think of me what they think of me. I decided from the beginning that pretending to lose a child was completely off limits. What I was doing was already so morally questionable, claiming something like that would have been . . . it would have been unforgivable. And I'm not just saying this because of your situation. I promise I'm not. It would be the ultimate disservice to anyone who actually had . . . you know. Had gone through that.' I swallow, despite my mouth being completely dry. 'There are so many people who would desperately love to have children, or have lost them . . . or, like Trish, having to fight for her stepdaughter despite being the best person to parent her.' I look at him, tears filling my eyes. 'I know I'm privileged that I've never been in that situation, and that faking a pregnancy on impulse was so . . . flippant. But it certainly didn't feel like that when I realised the amount of hurt I was going to cause.' I wipe a tear off my face with my sleeve and look up at him. 'Your . . . your friendship has meant so much to me and I betrayed it. I'm so sorry. For everything.'

Pierre takes my hand. It feels comfortable in mine. Not a jigsaw piece fitting perfectly into another, but more like a pair of novelty salt and pepper shakers side by side.

I think about the time he told me about his daughter and how in that moment all I could think about was myself. 'We have a short flight,' I say, putting my feet up on the seat opposite, hoping he doesn't clock the coffee granules smushed into the soles of my socks picked up from my kitchen floor when I cleared out the caddy earlier today. 'I would really like it if you would tell me about your daughter . . . about Margot.'

Pierre beams and I breathe. 'Yes. Margot . . .'

As we land, another chauffeured car is there to greet us. I turn to him for an explanation. 'Are you a scruffy unassuming Richard Branson?'

He smiles. 'Not even close. I sold my company a few years back. ComplyHi. It's a very boring compliance tech business, but it filled a gap in the market, so . . .'

I think about the battered coffee cup he's constantly sipping from. 'So, why bother with the Sea Fisheries gig?'

'Because I like to keep busy. I love the sea, and, despite having just chartered you a private jet, which, by the way, is an absolute one-off, I care about the environment.'

'Oh.'

'And between January and April every year, I get to ask the incomparable Barri Brown if I have permission to inspect her bucket.'

He greets the new chauffeur like they're old buddies, rendering me speechless on the bottom step of a private plane, wishing I'd taken the time today to do less sewing and more showering.

Chapter Forty-Four

It's dark outside. I feel like a car on a Scalextric track as we wend our way towards Pease Pottage services. Pease Pottage. What a bonkers name for a service station . . . makes me picture rows of medieval, wimple-wearing peasants supping on turnip soup.

As we turn off the roundabout I begin to grow nervous. According to Callum's TikTok account, he's back working here. He posted some silly videos sending up Pease Pottage like a Wes Anderson movie but subverting it to show the shit reality of a British service station. But what if he's not on shift? Or worse, he is here and won't hear me out?

I think about Sean and Ripley approaching this building the day Callum saw them here. What sort of day had they had? A fun adventure she will remember into adulthood or a day of bargaining, cajoling, and short fuses finished off with a service station sweetie sweetener so all is forgotten at the end?

We pull into the forecourt, a lot smoother than Sean would have, and I spy Callum immediately through the window, behind a fast-food counter. I watch him serve a customer, handling the items with care. Someone who knows the cost of things. I look at Pierre – *Are you not coming?* A shake of the head. He's right. This is a solitary endeavour.

Callum feels my presence the minute I step inside, which is unfortunate because I wanted some more time to watch him in his natural habitat before he tensed up at the sight of me. But Callum always was perceptive. He is serving a man who is talking loudly on his phone and not acknowledging Callum's existence and I feel affronted on his behalf.

Callum watches me as the man taps his card on the reader and leaves. It's eerily quiet. Pretty much just the two of us in the bright, bright food hall. An exposing light, not a warm one. Abrasive almost . . . it probably shows up every wrinkle, blemish and un-tweezered moustache hair.

I slide a piece of paper over to him and place the ormer shell on top. He turns it over and sees the etching of 'Fuck you, miss'. He smiles when he clocks I added a comma.

I wait patiently as he finally gets to read the personal statement I promised him I'd write but didn't.

> *I have thought long and hard about how I might best articulate why I believe that Callum should remain in Guernsey to complete his studies and be provided with safe accommodation in a suitable foster home.*
>
> *He is a gifted student whose inquisitive mind means he explores topics in depth beyond anything I was doing at his age. He is curious and intelligent and, apart from a few bad choices (because, let's face it, we all make those), he is a kind and impressive young man with a promising*

future ahead of him. I believe that he deserves safety and security and that he will be best placed to receive that here in Guernsey. But, more importantly, he is headed for greatness and by not allowing him to remain here, you will do a disservice to the island.

NOTE TO CALLUM: This was how my first draft of the statement began. A draft I admittedly didn't finish due to being a selfish 'trollop'.

Callum snorts when he gets to this bit.

I have since added the following (excuse the messy writing, I'm on a boat):

I let Callum down in an unforgiveable act of selfishness and, since we've been apart, I have come to realise that it is not just that he deserves to have the safety and security the island can offer him but that I would like to be the person to provide him with it.

Callum once told me that he doesn't believe anyone can truly care about a child who isn't biologically theirs, but I am here to tell him he's wrong about that.

There will always be an unconditional home for him with me.

It was on the boat over to Jersey when the penny dropped. Something Lara said as I talked about Callum. How I felt this overwhelming need to bridge the gap for him where others had failed. Lara smiled and pulled Harry – who had fallen asleep on her shoulder – closer to her to shield him from the wind.

'You know, you've said millions of times that you don't want a baby.'

'Yes, and I will die on that hill. Don't you—'

'All right. I promise I'll never question it again.'

'Praise be!' I yelled, causing Harry to stir.

'But,' Lara said, shushing me by lowering her voice, 'in all that moaning and groaning, perhaps justified . . . but only occasionally . . . In *all* that moaning, the one thing I've never heard you say is that you don't want to be a mum.'

That gave me the absolute ick. Twee, twaddle ick, ick, ick, ickiness, and I told her she was wrong yet again. But something also slid into place, like the time I bought a new mop with a head that fit *perfectly* in the floor space between the wall and the toilet.

For my sister, having her own offspring is additive to her life, whereas I know – and always have known – that having a baby would detract from mine. But the already-in-existence human being known as Callum Le Brocq adds to my life. And that's what finally clicked on the boat with Lara.

I don't want to be a mum. But I do want to take care of Callum. Nurture, and counsel, and console, and support, and guard, and champion, and love, and occasionally coddle (when he really needs it). To think he's brilliant, even when he's not brilliant. Or tell him that he's crap when he thinks he's better than he is. To unconditionally be there for him. To eclipse myself to make him gleam. And to show up every day until the day I die and even then – if I've done it well – his memory of me will continue to do the job for me.

And that's not a role reserved solely for mums or dads. That could be an auntie or uncle, a step-parent, a guardian. A sibling, a cousin, a grandparent, a friend. It can even be a teacher who dragged her miscreant teenage student into her disastrous fake pregnancy heist after he blackmailed her.

Callum may be the most high-maintenance bump of them all, but he's the perfect appendage to my life. I'm willing to lug him around for as long as he needs . . . and I'll do my best not to impale him on any sharp objects along the way.

Afterbirth

'Got them!' Dave calls to me from the main road above. He climbs down the steps with an armful of newspapers and joins me on my rug in the usual spot under the sea wall. It's a glorious morning on Cobo and my swimming costume is already dry after my morning dip.

Dave watches with amusement as I gather up my marking. 'How are the literary standards at Guernsey prison now they have Barri Brown there to show them what's what?'

'Oh, there is work to be done, Dave, but I'm up to the challenge.' I take a newspaper from him. 'It definitely helped when I dropped in that my dad did a two-stretch to get them on side a bit!'

He puts a playful arm around my shoulder just as I take a bite of my pain aux raisins, causing a raisin to fall out of my mouth. 'And your own reputation for being the most notorious teacher on the island!' he says.

As if to embellish his point, a young woman – twenty or so – passes by while filming me on her phone in the most unsubtle way possible. I give her a death stare as she passes, making her turn and run. The sensible long-sleeved shirt she wears to protect her shoulders from the sun does nothing to shield her proud buttocks dissected by a forensically thonged bikini.

'The True Crime TikTokers are the worst,' I say. 'They lull you into a false sense of security with their feigned innocence and blemish-free skin and then BAM, they destroy you with a well-edited video of you messily eating pastry products to back up their argument that you're a sociopath.'

I wasn't allowed back at school after the truth came out about my pregnancy. But I like teaching adults. And the prison is a humorous diversion for Dave. I hand him the pain au chocolat and coffee I bought for him and we both stand to watch Lara finish her final length across the bay, angular elbows cutting through the surface of the choppy water.

It's become a Sunday tradition for us all to meet here. Callum and I always visit Cedric in his care home first thing, where – like Kurt – he's a Big Name on Campus, and particularly enjoys delivering the post to each resident and charming the staff in the process. Then we head here to meet the others. A swim for those with the inclination followed by coffee and pastries for all while we read Lara's *Sunday Times* column.

Of course, the news got out eventually. Deep down, I know Yolande probably spilled and I'm OK about that. I'm facing it head-on. The articles followed. Interview requests, journalists ringing my house, but I knew there was only one person I wanted to have the exclusive.

Lara strides up the beach towards us in a chic one-piece, pulling off a silicone swimming cap.

'What bit is it today?' I ask as I locate the page in the newspaper.

'The strip search.'

'Oh God.'

'I changed all the details of the police officer, just like you asked.'

I think of PC Pluckrose and hope wherever she is – spilling her lunch, botching a tasering or making a mess of a minor crime – that she's content.

Harry, Luke and Callum kick a football around on the flat part of the beach where the tide has retreated. Luke nutmegs Callum and we all laugh as the latter lifts Luke over his shoulder and dumps him in the sea in mock fury.

'Who's the extra coffee for?' Lara asks.

'Pierre's coming down.'

Dave does a mock schoolgirl 'Ooooh' and I whack him with the newspaper. I see Pierre most days. We're just friends for now, but I'm hopeful. Both that we will make it work and that I can convince him to give up the Crocs.

'OK, while we wait for Pierre,' Lara says, 'I spoke to the podcast team . . .'

'Fine,' I say. Lara has been banging on about a podcast since her first column went viral. 'Pierre pointed out it's an income stream, so I've decided to relent.'

'OK, well that's great!' Lara picks up her phone to type an email to her editor.

I did have an ulterior motive for Lara's article, other than buttering up my sister after deceiving her so horribly. Me putting the story in the public domain kickstarted the legal proceedings against Sean. I was only able to claw a nominal amount of money back from him but the house is now in my name at least. A big chunk of the money he took went on his legal fees . . . which was a waste because Trish got custody of Ripley! I had provided a statement about the kind of man Sean is, which was confronting and difficult to write, but it felt worth it when I heard from Trish's legal team that it was the swaying factor in the final decision.

Trish sent me a letter thanking me with a gorgeous photo of her and Ripley smiling down from the top of a treehouse, which I put on the fridge.

Mine and Callum's fridge, I suppose.

I'm not sure Trish and I will ever be the firm friends we once were, but there's an open invitation for them to visit us, and I look forward to the nice bottle of red she'll bring.

Callum loves to refer to me as his 'benefactor' and himself as my 'ward' like we exist within a dystopian Charles Dickens novel. It doesn't irk me.

After getting permission from his dad, who in the end agreed being in Guernsey was what was best for him, I was granted a Residence Order. Callum's sticking around with me for his A Levels and then the world is his ormer. I'm not going to pretend it has been completely plain sailing. After however many years going out wherever and whenever he pleases, it's taken a bit of readjusting. He calls it 'The Barri Regime' – another nod to dystopia – but I think he secretly enjoys someone wanting to know where he is.

'I don't want it to be some worthy bullshit,' Lara says, still banging on about the podcast. 'With boring synth music. Let's get a really good comedian to narrate it. And it needs a punchier title than My Sister Faked a Pregnancy.'

I smile. 'Baby Sham.'

My mum rings me out of the blue one day as I'm getting ready to head out to the pub quiz with Suzie and some of my former colleagues, who are more palatable now I don't have to share tea-making facilities with them.

'Barri. You won't believe it but I got to the bottom of the premium bonds mystery.'

I perch on the windowsill in my living room, thinking back to that day all those months ago, not being able to relax in her house as she flapped the tatty old pieces of paper around. Distracted by the lack of compassion she had that Sean had left me for good.

After the initial shock of the pregnancy being a lie, Mum got over it surprisingly quickly. I guess having been married to Dad, she's more resilient than I gave her credit for.

'The premium bonds are yours. Your dad put them in your name before he died. Fifty K's worth for Edinburgh University.'

My laugh of surprise causes Callum to look up at me from the dining-room table where he's pretending to write an essay despite having his phone hidden in the page of his book. He gives me a questioning look and I wave my hand to signify I'll tell him later.

'You know what happened?' Mum continues. I pin the phone between my ear and shoulder as I pull on my cowboy boots. 'When that silly Irish girl who claimed to be Scottish looked you up on the system, she stupidly spelt your name B-a-r-r-y instead of B-a-r-r-i. It just occurred to me this morning that's probably what happened. So I called and asked them to check again with the right spelling. You know what the chap in the call centre said?! "Barri? What a bizarre name for a girl." Can you believe the cheek?'

'Well, he's right . . .' I readjust the ormer shell on the shelf, its iridescent interior gleaming in the light. 'But it's beautiful written down.'

Acknowledgements

Firstly, I would like to thank my agent Jemima Forrester for being a brilliant person and absolute rockstar in equal measure. Thank you for your faith in Barri, your belief in me, for pointing out that it is impossible to ever make the word 'snorkelling' sound sexy, and for coming up with the most perfect title for this book. I'm so grateful to have you as my agent.

Giulia, Sam and Kathryn in the DHA Foreign Rights team, and Georgie and Jem in the Film and TV department, thank you so much for your passion, excitement and support – I'm so grateful for everything you've done for me and this book. And to everyone else I've dealt with at DHA, thank you!

Katie Loughnane. The minute you sent through that fake pregnancy form, I knew you were the perfect editor. Thank you for your kindness, passion and humour throughout this whole process and for the many back-and-forth musings about whether or not Barri would use the word 'flange'. Thank you for taking such good care of this book baby; it couldn't have been in better hands. Thank you to Bella Bosworth, and also to the amazing team at Pan Macmillan, with special thanks to: Rebecca Needes, Sanjana Samaddar,

Rachel Vale, Josie Turner, Kimberley Nyamhondera, Zoe Coxon, Claire Bush, Mia Lioni, Stuart Dwyer and the UK sales team, and Leanne Williams and the international sales team. I'd also love to thank all the other editors who have taken Barri to their hearts and advocated for *Motherfaker* to be translated into different languages.

Thank you to: John Yorke and Suzy Cripps for setting the writing exercise that became the beginnings of this novel – and for the rejection from the BBC Writers' Academy for the second year in a row. It was the fuel I needed! To Harry Parkinson and Megan Reid for giving me the confidence I could do this. To everyone at The Novelry – in particular Libby Page for summing up what this story is really about so succinctly when I couldn't. And to Josie Humber for your belief, your excellent notes, and for steering me through the querying hellscape so brilliantly. My early readers: James Dangerfield, Rachel Holland and Karin Mitchell – thank you for your encouragement and invaluable feedback. My London Library pals, Jessie Norman and Amy Powel-Yeates for keeping me powering through that first draft. Smell and Schlongers for being the best hype women every step of the way; Kirsty Langley for the voice notes, daily moon musings and Lion's Gate Portal manifestations; Paul Chirnside for the much-needed (and always hilarious) coffee chats. Thank you to absolute powerhouses Nicole Cunningham, Jill McAusland, Esta Charkham, Belinda Campbell, Elspeth Rae, Lillie Allen, Rousol Al-Timimi, Monika Reinmann and Megan Smith. John Pocock for the support and wisdom. Uncle Andrew for double-checking all the Guernsey references. Nikki Allen and Janice Okoh for being my go-to author buddies. Thank you also to everyone at Corten Capital. All the times you stopped me in the kitchen to ask me how the writing was going, it meant more than you know.

This book celebrates all of the people in our lives who are not our biological parents but who play an important role in shaping who we are. For me, these are: Sarah and Andrew Dempster; Collette and Dave Parsons; Avril Hurley; my late, great Auntie Lynnie; and inspirational teachers whose advice, encouragement and wisdom I still think of often: Alyson Perrett, Ray Cook, Kate Whittaker, Sue Beard and Bob Dillinger.

Angela Nesi, my screenwriting partner and all-round incredible friend. Thank you so much for giving me the time I needed to write this book and for bringing your genius brain to the screen adaptation. You may always arrive to meetings eye-wateringly on time for my early person constitution but you are the best in every way.

To The Mad House – many already mentioned, plus Melva Stacey, Peter, Lisa, Lily and Jack Mitchell, Kirsty and Abigail Dempster, George Russell and Molly Parsons. You're all iconic, which is quite a feat for an entire family. I love you dearly.

Chris and Karin Mitchell, I am forever grateful to be your daughter. Thank you for never trying to steer me down a more sensible and conventional path despite, I'm sure, being tempted to! Thank you for surrounding me with stories, encouraging my imagination and for showing me the value in being curious and passionate about the world. A special mention to my dad for always keeping me humble ('What's a literary agent?') and to Mum who could definitely have been an editor in another life. I think she'd appreciate me saying here that Barri's mum is in no way based on her.

Finally, thank you to Danny for living (enduring!) this

process along with me. Thank you for the pep talks, the belief, the kindness and the occasional – but much needed – tough love. You inspire me every day to do and be better and I simply wouldn't be here without you.

About the Author

Anna Brook-Mitchell is a BAFTA Rocliffe Comedy-winning writer, actor and filmmaker. Her BBC Comedy Short Film, *Man Eater* – written with her screenwriting partner, Angela Nesi – aired on BBC Three in 2023 and was selected for BFI London Film Festival and Raindance. Anna lives in South East London. When she's not writing, she enjoys swimming, watching sport and playing the trumpet (badly) in an orchestra. *Motherfaker* is her debut novel.